"*A fast-paced future thriller that delivers on the promise of its high-concept premise.*"
The B&N Sci-Fi & Fantasy Blog

"*Appeals to my love of sci-fi, intelligent characters and puns.*"
Purple Owl Reviews

"*You'll want to hang in there for the entirety of the ride.*"
Strange Alliances

...g... engrossing and fascinating.
Manhattan Book Review

"*I've come away a fan of the author and the series.*"
Looking for a Good Book

"*Liege-Killer is a genuine page-turner, beautifully written and exciting from start to finish.*"
Locus

"*Hinz writes with skill and verve. His world is logical and alive, and he peoples it with credible and compelling characters.*"
San Francisco Chronicle

ALSO BY CHRISTOPHER HINZ:

Liege-Killer
The Paratwa
Ash Ock
Binary Storm
Anachronisms
Spartan X

Liege-Killer: The Graphic Novel
Duchamp Versus Einstein (co-written with Etan Ilfeld)

Christopher Hinz

STARSHIP ALCHEMON

ANGRY
ROBOT

ANGRY ROBOT
An imprint of Watkins Media Ltd

Unit 11, Shepperton House
89 Shepperton Road
London N1 3DF
UK

angryrobotbooks.com
twitter.com/angryrobotbooks
Blue dominion

An Angry Robot paperback original, 2019

Cover by Francesca Corsini
Commissioned by Etan Ilfeld
Set in Minion Pro

ISBN 978 0 85766 817 2
Ebook ISBN 978 0 85766 818 9

Printed and bound in the United Kingdom by TJ International.

9 8 7 6 5 4 3 2 1

This one is for my cousin, Barry Hawk, who was there at the beginning, offering support to a writer at the outset of the journey.

AUTHOR'S NOTE

Let's jump back a few decades and set the scene: a young writer, a cramped attic workspace, a passion for the exhilarating diversity of science fiction and fantasy. During an era when home computers still struggled through adolescence, the writer flayed the keys of a portable typewriter, blending the logical and the fanciful until he'd forged the novel *Anachronisms*.

The exotic thriller about an exploratory vessel far from Earth besieged by deadly forces was influenced by luminaries ranging from Frank Herbert and Arthur C. Clarke to Stephen King and A.E. Van Vogt – and with a nod to Ridley Scott's seminal *Alien* movie. When the manuscript initially failed to find a publisher, the writer dove into a more ambitious project. The success of *Liege-Killer*, issued by St. Martin's Press to critical acclaim, prompted an offer for *Anachronisms*.

However, this second novel didn't generate the level of enthusiasm that had greeted *Liege-Killer*. In retrospect, it probably should have been consigned to a drawer along with other fledgling efforts. Pride – and a most welcome advance – veiled critical perspective.

* * * * *

Long vexed by the novel's imperfections, I told myself I'd someday rewrite *Anachronisms* and render it a story I could be proud of. For years, newer projects consumed the workday but finally I made the commitment and plunged ahead with passion and naïveté. The latter quality arose from the misguided belief that a better story was possible by tweaking the text, smoothing over some rough spots and updating the science and technology. It soon became obvious that such minor changes wouldn't suffice, that nothing less than a total revamp was demanded.

And so *Anachronisms* was stripped to its foundations and rebuilt from the ground up. Although retaining some iconic tropes – first contact, autocratic AIs – those elements anchor a radically different tale that incorporates a kaleidoscope of fresh ideas.

Yet I desired even more for this novel, a way to bring back that sense of wonder about our amazing cosmos that long ago sprouted in parallel with my passion for the genre. It's said that the golden age of science fiction is twelve, a time when human beings are primed for physical, emotional and intellectual revelation. It's also true you can never go back. Still, we're never entirely cut off from those wonderlands of youth, when we could sprawl across warm summer grass and gaze up at the palpitating stars and snare the dream-spark of imagination from the infinite dark.

In celebration of such feelings, *Starship Alchemon* is dedicated.

Christopher Hinz, Reading, PA, USA, 2019

The mad grief of spectral gales
warping a spirit
grave and benign.

Systems betrayed by jagged deceit
and a storm out of time.

Homebound Visions.

The mad grief of spectral gales
bleeding the heart of anachronisms.

THE LYTIC'S LAMENT

MAJOR AI SYSTEMS OF THE STARSHIP *ALCHEMON*

LEVEL 0
SEN – Sentinel

LEVEL 1
SCO – Spatiotemporal Coagulators
PAQ – Primary Quantizer
POP – Primary Operating Power
NEL – Nucleonic Engines
NAV – Navigation

LEVEL 2
EHO – Ecospheric Homeostasis
SOP – Secondary Operating Power
SAQ – Secondary Quantizer
EAC – External Airseal Control
CON – Containment System
MED – Medical System

LEVEL 3
EPS – Elementary Probability Scanning
GEL – General Library
PYG – Primary Genesis Complex
FWP – Food/Waste Processing
GEN – Geonic Stability
HYP – Hydroponics

LEVEL 4

RAP – Robotics and Probes
IBD – Internal Bio Detection
LIS – Lander Interface System
ICO – Internal Communications
SPI – Storage Pod Interface

LEVEL 5

CYB – Cyberlink Network
HOD – Holographic Display
SYG – Secondary Genesis Complex
IAC – Internal Airseal Control
ICS – Internal Corrector System

LEVEL 6

ETI – External Telemetry Interface
NUB – Nutriment Bath
LUM – Luminosity System
TEM – Thermometry Regulation
LSN – Luxury System – Natatorium
LSD – Luxury System – Dreamlounge

CHAPTER 1

The assignor had a hunch the meeting would be unpleasant. He wondered if the young woman entering his office already knew the outcome.

LeaMarsa de Host wore a black skirt and sweater that looked woven from rags, clothing surely lacking even basic hygiene nanos. Whether she was making some sort of anti-Corporeal statement or whether she always dressed like a drug-addled misfit from the Helio Age was not apparent from her file.

The assignor smiled and rose to shake her hand. She ignored the courtesy. He sat and motioned her to the chair across from his desk.

"Welcome to Pannis Corp, LeaMarsa."

"Thrilled to be here."

Her words bled sarcasm. No surprise. She registered highly alienated on the Ogden Tripartite Thought Ordination. Most members of the bizarre minority to which she belonged were outliers on the OTTO scale.

"Would you like something to drink?" he asked, motioning to his Starbucks 880, a conglomeration of tubes and spouts. The dispenser was vintage twenty-first-century, a gift from the assignor's wife for his thirtieth birthday. "Five hundred and one varieties, hot or cold."

"I'll have a juggernaut cocktail with Europa cryospice. Hold the cinnamon."

"I'm sorry, that one's not in the menu."

She grimaced with disappointment, which of course was the whole point of requesting such a ridiculously exotic drink.

He unflexed his wafer to max screen size and toggled through her file. An analysis of her test results appeared.

"The Pannis researchers at Jamal Labs were most impressed with your talents. You are indeed a gifted psionic."

She flopped into the chair and leaned back. An erratic thumping reverberated through the office. It took the assignor a moment to realize she was kicking the underside of his desk with the toe of her flats.

He contained his annoyance. Someday, he hoped to have enough seniority to avoid working with her type. And this young woman in particular...

She was thin, with long dark hair hanging to her shoulders, grossly uncouth. His preadolescent daughter still wore her hair that long, but who beyond the teen years allowed such draping strands, and LeaMarsa de Host was twenty-three. Her skin was as pale as the froth of a milkshake and her eyes hard blue gems, constantly probing. She smelled of natural body scents. He didn't care for the odor.

"Let's cut to the chase," she said. "Do I get a starship?"

"At this time, Pannis Corp feels that such an assignment would not be in the best interests of all involved."

"What's the matter? Afraid?"

He'd been trained to ignore such a response. "Pannis has concluded that your particular range of abilities would not be conducive to the self-contained existence of stellar voyaging."

"What the hell does that mean?"

"It boils down to a matter of cooperation."

"Haven't I cooperated with your tests? I took two months out of my life. I practically lived in those hideous Jamal Labs of yours."

"And we're certainly pleased by your sacrifice. But when I'm speaking of cooperation, I'm referring to factors of which you may not even be conscious. Psionic abilities exist primarily in strata beneath the level of daily awareness."

"Really? Never would have guessed."

He paved over the snark. "You may wish to behave cooperatively but find your subconscious acting in contrary ways. And trust me, a year or more in a starship is a far cry from what you underwent in our labs."

"You're speaking from experience?"

"Actually, no. I've never been farther out than Luna."

"Then you don't know what you're talking about."

She stared at him so intently that he worried she was trying to read his mind. The fear was irrational. Still, like most of the population, he was categorized as a psionic receptor, susceptible to psychic forces, albeit mildly.

He forced his attention back to the wafer.

"Pannis is willing to offer you a choice of more than a dozen positions, all with good salary ranges. And the benefits of working for a mega are remarkable."

"What's the most exciting position?"

"Exciting? Why, I don't know." He tapped the wafer, scanned pages. "Ah yes, here's one that sounds quite exciting. Archeological assistant, digging up nineteenth century frontier cultures in the American southwest in search of lost caches of gold and silver."

"Blizzards?"

He looked up from the wafer. "Pardon?"

"Do you have anything with blizzards? I like storms."

Storms? Dear god, these people were a trial, and more trouble than they were worth. Still, he understood the economics behind the current frenzy among Pannis and the other megas to employ them.

Only last week the latest discovery attributed to one of LeaMarsa's kind had been announced, a metallic compound found in the swamps of the dwarf planet Buick Skylark. The mega funding that expedition, Koch-Fox, was touting the compound as key ingredient for a new construction material impervious to the effects of sunlight.

He scanned more pages on the wafer. "Yes, here's a position where storms factor in. The south polar regions, an industrial classification. You would utilize your abilities to locate ultra-deep mineral deposits."

"While freezing my butt off? No thanks. Anyway, no need to read further. I've made my decision."

"Excellent."

"I choose a starship."

The assignor couldn't hide his disappointment. "Again, you must understand that a starship is not in the best interests of…"

He trailed off as the door slid open. An immaculately dressed man with dark hair and a weightlifter's build strolled in. He wore a gray business suit with matching headband. A pewter-colored vest rose to his chin and a dwarf lion perched on his shoulder, a male judging by its thick mane. The cat couldn't have weighed more than two pounds. A genejob that small cost more than the assignor earned in a year.

The man was a high-ranking Pannis official, the InterGlobal Security VP, a rank rarely seen on this floor of the Manhattan office complex. His name was Renfro Zoobondi and he was hardcore, an up-and-comer known and feared throughout the corporation. The fact that Zoobondi was here filled the assignor with dread.

A black mark, he thought bitterly. *I'm not handling this situation correctly and my file will soon reflect that.*

Zoobondi must have been monitoring their conversation, which suggested that LeaMarsa was even more important than her dazzling psionic ratings indicated. The VP was here to rectify the assignor's failure.

He won't come right out and criticize me. That's not the Pannis way. He'll say I've done a fair job under difficult circumstances and then see to it I'm given a black mark.

Zoobondi sat on the edge of the assignor's desk and faced LeaMarsa. The diminutive lion emitted a tinny growl.

"You are being uncooperative, Mizz de Host." The VP's voice was deep and commanding.

She shrugged. He regarded her for a long moment then turned to the assignor.

"Access vessel departures. Look for a minor mission, something leaving within the next few weeks."

The assignor did as asked while cloaking surprise. *Is he actually considering such an unstable individual for a starship?*

Zoobondi wagged a finger at LeaMarsa. "Understand me, young lady, you will not be given a major assignment. But Pannis is prepared to gratify."

The assignor called up the file. He scanned the lengthy list, narrowed down the possibilities.

"The *Bolero Grand*, two-year science project, galactic archaeology research. Crew of sixty-eight, including two lytics–"

"Perhaps something smaller," Zoobondi suggested, favoring her with a smile. "We want Mizz de Host to enjoy the special bonding that can develop aboard vessels with a minimal number of shipmates."

"Yes, of course. How about the *Regis*, crew of six? Fourteen-month mission to Pepsi One in the HD 40307 system. They're laying the groundwork for new colonies and request a psionic to help select the best geographic locations on the semi-liquid surface."

"Perfect. Does that work for you, LeaMarsa?"

"No. Sounds boring."

"It does, doesn't it," Zoobondi said with a smile. "I'd certainly get bored traipsing across a world of bubbling swamps looking for seismic stability."

The assignor was confused. Something was going on here that he didn't understand. If Zoobondi wanted her to accept the *Regis* mission, he would have made it sound more attractive.

"Any other possibilities?" the VP asked.

"Yes. Starship *Alchemon*, eighteen-month mission to the Lalande 21185 system. Investigation of an anomalous biosignature discovered by an unmanned probe. Crew of eight, including a lytic."

Zoobondi shook his head. "I don't think so."

"Why not?" LeaMarsa demanded.

He hesitated, as if working on a rebuttal. The assignor understood.

He wants her to accept this mission. He's leading her along. The assignor had been with Pannis long enough to recognize applied reverse psychology, which meant that this meeting with LeaMarsa was part of a high-level setup.

It was possible he wouldn't get a black mark after all.

"Departing lunar orbit in seven days," he continued, following the VP's lead. "They'll be landing on the fifth planet, Sycamore, where the probe found evidence of bacterial life. It's a violently unstable world, locked in perpetual storms."

He glanced up at LeaMarsa, expecting the presence of storms to produce a reaction. He wasn't disappointed.

"Sounds perfect. I want it."

The VP adopted a thoughtful look, as if pretending to consider her demand. The dwarf lion rubbed its mane against his ear, seeking attention. Zoobondi ignored the animal.

"Where do I sign?" LeaMarsa pressed.

"Would you please wait in the lobby."

She strode out with that stiffly upright gait that seemed to characterize so many psionics. Renfro Zoobondi held his tongue until the door whisked shut behind her.

"You'll take care of the details, make sure she's aboard?"

It wasn't really a question.

"Yes sir. But I do have some concerns."

The assignor hesitated, unsure how forthright he should be. This was obviously a setup. For reasons above his security clearance, Pannis wanted LeaMarsa on that ship. But dropping a powerful and moody psionic into such a lengthy mission fell outside the guidelines of standard policy, not to mention being enticing bait to some Corporeal prosecuting attorney looking to make a name. He didn't want to be the Pannis fall guy if things went wrong.

"Sir, I feel obligated to point out that LeaMarsa de Host is no ordinary psionic. The Jamal Labs report classifies her in the upper one-ten-thousandth of one percent for humans with such abilities."

"Your point?"

"There are a number of red flags. And the OTTO classifies her as–"

"Most psionics have issues. A long voyage might do her good. Bring her out of her shell."

"She suffers from the occasional loss of consciousness while wide awake, a condition the Jamal researchers term 'psychic blackouts.' Even more disturbing, she's been known to inflict bodily harm on herself through self-flagellation or other means. Presumably, she does this as an analgesic against some unknown emotional torment originating in childhood."

The VP looked bored. He stroked the lion's back. The animal hissed.

The assignor tabbed open another part of LeaMarsa's file and made a final stab at getting his concerns across. "Sir, to quote the Jamal analysts, 'LeaMarsa de Host is a disturbing jumble of contradictory emotions. It is imperative that careful consideration be given to placement in order to prevent–'"

"The *Alchemon* is one of the newer ships, isn't it? Full security package?"

"Yes sir, the works. Anti-chronojacker system with warrior pups. And of course, a Level Zero Sentinel."

"A very safe vessel. I don't believe she'll cause any problems that the ship and crew can't handle."

The assignor knew he had to take a stand. "Sir, putting someone like her aboard that ship could create serious issues. And wouldn't it make more sense for her vast talents to be utilized on a mission here on Earth, something with the potential for a more lucrative payoff?"

"Better for her to be first given a less critical assignment to gauge how she handles team interaction."

"Yes sir, that makes sense, but–"

Zoobondi held up a hand for silence. He slid off the edge of the desk and removed a safepad from his pocket, stuck the slim disk to the wall. A faint, low-pitched hum filled the office as the safepad scrambled localized surveillance, rendering their conversation impervious to eavesdropping. The lion squirmed on the VP's shoulder, bothered by the sound.

"We're entering a gray area here," Zoobondi said. "Trust me when I say it's best you don't pursue this subject."

The assignor could only nod. If things indeed went bad, he likely would be the one to take the fall. And there was nothing he could do about it.

Zoobondi smiled and threw him a bone. "I believe you're due for a promotional review next month."

"Yes sir."

"Everything I've read suggests you're doing a fine job. Keep up the good work and I'm certain that your promotion will come through."

The VP deactivated and pocketed the safepad and strolled out the door. The assignor was relieved he was gone. There were dark tales murmured about Renfro Zoobondi. He was ruthlessness personified, supposedly having arranged for the career sabotage of men and women standing in the path of his climb up the corporate ladder. There was even a rumor that for no other reason than the twisted joy of it, he'd killed a man in armor-suit combat.

The assignor returned to the file on the *Alchemon* expedition. Reading between the lines, he wondered whether researching a primordial lifeform was really the mission's primary purpose. Could Pannis have a different agenda, a hidden one?

He closed the file. If that was the case, there was little to be done. He was midlevel management, an undistinguished position within a massive interstellar corporation. Going against the wishes of a man like Renfro Zoobondi was career suicide. The assignor had a wife and young daughter to consider. What would happen to them if he lost his job and possibly fell into the ranks of the "needful majority," those billions who were impoverished and struggling? It wasn't so farfetched, it had happened to a good friend only last month.

That night, the assignor slept fitfully. In the morning he awoke covered in sweat. He'd been in the clutches of a terrifying nightmare.

Thankfully, he couldn't recall any details.

CHAPTER 2

Morphing panels of abstract wall art caught Captain Ericho Solorzano's eye as he entered the *Alchemon*'s bridge, a six-meter-wide ovoid space with a vaulted ceiling patterned in delicate hues. Aesthetic effort had gone into the construction of the 200-meter-long starship.

A surveillance cam tracked Ericho, projected his moving image on a monitor. It revealed a tall slender man with sea blue eyes, a trim goatee and short auburn hair. The black-and-gold uniform of a Pannis captain completed the portrait of a seasoned veteran, fifty-nine earth-years young, not even halfway through his projected lifespan based on genomic and familial demographics. With a regimen of stem cell upgrades, microbiome reboots and old-fashioned luck, he'd be commanding ships until mandatory retirement for bridge officers at age one hundred and twelve.

"Can you truly see yourself, captain?" a moody voice asked. "Or are you lost in the shadows?"

The voice came from behind the HOD, the holographic display occupying the center of the bridge. The large sphere showed an animated swirl of clouds, its default setting. When activated it could display in 3D any object in the ship's library or within telescopic range.

Lieutenant Tomer Donner drifted out from behind the HOD in a motorized chair, his lanky frame oddly contorted as if resistant to comfort. Awkward posture was just one of the lieutenant's quirks although not as strange as applying a particle razor to his entire body five times daily to shave even the tiniest strands of hair.

Ericho had first met the lieutenant at the outset of the voyage. Back then, he'd seemed normal. No bizarre philosophical ramblings and no ungainly posture. Not to mention, a full head of brown locks.

A smile crept onto Donner's pale face as he uttered his favorite enigmatic phrase.

"We are but pawns within the realm of luminous dark."

A second chair floated into view, occupied by a slight man with thin lips and emerald irises streaked with silver. But his most notable feature was the flesh-colored umbilical attached to the center of his forehead that connected his prefrontal cortex to the *Alchemon*. The umbilical drooped across his shoulder like a snake, slithered across the deck to plug into the ship at the base of the HOD.

Jonomy J. Jonomy was the ship's lytic. Like all cyberlytic humans, he boasted identical first, middle and last names, the byproduct of an arcane judicial ruling at the dawn of the cyber age. Back then, the powerful *I-Human* movement, foes of artificial intelligence, had won a lawsuit demanding that lytics be assigned names that distinguish them from "organically pure citizens." As if a hole in the head wasn't enough to mark them as different.

Through Jonomy's umbilical flowed an immense amount of data. Every aspect of the ship could be monitored and controlled via the neuromorphic processors surgically woven into his brain in utero. He was the only crewmember capable of understanding at a fundamental level the vast network that was the *Alchemon*.

"Captain, we are maintaining prime geosynchronous orbit," Jonomy announced. "However, another storm epicenter has moved in below us. We have lost touch again with the lander."

They'd been circling the cloud-veiled world of Sycamore for the past three days, mapping the planet as best as they could through the disruptive storms. Ericho had finally granted permission for a surface mission in one of the *Alchemon*'s pair of landers. A few hours ago, four of the crew had touched down on the turbulent world.

The *Alchemon* was the first manned expedition to this star system, Lalande 21185, a red dwarf more than eight light-years from Earth and so old it had been shining when the sun was still a collection of swirling gases. Exobiologists long ago concluded that none of its planets could support life. Yet an unmanned probe had discovered bacteria on the fifth world, a Venus-sized rock with a nasty atmosphere, setting the stage for the *Alchemon*'s mission.

"Message coming through, Captain," Jonomy said. "Severe distortion. Audio only."

Amid high-pitched static, science rep Hardy Waskov's voice filled the bridge.

"We've concluded our studies here at alpha base. We're preparing to lift off for an area two thousand kilometers to the north. We'll reestablish contact at that time."

Ericho grimaced. "You know the rules, Hardy."

On a virgin planet, communication between a lander and mothership were to be maintained wherever possible. The science rep knew Corporeal exploration policies all too well.

That didn't stop him from circumventing them if it suited his aims.

"Relocation is necessary," Hardy said. "I've discovered that the bacteria has been migrating southward for half-a-million e-years. I suspect dissemination from a common source."

"If you use ground travel, we'd be less likely to lose the com link."

The boxy lander could operate like a tank, make reasonable speed across Sycamore's rocky but navigable surface. The electromagnetic anomalies in the atmosphere made communication all but impossible with airborne craft.

"Are you ordering us to waste a day in transit when we could fly there in a few hours?"

Rules occasionally needed to be sidestepped. But Hardy seemed to take that notion to the extreme. He'd been a thorn in Ericho's side since the *Alchemon*'s departure from lunar orbit nine months ago.

"Affirmative, Hardy. Consider it an order."

"In that case, I must refuse. Our psionic has experienced a psychic event."

That got even Donner's attention. The lieutenant leaned forward to concentrate on Hardy's voice.

"What sort of psychic event?" Ericho asked.

The intercom disintegrated into static.

"Atmospheric discharge," Jonomy said. "We will have to wait it out."

The science rep was within his rights to ignore mothership directives of a non-emergency nature, an example of the inflated importance of psionics in Pannis Corp's grand scheme of cosmic exploration and development.

That scheme was made possible by Quiets – Quantum intra-entangled transpatial systems – short cuts connecting the solar system with any other system reachable by unmanned probes. Thousands of such probes had been sent out over the past centuries, setting up Quiets to allow instantaneous travel.

However, the volatile nature of Quiets meant they had to be constructed at significant distances from large planets. It took months to travel from Earth to the growing collection of Quiets located at the edge of the asteroid belt, and a similar amount of time to reach a targeted world in a distant system.

Creating and maintaining a Quiets was notoriously expensive, even for a huge corporation like Pannis. Hundreds of them now linked Earth to faraway stars. But less than twenty percent had led to worlds with useful resources or capable of being terraformed to support colonies. Still, those few successes generated enormous revenue for Pannis and the other megas, the only entities wealthy enough to fund Quiets travel.

The Lalande 21185 Quiets would never be profitable. The star's planets were too far outside the habitable zone to sustain life, even with severe terraforming. Pannis had undertaken this mission only because the US – Unified Sciences, one of the few governmental entities not tax starved and dependent on corporate generosity – had insisted that the discovery of bacteria on a desolate world was worthy of a manned expedition. The corporation had agreed to foot the bill in exchange for unlimited mineral rights on another venture. Such trade-offs were common throughout the laissez-faire Corporeal.

Ericho enjoyed his role aboard these powerful vessels, journeying to distant star systems, helping the human species expand into the cosmos. That knowledge helped offset the fact that decisions about whether to undertake a particular mission remained far above his pay grade.

The storm interference passed. Hardy returned to the intercom.

"The psychic connection is based on LeaMarsa experiencing a strong emotion at the precise instant my calculations were pinpointing the source of the bacterial migration."

"Could be coincidental," Ericho said. He'd served with psionics on previous expeditions and not once had their abilities proved useful. But ever since one of LeaMarsa's brethren had led his crew to a treasure trove of new pharmaceuticals on the planet Nike Sneak, the megas had been scouring Earth and the settled planets for humans with potent extrasensory abilities.

LeaMarsa had been added to *Alchemon*'s crew a week before departure. That in itself was unusual, considering that extrasolar assignments were generally booked months or years in advance. Technically, she was in Hardy's department and therefore under the science rep's direct supervision, which was all right with Ericho. One weird crewmember, Lieutenant Donner, was enough of a challenge.

The HOD caught his eye. Donner had activated it to display his favorite doodled portrait, a skull-like face. It resembled a human one that had been stretched to accommodate an additional sensory organ, a marble-sized orb between the mouth and nose.

The lieutenant barked laughter and pedaled his chair closer to Ericho.

"Ah, Captain. You are poised at a juncture, drenched in the consequence of choosing between the unknown and the unknowable."

Ericho ignored Donner's latest verbal diarrhea and returned his attention to Hardy.

"For the record, I don't support your decision."

"Understood. We'll reestablish contact when we touch down at the new site. Waskov out."

"Wait. You said LeaMarsa experienced a strong emotion at the moment you discovered the source of the migration?"

"Yes."

"What sort of emotion?"

"I fail to see how that's pertinent."

"Humor me. Was she happy? Sad? What?"

The link remained silent. Ericho was about to conclude that Hardy had terminated the transmission or that Sycamore's unstable atmosphere had done it for him. But then the science rep's words abruptly came through loud and free of interference.

"LeaMarsa experienced a nebulous sensation of fear."

Lieutenant Donner lunged from his chair, charged at Ericho with an expression of mad rage. His hands were balled into fists, his posture that of a man ready to do violence.

Ericho's fight instincts took hold. He gripped the armrests, ready to springboard from the chair. But Donner abruptly froze.

"Is something wrong?" Ericho asked, keeping his tone even, the preferred technique for dealing with an unhinged individual. He watched Donner's face for any telltales that an actual attack was forthcoming.

The lieutenant's anger dissolved as quickly as it had appeared. Donner backed away, chuckling with delight. Ericho was reminded of a child who'd just gotten away with some outrageous playacting stunt.

"I caused you a fright, did I not?"

"Yes, Lieutenant, I would say so."

"I was merely making a point. A person's actions and reactions lie beyond the realm of predictive behavior.

What happens to any of us isn't our fault."

"Captain Solorzano, is there anything else?" Hardy demanded, unaware of what was transpiring on the bridge.

"No. *Alchemon* out."

Jonomy cut the link. Ericho kept a wary eye on Donner. The lieutenant settled back in his chair, stared blankly at the vaulted ceiling.

Ericho didn't know what to make of the incident. Had Donner truly been on the edge of losing control or had it merely been a bizarre stunt?

Whatever the case, one thing was certain. The unknown demons afflicting the *Alchemon*'s second-in-command were growing more inexplicable by the day.

CHAPTER 3

LeaMarsa de Host, the freaky ghost.

The disparaging phrase from childhood popped into LeaMarsa's head as she stood in the new locale where they'd touched down. It was daybreak on Sycamore, which meant fierce winds scouring the boulder-strewn landscape and thunderous energy storms ripping through the upper atmosphere. All were amplified into a cacophony by her shieldsuit's external mikes.

LeaMarsa de Host, the freaky ghost. Schoolmates had taken to calling her that. Mostly it was because they were frightened of her psionic abilities although sometimes it was simply because they were mean. She tended to recall the words whenever she found herself in an unpleasant environment.

And Sycamore was certainly that.

Everything was sporadically perceived here because of the atmospheric turbulence and swirling fog. Nearby hills seemed to blend into the brooding sky. The distant sun was a sickly halo when visible at all. Shiny green liquid the consistency of mercury huddled in small ponds. Violent gusts occasionally lifted the ponds off the ground and sent them shooting through the air like aquatic fireworks.

She could literally feel the planet's violence, even diluted by her shieldsuit gyros into meek wobbles. The heavy garment made her feel insignificant, a clump of flesh encased in mechanized armor.

And she sensed hidden forces at work here, disguised behind a veil of psionic interference the way the hills hid behind the fog. The notion triggered a dismal question, one that had been occurring to her with increasing regularity during the nine-month trip out.

Why did I come on this journey?

"Are you all right, dear?" Faye Kuriyama asked. "You look far away."

The scientist stood a few meters to the left, observing her with concern.

"I'm fine. Just thinking about what a strange place this is."

"No argument. Sycamore's as weird as they come."

Faye had piercing ruby eyes, wavy blond hair and an exquisite face and figure that placed her at the pinnacle of the Danbury Lustre Scale, the popular system for measuring the visual attributes of sexuality. Although the Danbury quantified males as well as females, LeaMarsa and many other women viewed it as a misogynistic throwback to male-dominated Helio Age cultures, where feminine value was too often equated only with physical beauty. But in today's Corporeal, voices such as theirs seemed increasingly in the minority.

Faye didn't come by her attributes naturally. She was a genejob, embryonically modified. Her parents had made a fortune cloning attractive twenty-first century actors and actresses from preserved DNA but limiting them to a low threshold of consciousness so they could be legally sold to wealthy families as house pets. Faye wasn't consciousness-restricted. But she was created to maximize sexual radiance and was equipped with pheromone secretors that could be activated by willpower alone, and which supposedly could incite lust from any man or woman within sniffing distance.

LeaMarsa liked Faye. The scientist resisted using her physical attributes for professional advancement, instead putting in seven e-years of concentrated study to become a GS, a multidisciplinary general scientist, a rarity in a Corporeal dominated by specialists. Still, LeaMarsa couldn't help wonder whether Faye had disappointed her parents by not following their genetic prescription for her life.

The scientist smiled. "I have to confess, dear, I'm beginning to share Hardy's enthusiasm for this place. The very instability of the planet is enticing."

For reasons LeaMarsa couldn't comprehend, Faye had taken to calling her "dear."

"Think of it," she continued, her voice rising in excitement. "Life exists here, has somehow managed to adapt itself. The Sycom strain is like nothing we've ever discovered."

She was Hardy's understudy, and at twenty-nine, six years older than LeaMarsa. In temperament, however, they remained far apart. What Faye found wonderfully strange and alien, LeaMarsa perceived as grim and dangerous.

"Any new psychic connections?" Faye asked.

LeaMarsa shook her head inside the bulky helmet, trying not to show frustration. Since touching down in this new area, Faye and Hardy had asked her variations of that question half-a-dozen times.

Any telepathic messages, LeaMarsa? Do you detect something, LeaMarsa? Are there superluminal impulses dancing in your head, parading through your body, tickling your spirit?

No!

How many times had she tried to explain that her so-called abilities didn't occur with the precision inherent to the hard sciences, that psychic impressions often occurred in jumbled ways. Back at the Jamal Labs, they'd subdivided her abilities into neat quantitative arenas in order to compare her with other humans possessing telepathic skills. They'd proclaimed her a psionic of the highest order, capable of tapping into that theoretical quantum jetstream believed to be the source of superluminals and psychic powers. The pronouncement suggested that they actually knew something about her.

"Nothing new," she said, maintaining an even tone.

"I wouldn't worry about it, dear. I'm sure things will happen in their own good time."

Hardy Waskov's booming voice cut in. "We're within the area of greatest bacterial concentration. I've just received confirmation from the *Alchemon*. The Sycom strain originated within this grid."

LeaMarsa glanced at her control panel, a collection of multicolored data readouts and diagrams along the inner surface of her helmet. She didn't understand all the readouts but knew enough to realize that a moving yellow blip sixty meters to her left represented Hardy.

"Can we pinpoint the migration source any closer?" Faye asked.

"Too much wild energy in the atmosphere," Hardy said.

"What about temperature spikes?"

"No discernible hot spots. One hundred twenty degrees is pretty much the average during daylight hours."

LeaMarsa glared into the gloomy skies, trying to locate the sun. It was hard to believe that this portion of the planet's rotation was referred to as daylight.

"There has to be some sort of anomaly," Faye insisted.

There is, LeaMarsa thought. *Me.*

At the instant Hardy was calculating the source of the migration she'd felt a shiver of fear, followed by what the researchers at Jamal referred to as a psychic blackout – a loss of consciousness in the here and now – a phenomenon that often accompanied her psionic impressions. The moment of fear and the subsequent blackout, lasting less than a minute, had come upon her without warning.

She'd never told anyone what happened during the blackouts, always insisting that she couldn't remember. Deceit was preferable to the truth, which likely would consign her to those regions of the OTTO scale inhabited by the delusional or hopelessly insane. In truth, she remained awake and alert, but with her consciousness transported elsewhere.

LeaMarsa called the place to which she journeyed during her blackouts *neurospace*. The name had popped into her head during the first blackout she could recall, at age thirteen, which had occurred at some point after her parents had died in a shuttle crash near one of the lunar colonies. She'd been 400,000 kilometers away at her New Haven, Connecticut, boarding school. According to the testimony of amused classmates, she'd been walking out of her dorm room when she'd frozen in an upright position, eyes wide open and face a blank.

Neurospace. It was an alternate universe that existed beyond the immediacy of her senses. Although she could *see* it – a vast starfield, pulsating specks of light against the black – she sensed that regular vision played no part in her perception. Eyesight was an analogue for what she witnessed when she journeyed there, a trick of the mind to process a form of information beyond normal sensory comprehension. She couldn't even be sure whether neurospace was an actual external universe or something that existed solely within her own head. Maybe it was a bit of both.

Her reverie was interrupted by a sudden wind lifting a pond into the air and scattering it into droplets. The action brought a touch of life to the gloomy atmosphere. The Sycom strain lived within those ponds. The periodic explosions served to distribute the bacteria across the planet.

The husky voice of the fourth member of the lander crew, their pilot Rigel Shaheed, entered the conversation.

"I scanned the target area for any formations that don't belong. No luck. Just more boulders and ponds typical for this latitude."

"Are you certain?" quizzed Hardy, sounding disappointed.

"As certain as shit floats in zero-g."

LeaMarsa was glad Rigel remained within the lander. There was a brutish quality to the *Alchemon*'s tech officer. She found his colorful language and in-your-face mannerisms annoying.

"Try running a basal geo," Faye suggested. "See if these rocks have any compositional differences."

"Doing it now," Rigel said.

"LeaMarsa, is there any particular type of scan you think we should try?" Hardy asked.

She sighed. "Nothing comes to mind."

"Anything at all, dear?" Faye prodded.

LeaMarsa gave a weary shrug. The shieldsuit translated the movement into a slight rising of her shoulder pads.

"Hey, got something," Rigel said. "A boulder that doesn't match the surrounding terrain."

"Location?" Hardy demanded.

"Close. Five meters northwest of Faye and LeaMarsa."

"Don't touch it until I get there! It is of the utmost importance that I be present."

Faye switched to a private channel, grinned impishly. "Hardy doesn't want some lowly researcher like yours truly upstaging him on a big discovery. That might jeopardize his dream of a Corporeal knighthood."

LeaMarsa followed Faye toward the rock. It was about three meters in diameter, with a craggy, weathered surface that made it indistinguishable from adjacent boulders.

"What's so different about it?" Faye asked.

"Check out the other side," Rigel said.

They circled the rock. The center of the far side was smoothly elliptical. Even more telling was its coloration, a shade of blue reminiscent of an Earth ocean in sunlight.

"Bless my odorous ass," Rigel said. "That blue stuff isn't rock. It appears to be the surface of a single, carbon-based multicellular organism."

"Alive," Faye whispered.

"And mostly encased inside the rock. Which means it must have been here for at least a billion e-years. That's the age of much of the surface debris."

Hardy's shieldsuit bounded out of the fog to join them, the excitement of discovery coloring his words. "It's unlikely the rock landed here as a meteorite. Possibly the organism is of subterranean origin, detritus from some lifeform that exists or existed underground."

"Unlikely," Rigel said. "Doesn't fit the geo profile. And Jonomy ran a preliminary compositional scan through GEL. Initial analysis indicates no known organic comparisons."

GEL was the general library. All the *Alchemon*'s major and minor systems had three-letter designations. LeaMarsa hadn't bothered learning most of the acronyms but GEL was an exception. On the voyage out, she'd frequently accessed

the library from her wafer, becoming enamored of vintage
novels of the late nineteenth and early twentieth centuries.
The characters were arcane, but she couldn't get enough of
the stories, particularly a Victorian detective called Sherlock
Holmes whose bohemian lifestyle and innate cleverness
enabled him to unravel the deepest mysteries.

"Don't ask how the damn thing's carrying on metabolic
activity," Rigel continued. "Even Jonomy's stumped."

LeaMarsa was reminded of the popular saying: *If a lytic
doesn't know, it's probably unknowable.*

"The organism must have been entirely encased within
the rock," Hardy said. "Erosion likely exposed part of it
half a million years ago. I think we can make a preliminary
assumption that that's when the bacteria was released from it
and began migrating across the surface."

"Makes sense," Faye said.

The scientist knelt in front of the organism, leaned in until
her visor was only centimeters from the blue surface. "Partially
translucent. I can see what appear to be thin interlacing
channels, almost like a venous structure. Should I risk taking
a sample?"

"By all means," Hardy said. "But to be on the safe side and
not disturb any unknown equilibrium, keep it minimal. Ten
cc's. Surface layer only."

Faye uncoupled a pistol syringe from her utility belt, pressed
the barrel gently into the bluish mass.

"Feels soft. Gelatinous."

The instant Faye's syringe touched the organism, LeaMarsa
felt a shiver vault the length of her spine. The shiver reached
her brainstem, morphed into a single word-thought.

Tragedy.

Tragedy in the past? Or in the future. Like many of her psychic impressions, clear interpretation remained a challenge.

Before Faye could depress the syringe, a loud screeching filled LeaMarsa's helmet. A sheet of emerald-green fire lanced across the sky. Bolts of lightning sliced through the fog, cracked against a distant hillside.

For an instant, everything was illuminated by an eerie light. And then the organism seemed to perform some energy counterpoint. Shafts of fiery red energy erupted from its surface, shot upward into the bleak skies.

A tremendous explosion lifted LeaMarsa's shieldsuit off the ground, sent her tumbling backward. She crashed hard on her back, five meters away. Fragments of shattered rock rained down all around her.

"Jesus!" Faye hissed. "What the hell was that?"

LeaMarsa realized Faye and Hardy had also been thrown onto their backs.

"Everybody check your suits," Rigel ordered.

"I'm fine," Hardy grunted. "All systems green."

"Same here," Faye said.

LeaMarsa turned her attention to the row of status indicator lumes on the control panel. She drew a breath of fear when she realized all of them weren't green.

"I have two yellow indicators."

"Which systems?" Rigel demanded.

"Thermal balance and mech symmetry." She had no idea exactly what those things were but was relieved by Rigel's response.

"They're noncritical. Just hit your main reset."

She did as the tech officer asked. A moment later, the two lumes returned to reassuring green.

"I'm good," she said, moving her legs to stand up. Servos

responded, motored her suit to an upright position.

"Jonomy says the energy transformation you just experienced appears to be a unique event," Rigel said. "Neither our mapping sensors nor the original probe registered anything like it."

LeaMarsa knew what the others only suspected. It was her presence here that had caused the violent energy eruption and the organism's subsequent release from the rock. She sensed the truth of that even if she couldn't explain how or why.

"Look," Faye whispered, pointing to where the boulder once stood.

The energy discharge had exploded away the rock, fully revealing the organism. To LeaMarsa, the blue clump resembled an extra-large medicine ball made of hardened jelly. It pulsated faintly, like some impossibly large human heart.

Faye pressed her hand against it. "Much cooler than the atmosphere. Glove sensors read it at nineteen degrees."

Hardy frowned. "Perhaps the rock protected the bulk of the organism from the heat..."

He trailed off. The two scientists exchanged intense looks.

"It might not be able to survive in a higher temperature," Faye said.

Hardy nodded. "Rigel, I want a capsule dispatched immediately. Never mind the internal adjustments. Just make sure the coolers are set to nineteen degrees."

"Got it."

"And inform the captain that he should begin prepping the *Alchemon*'s containment system."

"I'll pass along your request."

Hardy grimaced. "Please do so. But kindly make it clear to Captain Solorzano that Pannis would be most unhappy to learn that we'd discovered a unique alien lifeform, but then just as quickly lost it because of a captain's bureaucratic intransigence."

Rigel didn't respond.

Faye again knelt in front of the organism and leaned in close. But she immediately jerked back, startled.

"There's a smaller and denser object in the center. But that can't be right."

"What can't?" Hardy demanded.

Faye removed a scope from her utility belt, stuck it onto her faceplate at eye level and pressed the cylindrical end against the organism.

"Oh my god! The denser object, it has an internal skeletal structure. Something similar to a ribcage. More bones, though, and different spacing." She paused to adjust a setting on the scope. "It looks similar to a humanoid fetus."

"Astounding," Hardy said. "But what did you mean when you said that can't be right?"

"It wasn't there prior to that energy outburst."

"You must be mistaken."

"Take a look."

Faye transferred a replay of her suitcam video to Hardy and LeaMarsa. She was right. Prior to the outburst, the fetus wasn't there.

"It's about thirty centimeters long," she continued. "Two arms, two legs. The head appears to be more vertically elongated than ours."

"This is utterly amazing," Hardy announced. "We may be bearing witness to one of the most dynamic and important finds in the long and colorful history of the human species. We very well could be standing at the dawn of a new era of discovery."

LeaMarsa thought Hardy's remarks sounded rehearsed, a speech recorded for future media consumption. The science rep often came across like he was performing for an audience.

"Capsule dispatched," Rigel said. "You should see it approaching from the south."

A thick white cylinder drifted out of the fog. Microjets on its underside and stern were firing synchronously, keeping it aloft and moving forward.

The capsule halted three meters from the organism. The jets tapered off, allowing it to settle onto the surface. Its front end popped open, revealing an interior lined with delicate webbing.

"How do we get the organism into the capsule?" Faye wondered. "It appears delicate. We could tear it apart trying to lift it."

"Good point," Hardy said. "Perhaps we could slip a tarp underneath and gently slide…"

He trailed off as the organism rolled across the ground toward the cylinder. With a gentle bounce, it hopped over the lip of the capsule and nestled itself inside. The smart webbing tightened around the gelatinous blue sphere and the hatch closed. Exterior readouts turned green, signifying it was safely contained.

No one spoke for a few seconds. Faye broke the silence.

"Perhaps it sensed an environment similar to its previous one."

"Sensed how?" Rigel wondered. "It doesn't have any sensory organs."

"But that fetal creature inside it might."

"There may be a simpler explanation," Hardy said. "Perhaps some form of magnetoreception, similar to what certain Earth based organisms like sharks and honeybees use for navigation.

The capsule has a plethora of electronic instrumentation and projects fairly strong magnetic fields."

"Way too many coincidences going on here for my piece of mind," Rigel said. "The little buttwanker seems like it *wants* to go with us. I don't trust anything that's this damn cooperative."

"We mustn't leap to conclusions," Hardy warned. "We have no idea what we're dealing with."

LeaMarsa felt drained, as if she'd just gone through some sort of crisis, but one that transcended her understanding.

"Back to the lander?" Faye proposed. "Start running tests?"

"Yes, to your first suggestion," Hardy said. "But we need to hold off on any immediate testing and transport it straight up to the ship and into the proper containment area. We can then run a full battery of tests and study it at our leisure."

At our leisure. To LeaMarsa, the phrase suggested an optimism that was as far from reality as the *Alchemon* was from Earth.

CHAPTER 4

This was Ericho's fourteenth deep-space expedition and his ninth as captain. His commands had ranged from a simple recon flight through a fledgling Quiets to a massive colony vessel packed with seventy thousand settlers armed with new-frontier optimism.

The *Alchemon*, with its two modular decks configured to support a mere nine crewmembers, should have made for a fairly easy voyage. Instead, the last few months had ranked among the most difficult of his career.

Low on the psychosynchronicity scale, crewdoc June Courthouse had speculated. The crew was unable to mesh into a tight unit. Pannis and the other megas utilized psych algorithms to match individuals with missions. But such modeling could miss what was often obvious to an experienced spacefarer, statistically acceptable quirks at the outset of an expedition that ultimately could produce a troubling Tomer Donner.

It wasn't only the lieutenant who was a problem. Hardy Waskov was vexing in his arrogance, which was likely amplified by financial obligations to three ex-wives and seven children. And then there was LeaMarsa.

Ericho hadn't been completely powerless in terms of crew assignment. He'd been a captain long enough to work the system and had managed to get two friends assigned to the *Alchemon*, June and Rigel. Unfortunately, he'd seen no reason to protest when June asked him to also include Donner, a family acquaintance who supposedly was being blacklisted – denied assignments worthy of his experience – because of some sort of legal entanglements within Pannis. Ericho regretted not looking more closely into his background before granting June's request.

A cluster of green lumes on one of the bridge's main panels turned red. A pulsating alarm filled the air.

"Level Six, Captain," Jonomy said. "A break in a TEM line feeding Bono engine."

"Give me a schematic."

The diagram blossomed on Ericho's wafer. A mass of labeled geometry highlighted by red patches indicated the trouble areas.

"Bono engine is taking itself offline," the lytic said as he silenced the alarm.

"What about the other engines?" Although the quartet was not firing while they remained in orbit and the *Alchemon* could operate with a single engine, any such troubles could lengthen the trip home.

"Beyonce, Mick and Celine retain full functionality."

As Ericho watched, internal repair systems addressed the thermometry problem. The red patches on his display began to shrink. Finally, only one stubborn clump of scarlet refused to go green.

"I have notified RAP for manual correction of the last errant section," Jonomy said. "A repair pup is being dispatched into that tube. Duplex circuitry is handling the load without any problems."

Ericho turned off his display. There was no need for him to do anything. The malfunction was just one more in a series of routine issues that plagued a ship as complex as the *Alchemon*. He felt useless in such situations, knowing full well that the innate intelligence of the ship itself, with the support and assistance of a lytic, could easily handle such difficulties.

The captain needs to master that the master's not the captain. That classic saying had been drilled into him at Pannis command school in Barstow, California, and the dialectic phrase entered awareness whenever trouble occurred. Like most captains, he'd long ago adjusted to the true nature of starship command. For all practical purposes, the ship and its lytic were the ones responsible for day-to-day operations.

And if the direst projections of the Bridge Officers Union were to be believed, Ericho might be among the last generation of unmodified humans to command these ships. Many experts were predicting that a new wave of cyberlytic advancements, long stalled by lawsuits brought by *I-Human* and other anti-AI organizations, soon would lead to elimination of the megas' proprietary officer corps. Captains and lieutenants would become as redundant as car and truck drivers prior to autonomous vehicles. Vessels run solely by increasingly advanced lytics would become the new norm.

It was a sobering future to contemplate for a man in Ericho's profession, a far different scenario than he'd imagined as a child reading *Captain Clarke* novels. That popular series of juvenile adventures about a gifted starship commander had inspired his choice of careers.

Of course, real interstellar travel tended to be slow-paced and lacked the spikes of desperate action prevalent in the *Captain Clarke* universe. Still, Ericho enjoyed the nature of his profession, even the periods of boredom. And unlike many of society's long-lived humans who aspired to multiple careers, he had no desire to do anything else.

"The pup has arrived in the trouble area," Jonomy said. "RAP estimates an hour for repairs."

RAP was Robotics and Probes, the Level Four system that controlled the maintenance pups, the army of small specialized machines that lived in the bowels of the ship and handled repairs that couldn't be dealt with by the internal correctors. Scores of the basketball-sized pups patrolled the access tunnels that wound mazelike through the *Alchemon*, an entire domain too compact for human intrusion.

Donner, largely silent since that threatening outburst several hours ago, erupted into giggles.

"Ah, let us rejoice in the pain that will soon be upon us. For the voice of the plague blows like a fierce wind, singing of the storm."

Within the HOD, the lieutenant again began doodling his obsessive image, the elongated skull-like face. Ericho decided enough was enough.

"Override it, Jonomy."

The lytic responded. The holo dissolved. Donner's expression soured, like a child deprived of a favorite toy.

"Captain, you are a slayer of veracity. But truth will find a way, for we are but pawns within the realm of luminous dark."

"The bridge is adequately staffed," Jonomy said, catching Ericho's eye. "Although your shift is not over, I am sure that the Captain would agree to your early vacating."

"Absolutely," Ericho said. "You're free to go, lieutenant."

Donner responded with a cryptic smile, making it hard to tell if he'd take the bait.

"The lander has cleared the atmosphere," Jonomy said. "Contact reestablished. Estimated docking in twenty-six minutes. Hardy again requests a decision on the organism."

It was Ericho's chance to be a captain, issue a command decision. But he didn't know what to do.

Hardy wanted the organism brought into the containment, the isolated portion of the ship that theoretically could safely house any known lifeform. But based on the info transmitted by Rigel, what they'd found down there was not only unique but disturbingly bizarre. It was difficult enough imagining an organism surviving within a rock for a billion years, let alone with some sort of fetal creature inside it. Add to those anomalies the weird storm leading to its release from the rock and the way it had rolled obediently into the capsule, and even the most reckless captain would entertain caution.

The organism would have to be returned to Earth, of course. That was a primary purpose of this mission, or for that matter, any Quiets voyage that came upon alien life. Pannis would have Ericho's job if he failed such a basic obligation.

However, if a captain felt an organism posed a danger to the ship, he had the option of keeping it outside the vessel in the ecopod attached to the hull. The downside of such a choice would be having to spend the nine-month return voyage with a disgruntled science rep. Hardy's study of the organism would be severely limited if it wasn't inside the containment.

And if the organism later turned out to be in some way profitable to Pannis, his decision would be criticized for being overcautious, possibly resulting in a black mark on his record. Despite occasional misgivings, Ericho had every intention of continuing to command starships for as long as they'd have him.

"What kind of probabilities are we looking at?" he asked the lytic.

Jonomy rubbed a hand across his forehead umbilical, caressing the cable as if it were a pet snake.

"In regard to potential danger, EPS concludes that the organism's composition and behavior produce too many unknowns for accurate projections."

EPS was Elementary Probability Scanning, the Level Three system tasked with calculating odds.

"That said, a basic analysis reveals a forty-nine percent probability that our best course of action would be to bring the organism into the containment, versus a forty-eight percent probability that it should be housed externally. The difference is statistically irrelevant."

There were times when EPS calculations could be helpful. This clearly wasn't one of them.

"Returning the organism to the planet's surface registers two percent. Naturally, that does not take into consideration potential career fallout, particularly for an expedition's commander."

"And the remaining one percent?"

"Destroy it."

Donner muttered something. Ericho couldn't make out the words.

"Under Pannis guidelines," Jonomy continued, "those latter two options are unacceptable."

The HOD darkened into an image of the approaching lander against the shrouded backdrop of Sycamore. Jonomy magnified the 3D picture until the cylindrical capsule attached to the craft's flat underside became visible.

Donner rose from his chair and ambled to the starboard

airseal. As the door slid open at his approach, he paused and turned back to them.

"May dreams from beyond blister my soul and serve as my epitaph."

Grinning madly, he dashed through the airseal. It whisked shut behind him.

"His ideation is increasingly obfuscating," Jonomy said.

One way of putting it, Ericho thought. But the lytic was right. Donner was beginning to sound like a walking malfunction. And that incident a few hours ago when he seemed ready to erupt into violence suggested a man with an overloaded fuse.

Ericho realized he'd ignored the problem long enough. He would have to do something about the lieutenant before the situation degenerated further.

"Captain, Hardy insists on speaking to you. He is impatient for a decision."

The science rep usually sounded impatient. That didn't mean Ericho had to talk to him. All too soon, Hardy would be back aboard, bombarding him with petty grievances. But perhaps with his precious organism to study, he wouldn't be as bothersome.

Ericho realized he'd arrived at a decision.

"Inform Doctor Waskov that the containment will be ready."

From the files of Lieutenant
Tomer Donner, Pannis Corp
bridge officer

His name is Renfro Zoobondi. He's an icy-assed errand boy for Pannis' executive team, a fixer who handles the dirtiest assignments.

And Renfro Zoobondi enjoys his work.

I was on the Theodoris, *returning home from a seven-month passenger run through the Earth-Karama Quiets. It was the first voyage out for my young cabin mate and Pannis trainee, Karl Mingus.*

The two of us had begun an affair on Karama after discovering a mutual interest in twentieth-century jazz musicians. In short order we'd fallen madly in love and were intending to marry when we returned.

Never in my life had I felt this way about someone, felt linked to another human at such a fundamental level. Just being in Karl's presence often gave me incredible feelings of joy. I dreamed of us exploring the stars together, of being intimate on so many different planets that we'd be invited to join the exclusive Lightyears Club, whose members had experienced verified sexual encounters on at least six inhabited worlds.

Sensual fantasies aside, I was looking out for Karl on a professional level, trying to make sure his apprenticeship resulted in the best possible outcome: a junior crew license.

Renfro Zoobondi was hitching a ride back to Earth on the Theodoris *after addressing some labor problems at the mega's mineral-processing facility on Karama. Many of those "labor problems" were onboard, returning to the home world with bleak job prospects after having been fired by Zoobondi. Not surprisingly, tensions were running high.*

There was even talk of the most dire form of mutiny: chronojacking the ship, defeating its safeguards and energizing the spatiotemporal coagulators before the vessel entered a Quiets. Theoretical physicists remained fuzzy on calculating the extent of the weird energies unleashed but the physics of spacetime dictated the strange outcome. The ship would be propelled forward into a random future and locale.

You'd have thought Zoobondi would have kept to himself in his first-class cabin. But he was too arrogant for that. He walked freely through the ship, ignoring the enraged looks and whispered threats of the fired employees. He seemed to relish the fact that he was hated.

The incident happened only a few hours before the Theodoris *was to enter the Quiets. Karl and a man named Emil — one of Zoobondi's labor victims — were in the gym working out when Zoobondi entered to begin his own exercise routine. Angry words were exchanged between Emil and Zoobondi. One thing led to another, and soon the hotheaded former employee was challenging the Pannis fixer to a fight wearing X-7 armor suits.*

The X-7s aboard the Theodoris *weren't the military versions and boasted no weaponry. They were meant for use by the ship's security contingent, to be donned only in the event of some form of social unrest that demanded serious crowd control. But weaponized or not, a person encased in one could still inflict serious damage via servo-enhanced kicks and punches.*

According to later testimony, only the three men were in the gym at the time of the incident: Emil and Zoobondi in the bulky armor suits and my Karl, who'd been reluctantly recruited by the pair to serve as fight referee.

Zoobondi somehow managed to disable the gym's security cameras, perhaps using a safepad. In any case, he made sure there would be no official record of the fight.

Emil later admitted that he was no match for Zoobondi. Emil was attacked savagely, and even with the protection of the X-7 received enough serious injuries to spend two days in the Theodoris' medcenter. Emil testified that as the fight neared its end, Zoobondi wrestled him to the mats and landed punch after punch. According to Emil, on three occasions Karl loudly declared the fight over and Zoobondi the winner. But Zoobondi refused to end the brutal beating.

Emil was too dazed from being pummeled to recall the details of what transpired next. He thought he remembered Karl trying to grab hold of Zoobondi's arm to pull the fixer off him. He believed he heard the sickening punch that Zoobondi landed on Karl's unprotected face with the X-7's power glove, the blow that killed the love of my life.

Zoobondi claimed it was a tragic accident. There wasn't enough evidence to bring manslaughter charges. But even if there had been, the bastard was too well connected for such charges to stick.

Shortly after the civil case I filed against Zoobondi was dismissed with prejudice by a Corporeal court — not so much as a blemish would appear in Zoobondi's personnel file — I angrily confronted the killer. It took everything within me to hold back my outrage at the man, who seemed amused. He didn't bother trying to claim it was an accident as he had in court, as much as admitted that he'd gotten away with murder.

But it wasn't until that moment when he patted me on the shoulder and, with a sadistic smile, expressed his regret over my loss that I made my vow.

In memory of Karl Mingus, in memory of the annihilation of the love of my life, I will make Renfro Zoobondi pay for his crime.

CHAPTER 5

The containment area occupied a large portion of the port quarter of downdeck, in a section of corridor bounded by airseals at both ends. Past the stern-facing lock were the *Alchemon*'s twin lander hangars. Beyond the forward lock was downdeck's main expanse of shops and specialty labs, as well as the natatorium, dreamlounge, medcenter, main social room and various utility areas.

LeaMarsa stepped out of the elevator from updeck, where the bridge, crew cabins, dining area and hydroponic gardens offered a more soothing ambience. Although downdeck had similar styling, there was something vaguely unsettling about the lower level.

She passed through an airseal into a short corridor and approached the containment lab entrance, a door with a more imposing appearance than the others. According to Hardy it was pressurized to blow inward in the unlikely event of a breach to prevent contaminants from escaping. It also boasted a sureshutter. Should fast closure be required, the high-speed pneumatic blades would slice through any object positioned in the portal.

The door supposedly was smart enough not to close while a

human stood within its frame. But LeaMarsa had heard horror stories about sureshutters severing appendages or worse.

The walls surrounding the containment lab were equally shielded. Sensors constantly scanned for breaches. The entire containment area was overseen by a Level Two system, the second-highest echelon of the ship's six-tiered control network, the Sentinel notwithstanding.

None of the safeguards made LeaMarsa feel secure.

Why did I come on this journey?

She recalled the meeting with the Pannis assignor and that slick VP, and how she'd arrogantly demanded a starship assignment.

Her actions had been driven by exasperation. Over the years, she'd grown angry about her own identity, about feeling trapped in a culture that looked upon psionics as dangerous freaks. She'd come to resent that her abilities had isolated her from mainstream Corporeal life.

Many citizens avoided contact with potent psionics, supposedly because they feared having their thoughts or feelings read. Such apprehensions were mostly nonsense, the product of media distortions. Telepathic contacts rarely happened in such simplistic ways. Individuals who were strong psionic receptors might be disturbed by her presence, but for most people it came down to fear as an overriding reason. Not exactly a new idea in the history of the human species.

When Pannis had offered her a generous stipend and future employment in exchange for a battery of tests at Jamal, she'd eagerly accepted. She would take the mega's creds and proceed to make life miserable for them, punishing them in the name of all psionics, making them pay for the injustices in her own life. Along with those vengeance fantasies came an even more naïve notion, that journeying far from Earth would somehow provide a stability that had always eluded her.

She unleashed a bitter laugh. Since boarding the *Alchemon*, her role as the avenging outsider had given way to escalating anxiety. And as the ship drew closer to Sycamore, that anxiety at times threatened to become something even worse, the most terrifying aspect of her life, a miasma of dread that long ago she had come to refer to as *the reek*.

It had first manifested when she was five years old. She'd been playing with a doll in the bedroom of the Wisconsin condo where they'd lived at the time. While morphing the plastiform figure from one Disney princess to another, the doll's programming had malfunctioned, melting the face into an ugly blob.

At that instant, inexplicable shudders cascaded through her, accompanied by a vile odor of decaying flesh and a sensation of hands wrapped around her neck, strangling her. Gasping for breath, she'd erupted into mad screams.

Her mother had rushed in and tried to comfort her. The effort had proved futile; she continued shrieking under the torment of dread, death odor and invisible hands crushing her windpipe. Not until her mother had summoned the glimmering holo of a virtual medic, who'd prescribed a drowse drink – maternally forced down her throat – had chemically induced sleep brought relief.

Throughout LeaMarsa's childhood, the reek had returned on a number of occasions, enveloping her in its triple embrace of terror, decomposition and strangulation. She'd suffered a bout at age seven while watching a scary movie and another episode a year later after falling down a short flight of steps at school. She'd adamantly refused to discuss the reek with her parents or anyone else, afraid that merely talking about it would bring on a fresh attack.

The reek had struck increasingly during her teen years, including several incidents following the death of her parents in the shuttle crash. But by age fifteen she'd learned to gauge when an attack was imminent and take action to short-circuit it. Whenever she sensed the reek was close to penetrating waking consciousness, she would take flight by engaging in strenuous exercise. Long swims and vigorous runs had proven particularly effective.

She'd stumbled upon a more direct method for warding off the reek while fighting a hellish, nine-foot demon. The virtual game, *Jet Li's Shaolin Smackdown,* was played sitting in a haptic chair, and by overriding the chair's neural limiters – a trick learned from a schoolmate – she'd been able to feel the agonizing but non-injurious sensations of the demon's kicks and punches. The use of pain as an analgesic had opened up a whole new arena for countering the attacks.

Sometimes the reek came at night, in her dreams. Using biofeedback, she'd trained herself to recognize such onslaughts and awaken. Then she'd drive the terror back to its subliminal depths by lashing her thighs with a short length of fishing rod, later rubbing healcream on the marks so her parents wouldn't notice.

LeaMarsa didn't know what the reek represented or why it hovered within some deep chasm of her mind. All she knew for certain was that it could never be allowed to enter consciousness. As awful as its symptoms were, she sensed that at the heart of it was a thing so terrifying that it was beyond her capacity to confront. Vigorous exercise or self-inflicted pain – the method didn't matter as long as the reek was held at bay.

She reached the containment door and touched it with her palm. The door slid open. Recalling those sureshutter tales, she dashed quickly through the portal.

The compact lab was outfitted with workbenches and chairs, cabinets of test gear and a pair of superhaptic glove boxes. Sheets of white lumes beneath the translucent floor and ceiling provided shadow-free illumination.

Hardy sat at a bench observing scrolling data on a monitor, his chubby arms poking from a green lab shirt. A sliver of a smile crept across his jowled face as he spotted her.

"Welcome, LeaMarsa. Have you ever been in here before?"

She shook her head.

"Not much to see, I'm afraid. But for us research types, plenty to keep us occupied."

Faye emerged from behind a cabinet. "Recovered from decon, dear?"

"Uh-huh."

That had been another unpleasant experience. When they'd returned from the surface, Rigel had maneuvered the lander to an external airlock that led directly to the containment area. He'd guided the capsule with the organism through the outer lock, down a chute to the inner lock and, once repressurization was complete, into its new home.

After docking in a lander hangar, the four of them had been required to pass through a complex decontamination procedure. Melon-sized robots had scanned, sprayed and bathed them for the better part of an hour.

"Let us bring you to up to speed on what we've learned so far," Hardy said.

Faye walked to the blank wall at the back of the lab, swiped her fingers across a control slate. The electrochromic wall turned transparent, revealing the containment area itself. LeaMarsa was surprised to see the atmosphere bore a resemblance to Sycamore's, complete with gently wafting fog.

In the center was the organism. It pulsed contentedly, like a giant human heart. Its bluish coloration seemed lighter than how she remembered it from the surface, but that could have been just a difference in the lighting. Still, she had the impression it was somehow healthier. Faintly visible through its translucent skin was a darker lump, the fetal organism.

"I've named it," Faye said. "I call it Bouncy Blue."

"That is *not* its official designation," Hardy said with a scowl, concerned the name was too frivolous. "After we return to Earth, proper nomenclature will be assigned to it by the XBC."

LeaMarsa didn't recognize the acronym.

"Xenobiological Confederation," Faye said, reading her confusion. "It's responsible for classifying and naming all extraterrestrial organisms."

Hardy went on. "We're positive this creature is not native to the planet. No way could such an organism have developed there, even below the surface. Sycamore was never a living world. And we're certain the organism didn't arrive inside the rock via a meteor impact."

"How can you be sure of that?" LeaMarsa asked.

"The rock encasing it is indigenous," Faye said.

"We also believe," Hardy continued, "that the rock surrounding the organism was once significantly larger. Millennia of erosion whittled it down, exposing the organism and releasing the bacteria."

Faye nodded in agreement. "We're thinking that the Sycom strain was clustered only on the organism's surface and isn't native to it. Possibly the bacteria was a contaminant, the result of accidental exposure by whoever brought Bouncy Blue to the planet and embedded it in the rock."

It took a moment for LeaMarsa to register the impact of that last statement.

"It was brought to Sycamore? By whom?"

Faye couldn't disguise her excitement. "The most likely answer? An intelligent alien species."

Hardy raised a hand in protest. "At this point, that's pure conjecture. We have no proof to support such a conclusion."

"Admittedly. But there's plenty of evidence. And if it should turn out to be true…"

Faye trailed off. There was no need for her to state the obvious. Sophisticated plant and animal life had been found on scores of planets, but never had a lifeform been seen that came close to approaching the self-awareness of human intelligence. If Hardy and Faye could prove that Bouncy Blue was an extraterrestrial immigrant, deliberately or accidentally sent to Sycamore by some unknown species, it would be the find of the millennium.

Faye winked at her. "Fame and fortune for one and all, dear."

Hardy scowled, as if such thoughts were beneath him. But LeaMarsa knew that the science rep would hog any press conferences announcing the discovery of intelligent extraterrestrial life.

"Our initial fears about Bouncy Blue being harmed by severe temperature change appear to be unfounded," Faye said. "We've gradually varied the containment temperature a hundred degrees either way with no discernible effect. We need to study tissue samples to gain a clearer idea of its metabolism. But we're having a bit of a problem there."

"Bouncy Blue's tissue dies within microseconds of extraction," Hardy said. "Highly unusual, to say the least. One theory is that the organism generates some sort of life-enabling energy field that our instruments aren't sensitive enough to measure. This energy field could be shielding it from outside environments. Possibly, its tissue cannot exist beyond this field."

"Such a field could account for its survival on Sycamore," Faye added.

"What about that thing inside it?" LeaMarsa asked.

"So far, we're just looking, not touching. We don't know enough about what we're dealing with to attempt tissue extraction from the fetal creature."

"A proper scientist peels an onion from the outside in," Hardy said, sounding pompous. "In due time, we'll research the internal organism."

Movement in the containment caught LeaMarsa's eye. As Bouncy Blue rolled across the floor, she had the eerie notion it was somehow eavesdropping.

"It moves like that sometimes," Hardy explained. "Another mystery."

The airseal opened, admitting Ericho and Rigel.

"Captain Solorzano," Hardy uttered, his tone hinting of disdain. "To what do we owe the pleasure?"

Ericho ignored him and stared at the organism. LeaMarsa thought that the captain looked quite handsome in his black-and-gold uniform. Early in the voyage, she'd dreamed about the two of them having a sexual relationship. That was before she'd learned that crewdoc June Courthouse was Ericho's steady partner.

She felt no such attraction to Rigel Shaheed. The tech officer was taller and more broad-shouldered than Ericho, with thick muscled arms. Something beyond his brutish mannerisms made her feel anxious.

"Jonomy reviewed your experiment schedule," Ericho began. "We have some misgivings."

Hardy grimaced. "Do tell."

"Item forty-six on your agenda. You intend to place a fusion battery inside the containment?"

"Yes. We wish to learn whether the organism can tap into a raw power source, whether it's capable of direct energy absorption."

"Perhaps as a means of nourishment," Faye added. "It had to be feeding on something all these millennia."

"It's a necessary test," Hardy insisted.

Ericho pointed up at the containment ceiling, barely visible through the swirling fog. It was covered in a plethora of remote test gear, including foot-long canisters that could extend specialized appendages for extracting samples, and a permanently confined pup.

"You're aware that the pup carries a thermal HC for emergencies?"

"I'm aware of basic physics," Hardy snapped. "I'm certainly not so foolish as to allow a Higgs cutter to be activated with a fusion cell nearby."

"Not deliberately. But accidents happen."

"Not in my labs."

Rigel grunted. "If Bouncy Blue tries anything too weird or the containment is somehow breached, that pup could activate the HC. If it does, it'll carve your little friend into kitty litter. And if the beam touches a fusion cell, we'll be dealing with one nasty shitstorm."

Hardy gave an exasperated sigh. "There are precautions in place to prevent that. The *Alchemon* is intelligent enough not to allow such a stupid event to take place. It's not going to risk vaporizing a portion of itself."

"What you're saying does make sense," Ericho said, sounding reasonable.

LeaMarsa realized that the captain wanted her to see him as fair-minded and, by contrast, Hardy as dangerously reckless. It was the latest skirmish in a war that the two men, who disliked one another intensely, had been waging since the outset of the voyage.

"Anything else?"

"Item one-thirty-three on your agenda. It appears to be a reckless experiment."

Hardy's face darkened. "It's not slated until after an exhaustive range of other tests are performed. By then, the safety margin will undoubtedly be more than acceptable."

Rigel flashed a grin at LeaMarsa. "How about it? OK with you?"

She shook her head, confused.

The tech officer laughed. "Hell, he hasn't even told you."

"Told me what?"

"The good doctor here intends to have you put on a shieldsuit and go outside. You'll reenter through the containment airlock and once you're standing next to Bouncy Blue, you'll remove your suit. I believe the idea is for the two of you to engage in body-to-body contact. Still, I don't know how you're going to breathe that shit. Not a lot of oxygen in there."

"She'll wear an air mask," Hardy snapped.

"Yeah, good idea. Of course, you'll have to hope that Bouncy Blue doesn't get any notions while you're trying to psionically wake him. Cos you probably won't be able to get back in your suit and move your ass out of there if he gets other ideas, like trying to have you for dinner."

Hardy bristled. "LeaMarsa, this is nothing for you to be concerned about. He's just trying to frighten you."

"Damn right!"

"If and when we ask you to perform the experiment that Rigel has so inelegantly outlined, ample safety measures will be in place."

"Why would you want me to do something like that?"

"As you know, superluminals are known to be inversely proportional to distance. The closer you are physically, the greater the amplitude of the telepathic contact. Since it now seems probable that your presence on the surface was somehow a catalyst, you may be able to provoke a further reaction."

Rigel laughed. "Yeah, you'll provoke it all right."

LeaMarsa wasn't about to carry out such an outlandish experiment. Still, she saw no upside in bringing the issue to a head. Better to remain noncommittal and deal with it if and when the time came.

"It's my decision," she said. "Let me think about it."

Hardy's sneer suggested victory. "Satisfied, captain? Or are there more issues you wish to address…"

The science rep trailed off as he realized Ericho wasn't paying attention. The captain was prone on the floor, gazing through the containment glass at the organism.

"Jonomy, did you see that?" Ericho asked.

His voice came through on speaker. "Yes, captain, I did."

"See what?" Hardy demanded.

"The organism momentarily exhibited zero-g activity," Jonomy said. "For about five seconds, it elevated and suspended itself eleven centimeters off the floor."

They all moved closer to the wall, intrigued.

"Anything like this happen on the surface?" Ericho asked.

"It rolled itself into the capsule," Faye said. "But that trick didn't seem in defiance of planetary gravitation."

"I have checked for malfunctions," Jonomy said. "No geonic or electromagnetic anomalies in or near the containment that could have caused it to elevate."

"Astounding," Hardy whispered.

Ericho's expression didn't change. But LeaMarsa sensed he was deeply disturbed.

Rigel was easier to read. "If this bastard can do gravity tricks, no telling what it's capable of. Worse comes to worse, we might not even be able to blow it out the airlock. Bouncy Blue could resist decompression."

"The vacuum would probably kill it," Faye said. Her remark drew a sharp look from Hardy.

LeaMarsa felt another shiver vault up her spine, transform into that same word-thought she'd experienced on the surface.

Tragedy.

But this time, the word-thought seemed closer somehow. Stronger.

She wanted to be alone, away from this lab, away from all of them as well as that thing in the containment.

"Is there anything else you need me for at the moment?"

Hardy shook his head. LeaMarsa turned and headed for the door. Only a concerted effort kept her from bolting from the lab in panic.

CHAPTER 6

June Courthouse leaned back in her office chair and propped her bare feet on the desk. For as long as Ericho had known her, she'd been averse to footwear, donning it only when absolutely necessary.

"Tomer Donner suffers from a range of delusional fantasies," the crewdoc said in response to Ericho's request for her latest insight into the lieutenant. "Had any of this been apparent nine months ago, I never would have asked you to assign him to this mission."

June's med office was cool and dark, lit by soothing lume panels. The soft light revealed age lines on her dark skin, testimony to a departed youth. June disdained hardcore revitalizers, especially those elderly women, some one hundred and fifty or older, whose relentless enhancements gave them the faces and physiques of collegians even as age-related fragilities required biomech exoskeletons.

"How bad are these delusions?" Ericho asked. "Are we talking clinical madness?"

"I don't believe so. Tomer remains coherent and functional in terms of his duties, and clearly understands that he's afflicted. However, he also understands that no matter how thoroughly he perceives his problem, outside emotional guidance such as psychotherapy will not rectify it."

"How sure are you of all this?"

June smiled. "Don't trust my expertise?"

"No, it's not that."

He leaned deeper into the camelback sofa across from her desk, a four hundred-year-old heirloom from her late husband. François, a zero-G horticulturist, had died in only his sixth decade from a new cancer unknowingly brought to Earth in a shipment of medicinal roots harvested in the caverns of Eff Bee IV. Per his wishes, his remains had been reconstituted into the varnish used on the sofa's ancient woodwork.

June hauled the sofa along on all her Quiets missions, sidestepping Pannis regulations by classifying it as a "non-animated relaxation module." She had mentioned to Ericho that sitting on the sofa in the dark could invoke intimate memories of François, as well as their three grown children who'd romped on it as youngsters.

"There's nothing at all you can do to help him?" Ericho asked.

"I'm just saying that from Tomer's point of view, the various psychotherapeutic interventions wouldn't help. Without the patient's belief in and commitment to the process, those sorts of traditional treatments are largely ineffective."

"There are other options besides psychotherapy. What about optogenetic surgery or engram remodeling?"

"First of all, I can't legally order someone to undergo those. More to the point, opto wouldn't work. Too many light-activated enzymes we'd need to manipulate. The psych scan I did on Tomer during his most recent exam indicates that his delusional fantasies are global, impacting nearly every cerebral area. That leaves out en-rem as well. No matter how many false memories I'd implant, it wouldn't be enough to produce measurable behavioral change."

"All right, how about pharmaceuticals? You can order a crewmember to undergo a drug regimen."

"If I think it's justified, sure. And there are drugs that can block a wide range of the affected neurotransmitters. But in this instance, the intake regimen is complex and not without debilitating side effects. Nausea, migraines, a range of other physical ailments. I wouldn't recommend going the pharma route unless you're prepared to relieve Tomer of all duties."

"Do you think it'll come to that?"

She shrugged.

"Do you think he's dangerous?"

June's eyes sparkled. "That's a relative term, Ericho. Anyone who's been in deep space more than six months would qualify under my definition."

"Maybe. But I've never had a crewmember appear as if he was getting ready to attack me."

"You noted, however, that he didn't follow through. And you did say that you thought he might be playacting."

Ericho nodded. He'd reviewed the incident several times, both mentally and via bridge surveillance recordings. The lieutenant's faux attack could be construed as nothing more than an elaborate performance, an acting out of whatever strange fantasy was flowing through his head at that particular moment. Still, Ericho couldn't get over that intense look on Donner's face. It was just as reasonable to assume that the man had come close to losing control.

"Whatever his state of mind, I need your professional recommendation. Should I relieve him of duties? Curtail his workload?"

"Besides the incident, has he done anything else to give you cause for one of those options?"

"No."

"Then maybe you have your answer." She paused. "I'm getting the feeling that you have deeper concerns here."

"I do. It's been nearly a week since we arrived in orbit and three days since we brought that thing into the containment. During that time, Donner seems to have gotten substantially worse. His philosophical babblings are becoming even more bizarre. I've restructured our work schedule so he's never alone on the bridge."

Ship time remained based on the twenty-four-hour Earth-day. Ericho and the lieutenant shared daily five-hour bridge shifts, occasionally doubling up at critical junctures, such as when the lander crew had been on Sycamore's surface. Jonomy, whose altered brain required significantly less sleep than unmodified humans, legally could do up to a twenty-hour shift but in practice generally did less.

"Have you observed any unusual behavior in Tomer when he isn't on duty?" June asked.

"No, but that's hard to monitor. He tends to spend most of his time alone in the dopas."

Designated official privacy areas – dopas – were a Corporeal requirement aboard starships. On the *Alchemon*, surveillance cams and other forms of monitoring in the crew cabins, diner, natatorium, dreamlounge and medcenter weren't permitted, at least under normal circumstances.

Prior to the introduction of lytics, only private cabins were immune from surveillance. But with their all-encompassing abilities to see, hear and sense everything going on aboard a vessel, lytics had changed the game, prompting the megas to designate a certain percentage of crew areas as dopas.

Technically, only the awakening of a Sentinel could override a dopa. And that wasn't supposed to happen for anything short of an emergency threatening the security of the vessel.

Dopa or not, however, Ericho had heard rumors about shrewd lytics able to work around such restrictions. He wondered if there was a way of approaching Jonomy to institute covert surveillance on Donner but quickly decided against the idea. The man was a stickler for the rules and might well report Ericho upon their return for proposing such an illicit act.

June tabbed open a beaker of tea, sipped the hot beverage. "Until this voyage, I'd never served with a really potent psionic crewmember, so I'd never felt the need to know all that much about them. That changed this time out, of course, and I started doing research. How familiar are you with the basics of psionic science?"

Ericho shrugged. "I know about the three categories."

"Projectors, receptors and conveyors. Projectors generate these superluminals. Receptors receive them. Conveyors can relay and amplify the faster-than-light signals, function sort of like a com satellite by transferring data between two or more distant points. And a psionic rule of thumb is that as two people move physically closer to one another, the potential for psychic interaction increases geometrically.

"Researchers now know that most humans are receptors, albeit at such low levels that it has no real effect on our lives. A tiny percentage of us are projector-receptors or conveyor-receptors. But what distinguishes genuine psionics like LeaMarsa is that they have extremely high abilities in all three categories.

"I was able to access the classified Jamal Labs report on her, or at least the parts of it Pannis didn't redact. Even when compared to other psionics, LeaMarsa is uniquely gifted. She's an extremely powerful receptor and conveyor, can receive the thoughts and feelings of others and convey those thoughts and feelings between or among people. But she has even greater gifts as a projector. She's by far the most powerful one they ever studied, literally off the charts. Of course, most of this is happening at subliminal levels. She's largely unconscious of the extent of her own powers, as are most psionics."

June paused. "The truth is, no one really knows just how potent she is and what she's capable of. Bottom line, there's no way she should have been assigned to a long-voyage starship. We just don't know enough about the impact of such rarefied psionics in closed environments."

"Think we're guinea pigs? Some sort of Pannis experiment to determine how we'd react?" It wouldn't be the first time a mega had used the isolated environment of a starship to perform ethically questionable research.

June shrugged. "We were gauged for superluminal compatibility, of course. All starship crews are, to make sure there are no potential problems with projectors, receptors and conveyors being in a small closed environment for an extended period. The gauging methodology isn't perfect, so it doesn't give the exacting results that the more extensive exams at a place like Jamal might provide. For the eight of us, the test results were negative."

"But that was without LeaMarsa factored into the equation."

"Exactly. And it turns out that Tomer Donner is a potent receptor." June scowled. "I should have been given all this information before the mission. I only unearthed the bulk of it yesterday, and only then because I managed to dig up the results of our compatibility gauging. I believe the information was deliberately hidden."

"Does Donner know about his abilities?"

"He's known for a long time."

Ericho frowned. "Why didn't he express any concerns about this after LeaMarsa was added to the mission? We all knew she was a strong psionic. Did he say anything to you prior to takeoff?"

"Not a word."

"So, what you're saying is that you suspect the presence of LeaMarsa is having a damaging effect on him, that she's the cause of his behavior?"

"It's more than just a suspicion. I'm convinced that's what's happening."

"If it's true, someone at Pannis should have realized when they were making crew assignments that putting those two together in a confined space could lead to trouble."

June nodded. "There's another wrinkle here. Ever hear of a man named Renfro Zoobondi?"

"Sure. Pannis InterGlobal Security VP. Never met him but heard rumors. Supposedly, a nasty piece of work."

"We've heard the same rumors. A psychologist I know had a brief relationship with him during her college years. She believes that Renfro Zoobondi is a genuine psychopath, but one of such high intelligence that he's been able to hide his pathology from standard testing procedures, including the OTTO. There are unconfirmed reports of childhood sadism. Torturing cats and other helpless animals, that sort of thing."

"A sadistic psychopath. He'll probably be the next Pannis CEO."

"When I interviewed Tomer a couple weeks ago for his regular psych analysis, he mentioned Zoobondi. He wouldn't go into detail, but it's obvious he nurses a powerful hatred of the man. I believe it was Zoobondi who'd been blacklisting him, making it difficult for Tomer to get a starship assignment."

"Until I intervened on his behalf. Our psycho VP is probably pissed at me as well."

"Maybe. But I believe Zoobondi was able to adapt to the altered situation."

"Anything in the files about this?"

"Yes and no. There was some sort of incident between them during a voyage nine years ago. The *Theodoris*, through the Earth-Karama Quiets. But most of the file's been redacted, ostensibly for reasons of Pannis security."

"You believe there was a coverup?"

"I think Renfro Zoobondi is in a position to make information disappear or limit its access. I also believe that a true psychopath would have no qualms about putting a personal vendetta above the safety of a starship crew."

"You can't believe Zoobondi assigned LeaMarsa to the *Alchemon* in order to drive our lieutenant crazy."

June sighed. "Believe me, I know how bizarre that sounds. But we have to at least consider it. And then there's a whole other factor to the equation, something Renfro Zoobondi wouldn't have been aware of."

"Bouncy Blue."

She nodded. "You mentioned that you thought Tomer's been getting worse since our weird little friend in the containment was brought aboard."

"That seems to be the case."

"I have no proof, but I strongly suspect that Bouncy Blue, or that organism inside it, is also a potent source of superluminals. I believe LeaMarsa could be functioning as a conveyor, amplifying and spreading Bouncy Blue's superluminals throughout the ship. And if that's true..." June hesitated. "Tomer could be just the tip of the iceberg."

"What are you saying? That all of us are being affected by that thing?"

"With one exception, we all have minor receptor abilities."

"Who's the outlier?"

"Our tech trainee. Alexei has no testable abilities, which puts him in a league with less than one percent of the Corporeal population. You told me the other day you had an urge to throw Tomer off the bridge. And what about this ongoing feud you've been having with Hardy? We've known each other for a lot of years, Ericho, and I know you've dealt with your fair share of challenging crewmembers. But I've never seen you quite so agitated."

"Donner and Hardy are special cases. They could drive anyone around the bend." Ericho paused as June's concerns sank in. "You really think I'm being affected?"

"It's subtle, but yes, I believe you are. I can't say for certain the change is caused by superluminals, but I have a feeling I'm on the right track."

She hesitated, as if wanting to say something more, then apparently changed her mind. But Ericho knew her too well, knew where her thoughts were headed.

"You've noticed something in your own behavior, haven't you? Something that makes you suspect psionic influence."

She nodded. "Last night, after we had sex and you went back to your cabin, I had a nightmare. I haven't had one of those since I was an adolescent."

June sat up straight, planted her bare feet on the floor. She stared at some blank space above Ericho's head. A shiver seemed to pass through her.

"Must have been pretty bad," he offered, unaccustomed to seeing anything rattle her.

"Massively creepy. And frankly, I've never had one that was this intense. Anyway, I don't think my nightmare was coincidental. I wish there was a way to better understand the real-world effect of psionics. The science behind them remains in its infancy. And the inherent weirdness of the entire field of study renders traditional research methods challenging."

Ericho wondered if June's theories weren't venturing too far afield. "You told me a while ago that this crew is low on the psychosynchronicity scale, that they simply can't mesh into a functional unit. Maybe that's the real explanation for what's been happening."

He wasn't ready to believe that everyone's behavior was being weirdly influenced by LeaMarsa, or that thing in the containment, or some combination of the two. But it would be foolish to ignore her concerns.

"Whatever's going on," he began slowly, "Donner would seem to be the most affected, the one we need to worry about. So, assuming for a moment that his problem is psionic in nature, is there anything we can do about it?"

"The literature suggests that separating a potent receptor from a projector or conveyor can help. Physical distance does have a measurable impact on the strength of superluminals. Certainly, LeaMarsa and Tomer shouldn't come in physical contact with one another, which can lead to dramatic spikes in superluminal interaction."

Thinking back on it, Ericho couldn't recall ever seeing the two of them within ten footsteps of one another. "I never really considered it before, but I get the impression that Donner tries to avoid her. He'll leave a room when she enters or turn and walk the other way if they're approaching one another in a corridor."

"Smart of him," June said. "Or maybe he subconsciously senses that proximity to her is dangerous. Still, in psionic terms, the *Alchemon* isn't spacious enough for a proper separation. LeaMarsa, that thing in the containment – we're all just too close to one another.

"That said, we might come at this from a different direction, try to lessen the impact on Donner as well as upon the rest of us. The overall strength of a psionic, their ability to project or convey superluminals, can be reduced for a time by engaging in spirited physical activities."

"You mean sex."

"Actually, anything but that. Sex could have the opposite effect, heighten her psionic impact. Something to do with its intimate nature. Fortunately, as far as I know, LeaMarsa isn't sexually active with anyone onboard. And the dreamlounge logbook indicates she's never gone there."

Most crewmembers used the dreamlounge to fulfill longings. Millions of customizable fantasies, erotic and platonic – as well as full-immersion videos and games – could be downloaded into subcortical regions. Some of the crew hooked up for physical sex on occasion, particularly Faye and Alexei, and even Faye and Hardy if credence could be given to one of the ship's more outlandish rumors. As far as Ericho knew, he and June were the only two in an exclusive pairing.

"I'm thinking more in terms of exercise," June said. "Maybe you could give her a nudge by spending some time in the natatorium with her, swimming or working out."

"I'm probably not the best choice to be her prompter. We

really don't have much in common."

"Maybe. But early on she had a crush on you."

"Really? How do you know that?"

June laughed. "Men. How do you *not* know?"

"OK, I'm occasionally oblivious. But I still don't think I'm the one for the job. I'm older. And frankly, I've already got Donner and Hardy to deal with. I don't need to get entangled with another emotional mess."

"She's that, no doubt. Apart from her psionic issues, she suffers from some deep torment, a repressed pain probably originating in childhood."

"Has she ever talked about it?"

"No. But whatever the source of this pain, it scares the hell out of her. I was able to access some of her school reports from her younger years where she mentioned it. She didn't provide any details back then either, other than to give it a name. She calls it the reek."

June tapped her fingers on the desk as if considering other possibilities. "I'm not a good choice for a workout partner either. LeaMarsa has an inherent distrust of med doctors."

"What about Faye? They seem reasonably friendly."

"The problem with Faye is her secretors."

"I get the impression she wouldn't use them without first informing a partner."

"You're right, she adheres to a strict moral code. Trouble is, secretors can sometimes be triggered unconsciously in high-stress situations. Last thing we need is for LeaMarsa's libido to be enhanced, however accidentally. That could potentially worsen her psionic influence."

Ericho nodded and considered other possibilities. Rigel was out. LeaMarsa noticeably disliked him.

"Hardy wouldn't do," June mused. "He sees her in terms of career advancement and practically treats her like a lackey."

"Jonomy?"

"Strictly a solo exerciser. And lately he's not even doing that much. Instead, he's been spending an inordinate amount of time engaging with dreamlounge fantasies."

Ericho was surprised. "How'd you find that out?"

"At his request, we've had some psych sessions." June hesitated. "This is touching on areas of doctor-patient confidentiality. I'd rather not say more."

Medical ethics had permitted her to divulge details about Donner because of what had occurred on the bridge. A potential threat to a captain trumped confidentiality issues.

Still, Ericho couldn't help but be concerned at the idea of a lytic having psych sessions. The breed tended to behave more like AIs than humans, which was in some ways comforting given their level of control over systems and networks.

"That leaves only one possibility," June said, getting the discussion back on track.

"Alexei."

"He's the closest in age to LeaMarsa. More importantly, his lack of psionic abilities means that she shouldn't be able to influence him in that way. Will you talk to him?"

Ericho hesitated.

"You wouldn't have to make it an order. Alexei looks up to you. A subtle suggestion presented with just the right touch of paternal encouragement should do the trick."

"Let me think about it."

Ericho rose from the sofa. He was due on the bridge in ten minutes to start his shift. But as he headed for the door he hesitated and turned back to June.

"What was your nightmare about?"

For a long moment she didn't respond. Finally...

"Would you mind if we didn't talk about it right now? The feelings are still close to the surface."

"No problem. Maybe later."

He headed for the bridge, feeling more anxiety for a ship and its crew than he had in his entire career.

CHAPTER 7

LeaMarsa awoke lying at the edge of the pool with knees dangling over the padded lip and feet submerged in the cool liquid. Ultraviolet refractors dotted the natatorium walls. The overhead dome was tinted blue and overlaid with televised stratus clouds in imitation of an Earth sky.

It didn't remind her of home.

Fighting sluggishness, she adjusted a fallen strap on her one-piece bather and struggled to her feet.

Two figures splashed noisily in the water. She ignored them, stumbled between two multifunction exercise machines that resembled a pair of slumbering octopi and onto a winding path amid a garden of roses and hyacinths. She tabbed "lemonade" on the dispenser, downed the beverage in five quick gulps and crushed the cup. It disintegrated into powdery gases, recycling itself into the atmosphere before any remnants could touch the floor.

An analog clock above the door revealed she'd been asleep nearly an hour, which explained why her legs from the knees down were pruned. She'd come for a swim but after only a few laps had been overcome by tiredness.

"LeaMarsa!"

The male voice emanated from the water and was followed by a loud splash. She ambled back to the rim, stared at the two figures swimming toward her.

Alexei Two Guns hopped from the pool and shook his head, sending a fine spray of water from reddish hair styled unfashionably long like her own. The tech trainee was a bit taller than LeaMarsa. Slim and deeply tanned, he was naked except for a yellow crotchpad.

"We need a third for waterball," Alexei said, gesturing to Faye in the water. "Come in and get wet."

"No thanks."

"Don't think about it, LeaMarsa. Just do it!"

Alexei was pleasant enough, but she didn't understand how a person could be so relentlessly exuberant. And since yesterday he seemed to be hanging around her an awful lot, pushing her toward doing physical exercise with him.

Did he want more than that? Sex? She couldn't be sure. His intentions remained unclear. Odder than that, they seemed to have come out of the blue, as if he was following some mandate rather than his feelings.

Yesterday, during a random encounter in the updeck corridor near her cabin, he'd complimented her for wearing a simple skirt and blouse. The apparel, outputted from a PYG receptacle, was a generic ensemble she'd selected from among the thousands of fashion templates stored in the primary genesis complex. It wasn't even smart clothing. As usual, and against PYG's recommendation, she'd chosen the nano-free option.

Alexei had seen her dressed in such attire since the outset of the voyage and had never before said a word, which made the praise all the more bizarre, as did his subsequent proposal that they go swimming together. In any event, since that brief infatuation with the captain at the start of the voyage, she'd had no desire for sex, if that's indeed what he was awkwardly leading up to.

Faye propped her arms on the pool's lip and rested her chin in her hands. "Come play with us, dear."

"Maybe later."

"Not afraid of the fish, are you?" Alexei challenged.

LeaMarsa shook her head.

The pool was multifunctional, also serving as a reservoir for the *Alchemon*'s carefully maintained biosystem. Today, there were only a few fish darting about, but on occasion the water became saturated with schools of bass and groupers. Then some complex feedback system would be triggered, and klaxons would sound. Water and fish would be piped elsewhere, and the pool refilled and revitalized. Such transformations provided some of their food and potable water.

"Were you ever down here when Rigel was swimming?" Alexei asked.

LeaMarsa shook her head.

"You're really missing out." The trainee winked at Faye, sharing some private joke. "Rigel likes to swim with the fishes. Sometimes he catches them with his teeth. I've heard he eats them raw!"

"Gross," Faye said, making a face.

"He scares me," LeaMarsa said.

"Rigel? His bark is worse than his bite." She laughed at the double meaning of her remark. "Did you know he's taken a vow of celibacy for the duration of the voyage to honor his fiancées, whom he plans to marry in a joint celebration when we get back?"

"One's from Salt Lake City, the other from Dubai," Alexei added. "The three of them are getting married in a non-denominational ceremony aboard one of those submarine cruises in the middle of the Atlantic, halfway between the cities."

LeMarsa nodded, feigning interest. Alexei sat cross-legged at her feet, stared up at her. "You're coming to the Homebound, right?"

"I don't like parties."

"You'll like this one. You know about Homebounds, don't you?"

She shrugged.

"They're special events," Faye said. "Exceptional times when you can lose yourself. Follow the yellow brick road to wherever it takes you, right Alexei?"

The trainee grinned. His passion for that famous movie, *The Wizard of Oz*, was well known among the crew.

"Homebounds are where you can let it all hang out," Alexei said, his excitement building. "An ancestor of mine, a great-great-great-great whatever, was a crewmember on one of the first starships to leave the solar system through a Quiets. I remember reading about his adventures when I was young."

"When *he* was young," Faye mocked. "When was that, junior, like three hours ago?"

"I'm just saying, Homebounds are a tradition with a long history."

"You have to come," Faye added. "Main social room, tomorrow at thirteen hundred hours. Be there or be square."

"High five!" Alexei snapped.

The two of them raised their right arms and smacked their palms together. LeaMarsa had seen them use the vintage celebratory gesture on numerous occasions.

Alexei and Faye were Helioteers, the popular movement whose adherents practiced the customs and phraseology of the Helio Age, that period prior to humans emigrating in large numbers from the solar system. The megas, ever ready to incorporate fashionable memes, had amplified the public's enchantment by naming new planets after Helio Age commercial products such as Toyota Corolla and Big Mac, and the terraformed desert world, Viagra Hard.

Some Helioteers outfitted themselves in elaborate vintage attire and spoke only the various dialects of the era. LeaMarsa had picked up some of the lingo, although nowhere near the level of Faye and Alexei, as well as Rigel, who relished the profanity and insult-laden syntax then in common use.

Alexei had once proclaimed that if he had the power to go back in time he'd settle in the midst of the Helio Age, and within that mythical entertainment enclave known as Hollywood. There, he would aspire to dual professions: by day, a multimedia actor doing *Wizard of Oz* sequels; by night, the owner of something called a hip-hop club.

Alexei's face twisted into a cocky smile. "Rigel told me that Captain Solorzano is going to allow a full array of ingestors. Pannis frowns on that and a lot of ship commanders won't do it. But our captain's no mega lackey."

"So tomorrow we leave for home," LeaMarsa said. The thought of returning to Earth should have made her feel better but didn't. Not with that creature onboard.

She had a sudden memory from adolescence, of the awful discovery she'd made shortly after her thirteenth birthday, when she'd learned of her parents' abominable manipulation. It was something they'd taken great pains to keep from her.

Her discovery had been accidental. At school, she'd been accessing her parents' home system for some research notes she'd forgotten to transfer to her scholastic wafer. She'd come across one of her father's files that he'd apparently forgotten to encrypt. It detailed the injection of a unique strand of mitochondrial DNA into her mother's womb, and into the tiny embryo that months later would become their only child.

But before LeaMarsa could confront her parents about what they'd done to her in utero, they'd perished in that shuttle crash while on a business trip to Luna.

Afterwards, besides dealing with her grief, LeaMarsa had experienced surges of anger toward her parents. They'd made her into a genejob for completely selfish reasons. She'd felt cheated by their deaths, denied the opportunity to lash out at them for doing such an awful thing.

The vile odor of something dead assaulted her nostrils. Her first thought was that it came from the pool. Covering her mouth and nose didn't help – it kept getting stronger. Only then did she realize it was of psionic origin and that it was the smell that accompanied the reek. As if on cue came the mind-numbing dread and sensation of being strangled.

Yet the symptoms didn't achieve full strength. Instead, a psychic blackout overtook her. The reek retreated into the subliminal depths from which it had sprung. The voices of Alexei and Faye dissolved into a mush of indecipherable sounds.

And then she was floating in that alternate universe, neurospace – countless pinpoints of starlight against a tapestry of black. Not its true nature, she again sensed, merely the best interpretation vision could offer, a way for her mind to depict a thing wildly distinct from normal comprehension.

Another strange aspect of this realm of luminous dark was the sensation of being able to perceive billions – or perhaps it was trillions or quadrillions – of those stars at the same time. Such a thing was impossible in the real universe. But here, vision, or what passed for vision, didn't adhere to logic. Neurospace functioned by its own rules.

From somewhere amid those stars came a gravelly female voice, straining to be heard as if from a great distance.

"Sentinel Obey."

"Who are you?" she whispered. "What does that mean?"

There was no response. LeaMarsa's focus abruptly returned to the natatorium to meet the worried frowns of Faye and Alexei.

"Dear, are you OK?"

"Fine."

"You looked like you'd blacked out for a moment. And you were talking to yourself. Maybe you should go to medcenter for a checkup."

She shook her head.

"Let's swim," Alexei suggested, gripping LeaMarsa's elbow. "You'll feel better after exercise. That always helps me."

"No."

Alexei released her arm and dove into the pool.

"Anything you'd like to talk about?" Faye asked, still concerned.

"No. And even if I did, you wouldn't understand."

"Maybe not. But sometimes it's good to let things out. A girl chat might make you feel better."

LeaMarsa had no desire to discuss the psionic incident. But she was intrigued by the phrase uttered by the phantom woman.

"I've heard people mention the ship's Sentinel. I don't really know much about it."

Faye looked surprised by the abrupt change of subject. LeaMarsa pressed on.

"I know there are six levels of control and that the Sentinel somehow sits above it all. But I'm not up on the technology."

"Well, you pretty much have the basics. Six levels, with each level generally having a greater degree of control and more critical responsibilities than the one beneath it. Although actually it's more complicated than that.

"For instance, this natatorium – LSN – is Level Six, a rather lowly system. Most of the other luxury systems, such as the dreamlounge, are sixers as well. However, LSN is also part of FWP – food and waste processing – which is a Level Three system. And other Level Three systems get involved in the pool's operation as well, such as hydroponics and geonic stability.

"And since this is a crew area, the pool has to have a breathable atmosphere, so that involves a Level Two system – EHO – ecospheric homeostasis. And we have to have power, and that's routed by Level One systems like POP and NEL – primary operating power from the battery banks and the four nucleonic engines that provide our main propulsion." Faye smiled. "Confused yet?"

"It seems to make sense."

"It does, at least in a general way. But my point is, hardly anyone really understands or can make sense of it all. The interactions among these systems have grown too complex for a regular person to assimilate. That's why most of the newer ships have lytics. Still, I have a hunch that not even Jonomy and his ilk fully understand all the complexities.

"And the Sentinel?"

"Ah, yes, the big bad Sentinel. It fascinates people but there's really no great mystery. First of all, although there's only one Sentinel, it's capable of being in more than one location simultaneously. Think of it sort of like an octopus, an entity with one brain but possessing multiple arms.

"SEN is the Level Zero system designed to protect the *Alchemon* from dangerous programming commands, internal or external threats, malevolent humans, whatever. Anything that menaces the safety and security of the ship and its mission.

"In the event of such a menace, a Sentinel is awakened, which means that SEN generates and projects electrical signals throughout the ship via an overlapping superconductive network."

Faye hesitated, reading LeaMarsa's confusion.

"Sentinel signals travel at a speed infinitesimally faster than the ship's regular systems, nearer the actual perfect speed of light when unimpeded, such as in a vacuum. Actually, what goes on can be even more convoluted. The velocity of SEN signals sometimes exceeds the speed of light according to the somewhat paradoxical theories that form the basis of subatomic physics."

"You're talking about superluminals?"

"Same principle. Call it a cousin to what you're familiar with, those faster-than-light impulses known to have something to do with psionic interaction. Anyway, a Sentinel can literally outrun the ship's normal circuitry transmissions, which allows them to take control of whatever system they enter."

"How does this Sentinel know what to obey. I mean, someone must program it, right?"

"Sentinels follow guidelines laid down by the director's board of the Corporeal, which is made up mainly of representatives from Pannis and the other megas." Faye gave a wry grin. "In other words, a bunch of bitchpricks not overly concerned about the welfare of lowly crewmembers.

"Still, at the end of the day it's challenging for anyone, even lytics, to forecast exactly what will or won't awaken a Sentinel, or exactly what it will do once it's up and running. They tend toward the unpredictable."

"I heard the phrase 'Sentinel Obey.' Does that mean anything?"

"Something of a non sequitur. Once a Sentinel gets activated, it's in charge and calling the shots. The whole idea is that Sentinels don't obey anything or anyone. They might take input from humans, but they don't have to follow it. They're their own masters."

LeaMarsa felt a sudden chill even though the natatorium air remained comfortably warm.

Faye glanced at the clock. "I should get going. Soon time for me to be back in the salt mines."

"The salt mines?"

"Hardy. The containment."

"Have you learned anything new about the organism?"

"We're finally probing the fetal creature inside Bouncy Blue, which by the way, I'm calling Baby Blue. Of course, Hardy absolutely *hates* the name." Faye's eyes sparkled, amused at Hardy's conventionality.

"Anyway, Baby Blue is fascinating. We see the morphogenetic beginnings of an advanced, undoubtedly intelligent lifeform. A head, complete with eyes, ears, nose and mouth, plus an additional sensory organ located between the mouth and nose that we can't identify."

LeaMarsa recalled being on the bridge several weeks ago and seeing Lieutenant Donner draw a skull-like face in the holographic display. It seemed to match Faye's description of Baby Blue's face. She had no idea what that might mean.

"A central spinal structure is present. Internally, there are some tantalizing organs that resemble the valved heart and kidneys found in our own species."

"So it could be a human variant?"

Faye shook her head. "Too many structural differences. We're certain it's not one of us, although it likely developed in an ecosphere similar to that of Earth. It has a respiratory system that seems perfect for the exchange of oxygen and carbon dioxide. The lungs are almost a dead match for ours.

"Its brain is highly developed but possesses what appears to be a variation of the tripartite human brain – roughly speaking, the three interwoven neurological systems that enable us to function simultaneously on physical, emotional and intellectual planes. But Baby Blue has a fourth distinct system overlapping the other three, suggesting a later evolutionary development. We have no idea of the purpose of this fourth system. But there are neural pathways connecting it to that unknown sensory organ."

"It sounds like the creature is in some sort of suspended state."

"Closer to a fetal state," Faye said. "Yet even that's not quite correct. Baby Blue seems to be bypassing the normal entropy process inherent to living organisms. It bears all the hallmarks of an evolutionary creation, yet it doesn't appear to be evolving. Nor decaying, for that matter. More like it's frozen in time. Some sort of fantastic hibernation process is probably the closest analogy. And yet..."

Faye trailed off with a puzzled look.

"What?" LeaMarsa prodded.

"I still can't wrap my head around the fact that it apparently didn't exist prior to that energy storm on the surface. According to our understanding of biological principles, which as far as we know apply to lifeforms on every planet we've explored, that should be impossible. It's as if the fetal creature came into spontaneous existence."

"Has it elevated again?"

"Five more times, the last I checked. Periodically, the damned thing simply ignores gravity and lifts itself off the floor. Once, it rose nearly a meter and stayed aloft for thirty seconds."

Faye shook her head in wonder. "Totally bizarre. The only possible explanation is that it possesses its own form of geonic nullification, which has never been seen before. The *Alchemon* simulates gravity, of course. But that's based on sophisticated pressure variations and subatomic fields that grant us a polarity in reference to the ship. Those are scientifically understood methods that trick us into believing there's an up and down. They don't violate scientific principles. But Bouncy Blue…"

She trailed off with a shrug and glanced at the clock. "OK, I'm out of here. And dear, don't forget you're coming to the Homebound tomorrow. No excuses."

"We should turn the ship around," LeaMarsa blurted out. "We should return the creature to Sycamore and leave it there."

The scientist regarded her with a look bordering on pity. LeaMarsa knew that Faye and the rest of them perceived her as a troubled soul, ping-ponging from one fear to the next. Yet for all their reliance on perceiving the world through the lens of science, none of them seemed to comprehend the greater reality.

Her fears, and what they would bring down upon them all, were real.

From the Files of Lieutenant
Tomer Donner, Pannis Corp
BRIDGE OFFICER

Renfro Zoobondi.

I turn the name over in my head nearly every day now, trying to see the killer of my lover from different angles, trying to look for his weaknesses. I know he's become an obsession with me but I'm powerless to do anything about it. I'd like to kill him with my own two hands, but I realize that such a thing is destined to remain in the realm of fantasy. I know my own limitations. I don't have the strength and courage necessary to murder another human being, even such a vile perversion as Zoobondi.

Today is the third anniversary of Karl's murder – the day my obsession took hold – and I've used every spare moment to secretly look into the VP's affairs. I've hired investigators to track Zoobondi's movements and a forensics auditor to unearth and review his complex finances. I'm fairly certain he's been using some dodgy bookkeeping to embezzle funds from various Pannis accounts.

I've talked to several people who were victimized by Zoobondi during his rapid ascent up the corporate hierarchy. I'm also pretty certain Karl wasn't the first man that Zoobondi killed in hand-to-hand fighting. There've been two additional victims I've been able to confirm, although not to the point of being able to prove it in a criminal court. Having come to know this sadistic bastard as well as I do, I'd be willing to bet there are others too.

Yet so far, nothing I've turned up is strong enough to instigate an official probe. Zoobondi is smart and covers his tracks too well. I have to admit, a sense of frustration has begun to set in.

Still, I've vowed that my determination will not flag. I'll keep trying to nail Renfro Zoobondi until the day I die.

CHAPTER 8

The main social room was the largest space on the ship. Over thirty meters in length from forward to aft airseals, a portion of it had a high ceiling that intruded into updeck. A double row of columns, purely decorative but suggestive of ancient Roman architecture, rose along the room's length to encompass both levels.

One column housed a freelane, a transparent cylindrical shaft. The artificially generated geonic forces present elsewhere were held at bay inside the recreational tube. Floating in a microgravity environment was believed an excellent stress reliever.

Today, the room also served as a gallery. Animated picture frames dotted the walls. In deference to the crewmembers who were Helioteers – Faye, Alexei, Rigel and, prior to his erratic behavior, Lieutenant Donner – Jonomy had programmed the frames to display brief videos of Helio Age personalities.

Ericho felt that one of the most remarkable heritages of the Helio Age was also one of the simplest: offering a window into the past through imagery of people long-dead. Nevertheless, Helioteers tended to romanticize the era preceding starflight and human expansion into the galaxy, ignoring its dark undercurrents. The Helio Age was a time of bigotry run amok, when an individual's skin pigmentation, spiritual belief, ethnic background or sexual preference could incite violent personal attacks or propel nation-states into horrific wars.

Still, he understood some of the era's fascination. He wondered what it must have been like when most institutions were controlled by governments rather than the all-powerful megas. And whether corporate ascendance at the expense of democratic institutions was to blame, historians often pointed out that contemporary society had produced an exceptionally large underclass, the needful majority.

Ericho turned his attention to a wall of picture frames featuring videos of famed twentieth-century political figures. As he recalled, John F. Kennedy, Winston Churchill, Martin Luther King and Mahatma Gandhi had achieved fame during times of incredible carnage, with three of the four being assassinated. The way they smiled and waved brought to mind present-day politicians that the megas put forth for election to the Corporeal Congress.

Each frame was programmed to cycle through multiple personalities. Kennedy, Churchill, King and Gandhi morphed into figures whose imprinted names Ericho didn't recognize. He wasn't interested enough to tap the frames for biographical readouts. Marilyn Monroe, J.D. Salinger, Coco Chanel and a being called André 3000 – perhaps an early android model – would remain enigmas.

"I feel luscious!" Faye Kuriyama hissed as she intersected Ericho's wandering path.

He raised his glass in salute and took another sip of Topaz lime brandy. It was his favorite recreational drink, made with a pseudo-alcohol formulation to prevent hangovers.

"Luscious," Faye repeated, licking her lips with unfettered sensuality.

She was dressed from neck to ankles in a natal suit, which accounted for her mood. The flesh-colored garment magnified the sensation of touch to such a degree that even the gentlest of breezes could feel like a soothing massage. Ericho had worn them a few times in his younger years. These days he preferred to experience his massages a more natural way, through June's talented hands.

"Touch me," she ordered.

He patted her shoulder. She smiled with delight.

"I felt that all the way to my bones. You should put on a suit, captain."

"Tempting."

A frame behind Faye changed to a skinny man with a goatee in a black turtleneck demonstrating an iPhone, a brand of that ubiquitous com device of the early twenty-first century. Smartphones were obsoleted by wearable com, in turn made redundant by implants. Now even that latter technology was disappearing, a victim of Helioteer fascination with older technologies and the cultural coolness of owning shrinkable wafers.

The animation cycled into its next incarnation, a colorful, bandana-clad musician wildly gyrating with a guitar, even playing it with his teeth. Ericho was puzzled why the video ended with him setting fire to the stringed body of his instrument and smashing it to pieces. Best guess, he'd thrown the fiery tantrum because the crowd was disappointed by his performance.

A hand touched Ericho's shoulder and he turned to face Tomer Donner. The lieutenant had chosen to attend the

Homebound barechested and barefooted, accentuating his hairless state. He wore only outlandish silver jodhpurs with deep pockets. An icicle earring – a stylish sliver of frozen mineral water formed over a microfridge – hung from his right lobe.

"I am an artisan of recreation," Donner began, "tasting both sides of the equation beneath skies of excitation."

A droplet melted from his earring, splattered on his shoulder.

Faye grinned. "You sound like a mad poet."

"Indeed. A poet prepared, for we are but pawns within the realm of luminous dark."

"What have you ingested?" Ericho asked, for once not bothered by the lieutenant's ramblings. It was too bad Topaz brandy was prohibited on duty.

"Ingested? Nothing other than a snack of cheesebread and sugarham. I intend to maintain pharmaceutical abstinence for the duration of the Homebound." He smiled. "Call it my own special Donner party."

"Sober is a bummer," Faye said, sighing with pleasure as she rubbed a hand across the belly of the natal suit.

"And a bum is sober!" Donner exclaimed.

The phrase shouldn't have been funny but Ericho found himself chuckling. Brandy was stripping Donner's wit of its worrisome madness.

He felt better than he had in days. The Homebound was the perfect remedy for LeaMarsa's unsettling presence, Donner's instability and Hardy Waskov's intransigence, not to mention that thing in the containment. Should he choose, he could even get drunk and sleep it off before his next duty stint, as Jonomy remained on the bridge. Ericho had served with lytics who were to some extent social creatures interested in joining such festivities. Jonomy was of the other variety.

Ericho spotted June conversing with Hardy. She'd prescribed a list of acceptable drugs for the Homebound, making certain that none of the more potent psychotropics and amphetamines were available. The limitation had been imposed on everyone even though its main purpose was to ensure that Donner was denied anything that might worsen his neurotic behavior.

Rigel and Alexei were off in a corner, laughing as they arm-wrestled. Only LeaMarsa stood alone, leaning against the wall sipping a blue drink. As usual, her expression, sadness coupled with disinterest in her surroundings, suggested a lost soul. Not for the first time, Ericho felt pity for her.

He turned back to Faye and Donner, who had segued into a lively discussion about Helio Age jazz music. For once, Donner sounded reasonably sane as he explained to Faye the subtle distinctions between the styles of two horn players, Charlie Parker and Louis Armstrong. Ericho wasn't familiar with the musicians but idly wondered whether the latter man was related to Neil Armstrong, first human to set foot on another world.

LeaMarsa and Donner were at opposite ends of the room. Because of the potential for dramatically escalated psionic interaction should they venture too close, Ericho had taken it upon himself to keep them separated. So far, it hadn't been an issue. As he'd noted earlier, the lieutenant seemed wary of LeaMarsa and kept his distance.

He wandered over to her, asked how she was doing.

"Fine," LeaMarsa said, avoiding his gaze.

"What do you think of your first Homebound?"

"It's OK."

A conversationalist she wasn't. He pressed on.

"You're from Wisconsin originally, right?" he asked.

"Milwaukee."

"Passed through there once when I was a kid. Seemed like a nice city although I didn't really see much of it. I was on one those old bullet trains with my mom and dad. Did you always live there?"

"We moved to Connecticut later," she said, turning to an animated frame of Pablo Picasso. The artist was drawing a curving series of black lines on a large white wall.

Ericho was about to give up trying to jumpstart a conversation when LeaMarsa surprised him with a question.

"Are your parents alive?"

"They are," Ericho said, smiling as he thought of them. "They live on an island formerly known as Great Britain, in a small seaside town on the English Channel. Mom runs a company that makes deep-sea engineering pods. Dad designs and retrofits vintage sailing ships. They both love the ocean."

At the end of every voyage, he looked forward to spending a few weeks at their seaside home, as well as seeing his sister and older brother who lived nearby.

"Any siblings?" he asked. He knew about LeaMarsa losing her parents in that shuttle crash but little about the rest of her family.

"Just me."

She went silent again. He was about to walk away.

"My parents were bioresearchers specializing in mitochondrial DNA," she said quietly.

"Mitochondrials, huh." He didn't know much about them but recalled reading that they had something to do with superluminals.

She looked sadder than usual. He changed the subject. "What do you plan on doing when we return to Earth?"

For a long moment she didn't respond. Then...

"I'd like to go live somewhere where there aren't many people. A farm, maybe. Spend time taking care of animals. Cows and sheep. And horses. I used to ride them when I was little. It made me feel free."

The faintest of smiles touched her lips but was quickly overwhelmed by a darker expression. Her voice fell to a whisper. "But none of those things are going to be possible."

"Why not? There are still plenty of horses to ride."

"I don't think we'll make it back to Earth."

Her eyes seemed to lose focus. She scurried away. As much as he hated to admit it, her final words instilled a vague sense of fear.

The Pablo Picasso video she'd been gazing at snared Ericho's attention as it morphed into its next image, an attractive dark-haired woman in a black dress with bare shoulders. Unlike the others, this one wasn't animated. It was rendered in sepia tone, suggesting that the woman in black had achieved fame before the development of video. Her name, Mary Shelley, triggered a vague association. Ericho believed she'd had something to do with proposing a novel use for electricity.

His attention returned to LeaMarsa. Alexei had cornered her against one of the pillars. Ericho was too far away to hear what was being said but it was clear LeaMarsa wasn't interested. She beelined away from the trainee.

Alexei spotted him, approached.

"She's not easy to talk to, sir."

"Definitely not."

Ericho had subtly broached the idea that LeaMarsa seemed lonely as well as physically inactive, and perhaps could use a friend close to her age to be a workout or swim partner. Alexei had jumped at the bait, leaving Ericho feeling a bit guilty about the ploy. He sensed the trainee was more interested in pleasing his captain than having a closer relationship with LeaMarsa. He also was concerned he'd been too subtle and hadn't made it clear that the two of them pursuing a sexual encounter wasn't his intent.

"Maybe I'll try again with her," Alexei said, withdrawing a pair of stroke lenses from a pocket and pasting them over his eyes. "Right now, if you don't mind, sir, I'm aiming for some mental expansion."

"A man has to see what he has to see," Ericho replied, using the familiar refrain for stroke lensers.

Alexei headed off, his face blossoming with awe as the lenses activated. "Whoa!" he hollered. "I'm not in Kansas anymore!"

The devices augmented what the eye naturally perceived by creating feedback loops from random areas of the brain. Some people called stroke lenses mirrors into the soul. Ericho had tried them in his younger days, had concluded that they merely distorted perception until nothing was real.

"Look!" Rigel hollered, pointing to the freelane.

Ericho turned. Donner and Faye, naked and holding hands, were upside down inside, rocketing the length of the transparent chute between the two decks. As they reached the bottom, they pushed off with their hands and soared back to the top, then reversed direction by kicking their legs against the updeck terminus.

Over and over they repeated the action. The shaft was soundproof but judging by their expressions, they were laughing madly. Ericho smiled but then caught sight of LeaMarsa exiting through the aft airseal. He recalled her disturbing remark about not making it back to Earth.

Gulping the rest of his brandy, he headed to the dispenser for a refill.

CHAPTER 9

LeaMarsa left the Homebound and made straight for the containment. Entering the deserted lab, she swiped her fingers across the control slate, turning the wall transparent. She gazed in at the creature, unsure why she'd come here. A part of her wanted to be as far away from the organism as possible. Yet another part remained curious.

"You want something from me, don't you?" she challenged, half expecting a response from Bouncy Blue or that thing inside it.

Even as she uttered the question she sensed her darkest fear trying to claw its way up from the depths, seeking to thrust itself into consciousness. She smelled those distant whiffs of decay, felt those strangling hands closing around her neck.

She short-circuited the reek's latest assault by dropping to the floor for a series of strenuous pushups. The workout did the job; the reek settled back into its subliminal crypt. But as she rose, another emotion surfaced. Anger.

Her existence was unfair. The universe seemed to conspire against her.

"Why are you here?" she demanded, smacking her palms against the glass. She was aware the question referred not only to the creature but also to her own presence on the *Alchemon*.

"That remains unknown," a voice answered.

Startled, LeaMarsa spun to see Jonomy's face peering from a monitor.

"I am sorry," the lytic said. "I did not intend to alarm you."

"It's OK."

He was plugged into the umbilical, communicating from the bridge.

"What are you doing in the containment lab?" he asked. "I thought you would be enjoying yourself with the others at the Homebound."

"I got tired of it. I wanted to be alone." She turned back to the containment wall. Bouncy Blue had elevated again, this time floating a half-meter above the floor.

"Why does it do that?" she wondered.

"The most likely theory is that it, or perhaps the fetal organism within, is practicing a long-dormant skill. Like a human whose muscles have withered from inactivity, it is trying to get back in shape."

In shape for what? she wondered.

"A more interesting question concerns its morphology. How and why such an organism exists in the first place."

"Any ideas?"

"None that come close to aligning with current theories. There are no biological correlates. This creature is truly a unique find."

"What do you think it was doing on the planet?"

"No single explanation tracks high enough on a probability matrix to be considered credible."

"You must have some idea, a best guess."

"In a realm of such low probabilities, I prefer not to speculate."

Jonomy didn't think or talk like the others. He also seemed to be the only person aboard the *Alchemon* who didn't want something from her, who wasn't trying to manipulate her in some subtle or not-so-subtle way. Conversing with him was oddly comforting.

"Are you a hundred percent certain it can't escape the containment?" she asked.

"Such a level of certainty does not exist. However, containments are designed with a high safety margin."

"I was reading up on the ship's control network. The containment is only a Level Two system."

"Level Two systems are quite powerful."

"Not as powerful as those of Level One." *And not as powerful as the Sentinel.*

"Correct. But from a statistical basis, there is little to be concerned about." Jonomy paused. "Have you given further consideration to Doctor Waskov's research agenda, specifically item one-thirty-three?"

"Not really." That was a lie. She'd indeed thought about it and still had no intention of entering the containment with that thing in there. But she was curious as to what Jonomy thought of the idea.

"Would you do it? If it were your choice, would you go into the containment?"

"The question is unanswerable. I am not you."

"But if you were?"

"But I am not."

She gave up trying to pry a response from him, tried another question.

"This mission, do you think it's going to be a success?"

"In what terms are you defying success?"

"Getting back to Earth."

She assumed Jonomy would answer in calculated percentages, with the odds highly in favor of their safe return to the solar system. But he surprised her.

"There are facets of existence that remain impervious to comprehension, and thus defy all means of calculation."

Maybe he senses what I sense, that the Alchemon *is a doomed vessel.*

CHAPTER 10

Remnants of the Homebound were visible throughout the main social room. Faye's natal suit lay crumpled along the wall where she and Donner had stripped to enter the freelane. Non-recyclable plates and utensils littered the floor. A beverage had been spilled or thrown onto a frame displaying a portrait of Charles Darwin, and the incursion was preventing the frame from evolving to its next image.

Janitorial pups would arrive soon to clean up the mess. The robots were waiting for Ericho to exercise a captain's prerogative and officially declare the Homebound over.

Only June, Faye and Donner remained in the room. Faye, in her underwear, was wandering aimlessly, rubbing her forehead as if nursing a hangover. Donner, still naked, was curled up in a fetal position near a dispenser, sound asleep.

Time to get back to reality, Ericho thought, vaguely troubled by the idea. It meant again dealing with the lieutenant and Hardy Waskov, not to mention whatever negative impacts LeaMarsa and the organism in the containment might be having on them.

The return trip was always the dullest part of a voyage. Outward bound, anticipation produced a certain edge, an excitement that served to keep him energized even during the most routine duties. Going home offered no such relief, not until that flurry of activity five months from now when the *Alchemon* reached the Lalande 21185 terminus of the Quiets.

The ship would enter a hundred-cubic-kilometer void surrounded by warning beacons. The vessel's spatiotemporal coagulators would be phased into the odd energy patterns present within the Quiets and the *Alchemon* would emerge instantaneously at the solar system terminus. From there, the nucleonic engines would fire up again and the ship would embark on its final four-month journey to Earth. Shortly thereafter, Ericho would hire out on another Pannis vessel and return to the stars.

His parents and siblings, all contentedly Earthbound, wondered when he'd outgrow his roving existence. Extended lifespans made it possible for citizens to enjoy multiple careers, and mega psychologists believed that people should experience a minimum of three professions in their lives to maximize emotional health. His family, all high achievers, had done that and more, and boasted accomplished resumes in multiple fields.

But Ericho had never wanted to do anything beyond voyaging on starships. He had no desire for additional careers, no desire to compete for accolades. He realized he was ensnared in a repetitive life pattern. Yet it was a pattern he had no desire to outgrow.

You can't stay a grunt forever, you need an adult job, his older brother would tell him, an opening volley in what inevitably would grow into a fierce debate.

But Ericho would argue that it's what he loved to do, even while a faint voice in his head suggested that his brother wasn't completely off the mark. A bridge officer certainly transcended being a grunt. He wasn't trapped in the ranks of the needful majority, doing some lowly job like scrubbing miasma tanks in a nucleonic fuel plant. Modest family income had enabled him to avoid such a fate. Still, with lytics and AIs essentially running starships, few instances of pivotal decision-making were required of him.

A Helioteer phrase sprang to mind: "go with the flow." It could well describe his attitude toward being a captain. And that was the core of his brother's argument, that Ericho was comfortable in circumstances that didn't require him to confront real challenges, and thus take the next step in personal growth.

"You look far away," June said, coming up behind him and rubbing his shoulders.

"Just reviewing the state of my irresponsible existence."

"Dwelling on your brother again, I see. Did I ever tell you that I think he can be a bit of a jerk?"

"Once or twice."

She broke into a smile. He loved the way she smiled at him, how it could consign his troubles to a recycle bin.

"Just feeling a bit philosophical," he offered. "What'd you think of the Homebound?"

"A reasonable success." She gazed at Donner's sleeping figure. "Most of us had an opportunity to cut loose or relax in our own unique ways."

"Most but not all."

June nodded. "I saw you talking to Alexei. Nothing on the workout-partner front between him and LeaMarsa, I gather."

"She's a challenge. Any other ideas?"

"I've been doing further study. There's some preliminary

research that certain forms of relaxation can also lessen a psionic's impact."

"Such as?"

"A nutriment bath."

"Worth a shot. So, get her into NUB."

"Believe me, I've been trying. So far she's resisted." June paused. "I'll push the issue, tell her it's a medical recommendation."

Ericho related LeaMarsa's warning that they probably wouldn't make it back to Earth. He forced a grin as he said it, hoping June would be amused.

The crewdoc's voice fell to a whisper. "Did LeaMarsa say why she believes that?"

"No." He recalled another aspect of their conversation. "Mitochondrials and superluminals. I read an article, but I don't remember the details. There's some kind of correlation, right?"

"Now there's a question out of the proverbial left field."

Ericho nodded. "It relates to something I said to LeaMarsa and the way she reacted. I definitely touched a nerve."

"Well, first of all, superluminals, especially the type found in humans, aren't easy to understand. We know they exist and we can reach certain mathematical conclusions about them, such as that their effects intensify in direct proportion to physical distance. But when you really try to examine them in detail, the quantum observer effect and Heisenberg uncertainty kicks in. Basically, the deeper you study superluminals, the less sense they seem to make."

"And mitochondrials? Power plants of the cells, if I remember my bio courses."

"They supply the chemical energy," June said. "They have

other functions as well, such as signaling and cell growth. Their connection with superluminals comes from a body of research pointing to mitochondrials as the primary genetic carriers of superluminal abilities."

Her explanation triggered another fact from the article. "Psionic abilities can be passed on from parent to child, right? And they tend to run in families."

"That's the current thinking."

"LeaMarsa said her parents were bioresearchers specializing in mitochondrial DNA. What do you know about that?"

June hesitated. Ericho had a hunch she was faced with a medical ethics conundrum.

"You can't tell me without violating confidentiality," he concluded.

"I've learned some things about LeaMarsa through standard GEL and MED files. Those I can talk about. But other things were revealed during private sessions."

"Got it. Still, give me what you can. In fact, I'd like a comprehensive med file on LeaMarsa as soon as possible. Put in anything and everything you can dig up on her history."

"Care to tell me why?"

"I don't know."

June's frown implied that Ericho was being evasive.

"Honestly, I don't. I just have this feeling it's important." Ericho couldn't analyze his request any better than that.

He activated his mike. "Jonomy?"

"Yes, captain."

"I'm declaring the Homebound over. Normal duty shifts from here on out."

"I'll issue notifications."

Ericho sensed movement behind him, turned. Tomer

Donner approached in a swerving gait, on the edge of drunkenness. The lieutenant had restored his minimal attire, the silver jodhpurs and icicle earring.

"Homebound's over," Ericho said, trying to waylay Donner with rational thought before the man could launch into fresh ramblings. He should have realized the effort was futile.

"I am the offspring of excitation, the skulking metaphor extracted from synergy and made real."

Donner teetered. Ericho grabbed his shoulder to steady him.

"Why don't I walk you to your cabin. You look like you could use a bed."

"Bravo, captain. You don't insult directly by questioning my sanity but instead utilize a diversionary tactic. Still, I believe you're right. It's time for me to leave this place for a more lasting arena of slumber."

Ericho guided Donner through the forward airseal and into downdeck's main transverse corridor. The lieutenant walked slowly, lost in thought. Ericho remained silent, not wanting to provide fuel for fresh effluence.

They crossed through a central airseal that divided port and starboard halves of the ship. As the door whisked shut behind them, Donner raised his gaze to the lume-encrusted ceiling.

"Something wrong?" Ericho asked.

"An infinitely speculative question."

A faint shiver seemed to pass through the lieutenant, followed by a bout of nervous laughter.

"Ah, captain. You think you are in control, but you are not. Other forces are at work, disjunctive forces that will soon rip us asunder. Be forewarned. There are consequences for not recognizing the truth."

"Which is?"

"That you cannot command that which cannot be commanded."

"I'll keep that in mind."

Donner walked on, at an agreeably faster pace. *Almost there*, Ericho thought, concentrating on the elevator up ahead. A quick ascent to the crew cabins and the man would be out of his hair, at least for a time.

They entered the elevator. The door closed. Before the compartment could move, Donner slammed the emergency stop button.

What now? Ericho wondered.

The lieutenant backed into a corner and fell into a crouch, arms dangling loosely at his sides, fingers bent inward at the first joint. There was no mistaking a fighting posture.

Ericho assumed a matching stance, not about to take the chance that this was more playacting. He kept his tone light, hoping to steer the lieutenant back to reality.

"You're probably as fatigued as I am. It'll be good to get some real sleep, huh?"

"I wish things could be different." Donner's words echoed heartfelt emotion. "Please know this isn't my fault."

"I'm sure you're just tired."

"I'm not completely without blame. I did elect to come on this voyage, allowed things to get so out of control."

Ericho suspected he was referring to LeaMarsa's presence. He wanted to ask why Donner hadn't backed out of the mission, knowing she could have a negative impact on him. But at that moment, he attacked.

Ericho jerked his head back. Donner's left hand swept past his neck, a vicious karate swipe.

Purgefire!

Donner swung his right foot upward, aiming for Ericho's crotch. The blow went wide. Ericho grabbed for the arcing foot but missed.

The lieutenant pivoted, rammed his bare heel into Ericho's guts.

Doubling over in pain, he backpedaled toward the opposite corner. Donner charged again. Ericho deflected another wild kick with his elbow and went on the offensive, swung a haymaker toward the lieutenant's face.

For a man who looked drunk, Donner moved with surprising speed. He sidestepped the fist and unleashed a brutal left jab into Ericho's windpipe. Gasping, Ericho's hands instinctively shot up to protect his neck from further hits. But that opened up his midsection.

Donner's heel caught him full force. Ericho flew backward, slammed the wall. Stunned, he collapsed to his knees.

The lieutenant unleashed a mad wail of triumph. Unpinning the icicle earring, he crushed it beneath his heel. For a fragile moment, the craziness seemed to leave his face.

"The Quad awakens," he said, looking infinitely sad.

Donner opened the elevator and dashed back into the downdeck corridor. The door slid shut, leaving Ericho on his knees fighting a wave of dizziness.

He struggled to his feet, tabbed his mike. "Jonomy, Donner's out of control. He just attacked me."

"Already tracking him, captain. I believe he is heading for the containment."

"Seal the door."

"Done. However, as a bridge officer he possesses the override code for all internal seals."

Ericho cursed under his breath. The door had innumerable security features to prevent anything from escaping the containment and its lab. But entry *into* the lab wasn't considered such a major issue. Only modest safeguards were in place.

He staggered out of the elevator. His neck and midsection were sore, as was his upper back where he'd slammed the wall. Fortunately, it didn't feel like anything was broken.

"Captain, the airseal into the containment area has been overridden. Lieutenant Donner has entered the lab."

Ericho recovered his strength. Ignoring the pain, he dashed toward the containment. He would be more aggressive when he caught up to Donner. Even though he'd been alerted to the assault, his desire to soothe the lieutenant had caused him to hesitate, not respond fast enough to the violence. He wouldn't make the same mistake twice.

"I have lost surveillance video inside the lab," Jonomy's voice came over the link.

"How's that possible?"

"A simple means. The lieutenant has draped the overhead cameras with adhesive fabric."

"Where the hell did he get that?"

"He had it with him, in one of the pockets of his jodhpurs."

He doesn't want us to see what he's doing. A more ominous conclusion surfaced. *Whatever it is, he's planned it in advance.*

"I am modifying the camera's EM characteristics. I should be able to incorporate wavelengths that can penetrate the cloth and allow us to see–"

A vibration shook the corridor. The rest of Jonomy's words were lost in a wail of alarms. It sounded as if half a dozen systems had just gone to emergency alert status, each with a distinctive bell, klaxon or pulse. The shrieking mélange filled the air. It would be wailing away in every corridor and crew area of the ship.

"Jonomy! What happened?"

The mix of alarm frequencies blotted out his response. Ericho raced down the corridor toward the containment, trying to make sense of the warning signals competing for his attention. The highest pitched one was a Sentinel alert, in and of itself indicative of major trouble. A harsh beeping indicated the problem was internal and a thumping bass horn proclaimed a complete airseal shutdown, meaning the ship was being automatically compartmentalized against some hazard.

The doors between Ericho and the containment whisked open seconds before he reached them. Jonomy must have been tracking him, overriding the airseal shutdown and clearing a route.

He listened closely, distinguished other warnings. A rhythmic drumming indicated that the *Alchemon* had lost a portion of its internal telemetry system. A tinny pulse indicated a gravity aberration and a birdlike chirping, a radiation release. Each alarm by itself was bad news. But all of them combined...

Comprehension slammed through him as he dashed through a final airseal to enter the corridor leading to the containment.

An internal explosion. It seemed the likely explanation for this particular mix of alarms.

An airseal at the opposite end whisked open and Rigel came rushing toward him. The two of them reached the containment door at the same time.

There was abrupt silence. Jonomy had killed the alarms in this corridor. Only flashing red ceiling lumes indicated they remained on emergency status.

The lytic's words came through loud and clear. "The event occurred in the containment lab, twenty-three seconds after Lieutenant Donner entered."

"Is the containment breached?" Ericho asked.

"Unknown. Total sensor loss in both areas. Every system within the containment and its lab has been terminated. Thus far, all seals are holding. However, there is low level gamma radiation in that corridor and other areas bordering the containment."

"How bad are we getting juiced?" Rigel demanded.

"Radiation leakage is minimal. IBD reports that you are well within safety parameters."

"As long as we don't open the door."

"You cannot open it," Jonomy said. "None of us can. The Sentinel has taken control of that airseal.

Jesus of Naz! Ericho thought. *What had the lieutenant done?*

"There is no clear indication of what has happened. Every piece of hardware down there registered a near-simultaneous overload and dropped out of the net. I am trying to locate and restore the surveillance cam files of those final seconds after the lieutenant entered the lab and apply those modified wavelengths to penetrate the adhesive fabric. The explosion was severe enough to send a pulse into data storage, scrambling recent files. The *Alchemon* has quite literally received a traumatic shock. It is trying to restructure itself, reroute misplaced data into undamaged regions."

"What about the air vents?" Rigel asked. "The containment's totally self-contained but the lab feeds off some of EHO's subsystems. There could be radiation leakage there."

"The vents were sealed by the Sentinel within microseconds of the explosion."

"Donner was alone in the lab?" Ericho asked.

Jonomy hesitated. "That has not been confirmed."

"Crew status?"

"Per emergency conditions, they are isolated in whatever section they happened to be in at the moment of the incident. June, Hardy and Alexei are in their quarters. Faye is still in the main social room. Do you want any of them routed elsewhere?"

"Send June to med. Keep everyone else where they're at. What about LeaMarsa?"

"Unknown."

"How's that possible?"

"For some reason, the trackers can't locate her. It may have to do with that traumatic shock the ship received, temporarily disabling some of our systems. However, I can confirm that she was in the containment lab approximately ten minutes prior to the explosion."

"You're sure?"

"I spoke with her."

"Then she could have been in there with Donner."

"Unknown."

"All right, Jonomy. I'm heading up to the bridge unless you have a better idea."

"There is nothing further you can do outside the containment. The Sentinel will not permit access. Repair pups are being dispatched into all adjacent areas to scour the radiation leakage."

"Any damage to the Big Three?" Rigel asked.

The tech officer was referring to the trio of Level One systems that provided the means for a ship to enter a Quiets. The delicate spatiotemporal coagulators were the most vital since not all of their complex functions had full backup. The other two, primary power and the main quantizer – the latter performing trillions of nanosecond-to-nanosecond calculations within Quiets space – had auxiliaries.

The Big Three – SCO, POP and PAQ – needed to be working in perfect tandem to enter and exit a Quiets. They represented the ship's ticket home. If any one of them and its backup had been severely impacted by the explosion, the *Alchemon* would be stranded out here, lightyears from Earth. And given Pannis' miserly policies for dispatching search-and-rescue missions, the expense might not be justifiable to a corporate retrieval committee.

"No apparent damage to the Quiets systems, captain. Secondaries are stable as well."

Ericho sighed with relief. But the feeling was short-lived as Jonomy continued.

"However, I cannot at this time be one hundred percent certain of that diagnosis, particularly in regards to SCO. We will not have confirmation until the impact of the explosion is fully addressed and all major systems go through a reset process."

Ericho spun to Rigel. "I think you'd better–"

"Way ahead of you," the tech officer snapped, dashing toward the stern.

Jonomy might be unable to guarantee the proper functioning of SCO, POP and PAQ directly through the *Alchemon*'s network, but Rigel could do a manual check from the Big Three nexus. The site was accessible via a maintenance shaft from the port lander hold.

Ericho headed in the other direction and boarded the nearest elevator. A quick ascent to updeck and transit through two airseals brought him to the bridge.

The lytic's chair was slowly rotating around the HOD. Jonomy's eyes were pinched shut, indicating he was in a deep stage of communing with the network. Ericho didn't want to bother him with more questions while he was interfacing. He plopped in the command chair and accessed the network from his control panel.

The first wave of scrolling data induced a grimace. IBD – internal bio detection, a Level Four system – was reporting a thermal increase of six degrees at the containment entrance where Ericho and Rigel had stood only moments ago. Even though the temperature escalation was relatively mild, IBD was now declaring that section of corridor an unsafe zone and suggesting that all access be restricted unless crewmembers wore biosuits.

It wasn't the thermal leakage itself that concerned Ericho but what the reading indicated. If that much heat was penetrating the reinforced lab walls and door, the interior must be superheated, perhaps even molten.

Jonomy opened his eyes. Ericho took the opportunity to bark a fresh question.

"Could it have been a micronuke?"

"No, captain. If it had been that severe, we would have registered shock waves all over the ship."

Ericho wasn't convinced. "I felt a strong vibration when it happened."

Rigel came over the intercom. "A micronuke would have taken out half the ship. We wouldn't be here talking about it."

"Captain, I've located the final surveillance video from inside the lab."

Jonomy piped the imagery to Ericho's wafer. The viewpoint was from a ceiling camera. Ericho watched in mute fascination as Donner burst into the containment lab and proceeded to throw a wad of adhesive fabric at the camera. The video disappeared for only an instant, then took on a greenish pallor as the lytic modified wavelengths to see through the fabric.

"Here are the final twelve seconds," Jonomy narrated. "Notice what the lieutenant is withdrawing from his jodhpurs."

Ericho grimaced as Donner slipped a stubby metallic cylinder from a wide pocket. "A Higgs cutter."

"He must have swiped it from the mech shop," Rigel said. "We only have two manual ones aboard and that's where they're stored. All the other HCs are attached to robots or specialty pups."

Ericho felt drained, his adrenaline rush from the incident starting to wear off. It didn't matter where Donner had procured the device.

"The lieutenant must have had the cutter with him at the Homebound," Jonomy said.

Ericho should have searched him. He should have been far more concerned about Donner's behavior, about the crazed philosophizing, about the earlier faux attack on the bridge. He could have stopped this.

He sighed; realizing now wasn't the time for self-recrimination. He watched in silence as the inevitability of the incident played out on the monitor.

Donner used the cutter's laser-like beam to burn through the lock of one of the lab's secure storage closets. He yanked open the cabinet door to reveal a boxy fusion battery on the top shelf. Pointing the Higgs cutter at it, he depressed the trigger. The incinerating beam again ignited, the HC emitting a distinctive whine as it ramped up to maximum output. It took only three seconds for the beam to pierce the battery's shielding.

An instant of frozen time. The screen went white as the camera signal was lost.

On a starship that possessed safeguards against the unimaginable, an insane man had carried out a relatively simple act. A powerful Higgs cutter, restricted for shipboard use except in emergencies, had been directed at the unstable elements of a fusion cell. Precisely calculable physics had determined the result: a melt, an expanding ball of intensely hot fire absorbing all surrounding matter within nanoseconds.

Rigel, who must have been watching the surveillance feed on a monitor from the bowels of the spatiotemporal coagulator system, broke the silence. "I guess we're lucky it was the lab. Most other areas of the ship don't have such thick walls."

Ericho nodded. Had Donner vaporized himself elsewhere, the *Alchemon* likely would have been destroyed.

"Captain, crewmembers are asking to be released from their secure areas."

"Do it." There was no reason to keep them sequestered at this point.

"I am receiving updated data. The melt has definitely breached the electrochromic wall separating the lab from the containment. Status of the organism remains unknown."

"All right," Ericho said, trying to get a handle on the situation. "Let's assume for a moment that Bouncy Blue has been destroyed. That means we have two useless chambers down there, both hot as hell and filled with radioactive gases. We might be able to clean up the outside corridor and control any air leakage through EHO, but that mess in the lab and containment is going to stay hot for a long time."

"And it could start leaking," Rigel added. "With that much

of a heat source in the middle of the ship, we run the risk of thermal baffles failing. So, we blow the containment airlock and give the whole goddamn radioactive mess a vacuum enema, purge it into space."

"Exactly."

"In theory, the suggestion is sound," Jonomy said. "Sudden depressurization should work and make the eventual cleanup easier.

"However, there are two issues we must address before taking such action. First, we are not positive the organism is dead. Remember, this is a creature that apparently survived in a harsh environment on Sycamore for more than a billion years. For all we know, it is capable of surviving a melt."

"No way," Rigel said.

"The second issue is more fundamental. We can no longer open the inner seal of the containment airlock. That subsystem is offline and presumably suffered damage from the melt. And even if we could reroute the controls, the mechanism itself may have been fused by the intense heat."

"Then we do an EVA," Rigel said. "Someone goes out there and opens the outer seal, enters the airlock, plants a low-intensity explosive at the inner hatch. We blow it manually. Same result."

"You're forgetting about the organism."

"Fuck Bouncy Blue. We're dealing with a goddamn melt! We have to dump that mess. And we got to do it before we go through the Quiets."

Rigel was right. Ericho had gone through enough Quiets to know that odd things could happen to a vessel during one of the instantaneous passages. The engineers who designed and worked on Quiets travel were well aware of the strange forces that came into play when the spatiotemporal coagulators were activated.

On one of Ericho's early flights, dozens of airseals had mysteriously opened during the transition. On another trip, his vessel had emerged from its Quiets passage in geonic turmoil, with simulated gravity flipped ninety degrees, transforming walls into floors or ceilings. Traveling through a Quiets with a highly radiated compartment... there was no telling what might occur.

June came over the intercom.

"Faye and I found LeaMarsa. She appears to be in a deep sleep. We can't seem to wake her up."

"Where was she?" Ericho asked.

"Downdeck, corridor B-1. Near the dreamlounge. She was just standing there, frozen."

"You're taking her to medcenter?"

"On our way."

Hardy joined the conversation. "Captain, I heard Rigel's suggestion and must insist that you hold off on any decision about purging the containment. I believe there's a distinct possibility that the organism survived the incident."

"We're still evaluating the situation." He faced Jonomy. "Can we get a pup in there with a camera?"

"I am afraid not, captain, at least not yet. Not even the most shielded pups can handle that level of exposure. The mix of radioactive isotopes in the lab and the containment are still too hot. However, most of those isotopes have short half-lives. They will decay relatively fast."

"How long?"

"Eight to ten hours before a pup can survive for any reasonable length of time."

"What about the links?" The ship's pair of virtual reality-controlled robots had far better shielding than the pups.

"Minimum of three hours," Jonomy answered.

"We could cut that time in half," Rigel said. "Outfit one with additional shielding."

"There is an obvious problem with any of these options."

Ericho nodded grimly. "How do we get them in there without contaminating more of the ship?"

"And in either case, robot or pup, there will be fatal contamination to the unit. Pannis guidelines for such a scenario suggest not using a link."

"Why the hell not?" Rigel growled.

"Replacement cost for a robot is approximately six times that of the most expensive pup, excluding the warrior pups."

"Screw those buttmeisters in Pannis accounting! Our asses come first."

"No argument. Those are only guidelines, not dictates. The decision is left to a ship's captain. Before we proceed much farther down this path, I would remind you of a more fundamental issue. The Sentinel is controlling that airseal, which is the only way into the containment area other than the external chute. The Sentinel may decide not to allow the door to be opened for either a robot or a pup. Furthermore, the corridor airseal also may have been damaged and be inoperable."

Ericho took Jonomy's concerns in stride. They'd figure out how to deal with the Sentinel and a possibly nonfunctioning airseal when the time came.

"Rigel, are you in SCO yet?"

"Yeah, I'm here, checking systems now. So far, everything's green. But I've got a few tests to run."

"How long?"

"Twenty minutes."

"When you're done, prep a link robot for a hot environment. Extra shielding, whatever else you can think of. We need to get in there."

CHAPTER 11

LeaMarsa floated within the alternate universe of neurospace but there was something different about it. Several clusters of the faux-stars – each grouping hundreds or perhaps thousands strong – were cloaked in ominous shadows.

"Coalesce and Target."

It was the same gravelly voice that had uttered *Sentinel Obey*. LeaMarsa again sensed that the phantom woman was straining to be heard from somewhere amid those stars. Yet it was as if she was on the far side of a vast ocean. And as with the earlier utterance, the significance of *Coalesce and Target* remained unfathomable.

"Who are you?" she demanded. "What are you trying to tell me?"

There was no response.

A burst of light from one of those shadowy clusters snared her attention. A single star from within the cluster shot out of neurospace like a renegade comet, coming toward LeaMarsa at high velocity. But before the ejected star could reach her, it dissolved into nothingness.

The incident provided fundamental insights about the realm of luminous dark. Each star was the analogue of an intelligent lifeform, and the star that had been ejected was the analogue of an entity whose life had been extinguished. Furthermore, it was someone she knew.

Lieutenant Donner.

LeaMarsa bolted awake to find herself sitting upright in an unfamiliar bed. Two pairs of hands grabbed her shoulders, gently pushed her back down into the mattress. She squinted under bright overhead lights, unable to discern faces.

Vision cleared. She recognized her surroundings, realized she was in a medcenter treatment room.

June and Faye flanked the bed. Above, the tentacles of a multi-pronged clinician drooped from the ceiling, its hands clutching a variety of diagnostic modules.

"Let me up!" she demanded.

They allowed her to rise. She looked into their faces, saw deep concern.

"I'm OK. I'm fine now."

She got to her feet. A rush of dizziness forced her to sit back down.

"Take deep breaths," June suggested.

LeaMarsa inhaled and exhaled slowly. "What happened to me?"

"We found you near the dreamlounge in a deep sleep," June said.

"It's like you were in a coma," Faye added.

It was neither sleep nor coma but another psionic blackout, albeit one apparently lasting longer than usual. She remembered leaving the containment and heading for an elevator. That the blackout had occurred near the dreamlounge was probably coincidental. She hated such places and had avoided them since she was fifteen.

Back then, she'd become fascinated by avant-garde artists

and writers. She splashed random globs of paint on vintage canvases and wrote brooding poetry and dreamed of losing her virginity to Ryla Eun-Jung, the storm singer who'd died in the same shuttle crash that killed her parents.

A solo day trip from her New Haven boarding school to an underground dreamlounge parlor in the Bronx made the sex fantasy possible. She'd programmed the liaison with the famed musician when he was thirty and deep in his squall period, incorporating thunder and oceanic wind sounds with lilting string ensembles. The setting was a villa on the Korean peninsula crafted from a customizable template and decorated with the works of Helio Age artists Marcel Duchamp and Henri Matisse.

Programming a chance encounter at a nearby café, she'd had Eun-Jung invite her to the villa, where they'd made virtual love on the balcony of a second-floor bedroom in view of a beautiful golden waterfall.

He'd proved a gentle lover. Although a part of her recognized that the kisses, caresses and ultimate penetration were happening only in her head, the impact of the encounter had been intense. Too intense, in fact. Not realizing that subcortical dreamlounge fantasies required well-defined parameters to prevent side effects, she'd left the Eun-Jung program open-ended, thereby providing a doorway for her deepest fear to slither into the virtual world. Upon climaxing, the reek had swarmed up out of its subconscious chasm. Screaming, she'd bolted from the dreamlounge.

Three days later, having suffered flashbacks of the incident, she'd seduced a random boy at a local tavern in the hope that physical lovemaking would blot out the impact of the virtual.

It hadn't.

Her thoughts returned to the present as she recalled the phantom woman's latest utterance.

"Coalesce and Target?" she asked. "Do you know what that means?"

June and Faye looked mystified.

"Dear, did you have some sort of psionic experience?"

"No."

"Discussion can be healthy," June prodded. "Whatever happened, you might feel better sharing it."

"I won't feel better."

The crewdoc adopted a sharper tone. "LeaMarsa, this isn't just about you anymore. I believe that this ship and its crew are being impacted by psionic forces. Your personal insights could be important for everyone's sake, especially in light of the tragedy."

She knew who they were talking about. "How did the lieutenant die?"

June and Faye looked surprised that she knew. They told her about his suicide and the containment melt.

"I'd like to return to my cabin now."

"It might be better if you stay here for a while," June said. "I don't think you should be alone right now."

But I am alone. And I'm the only one who realizes that what happened to the lieutenant is just the beginning.

CHAPTER 12

"Move your right foot forward," Jonomy instructed.

Ericho could see nothing but a gray haze. The lytic's words came to him from speakers inside the weighty headpiece.

Link gear for general usage was lightweight. But for critical applications, including use aboard starships, psychologists dictated that the control suits be heavy and cumbersome. Supposedly, this induced an unconscious reaction, impressing upon the wearer the importance of their task. Bulky suits had been statistically shown to improve safety ratios and reduce accidents.

Ericho strained to lift the leaden boot and drag it in front of him. The movement activated the servos, filling the helmet with a background hum and decreasing the suit's weight to a less bothersome level.

The interior of the visorless helmet came to life with virtual screens, letting Ericho know that the link was correctly positioned within the bridge's multi-directional treadmill.

"Captain, the robot you will be using is in downdeck port quarter, closet twelve."

Ericho mentally situated himself in the locale. "Got it."

The screens showed him a stereoptic view of the storage closet's dim interior through the robot's eyes. For all intents and purposes, he was now a hundred meters away from his body, inside the machine. The robot, covered in a rubbery skin, had inhumanly thin arms and legs that were stronger and more flexible than flesh-and-bone appendages. Rigel had attached extra radiation padding to protect critical areas.

The head vaguely mimicked its human prototype, with eyes, ears, nose and mouth. Still, a link face would never be mistaken for a person. It was more like a bizarre cross between an early com satellite and one of those carved pumpkin heads used during Helioteer celebrations of some long-ago holiday.

Ericho could still feel his own body. Yet physical sensation felt distant, as if his flesh and muscles were in a deep sleep. A specially formulated atmosphere within the suit included an anesthetic that deadened certain nerve endings, maximizing the perception that his consciousness was inside the robot.

The link incorporated a haptic system, enabling him to experience tactile sensation through the robot's skin. He could also see, hear and smell anything in the machine's immediate environment, as well as taste any object inserted into its mouth. He didn't anticipate using that latter function, having no desire to taste white-hot irradiated matter.

Bright light from a corridor filled his visual field as Jonomy opened the closet. He walked out of the closet and headed aft. After a few dozen steps, the telepresence felt natural. In reality, he would never step beyond the perimeter of the bridge treadmill, which constantly readjusted to keep him centered.

"Radiation leakage has stabilized," Jonomy said. "The cleanup pups are holding their own."

Ericho passed through an airseal to reach the section of corridor outside the containment.

"Remember, captain, you are going to have to move fast

once I open that door. EHO has created a pressure differential to minimize the corridor's exposure. Even so, the Sentinel has determined that it will allow only two-point-five seconds for you to enter the lab to prevent escaping contaminants from exceeding manageable levels. Should you surpass that interval, the Sentinel will activate the sureshutter."

Ericho had never been chopped apart by pneumatic blades. He had no desire to experience the sensation, even in telepresence.

He found himself wondering why the Sentinel hadn't awakened in time to stop Donner from vaporizing himself. But even as he framed the question, he suspected the answer. As powerful as a Sentinel was, it wasn't omnipotent. SEN was known to be at its weakest when trying to predict the actions of humans, especially those with behavioral quirks that put them at the extremes of psychological bell curves. Predicting the actions of a crazy bridge lieutenant no doubt posed as much of a challenge to a shrewd AI as it did to Ericho.

"OK, Jonomy. I'm ready."

The heavy seal whipped open. He lunged through, twisting his neck sharply to the left. In response to the abrupt movement, the robot performed an inhuman act, rotating its head one-eighty degrees in order to show him a rear view of the door whisking shut as he cleared it.

A second twist of the neck rotated the robot's head back to its normal position. He surveyed the containment lab, or what was left of it. Even though he had an idea of what to expect, it was an eerie scene.

The room was filled with a cloud of grayish smoke, which had been disturbed into gentle swirls by his sudden entrance. The robot's eye sensors made a spectral adjustment, inserting a sequence of filters until he was able to see clearly.

The center of the lab was gone – no consoles, no test equipment, nothing. At the spot where Donner had activated the Higgs cutter, a small molten pond bubbled where the flooring had been. Only the reinforced subfloor had prevented the red-hot mass from burning its way out of the containment lab and possibly through the hull.

Overhead, the ceiling was badly warped, looked like a slab of mottled cheese. Walls had suffered similar damage. Cabinets and test canisters had melted into grotesque forms. It took him a moment to realize that a pair of twisted stalagmites growing out of the deck had been chairs.

The floor around the perimeter remained intact, although now bore a resemblance to the dusty lunar surface. The lab was silent except for a faint hiss emanating from the molten pond.

"Quite a mess," Jonomy said, his serene tone accentuating the understatement.

"Smells bad, too."

A few sniffs of burned air was enough. Erich blinked his eyes at the link's sight typer and disengaged the nasal function.

There was no sign of Donner. Ericho was thankful for that. They were operating under the assumption he'd been instantly vaporized. Still, the bizarre forces unleashed in a melt could cause greater energy flashing in one direction. He'd seen a training video of a similar accident at a Pannis nuclear reprocessing plant. A worker had been only partly incinerated. The entire right side of her body, including arm, leg and half a head, had remained perfectly intact and eerily upright.

The electrochromic wall was gone except for a few shards hanging from the ceiling like frosted icicles. Ericho stepped through into the containment. The damage wasn't as severe;

the wall likely had absorbed a good amount of the melt's initial burst of ravaging energy. Test equipment drooped from the ceiling but the canisters and their mechanized appendages appeared intact.

In the far corner, beside the hatch that accessed the airlock chute, lay the organism. Bouncy Blue had lost its distinctive coloration. The gelatinous skin was badly charred.

"No signs of metabolic activity from your sensors," Jonomy said. "EPS calculates a ninety-nine percent probability that the fetal organism is also dead."

Ericho heard a crackling sound behind him. Startled, he rotated his head but there was nothing there.

"Sensor burnout," Jonomy explained. "I have shifted the system over to the secondaries."

The sound hadn't come from behind Ericho but had originated within the robot's head. Telepresence had its quirks.

"I have received an update from the Sentinel. It has determined that even the small amount of radioactive contamination leaked into the corridor during those seconds the door was open is unacceptable. It will not permit the door to be opened again."

"Got it."

SEN's decision wasn't unexpected. Even if the Sentinel permitted an exit, the intense heat and radioactive isotopes ultimately would cause severe damage to the robot. Should they embark on the plan to open the outer airlock and eject the entire mess into space, it would be dispatched as well.

"Any suggestions for moving Bouncy Blue's carcass outside the ship?" Ericho asked.

Hardy had made the request in the strongest possible terms. Dead or alive, he wanted the organism transferred to the external ecopod for their return to Earth.

"Can you open the hatch to the airlock chute from inside?" Jonomy asked.

Ericho examined the lock's control panel. It didn't look damaged, but its status lights were dark. He tried a keyboard reset. Nothing.

"Automatics must be burned out. I'll attempt a manual release."

He disengaged the windup lever from the mechanism. But when he applied the robot's considerable strength and tried to crank the handle, it wouldn't budge.

"The heat must have warped something," he concluded.

Rigel jumped into the discussion. "I know how we can purge the containment and still salvage Bouncy Blue. One of us does the EVA, opens the outer lock, plants the explosive at the inner lock. But before we trigger it and purge the mess, we cut a small hole through the inner lock, reduce the pressure differential. That way when we blow it, the purge will be less forceful. It should enable Bouncy Blue to be snatched with a net as it flies out."

"Such a maneuver carries a high-risk factor," Jonomy said. "EPS calculates—"

"Not if we do it right," Rigel snapped.

But Ericho agreed with Jonomy. It sounded dangerous. He wasn't about to chance using a crewmember for such a stunt. Still, they might be able to implement the plan with the second link robot or one of the repair pups outfitted for extravehicular ops.

He broached the idea. Jonomy was skeptical.

"Pups are not designed to handle the contingencies that could arise during such a complex task amid a debris field.

There is another issue. Whether carried out by a link or a pup, the Sentinel might perceive the venting of a compartment as a threat to the vessel's integrity."

"That's crazy," Rigel said. "SEN would never do that."

"Historically, Sentinels have taken a dim view of purges, no matter what their purpose, since they often result in unforeseen side effects."

"Sentinels aren't stupid," Rigel argued. "Ours isn't going to stop us from ejecting a hot mass."

"For the moment, we're not doing anything," Ericho said. "Let's debate this later and focus on the task at hand."

"Captain, I am reading unusual voltage surges in the robot's power modules. Have you suffered any damage, such as being struck by a falling object?"

Ericho ran his hands across the thick shoulders. Tactile sensation through the finger pads detected nothing out of the ordinary.

"Everything feels OK."

"The malfunction rate may be creeping higher than initially calculated. The robot's demise may happen earlier."

"Worst case?"

"Less than two hours."

"All right. Anything else you need me to do in here?"

"No. It can continue essential monitoring without your presence."

"I'm coming out."

Ericho took a final look at Bouncy Blue's charred remains and disengaged from the link. As consciousness reverted into his body, he had a grim thought. He might go down in history as the man blamed for destroying the greatest discovery of the millennium.

CHAPTER 13

There were places on the *Alchemon* that felt bad. LeaMarsa disliked the hydroponic gardens, with their claustrophobic conglomerations of submerged plants and twisted piping. The twin lander hangars and the storage pods, cold spaces filled with dark shapes, made dreariness tangible. And the containment lab...

She'd thankfully never have to go there again.

Still, none of those places were as disturbing as the dreamlounge. Yet here she was, standing in the largest of its four pods, a space that appeared to have limitless dimensions. A golden desert swept out before her to a distant mountain range, its flanks splotched with organic green, its molasses-hued peaks framed against a cloudless sky.

The illusion extended past peripheral vision. Only when she turned around did the vista morph into drab curving walls and a plain airseal, revealing the pod's actual dimensions at a mere twenty-five square meters. The pod was also programmable for multiple subcortical hookups, enabling individuals to share the same fantasy.

LeaMarsa would have refused to take part in such a hookup, which would have required donning a sensor cap like the one worn during her ultimately terrifying Eun-Jung seduction.

Fortunately, it was being utilized in a simpler fashion. The desert holo was one of thousands of archived vistas, none of which required subcortical linkage.

Nevertheless, the multisensory scene made her uncomfortable. She heard the wind stirring up sand and whistling through spiny cacti. A warm breeze touched her face, so dry it sucked the moisture from her lips. It wasn't the scene itself that bothered her but the fact it wasn't real, that illusion trumped the reassurance of physicality. Her grip on reality seemed to be growing more tenuous. Counterfeit environments tended to make her more aware of the reek lurking in the depths.

But this ceremony had to be endured. Her shipmates already viewed her with suspicion and alarm. It would be perceived as an unforgivable insult if she couldn't tolerate a funeral.

The seven of them stood in a semicircle facing the desert. LeaMarsa was at one end beside June, who wore the ceremonial blue suit of a Pannis medical officer. Next was Faye in a long black dress, her body stiff and her eyes locked into an unreadable stare.

Ericho occupied the middle position. Like June, he was in formal attire, a black and gold captain's outfit brimming with medals and commendations. He looked older and more tired than LeaMarsa could recall. Beyond him stood Rigel, Alexei and Hardy, also dressed in their finest.

Ericho cleared his throat. "We're ready, Jonomy."

A ball of hazy white light took shape above the distant mountains. Music faded in: a full orchestral melody of Pachelbel's 'Canon in D Major'. LeaMarsa had read that back in the Helio Age, the music had been popular for weddings. It and the desert vista had been listed as favorites in Tomer Donner's personnel file.

The ball of light moved slowly toward them and morphed into Tomer's face. The holo must have been recorded long ago or else had been artistically enhanced, for the image didn't match the man that LeaMarsa had come to know over these past nine months. He had a full head of hair, and his face seemed warm and relaxed, suggestive of someone at peace with himself.

Ericho began the ceremony. "We gather here to honor the spirit of Tomer Donner, Class Four bridge officer of Pannis Corp, lieutenant of the starship *Alchemon*. Born forty-four standard e-years ago in the former Third Israeli Republic. Trained at the Pannis schools in Holbrook-Hastings. A graduate, with honors, of the Academy of Primary Sciences..."

The face in the sky grew larger as the captain continued the eulogy. LeaMarsa found herself caught up in the power of the event. *Tragedy*. Although the current experience of that feeling was rooted in Donner's death, she was reminded of the psychic turbulence she'd gone through on Sycamore's surface when they'd discovered the creature.

Ericho concluded on a personal note. "Tomer Donner had his troubles, his demons. And obviously those demons were partially the cause of his demise. I couldn't honestly call him a close friend. But I will to choose to remember him on better days, as a loyal shipmate and as a man dedicated to fulfilling our mission."

Donner's holo dissolved into sparkling white granules that gently wafted onto the desert sands. The music faded. LeaMarsa heard sobbing, realized it was Faye. "Ashes to ashes, dust to dust," June whispered.

"Does anyone wish to add anything?" the captain asked.

No one spoke. Ericho went to the control panel and

deactivated the holo. The desert vanished, leaving the seven of them in a room stripped of hallucinatory eloquence.

Faye, crying uncontrollably, dashed out the door.

"All right, we all have our duties," Ericho said. "We're still on emergency status but that's mainly precautionary. With the exception of the containment and some related subsystems, the ship is functioning well. We've come through a serious incident in pretty good shape."

LeaMarsa noted the grim faces. The captain's upbeat assessment wasn't registering.

"Have you considered my requests?" Hardy asked Ericho.

The science rep not only wanted to preserve the organism's remains but wanted the ship to return to Sycamore for fresh samples of the bacteria to replace those lost in the melt.

"Going back to the planet is a bad idea," Rigel said.

"It's the captain's decision, not yours," Hardy argued.

"*Very* bad idea," Rigel snapped.

"We're still considering what to do about the remains," Ericho said. "But Rigel's right. We've had a serious accident and the ship is damaged. Besides that, returning to Sycamore would put us close to the edge of our fuel reserves."

Hardy protested. "The Sycom strain provided the initial focus for this expedition. Our entire voyage has already turned into a scientific disaster. Be that as it may, it would be doubly foolish to return to Earth with nothing to show for our efforts."

"Hardy, I concur with the captain," June said. "There are forces at work here that may have caused Donner's suicide. Those forces could ultimately affect us all."

"What forces? What are you talking about?"

June lowered her voice. But LeaMarsa could still make out her words.

"I believe a psionic chain of events, at least partly having to do with the presence of that creature, led to the lieutenant's death."

"She means me," LeaMarsa said, stepping forward.

"No one's blaming you for what happened," June said. "I'm talking about forces beyond anyone's control."

"Even if you're right," Hardy argued, "whatever effects you're referring to perished with the organism."

"Not necessarily. We could still be in danger."

"I don't follow."

"Bouncy Blue is dead. But we can't say the same for Baby Blue."

"What are you talking about?" Rigel demanded. "The damn thing was charbroiled."

"Bouncy Blue may have shielded Baby Blue from the harsher effects of the melt. If that's the case, the organism might still be a strong projector of superluminals."

"The robot's sensors read no signs of life," Hardy said.

"There are other ways to gauge whether it survived."

"Such as?"

June glanced at Ericho as she continued. "I've been having a recurring nightmare. And it came to me again less than an hour ago when I laid down for a nap, well after the melt occurred. In this nightmare, something we brought aboard this ship returns to Earth with us and begins to carry out rampant destruction. Our cities come under attack in ways that we have no defense against, brought down by some powerful invisible force."

She shook her head, as if unable to describe it better. "This force appears out of thin air and devastates the world. It shatters everything our civilization has built, sends our mightiest skyscrapers crumbling to the ground. I'm with my family and friends, everyone on Earth I know and love. We're standing in a field outside a city, watching the destruction. And then the force comes for us."

June's voice fell to a whisper. She struggled to continue. "This terrible feeling of simultaneously freezing and burning comes over me, comes over all of us. We're slowly consumed by this icy fire, but not just in a physical sense. Our minds, our emotions, everything that's unique about us is also stripped away." She paused. "It's the most horrifying thing I've ever experienced."

Hardy seemed oblivious to the shudder passing through the crewdoc.

"Yes, June, that sounds quite appalling. But it provides no evidence that the fetal organism survived."

Alexei chimed in. "I've been having nightmares like that too."

"Coincidental," Hardy said, increasingly annoyed. "As professionals, you should be aware of the irrationality of what you're saying. Nightmares are just nightmares. They do not foretell real-world events."

He's wrong, LeaMarsa thought. *Our fears can showcase the future.*

"The organism is dead," the science rep insisted. "If there was even the slightest sign of life, we would know."

"Not necessarily," June said. "According to Jonomy, EPS registers a ninety-nine percent likelihood of fatal injuries to the organism. However, the one percent uncertainty is based on the notion that Baby Blue may have survived but that its vital signs are too low to register."

Ericho tabbed his mike. "Jonomy, are you following this discussion?"

"Yes, captain."

"Is there any way to increase the sensitivity of the robot's sensors?"

"I could attempt downloading an enhancement package. However, given the robot's highly contaminated environment and the amount of time it has been in there, there is a strong possibility the package would not properly install. I am already experiencing problems with the robot's telemetry."

"Give the enhancement a try."

"Affirmative."

The captain headed away and the rest of them followed. At a transverse corridor, the group dispersed, each person off to resume individual duties. Everyone looked even grimmer. LeaMarsa knew they were all dealing with troubling thoughts provoked by June and Alexei's revelations about their nightmares.

But the true nightmare is just beginning.

From the files of Lieutenant Tomer Donner, Pannis Corp

BRIDGE OFFICER

Seven years, eight months, fourteen days. That's how long it's been since Renfro Zoobondi killed my beloved Karl and my obsession took root. I know it's not healthy but my rage over the incident hasn't relented. I'm as angry today as I was then.

Yesterday, two days before Christmas, I found myself in the same room with the murderer. It was the first time I'd seen him since that confrontation shortly after Karl's death.

Zoobondi was part of a group of high-ranking Pannis execs giving an instructional presentation in a large Boston auditorium. Considering that I was seated at the rear of the balcony and within a crowd of more than a thousand starship officers and midlevel execs, I assumed Zoobondi would be unaware of my presence. I took the opportunity to glare with such intensity that had my eyes been weapons, his flesh would have been incinerated.

His time at the podium began with a projection of Corporeal trends featuring a technohistorical grid of the next thousand e-years. Graphically enhanced by data-dripping HODs floating over the audience, the presentation was being simulcast to multiple venues.

Zoobondi, passionately animated, paced the stage like a master showman as he quoted the latest Pannis profitability update. He related the figures to the continued growth of the interstellar population, which was expected to undergo a spectacular geometric escalation that would peak eight hundred e-years from now. During that time, the Corporeal would experience a twentyfold increase, reaching a pinnacle of nearly half a trillion souls scattered across a thousand-plus settled worlds.

The formidable human explosion was partly due to recent discoveries of numerous planets in the stellar neighborhood suitable for terraforming and on the development of ever-faster exploratory probes for anchoring new Quiets in more distant systems. Also contributing to the population increase was the multiplying birthrate, with centenarians becoming parents even as their own great-great-grandchildren and all generations in between continued making babies.

Those facts taken together would produce a scenario that, to quote Zoobondi, "will offer wealth-harvesting opportunities beyond the wildest fantasies of our Helio Age ancestors."

After warming the crowd with a few more gems of rapacious mega wisdom, Zoobondi segued into the heart of his presentation by outlining the latest advances to thwart chronojackers. The temporal pirates were becoming a major problem, and Pannis and the other megas that funded Quiets were understandably up in arms. A part of me not consumed by fantasies of vengeance listened with interest as Zoobondi outlined the physics and methodology of the crime.

How far forward a chronojacked vessel would be sent couldn't be accurately determined, although the ships generally reconstituted from a few centuries to a few millennia in the future. Spatial displacement also occurred, with chronojacked vessels often emerging lightyears from their initial locales.

Chronojacking was no longer limited to pure fanatics. Severing all Corporeal ties, abandoning friends and family to leap ahead into an unknown destiny, once had attracted only devil-may-care adventurers and certifiable crazies. But for many, it had now become a kind of holy grail.

The new breed of chronojackers included gamblers who put all their creds into the underground banking system, hoping to return to future riches through the tried-and-true method of long-term compound interest. Others were anti-corporate revolutionaries seeking an age when the megas were no longer dominant. But most came from the needful majority, whose stagnant wages and decreasing opportunities provoked desperate measures, prompting them to risk all in order to cross a temporal border into a hoped-for better life.

Starship owners naturally disliked having their vessels hijacked into such unreachable future realms, a situation made worse by the insurance megas refusing to write policies to cover such losses. And despite intense lobbying, the Corporeal Congress thus far had resisted extending the statute of limitations beyond its current seventy-seven years, which made criminal prosecution of most chronojackers unlikely.

Zoobondi brightened as he explained the unpleasant surprises being introduced to dissuade chronojackers.

"New ships are being equipped and older vessels retrofitted with warrior pups. Upon an attempt to fire the spatiotemporal coagulators outside of Quiets space, the Sentinel will activate these robots. The warrior pups will regard chronojackers as malfunctioning units and take lethal action. Even if a ship is successfully chronojacked, those responsible will face the prospect of being hunted down and terminated."

Zoobondi couldn't hold back a grin at the idea of robots murdering transgressors. He concluded his presentation at that point by wishing everyone happy holidays.

Later, as I filed toward the exit with the rest of the crowd, I was surprised when he caught up to me.

"You've been doing some investigating," the VP said, flashing that superior smile of his. "Digging into my finances, my personal life."

I stood there in a cold rage and denied knowing what he was talking about.

"I understand your desire for vengeance, Lieutenant Donner. Really, I do. But I believe it's time for you to move on."

There was no misreading the threat in his tone and in those cold eyes. Zoobondi would have liked to murder me with his bare hands, or maybe hire some lowlife member of the needful majority to carry out the task for him.

But through my efforts, I'd gathered plenty of evidence against him, and he would know that I'd made arrangements for that evidence to go public should anything suspicious happen to me. I knew he had ambitions to reach even higher in the Pannis hierarchy, become the next CEO. Such rarefied air was incompatible with public scandal, so even if he took pains to make it look like an accident, there was always the chance that killing me could backfire and harm his career.

A young woman who'd been lingering in the background approached. Her hourglass figure and long black hair trimmed into bangs not only put her high on the Danbury Lustre Scale but marked her as a Pager, one of the thousands of genejobs crafted to emulate Helio Age sex personality Bettie Page.

The Pager wore sidearms – she was one of Zoobondi's personal bodyguards. Cradled in her arms was a dwarf tiger, a gaudy thing with phosphorescent red and green stripes, probably engineered with a genetic kill switch for expiration after the holiday season. She placed the Christmas-themed cat on Zoobondi's shoulder and backed away, her killer eyes never straying from my face.

The VP stroked the tiger's back as he leaned close and whispered in my ear.

"Accept what happened and continue your Pannis career without impediment. If not…"

Zoobondi pinched the tiger's flank. It reacted by snarling and scratching my cheek. I winced in pain and pulled away, glaring in *fury at the VP. It took all my willpower not to smash his face in.*

"Sorry about that," he said with a smile. "But I hope our little talk clarifies that it's a mistake to declare war on me. My defenses are more potent than you can imagine."

He turned and walked away. I dabbed at my bloody cheek and tried to convince myself that his threat didn't scare me. But of course, it did.

Nevertheless, if it is the last act of my life in this universe, I will see that this man suffers justice.

CHAPTER 14

The diner was located just off the bridge, a small ovoid room flanked by cabinets, stoves and thermal and microwave cookers. Three tables with attached seats mushroomed from the floor. A server pup with lifelike human arms hung from the ceiling, awaiting orders.

Ericho usually preferred making his own meals. This evening he was tired, however, and had permitted the pup to handle the cooking. The faux chicken in bean sauce with lemon-curry rice was good, though if he'd been the chef he'd have been more creative with the spices.

June and Rigel sat with him. The diner was a dopa, as good a place as any for a private conversation.

"I say we give LeaMarsa a high dose of loopy," Rigel proposed as he chomped into a codburger leaking tomato sauce. "Keep her neurons scrambled for the rest of the voyage."

"We can't do that," June said.

"Why not?"

"I think you know why."

Ericho did too. Still, Rigel's idea was appealing.

The drug Loopaline B4, aka loopy, was as necessary for safe Quiets travel by humans as the proper functioning of the Big Three systems. Early Quiets voyages had ended in disaster when crewmembers came out the other side suffering various psychological ailments, the worst being psychotic autosarcophagy. Those cases of self-cannibalism ranged from the mild, such as gnawing bits of skin off one's own arms and legs, to the more severe, where sufferers chewed and swallowed their own tongues, fingers or worse.

Although numerous theories had been put forth to explain the bizarre syndrome, neurological researchers had never pinpointed a cause. However, a cure had been found. Loopaline B4, a unique blend of soporifics that acted upon the most evolutionarily ancient regions of the human tripartite brain, had tamed the urge to consume oneself.

But having crews take a small hit of the drug prior to engaging the Quiets engines was one thing. What Rigel was suggesting would render LeaMarsa comatose.

June shook her head. "I can't declare a crewmember a menace and prescribe drugs to vegetate her without clear proof the individual is causing serious harm."

"Bullshit. We all know what's happening here."

"Maybe, but there's no way of proving it. We have only circumstantial evidence putting LeaMarsa at the root of some psionic-based malady. And even if I vegetated her, there's no guarantee it would hinder her abilities. Some of the psychic literature indicates that superluminals can become even more potent when the psionic is unconscious."

"Yeah, but I'll bet we'd all feel better if she was in cold storage. Want to spend the rest of this trip having those freakish nightmares of yours?"

"Of course not."

"Me neither, goddammit."

"So, you're having bad dreams too."

"Just don't ask me to talk about them. Not going to happen."

June laid a soothing hand on the tech officer's arm. "Believe me, Rigel, I understand how you feel. But your idea is unrealistic."

"You call saving our asses unrealistic?"

Ericho had a thought. "You mentioned that a nutriment bath might reduce her psionic impact."

"I've scheduled her for one about an hour from now. I'm going to drag her there myself."

Rigel looked incredulous. "She's making us crazy and you're gonna give her a fucking bath?"

June sighed and turned to Ericho. "How close are we to vacuuming the containment?"

"Jonomy's finalizing a plan using the other link robot. It'll give us the best chance of capturing and preserving Bouncy Blue's remains."

"I've changed my mind about that," Rigel said. "I say we eject that thing along with the rest of the debris."

"I agree," June said. "And I don't care what Jonomy's sensor-enhancement package revealed, that there's no measurable signs of life. My gut tells me otherwise. My nightmares tell me otherwise. That fetal creature is still alive. We need to get it off the ship, get it as far away from us as possible."

"Amen," Rigel said.

The fact that the two people aboard who Ericho trusted the most were lobbying for the plan, carried weight. He thought about it for a moment and came to a decision.

"All right, we'll do it. Eject everything."

He wasn't looking forward to breaking the news to Hardy. The science rep would go ballistic.

Jonomy's urgent voice came over the speakers. "Captain, report to the bridge."

He tabbed his mike. "What's up?"

"A new problem in the containment."

"We're in the diner. Put it on monitor."

A wall screen blossomed to life. The image showed a tight view of the devastated containment lab, obviously originating from the link robot. The scene was constantly changing as the robot ambled around the perimeter, panning its camera eyes as if searching for something. Ericho gazed closely at the damaged walls and furnishings but nothing appeared out of the ordinary.

He glanced at Rigel and June. They seemed equally puzzled.

"Jonomy, what's it looking for? What are we missing?"

"It appears to be scanning its environment. But that is not the relevant issue. No one is controlling the link. It is operating by itself."

"Did you try regaining control?"

"Direct programming commands are having no effect."

"Mechanical failure," Rigel proposed. "It's been in there for hours. The heat and radiation finally got to it."

"Unlikely," Jonomy said. "Microseconds before the robot initiated this behavior, it severed the com linkages. That action was deliberate, not a mishap."

"Does EPS have an explanation?" Ericho asked.

"It does not. The incident defies logical interpretation. Rigel's suggestion of a mechanical failure offers the highest probability. But even that percentage is far too low to be given statistical relevance."

Onscreen, the robot stepped into the containment and approached Bouncy Blue. As they watched in silent fascination, the robot knelt in front of the organism and withdrew a pair of knives from its utility belt.

With a blade in each hand, it began cutting a large hole in Bouncy Blue's gelatinous outer skin, employing the rapid movements typical of mechanical beings. As it sliced deeper, it withdrew and haphazardly cast aside the gelatinous refuse. The floor was soon littered with blue chunks of carved membrane.

"What the hell is it doing?" Rigel muttered.

The robot sheathed the knives and plunged its hands deep into the ragged opening. When it withdrew, its arms cradled the fetal organism.

"Like delivering an infant," June whispered.

"Captain, I am now registering strong vital signs through the robot's sensors. The fetal creature is indeed alive."

They could see the evidence themselves. Baby Blue squirmed gently. A chill went through Ericho and he recalled Donner's final words.

The Quad awakens.

He was certain that Baby Blue, and what Donner had referred to as the Quad, were one and the same.

"Maybe the lieutenant wasn't only trying to kill himself by destroying the containment," Ericho proposed. "Maybe he was trying to destroy this thing before it could hatch."

"Or just the opposite," June said. "Create the conditions enabling it to be born."

The creature was about a foot in length from the top of its elongated head to the tips of its triple-toed feet. Arms ended in six-fingered hands, the digits separated into three distinct pairs.

"Triple sets of opposable digits," June said. "From an evolutionary standpoint, that would suggest a high degree of dexterity."

"Dexterity my ass," Rigel said. "What I want to know is

how the hell it's managing to breathe in there. The heat and radioactivity should kill practically any living thing."

"It doesn't look like it's having any problems," Ericho said.

Baby Blue's skin was a deep blue, a shade darker than the membrane. Its eyes were closed. The presence of a mouth, nose and ears made the face appear vaguely human. But it was longer and narrower than a human countenance to make room for that additional sensory organ, a protruding silvery marble between its mouth and nose.

Ericho recalled the skull-like image Donner had frequently doodled in the HOD. That obviously had been the lieutenant's prescient representation.

"Jonomy, you'd better notify Hardy and Faye."

"Already done, captain. They're observing as well."

"It must be controlling the robot," Rigel said. "Any ideas how *that's* happening?"

"Some sort of crossover between psionic superluminals and the electromagnetic spectrum?" June speculated.

"Possibly," Jonomy said.

The robot stood. Holding Baby Blue in its arms, it walked out of the containment and back into the devastated lab. The creature writhed gently, in the manner of a newborn human infant.

"Incredible," June whispered.

"Not so incredible," Rigel pointed out. "Look where it's headed."

The robot made its way to the airseal through which it had originally entered the lab. It stopped a pace from the door. Its gaze zeroed in on the control panel.

"Looking for a way out," Rigel said.

"Captain, SEN has deduced that the robot intends to attempt

an escape. It will stop that from happening."

"How?" June asked.

"I've got a pretty good idea," Rigel said. "Warrior pup."

Ericho grimaced. There were three of them aboard the *Alchemon* and as far as he was concerned, that was three too many. He'd never liked the idea of lethal robots in the bowels of starships, waiting to be activated by a Sentinel to destroy what Pannis publicly referred to as "malfunctioning entities." Whether such entities were robotic or human made no difference.

"The Sentinel has activated a warrior pup and dispatched it into airlock three," Jonomy reported. "The pup will enter the containment airlock from outside the ship to deal with the problem."

Hardy's angry voice erupted from the speakers.

"Captain, you cannot allow this to happen. If that pup terminates the robot, it could inadvertently destroy the fledgling organism. We are looking at what clearly is one of the most unprecedented events in the history of extraterrestrial discovery. We must do everything possible to keep this creature alive. It is without doubt the product of a high intelligence."

"A *dangerous* high intelligence," Rigel countered.

"There is no evidence to support that supposition."

"Are you blind? Don't you even know what's been going on?"

Ericho raised his hand, cutting Rigel off before the argument could escalate. "Hardy, even if I agree with you, your point is moot. Talking and arguing about this won't make the slightest difference in terms of what's about to happen. I can't control the Sentinel any more than you can."

"You're obligated to make the attempt."

"I've tried," Jonomy said. "I've been in communication with

SEN and have made it aware of your concerns. However, its priority is keeping the organism contained."

"Does SEN have any explanation for what's happening here?" Ericho asked.

"It does not. However, bear in mind that such analyses are not native to its function. It is guided by practicalities – in this case, safeguarding the ship. The cause of a problem is of less interest to it than finding a solution to the problem."

The science rep muttered something indistinguishable and exited the intercom.

"The warrior pup is in transit," Jonomy said.

"Give us video."

A hull cam showed a sphere with a reflective surface exiting a midships airlock. The warrior pup was slightly larger than the regular pups. Dozens of microjets fired a sequence of short targeted bursts, enabling it to roll along the ship's flank a few centimeters above the undulating hull. It was headed for the containment airlock at the stern.

"Armed with HCs and mag projectiles," Rigel said, admiration in his tone. "Plus, Halliburton defensive shielding and the nastiest attack guidance system ever designed. Wouldn't want one of them pissed at me."

The warrior pup reached the containment lock, paused before the closed hatch.

"Sentinel is opening the outer seal," Jonomy reported. "SEN is clearing the way."

"I just thought of something," Rigel said. "Maybe the pup won't bother entering the containment. Maybe it'll just do what we were planning to do, blow the inner hatch and vacuum everything into the void."

"Unlikely. Sentinel responses tend to be very specific. I do not believe that dealing with the original contamination from the melt is within the scope of the Sentinel's duty at this time. Besides that, there is still SEN's historical aversion to purges. I believe the Sentinel will stick to its primary function, ensure that the robot does not exit into the corridor and spread further pollution."

The outer lock opened. As the warrior pup dropped into the containment chute, the screen split into two images. On the left was the camera view from the pup as it slithered down the shaft toward the damaged inner seal. The right image emanated from the malfunctioning robot, still poised before the containment lab door.

The robot shifted Baby Blue to one arm and used its free hand to reach for the door's manual opening mechanism. Ericho tensed as the robot withdrew the emergency hand crank from its cavity and began winding the handle.

"Do not worry, captain," Jonomy said. "The door cannot be opened by that method. The Sentinel is overriding the manual egress unit at the airseal."

Onscreen, the robot turned the handle three revolutions. Under normal circumstance, that should have opened the door. When the airseal failed to slide back, the robot jerked away. To Ericho, its action seemed oddly human, as if the robot was startled by the handle's failure to adhere to its function and open the door.

The warrior pup reached the inner hatch.

"Outer hatch closed," Jonomy said. "The airlock is repressurizing."

The pup extruded one of its Higgs cutters. The beam ignited, burned through the inner lock. In the lab, the robot's ears must have picked up the hissing of incinerating metal. It whirled and zoomed in on the airseal.

"It knows it's screwed," Rigel said gleefully.

The pup extruded a pliers-like hand. Grasping the handle, it jerked sideways. The action wrenched open the hatch.

The pup lunged into the containment and yanked the hatch shut behind it. Spotting the robot in the adjacent lab, it shot through the opening between the two areas and halted three paces away.

The two machines seemed to stare at one another. Ericho was reminded of a twentieth-century video excerpt he'd seen as part of a museum display. A style of vintage movie – he believed they were called westerns – featuring two men in a face-off, ready to shoot one another with holstered projectile weapons.

The containment scene boasted one big difference. The robot lacked true offensive capabilities, although it did have the utility knives and a low-powered Higgs cutter. But it was no match for the weaponry of the diminutive warrior pup.

The robot gently laid Baby Blue on the floor and moved to the far corner, as if trying to get as far away as possible from the creature.

Like a parent trying to spare its child from harm, Ericho thought, fascinated by the behavior.

The robot's shoulders appeared to slump, almost as if it knew its destruction was imminent. In a sudden blur of motion, the pup attacked, firing its Higgs cutters. Three shafts of intense light flashed between the machines. Puffs of gray smoke poured from a triplet of holes in the robot, two in its chest and one in the forehead. The initial volley had targeted control and stability systems.

"Burn that sucker," Rigel muttered, enjoying the lopsided battle.

The robot staggered drunkenly out of the corner, flailing its arms. The pup fired again, this time using pencil-thin HC beams to chops off its arms. More flashes severed the robot's legs above the knee joints.

Its appendages amputated, the robot collapsed to the deck. It tottered for a few seconds on hinged kneecaps before falling forward. Its head slammed the floor and its camera eyes went dead.

The split screen vanished. The only imagery now emanated from the victor.

The pup hovered over the downed robot and shot a mag projectile into the top of its skull. The projectile exploded with a loud hiss, sending a shock wave of electromagnetic pulses into whatever remained of its control circuitry. The robot shuddered once and became still.

"End of malfunction," Rigel said.

But there was no time to savor the pup's victory. Jonomy's voice rose in alarm.

"Aberration signal, captain. It's coming from the warrior pup."

The pup seemed to go crazy. Firing its thruster jets, it darted back and forth across the lab with dizzying speed, tumbling and rolling madly, yet somehow managing to avoid plowing into the walls. The jerky scene on the monitor reminded Ericho of a ride he'd once taken on a suborbital rollercoaster.

"Stabilizer failure?" Rigel suggested, not sounding convinced.

The pup froze in the midst of a violent gyration. Rotating slowly, its camera eye zoomed in on the lab's airseal.

It lunged at the door, multiple HCs firing in tandem. One beam pierced the lock mechanism, presumably disabling the sure-shutter. The other beams combined to burn a square opening in the center of the airseal, slightly larger than the pup's diameter.

The pup crashed into the square. The weakened slab tumbled out into the corridor.

The pup lunged through the opening.

The screen went dead.

A radiation alarm chirped, indicating the airseal breach was allowing contaminated wastes to pour into the corridor. Ericho leaped up from the table and raced toward the exit with Rigel on his heels.

"Sentinel overrides on all adjacent airseals," Jonomy said. "Automatic pressure-differential systems activated to contain the radiation."

"This is crazy!" Rigel yelled as the two of them ran toward the bridge.

"No argument."

"Captain, the malfunctioning pup has reached the next airseal. It is burning through that door as well."

"How do we stop it?" Ericho demanded. Pressure differentials or not, if the warrior pup penetrated too many airseals, the entire ship could be flooded with radiation.

"The other two warrior pups have been Sentinel-activated. They're heading for a position on the other side of that door, waiting for the errant pup to come through."

Ericho and Rigel reached the bridge. As Ericho assumed his command chair, the HOD came to life. Interlaced corridor cams provided a 3D view of the two newly awakened warrior pups floating near an airseal. A square section in the center of the airseal was being cut through from the other side.

Ericho held his breath as the crazed pup smashed through

the cutout section. But it wasn't prepared to encounter two of its deadly shipmates.

The waiting duo struck first, launching a volley of HCs and mag projectiles that caught the malfunctioning pup in a crossfire. The battle was over in seconds. The crazed pup fell to the deck, a smoldering mass. The victorious pups picked up their victim with pincer hands and dragged it through a small access opening in the ceiling.

"Hauling its ass to pup heaven," Rigel muttered.

"Radiation contained to the affected corridors," Jonomy said. "RAP is dispatching repair and radiation-scrubbing pups."

"This makes no sense," Rigel said. "That warrior pup was under Sentinel control when it went crazy."

"Actually, it was not. At the moment the link robot was terminated, SEN fulfilled its duty. The Sentinel deactivated and its control link was broken. The warrior pup was momentarily acting on its own accord."

But not for long, Ericho thought. Something else had assumed control of the pup, the same unknown thing that minutes earlier had taken over the robot.

He kept his attention on the HOD. In less than a minute, both sections of contaminated corridor were swarming with dozens of maintenance pups pouring from access shafts. Some were specialized rad scrubbers, unfolding particulate filtering nets. Others began welding plates over the damaged airseals.

"EPS and EHO estimate fifty minutes for repairs," Jonomy said. "Only minor radiation leakage into the pup access shafts. They should be scrubbed clean within the hour."

Ericho leaned back in his chair with a deep sigh, wondering what bizarre craziness would come upon them next.

CHAPTER 15

LeaMarsa followed June into the subshaft branching off downdeck's main corridor and up a curving ramp. She was no fan of nutriment baths but the crewdoc had insisted.

"I hear the malfunctions are under control," she blurted out, eager to concentrate on something else. "Faye told me everything's been fine since the robot and warrior pup were destroyed."

June nodded. "I believe the worst of our troubles are behind us."

LeaMarsa read doubt in her voice. "Have they figured out what happened to the robots?"

"Evidence suggests that Baby Blue can take command of electronic systems that venture too close."

The ramp ended in an airseal. June opened it and they entered a small circular chamber. The deck had a quartet of outlined circles.

The crewdoc stripped to a bikini. Her dark flesh revealed the imperfections of her years, including stretch marks from having given birth. LeaMarsa had once heard June mention a desire to have more children. With pharmaceutically delayed menopause and stem cell enhancements, safe pregnancies were possible even in a woman's ninth decade.

"Clothes off," June ordered.

LeaMarsa reluctantly let her jumper fall to the floor. Bikini-clad, she stepped onto the outlined circle beside.

"Ready?" the crewdoc asked.

"Not really."

June swiveled her head to a wall sensor and spoke in a commanding tone.

"Nodes one and two ready to drop."

NUB, the Level Six system that controlled what awaited them below, spoke in a lyrical female voice.

"Drop authorized. Countdown commencing. Three... two... one."

The node beneath LeaMarsa dilated with such speed that the floor seemed to simply disappear. She plunged downward. Geonic counterforces broke the fall, suspending her in the freefall zone in the center of the bath.

The warm and humid atmosphere was a spectral wonderland. Shafts of light from above and below illuminated the bath's marble-sized nutriment globules, their colors ranging from aquamarines and violets to bold teals and fiery reds.

June bobbed gently up and down a few meters away, looking absurdly happy. The crewdoc curled into a ball and rotated her body until she was upside down in relation to LeaMarsa.

"Doesn't this feel good?"

No. The globules were already crawling over her moistened flesh like hungry leeches. She remembered why she so disliked these cleansings.

"Don't fight it," June said. "Let the bath soothe you."

The motion-activated globules released vapors that osmotically penetrated skin pores or entered the bloodstream via breathing. June clapped her hands, smashed a cluster of them to release antioxidants and other beneficial chemicals.

"Crush as many as you can," the crewdoc urged. "The more chemicals liberated, the better the bath will remove toxins from your body and restore peak microbiome efficiency."

LeaMarsa clapped gingerly, trying to ignore how the globules kept trying to attach themselves to every part of her body. The ones swarming at her mouth, nose and crotch made her especially jumpy; she kept batting them away. In contrast, June allowed the globules to crawl freely over her. She soon resembled a piñata encrusted with liquid jewels.

"It feels like being back in the womb," June said with a smile.

"I don't remember being in the womb."

"Our intellects and emotions might not remember but our bodies do. It's the nature of our tripartite minds. The earliest memories are encoded in purely physical form."

LeaMarsa was reminded of what Faye had said about Baby Blue having a fourth system, a later evolutionary development that overlapped its physical, emotional and intellectual selves, and whose purpose remained unknown.

"How are they dealing with the creature? Do we know what it's doing down there?"

"No way to tell," June said. "With the link robot out of commission, we have no sensor presence. And in light of what happened, the Sentinel won't permit access to the containment, at least not from inside the ship. The main effort at the moment is to make sure the contamination stays confined."

"We should dump the creature into space."

"Pretty much everyone agrees with that except Hardy. However, the devil's in the details. There's real concern that if a robot or pup enters the containment shaft to open the inner hatch, it'll get within the creature's range of control and be taken over like the other robots."

A globule floated into LeaMarsa's mouth. She inadvertently bit down, crushed it into a wet powder. The sour taste, reminiscent of lemons, triggered a childhood memory.

She was maybe five years old, sucking a lemon icicle while holding her mother's hand. They were wandering through some sort of terrarium full of exotic foliage.

"Try looking at that one as hard as you can," her mother instructed, pointing to a plant with orange flowers. "Try seeing it through your exceptional abilities."

LeaMarsa made the attempt, as she always did during her younger years when her parents prodded her to exercise her psionic talents – what they referred to as her "exceptional abilities." But the plant had suddenly seemed menacing to her, and she'd yanked free of her mother's hand and ran from the terrarium.

As the memory coursed through LeaMarsa, the nutriment bath vanished. In its place appeared that other universe, neurospace. She was again in the midst of a blackout.

More of those shadow clusters had come into being. Even as she contemplated what that meant, the voice of the phantom woman returned, again struggling to speak as if from a great distance.

"Implement Synchronicity."

LeaMarsa sighed in frustration. Did these cryptic phrases even have meaning? Maybe this latest one, along with *Sentinel Obey* and *Coalesce and Target,* were just random nonsense, synaptic flotsam inherent to neurospace.

She tried willing the blackout to end, forcing consciousness back to the nutriment bath. When that had no effect she flailed her arms and legs, hoping motion might jar consciousness back into the real world. But her appendages moved sluggishly, as if encased in thick mud.

She sensed that some unnatural force was causing the clusters, and that it was growing stronger. Or perhaps the force had grown stronger in the past or would go stronger in the future, for she sensed that neurospace wasn't in alignment with the relativistic passage of time throughout the real universe. Here, past, present and future were jumbled together, with each star simultaneously existing at multiple points along its analogue's timeline.

The blackout ended abruptly and she was back in the nutriment bath, still thrashing. Swarms of globules attracted to her gyrations enveloped her.

"Get away from me!" she screamed.

"It's all right, LeaMarsa," June soothed. "Try to relax."

She couldn't. Panic overtook her. The globules kept attaching themselves, as if wanting something from her that she couldn't give.

"All right, we're going," June said, grabbing her arm and guiding her toward the exit hatch at the bottom. Gravity increased as they descended. The globules detached and drifted away.

June opened the hatch. They exited into a downdeck corridor. The crewdoc looked at her with deep concern.

"We should go to medcenter."

"I'm fine."

"We both know that's not true."

There was nothing in June's medical bag of tricks that would stop LeaMarsa's torments. Why couldn't the crewdoc realize that?

Just leave me alone!

CHAPTER 16

The *Alchemon* was the first manned vessel to venture through the Earth-Sycamore Quiets according to the most recent files in the ship's library. Those files were last updated five months ago when the ship passed through the Quiets and went dark – lost touch with the com beacons that transmitted data throughout the vast Inet-29 net linking the planets of the Corporeal.

As of then, no expeditions had been slated to follow. And the only vessel venturing anywhere near this sector prior to the *Alchemon* had been the original robotic explorer that discovered Sycamore's bacteria and set up the transpatial corridor. That spacecraft, according to records, had returned safely to the solar system.

Then who the hell is out there? Ericho wondered. He stood behind Jonomy at the perimeter of the HOD, impatiently waiting for him to establish a clean image. Rigel sat in Donner's chair, accessing info from a wafer.

Some sort of last-minute adjunct to our mission? Ericho had heard of such things happening. Still, the reasons were always extraordinary. Pannis was not known for spending more creds than budgeted for a deep-space venture. Even the *Alchemon*'s expensive nucleonic fuel was precisely allocated so that the ship could perform only limited course changes and maneuvers over its eighteen months away from home. And a search-and-rescue mission didn't fit the equation.

Then again, they did have aboard the most powerful psionic ever studied. Perhaps that was enough of a reason for Pannis to send an extra ship for back-up.

A jumble of rapidly changing textures and colors flashed across the HOD, impossible to assimilate. The streaming images represented the high-speed processing of Jonomy's umbilical-linked mind. However fast the HOD, it couldn't keep up with the tempo of a fully interfaced lytic.

Jonomy slowed the stream to a level of human comprehension. Textures and colors morphed into a white smudge against the darkness of space, the HOD's representation of the unknown vessel.

He opened his eyes, emerged from his deep commune with the network.

"Can you clean up the image?" Ericho asked.

"No, captain. The vessel is too far away. About three hundred thousand kilometers, maintaining a parallel course. It is using nonstandard EM and visual-field distortion to disguise its signature."

They'd detected the mystery ship during a routine course correction meant to put them on a more accurate trajectory for the Sycamore Quiets. Within seconds of that event, the other vessel had instituted a correction to match their own.

"It is probable the vessel has been out there for a while," Jonomy said. "If we had not gone through the course correction, we likely would not have spotted it."

Rigel looked up from his wafer. "Explain to me why EPS has no theories about what another ship's doing out here."

"EPS can only calculate probabilities based on established

statistical ratios among quantifiable information. It will not postulate theories in situations where a high percentage of unknown factors are present."

Rigel rolled his eyes, indicating what he thought of Jonomy's explanation. "Maybe somebody needs to teach EPS the concept of an educated guess."

"A so-called educated guess is no better than–"

"With EPS out of the picture," Ericho interrupted, "it's up to us to figure things out." He faced Jonomy. "You're postulating a Corporeal vessel, correct?"

"Yes, unless we assume the existence of an alien civilization with nearly identical starship development. PAQ has done a rudimentary shape analysis based on our meager data collected at the moment of contact. They appear to be standard slab configuration, slightly smaller than us. Those EM distortion patterns match Corporeal standards."

"But no caste code."

"Correct."

All Corporeal computers, whether space or planet-based, broadcast unique telemetry beacons. The caste codes enabled disparate equipment to communicate. But the mystery vessel had thus far ignored all attempts by the *Alchemon* to establish contact.

"The absence of a caste code puts them in violation of numerous regulations," Jonomy pointed out.

"I'm guessing that's not keeping them up at nights," Rigel grumbled.

"Any suggestions?" Ericho asked.

"Make a flat-out run at them," the tech officer proposed. "See how they respond."

"Unwise," Jonomy said. "At best, a waste of fuel. Assuming

a similar power plant, they would likely just change course to maintain the same distance between us. Even if we could get close enough for our sensors to overcome their EM field, without a caste code we would probably learn little."

Ericho sighed and rubbed a hand across his face to wipe away drowsiness. He'd been awake for twenty-plus hours. There was a limit to how long stimulants could keep body and mind alert. Very soon, he was going to have to close his eyes.

But despite Jonomy and Rigel being available to cover his absence, he worried about missing the next critical incident. And there would be more incidents. Of that he was certain.

"What about chronojackers?" he wondered. "That would explain why the ship would be wary of us, why they're broadcasting no caste code."

A hijacked starship from some past era would want to avoid contact, at least until its crew made certain enough time had passed so that the Corporeal statute of limitations would spare them from arrest and prosecution.

Jonomy shot down the idea. "A chronojacked vessel would project a unique energy signature that even the best EM field could not disguise."

"You sure about that?" Rigel challenged.

"Absolutely certain."

"Seems to me you randomly pick and choose what you're certain of."

"My actions are not random. Your statement is nonsensical."

Rigel rose angrily from his chair. "Nonsensical, huh? What I want to know is, why don't you know what's happening to us? And don't give me more crap about EPS not having enough data to work with. Look at the whole picture, goddammit.

"We find an impossible lifeform on a bizarre planet. Our

lieutenant goes crazy and almost burns us to a cinder. We've got lunatic robots, an unstable psionic and enough problems for a dozen voyages. And now there's another ship out in the middle of nowhere following us?"

"We do not know if they are following us."

"They sure as hell ain't on a pleasure cruise."

"I cannot fathom a logical connection among these events. However, some type of connection likely exists. What we have been experiencing suggests a pattern, suggests purpose."

"Baby Blue," Ericho said. "It has to be at the root of all this."

"Maybe not," Rigel said. "What if we've got this whole thing backwards? Maybe Pannis is responsible. Maybe they created Baby Blue. Maybe it's an artificial lifeform developed by one of their armaments subsidiaries, something so dangerous that the only way to safely test it was to conduct an experiment far from Earth. Maybe the *Alchemon* and all of us are guinea pigs."

"That is paranoid speculation," Jonomy said.

"Is it? Remember how LeaMarsa was added to the crew at the last minute? Maybe Pannis put her aboard to influence this artificial lifeform somehow, or for it to influence her. Maybe this other starship followed us through the Quiets and is secretly monitoring us, checking on how their grand experiment is going." Rigel paused. "They could be armed with intercept missiles, ready to incinerate us if things get out of hand."

Pannis and the megas certainly could be ruthless. Ericho could accept that a psycho like Renfro Zoobondi might have sabotaged their mission for his own devilish reasons. But Rigel was talking about a conspiracy that would have had to involve hundreds or even thousands of people.

"Your theory runs counter to what we know," Jonomy said.

"First, the discovery of the organism. Hardy's data proves that it was encased in rock on the surface of Sycamore for more than a billion e-years. The erosion process that exposed the rock and spread the bacteria across the planet was a phenomenon that could not have been faked.

"Second, if this other starship was somehow monitoring us, Pannis would have had to install secret com gear on the *Alchemon*. If such an implanted subsystem existed, I would have detected it. And even if I somehow missed it, the Sentinel would not. One of its primary duties is to safeguard the ship against illicit tampering."

"You wouldn't need an entire subsystem," Rigel argued. "There's a simpler way to monitor us. All Pannis would need is a small shielded transmitter discrete from the network and someone onboard to use it."

Ericho frowned. "You're saying we have a spy? Who?"

"Who else? Our illustrious science rep, Hardy Waskov."

Jonomy hesitated, considering the idea. "In theory it is possible. However, you are making assumptions based on assumptions, a sure method for digressing farther from the truth."

"You want the truth?" Rigel growled. "Give me a power glove and ten minutes alone in a room with Hardy."

Alexei came over the intercom.

"Captain, I'm in the natatorium. I just came here following my duty period. I realize I should have gone straight into a sleep cycle, but I was kind of tense from worrying about everything that's been going on. So I came here for a quick swim and–"

"Get to the point."

"Yes sir. You probably have this on your monitors, but the pool is messed up. I've never seen so much pollution in a biosystem. The water is full of algae and these pulsating globules. They seem like something from the nutriment bath, but a lot bigger. Plus, it's really hot and humid in here."

Jonomy shook his head. "The ship is not reporting a problem. No abnormal indicators in any of the systems that interact with the natatorium."

"Give us a visual," Ericho ordered.

"Sir, LSN is a dopa."

I need sleep, he reminded himself. He was forgetting standard policy.

"All right. Alexei, you're going to have to do it the old-fashioned way. Set up a manual camera feed."

"Is that legal in a dopa?"

"Captain's orders."

"Yes sir."

Ericho turned to Rigel. "Let's pretend for a moment that this is the only problem the ship's experiencing. What could cause this sort of pollution?"

"Could be a fluid leak. A bit unusual that the ship's not registering it, but I've seen some odd mech breakdowns in a ship's piping. It would have to be a combination of malfunctions, though, probably involving NUB and TEM."

"So, the nutriment bath and thermometry regulation systems go haywire and start interacting with the natatorium?"

"I didn't say it was likely, just theoretically possible."

Alexei came back on the intercom. "You should be getting video now."

The HOD came alive from a 3D cam the trainee had stuck on the wall. His description didn't do justice to how strange the pool looked.

Much of the surface had a black sheen and was opaque, as

if covered by an oil slick. The remainder was splotched with clumps of what appeared to be green and violet algae. Scattered across the surface were dozens of multicolored globules similar to those from the nutriment bath. But as Alexei had indicated, they were larger, some the size of golf balls. A white mist hovered above the pool, probably due to the escalated temperature and humidity.

"No way that's a fluid leak," Rigel said.

Ericho agreed. "And we have no indications of an LSN malfunction?"

"That system remains green," Jonomy said. "EHO has registered the heat increase and the presence of the mist but has deemed those changes harmless. The only other anomaly I am reading comes from IBD, which is just now reacting to the pollution."

"Why the hell didn't it react earlier?" Rigel asked.

"I have no explanation for the delay. At any rate, IBD is closing off all feeder valves to and from the natatorium. It is isolating the pool from the rest of the biosystem."

"Can we get an analysis of the water?" Ericho asked

"IBD is undertaking that now. It will route samples of the algae, the globules and the oil-like pollutant to EHO for more detailed parsing."

"How long?"

"A full array of tests will take several hours."

Ericho shook his head. Whatever was happening in the pool, he sensed that it was too important to wait that long for an explanation.

Jonomy read his thoughts. "Hardy could accomplish the task manually considerably faster."

Ericho opened a line to the downdeck lab that Hardy and

Faye were working out of since the melt. Hardy came on speaker. Not surprisingly, he sounded annoyed.

"We're busy, captain. What is it?"

Ericho explained the problem and asked for Hardy's help with the analysis. The science rep went ballistic.

"Do you really think my time is so inconsequential that I would drop important work for such a simplistic task? *Do you*?"

"We need your expertise."

"Don't patronize me!" Hardy shrieked. "If you think you're getting back in my good graces, you are deeply mistaken. Your incompetent leadership has jeopardized an important scientific mission! And your unwillingness to return to Sycamore to procure samples of the bacteria can only be ascribed as the actions of a complete fool!"

Ericho kept his anger in check. "We need the pool water analyzed immediately. I'm making this an order."

"Fine! I'll send Faye. When I'm testifying at your court-martial for your malfeasance throughout this mission, I wouldn't want it said that I wasn't cooperative!"

Hardy cut the circuit. The bridge was silent for a moment as the three of them exchanged puzzled looks. The science rep could be arrogant, but they'd never heard him so infuriated.

"The man needs some happy time in the dreamlounge," Rigel said.

Ericho recalled June's concern that they all were being impacted by psionic forces. Perhaps Hardy's way of dealing with an ongoing subconscious assault was to unleash simmering rage.

He rubbed his temples, trying to ward off the beginning of a headache. Its likely cause was lack of sleep rather than Hardy's tantrum. In any event, the bridge could do without him for a short time. He'd be able to think more clearly after a bit of rest.

"I'll be in my cabin. Give me a wake-up call in ninety minutes or when Faye has an update on the pollution." He paused at the airseal and clarified the order. "Sooner if there's new trouble."

CHAPTER 17

I've fallen out of bed.

The thought wiped away the last traces of sleep. LeaMarsa was on her back on the floor of one of the private treatment rooms, garbed in a nightgown, her legs tangled in a sheet whose other end remained tucked in.

She couldn't recall how she'd gotten here. There was a vague memory of June asking her to come to medcenter this morning after what had occurred in the nutriment bath. But everything beyond that remained a blur.

Twisting free of the sheet, she retrieved her jumper from the closet. Underpants and shoes were nowhere to be found. She accessed the room's PYG recep and ordered new versions of those items. Seconds later they appeared in the output tray.

Dressing quickly, she opened the door and exited into the corridor separating the treatment rooms from medcenter's main expanse. A pair of ovoid windows provided a view into June's office. It was empty.

LeaMarsa left medcenter and entered downdeck's main corridor. A hundred meters toward the stern lay the containment. Just around a bend in the other direction was the mech shop.

Important places. Odd impressions trickled through her, fragmented thoughts of recent events. She remembered something from a few weeks ago.

The *Alchemon* had still been on its approach to Sycamore. Tomer Donner had been standing in the mech shop in front of a secure cabinet. The corridor airseal was open and LeaMarsa, passing by, had glanced in.

The lieutenant had stuck a safepad to the wall and apparently had used a command override to unlock the cabinet. He withdrew a Higgs cutter, lovingly caressed the barrel before tucking the weapon in his pocket.

He turned toward her, as if knowing she'd been watching. A sad smile came over him.

"We are but pawns within the realm of luminous dark."

With that cryptic remark, he'd brushed past her and headed down the corridor. At the time, she hadn't assigned any significance to the event. Only now did she understand. He'd been planning the destruction of Bouncy Blue even before they'd discovered it. But how could he know what they'd find on the planet?

The answer was obvious. Donner had been in psionic contact with Baby Blue. LeaMarsa had functioned as a superluminal conveyor, unconsciously transmitting the creature's thoughts to the lieutenant.

Tragedy. She hadn't merely touched the future and perceived his fate. She was partly the cause of it.

A familiar terror rose from the depths. Waves of fear washed through her.

"No," she whispered, dropping to the deck to begin a series of frantic pushups. But the reek was too potent this time. The odor of dead flesh filled her nostrils. She struggled to breathe as those strangling hands tightened around her neck. A more rigorous counteraction was needed.

She lifted her long jumper, dug fingernails into her thighs, raked the flesh until she drew blood. The pain did its job. She felt the reek retreating into the abyss.

"LeaMarsa, what are you doing?"

Startled, she lowered her jumper, hiding the bloody claw marks. Hardy Waskov stood two paces away, glaring down at her with stern disapproval.

"It's nothing," she whispered, getting to her feet.

"I've been looking for you. Why haven't you responded to my queries?"

She didn't answer.

"It doesn't matter. You're to come with me. I need your assistance with some experiments."

With everything that was happening, with the ship under deadly threat, Hardy was still trying to behave like a detached researcher. LeaMarsa stifled an urge to laugh. There was something insanely humorous about that.

"What kind of experiments?" she asked, struggling to keep a straight face.

"Telepathic enhancement. We've set up a research lab in the port storage pod adjacent to the lander hold. You'll wear an isolator hood and attempt to establish contact with the creature. We must not forget the scientific purpose of this mission."

The laugh broke through her defenses. Hardy scowled.

"I'm very serious, LeaMarsa. I refuse to allow our efforts to be crippled any further by an incompetent captain. With a revamped experimental roster, we can still return to the solar system as a successful expedition."

His words oozed rationality. Yet Hardy remained oblivious to the psionic storm that swirled around them.

Still, she would participate in his experiment. It would keep her occupied, keep her mind from being assaulted by the one thing that never could be allowed to break into consciousness.

CHAPTER 18

Ericho sat in the pilot's seat of the lander but he wasn't in control. The presence of gravity, as well as vibrations and crackling noises, cued him that they were in a descent. But the window shields were down. He had no idea what planetary atmosphere the lander was plunging through.

The automated descent seemed too fast. External temperature gauges indicated heat shields were close to the danger zone. But, somehow, he knew he was safe, as were the other three members of the crew. He could sense their presence behind him, securely strapped in.

He started to turn around, intending to reassure the trio that everything would be all right. But before he could swivel far enough to make out their identities, the shields peeled back.

They were plunging through a pocket of dense clouds. Moments later, vivid blue skies appeared as the lander broke free. A few thousand meters below was a vast desert. On the horizon beyond a range of mountains, streaks of amber, red and mauve revealed a sky ripening into dusk. Sunset over the Mojave, a beautiful sight.

He recognized the area by rock formations below and the contours of the mountains toward which the lander soared. In his younger days, he'd been stationed nearby, at Pannis' southeastern California base outside of Barstow. He'd flown numerous training flights over the area.

Yet something was wrong. He should have been able to see Barstow's most impressive skyscrapers piercing the heavens beyond the mountains. Like many Earth cities of the late Helio Age, adding illusory height via holographic extensions to buildings already hundreds of stories tall had become a competition among metro areas. It was as if the cities themselves yearned to reach the stars.

The tower of mega BNSF, with its distinctive holo of an animated steam locomotive chugging upward into the heavens, should have dominated the vista. But there was no tower, no locomotive. As the lander swooped over the mountains, he realized the entire city was gone.

Ericho bolted upright in bed. Sensors read his abrupt awakening and brought ceiling lumes to full power. He glanced at the antique mantel clock on his dresser, a gift from his parents. He'd been asleep nearly ninety minutes. Overcome by tiredness he hadn't even bothered undressing and had flopped across the covers.

The desert imagery clung to him as he got to his feet. He sensed it was important, that it was more than just a typical dream. But whatever meaning it might hold remained elusive, as shrouded from view as the mystery of the missing city of Barstow.

Could the dream be related to the swirl of psionic forces impacting them? It seemed possible. If so, he supposed he should be thankful not to be suffering the more horrific nightmares plaguing June.

Perhaps his dream was merely a yearning to return to those enjoyable years he'd spent at Barstow. His days had featured live suborbital flights as well as starship training in simulators. The nights had been given over to dance clubs and the bedrooms of numerous young women.

He headed into the bathroom, unable to stop dwelling on the dream. It seemed to possess a transcendent quality unlike any he'd ever experienced. Could it be related to what June had shared with them about her nightmares? Could that invisible force she'd spoken of have brought down Barstow's towers?

No answer was apparent. He stripped and entered the shower. As alternating jets of air and water blasted, scrubbed and dried his body, the dream's imagery drifted farther away. By the time he emerged and donned a clean uniform, only vague hints of it remained.

Jonomy came over the intercom. "Your wakeup call, captain."

"Any new developments?"

"Relatively peaceful. The unknown vessel continues to parallel us at three hundred thousand kilometers. Faye retrieved samples of the natatorium pollution but has not yet isolated a specific cause. Initial analysis indicates an esoteric mixture of biochemical ingredients that were introduced into the LSN feedwater system."

"Introduced from where?"

"Various other systems and subsystems."

"Is the *Alchemon* aware yet of the pollution?"

"Yes and no. The natatorium malfunction continues to display confusing parameters. Most of the network is now cognizant of the trouble. But in order for that to have happened, I had to indoctrinate the *Alchemon* with the concept that it was experiencing a serious malfunction."

"I don't follow."

"In essence, I had to create a new feedback loop within

the system so that data emanating from the pool was routed back into the network. Once that was accomplished, EHO, the system with overall responsibility for the natatorium, was able to respond. EHO now recognizes the existence of the problem. However, other systems maintain that there is nothing wrong with LSN. Overall, the situation would seem to indicate that we still have major glitches somewhere in the network."

"Is the pollution still limited to the pool?"

"Yes. And to err on the side of caution, I had Faye set up a contamination monitor and had Alexei mount additional cameras down there. The signals from those devices have been routed directly to the bridge on backup circuits that bypass the afflicted systems."

It was reassuring talking to Jonomy. He always seemed to have things under control. Of course, considering the extent of their troubles, a captain's faith might be little more than a pleasant illusion.

"On my way to the bridge," he said.

He left his cabin, thinking about strange pollutants, crazed robots and a starship where none should be. But in the back of his mind remained an image of sunset over the Mojave and the troubling mystery of what had happened to Barstow.

The bridge seemed inordinately crowded when Ericho arrived. Alexei was on the treadmill in the bulky link suit. Rigel stood nearby, ready to help him don the clamshell helmet. Jonomy was in his usual chair, umbilically linked. June paced in orbit around the HOD, her arms crossed tightly, her expression grim.

"What's wrong?" he asked.

"LeaMarsa suffered some sort of breakdown in the nutriment bath," June said. "And I did something unethical. I gave her a high-dose injection of Loopaline B4."

"You vegetated her?"

"Good for you," Rigel said.

But guilt marred June's face. "I didn't tell her what I was doing. I told her it was a sedative to help her sleep."

"So, she'll be out like a baby for nine months," Rigel said. "Don't worry, if it comes down to having to justify your actions to some dickhead Pannis investigating committee, we'll all testify you had no choice." He smacked the top of Alexei's clamshell helmet as he snapped it into place. "Ain't that right?"

A hearty "Yes sir" came from the trainee's suit speakers.

June grimaced. "There's a bigger problem. The drug didn't work. She woke up ten minutes later."

"I didn't think that was possible," Ericho said.

"It's not supposed to be."

"What did she say when she awakened?"

"I didn't get a chance to talk to her. I'd stepped out for a few minutes and she left. Apparently, she ran into Hardy. He persuaded her to don an isolator hood to assist with some experiment."

"Get down there," Ericho ordered. "Tell LeaMarsa she has to return to medcenter."

"I tried. Hardy wouldn't let me into the lab."

"Asshole," Rigel grunted.

Ericho balled his fists, trying to hold back a wave of anger. He'd had just about enough of their intractable science rep.

"As soon as the containment's vacuumed, I'll deal with Hardy."

"Sir, are you going to tell him we're dumping Baby Blue?" Alexei asked.

No one answered. Rigel tapped the trainee's helmet. "Concentrate on your task. You ready in there?"

"All green."

"Remember, take your time walking. Keep one boot in contact with the hull at all times."

"No problem. Even if I do step off the hull, I've got the emergency jets for maneuvering."

"Yeah, but don't count on those. These robots aren't designed for external environments. They can be tricky in zero-g so stay on the hull."

"Got it."

Ericho would have been more comfortable having Rigel do the link EVA. But the tech officer felt the trainee was up to the task. More importantly, Rigel believed he could better function as a coordinator of the virtual spacewalk, monitor any unforeseen obstacles and adjust Alexei's mission parameters accordingly.

The task was simple. The linked robot would do what Ericho in retrospect should have authorized immediately after the melt: depressurizing the containment and venting the entire hot mass into the void.

Alexei would stay as far away from the containment as possible, which hopefully would prevent Baby Blue from taking control of the robot. He would walk the virtual machine only as far as the outer lock. After opening that hatch, he would fire the robot's Higgs cutter at the inner hatch until it was weakened enough for the containment's internal pressure to blow it open.

The trainee lifted the link's right boot and stepped forward. The treadmill compensated by slithering in the opposite direction. In short order, the trainee was walking briskly, heading for airlock three.

Ericho gazed at the main screen behind Jonomy, which displayed the view from the robot's eyes. Alexei halted in front of the airlock and waited for Jonomy to open it.

"When you exit the lock," Rigel instructed, "you'll walk seventy-five meters toward the starboard quarter. The main sensor channel needs to be bridged so be careful when you step across it."

"Got it."

The robot entered airlock three and awaited depressurization. The outer seal parted, and Alexei nursed the machine out into the void. Ericho turned to the HOD. Jonomy had activated 3D video from the hull cams to monitor his progress.

"Approaching main sensor channel," Alexei said.

The channel was one of the depressions running across the width of the *Alchemon*. The robot paused at its edge.

"Preparing to cross."

On the treadmill, Alexei raised his right foot. Onscreen, the robot's corresponding leg mimicked the move. Alexei stepped across the depression, planted the robot's leading boot firmly on the other side.

"Halfway there." There was a long pause, then: "What an incredible starfield. I can see Sycamore in the distance–"

"Pay attention to what you're doing," Rigel snapped.

"Right. Got it."

Alexei lifted the link's left boot. But instead of completing the crossing, he stopped in midstride.

"Something's wrong. I can't move my left leg."

In the HOD, the robot seemed frozen, one boot across the channel, the other suspended. Alexei's position on the treadmill matched the odd pose.

"Unknown malfunction," Jonomy said. "Losing grip adhesion."

Alexei compressed his right leg, the one still planted. With a violent thrust, he leaped into the air and hopped off the treadmill. The link's boots made a resounding *crack* as the trainee touched down on the deck two meters away.

Onscreen, the robot mimicked Alexei's move and shot away from the hull. Ericho could only watch helplessly as the linked machine drifted into space.

"What the fuck are you doing!" Rigel hollered.

"I'm not doing anything!"

"Alexei, activate the emergency harness system," Jonomy instructed.

"No good. The pitons and cabling won't extract. Nothing's working."

Ericho whirled to the lytic. "Override it."

"I cannot. The entire CYB system has entered multi-failure mode. I am attempting to reroute and bypass the problem."

Jonomy closed his eyes, entered deep symbiosis with the network. Ericho spun back to the suited figure who now stood motionless.

"Alexei, see if you can–"

The trainee lunged forward, his arms thrashing wildly, his helmeted head jerking back and forth.

"I'm not doing this!" he cried out. "The suit's moving on its own!"

Ericho had never heard of a link behaving in such a way. The crazed movements reminded him of old videos of people with severe spasms from damaged central nervous systems, back before medicine had cured cerebral palsy and its brethren.

"Try your sight typer," Rigel ordered. "Red-yellow-red, the emergency override."

Even as Rigel spoke, the helmet began violently jerking back and forth.

"No good," Alexei said, his voice rising in pitch, on the verge of panic. "My head's moving too fast. Can't focus…"

"We need to get him out of there," Rigel said, motioning to Ericho and June.

The three of them moved toward Alexei, trying to avoid his wildly gyrating arms.

"Pin his wrists," Rigel instructed. "I'll get the helmet off."

Alexei swung his right arm at them. Ericho jerked back just in time. The blow missed his jaw but slammed June in the chest. She tumbled backward with a squeal of pain and crashed to the deck.

Rigel grabbed the errant arm, pinned it behind the link's back. Ericho managed to do the same with the other arm. But the appendages seemed to have a life of their own, twisting and fighting against the restraint.

"I'm not doing this!" Alexei screamed. "It's not me."

"Gotta stop you anyway," Rigel said. "This is gonna hurt!"

Rigel landed a brutal kick to the link's left knee. Alexei grunted in agony as his leg went out from under him. He crumbled to the deck, taking all three of them down.

But somehow the suit righted itself, even with Ericho and Rigel still hanging on. Alexei whirled toward the center of the bridge and into the HOD. Multi-hued streamers erupted from the holographic sphere as their bodies passed through the display.

"Enough!" Rigel hollered.

He grabbed the suit by the back of the neck in a horsecollar grip and yanked violently. Alexei slammed the floor with a resounding crack followed by a sharp cry of pain.

Rigel straddled the suit, his full weight on Alexei's chest. He pinned the trainee's wrists against the deck.

"Get his goddamn helmet off!"

Ericho knelt on one side of Alexei's head. June, recovered from her spill, rushed to the other side. Together they tried opening the clamshell. But the link fought their efforts, whip-lashing with such speed that Alexei's head became a blur of movement as it bashed against the deck.

The captain finally was able to grab an override switch. The front and back halves of the clamshell parted. He tore the headpiece from Alexei's head. The primary control circuitry was located within. The moment he got it off the rest of the suit went dead.

But not the helmet. It rolled eerily across the deck, servo motors still in the throes of the malfunction. The clamshell halves snapped open and shut like some bizarre mechanical mouth gasping for air.

Rigel grabbed the hinged halves, ripped them apart in a cascade of sparks. He smashed the two pieces against the deck until they stopped quivering then stomped on them for good measure.

Ericho and June turned their attention to Alexei. His eyes were closed. Nose, mouth and tear ducts leaked blood.

"Hemorrhaging from burst capillaries," June said, easing her fingers beneath the back of Alexei's head, where the suit had pounded him against the deck. When she withdrew her hand it was soaked red.

Gingerly, they removed the rest of the suit.

"Careful," June warned. "Don't move him any more than you have to." She whipped her attention to Jonomy. "We need an autobed up here."

"MED has already been informed."

June dabbed at Alexei's bloody face with a cloth while they waited. A minute later, the autobed wheeled itself onto the bridge. Two of the bed's sextet of mech appendages cradled Alexei to limit further injury. The remaining four arms extended to their full lengths, slithered under his legs, spine and neck, and gently lifted him onto the mattress.

Jonomy emerged from his communion with the network. Ericho sat, nursing a sore elbow cracked against the deck during the struggle. June sprinted out the door behind the autobed.

"What in the hell is going on!" Rigel yelled in frustration.

Jonomy remained calm. "The CYB malfunction exhibited the same parameters as the trouble in the natatorium. I attempted to create another feedback loop to make the network aware of the problem. However, that effort failed. The *Alchemon* maintains that the link incident was a human malfunction. It points to Alexei as the source of the trouble. EPS agrees and gives a ninety-eight percent probability that Alexei suffered a breakdown that caused him to input irrational commands."

"That's the most dumbass thing I've ever heard!"

"I am only reporting the ship's conclusion. I am not necessarily in agreement."

He gestured to the HOD, which now imaged an external camera view. In the distance was the link robot, motionless relative to the ship.

"The *Alchemon*'s weak geonic field offset its inertia. It is not drifting any farther out."

"How do we bring it back?" Ericho asked. Considering they'd already lost the first robot, Ericho didn't like the idea of losing the second one. Then again, if linking was no longer reliable...

"PAQ suggests sending a lander out for it."

"Do you agree?"

"PAQ's conclusion is partially based on a financial calculus, the cost of losing another expensive unit."

"Screw those goddamn Pannis bookkeepers," Rigel growled.

"Is that a yes or a no?" Ericho demanded.

"There is also the matter of the mystery ship, which could pose unknown threats to a recovery mission. Therefore, I find myself opposing the recommendations. For the time being we should abandon the robot. It likely will remain within our geonic field for a time, providing the possibility of recapturing it later."

Jonomy disagreeing with advice from the *Alchemon* was a rare event. But Ericho was in accord.

"What about remaining options for vacuuming the containment?" he asked.

"We could utilize a pup. That is still problematic, of course, and would require modifications to its programming to enable a complex external assignment. At this juncture, the most practical method would be a human EVA."

"Let's do it," Rigel snarled. "We need to stop fucking around and purge that son of a bitch."

Ericho hesitated. Considering everything that had gone wrong so far, he didn't relish sending anyone outside to blow the containment hatch. Assuming Baby Blue was responsible for the malfunctions, there was no telling what threats it might use against humans who ventured onto the hull.

"I'm not ruling it out," he said. "But first things first. Rigel, see if you can figure out what went wrong with the suit. Maybe there's a way to safeguard the system against external tampering."

The tech officer snatched up the helmet pieces, slung the heavy garment over his shoulder and stormed off the bridge.

"I'm going down to have a talk with LeaMarsa," Ericho said.

Somehow, she was the key to what was happening to them. But as he headed for the port storage pod, he found himself overwhelmed by a deranged anger directed at the science rep.

And if Hardy gives me any trouble, I'll purge his *ass out the nearest airlock!*

CHAPTER 19

LeaMarsa repressed a shiver. Hardy's makeshift lab was cold. Storage pods, rarely occupied by humans, had minimal heating systems.

The science rep had reworked part of the space into a work area using flex walls and lume-encrusted ceiling panels. A haphazard array of research gear had been scrounged from other parts of the ship.

"Are you ready?" he asked.

His voice came through speakers in the isolator hood LeaMarsa wore. It resembled a giant potato studded with antennas, parabolic dishes and signal deflectors. Hoods shielded wearers from a wide range of the electromagnetic spectrum, in theory heightening psionic sensitivity by blotting out sight and hearing, as well as radio and other frequencies swirling in a starship's techno-rich environment.

She'd donned hoods at the Jamal Labs but had never experienced any measurable level of telepathic enhancement. Still, seclusion from the outside world was her default setting. And nothing bad had ever happened to her while wearing a hood.

"Clear your mind," Hardy ordered. "Try imagining yourself in a comfortable environment with no distractions or worries."

The request seemed ludicrous in light of recent events. Still, she'd learned a few techniques at Jamal, and focused on slowing her breathing and heart rate.

"I'm getting good readings," Hardy said. "Now, plant an image of Baby Blue in your mind."

Using the video she'd seen of the newborn creature taken by the link robot, she formed a mental picture. An instant later she blacked out and was again transported into neurospace. Many more of those ominous clusters had appeared since her previous visit; vast arenas of the starfield seemed polluted by their presence. Dread washed over her as she contemplated what that might mean – or what it *had* meant or *might* portend.

"Sentinel Obey. Coalesce and Target. Implement Synchronicity."

The voice wasn't strained this time and no longer seemed as if it emanated from a great distance. Instead, it resonated through LeaMarsa with sublime clarity. She realized that the inscrutable phrases weren't nonsensical flotsam or some side effect of neurospace.

They're a set of instructions.

But instructions to do what?

Neurospace vanished, replaced by a strange vision in which she was a participant. She sensed that the vision was also courtesy of the phantom woman.

LeaMarsa stood on a riverbank, her bare toes touching warm pebbles at the water's edge. It wasn't Earth. The sky was the color of weathered ivory and peppered with delicate silvery clouds. She had a feeling that this alien world no longer existed, that she was seeing it in some distant past.

The river's far shore rose steeply into a mountain range covered in ground-hugging crimson foliage. Beyond the mountains, a cluster of ultra-thin buildings pierced the clouds. None of the skyscrapers were vertical; each ascended at a slight angle. She sensed that the slantings were deliberate, an esthetic choice. The vista brought to mind a tightly packed bundle of pick-up sticks held upright in preparation for release into a random scatter.

As she admired the city's delicate beauty, it came under attack. Some invisible force shattered the off-kilter skyscrapers, crumbled them into fountains of dust. In a matter of seconds, nothing of the city remained visible above the mountains.

The middle of the river grew agitated. A vessel reminiscent of a circular raft, maybe five meters in diameter, ascended from beneath the waters. It was topped by a shimmering translucent hemisphere, a shield of some sort that enabled it to function as a submarine.

A dozen humanoid creatures stood on the raft. Tall and lean, they had bluish skin, long gray hair and elongated faces. Other than lacking that additional sensory organ between mouths and noses, they appeared to be adult versions of the same species from which Baby Blue originated. A mix of males and females, they were garbed from the waist down in brightly colored garments that resembled culottes.

Whatever invisible force had destroyed the city was now attacking the humanoids. LeaMarsa was close enough to see them being consumed by some form of fire that illogically seemed both cold and hot. In moments, all that remained of them were charred stalks, icicles of flame dripping from their scorched flesh.

Somehow, she knew that Baby Blue was the invisible attacker, and that it had destroyed their civilization. June's nightmare suggested Earth would suffer a similar fate. This vision from long ago was a preview of what it had in store for humanity.

"**The creature is called the Diar-Fahn, the doom that we brought upon ourselves.**"

Whatever limitations had hindered the phantom woman's conversational ability had been overcome. Perhaps the isolator hood was responsible, enabling straightforward communication. Whatever the case, the words flowed through LeaMarsa with clarity and purpose.

"Who are you?" she whispered.

"**I am Nanamistyne of the Avrit-Ah-Tay. I am the jailer.**"

"I don't understand."

"**The Diar-Fahn was an experiment in genetic engineering. It was created for a benign purpose, to access a sub-nanoscale domain we had discovered, a compacted dimension, an essential element of spacetime.**"

"Neurospace."

LeaMarsa sensed the phantom woman acknowledging her conclusion.

"**Like humans and all other intelligent species, we of the Avrit-Ah-Tay possess a tripartite consciousness based on the sequential evolutionary development of the physical, emotional and intellectual components of the brain. Neurospace contains an analogue of every such intelligence – every organic tripartite consciousness alive in the universe. It is the heartland of superluminal interaction, the source of what you refer to as psionic abilities.**

"**Yet no intelligence with which we were familiar could gain full conscious access to neurospace. Our tripartite selves are only able to catch glimpses of its true nature. In our hubris, hoping to overcome that deficiency, we reengineered our DNA to create an entity possessing a fourth level of**

consciousness. We nurtured this entity until we felt it had the maturity to carry out its purpose, to directly access and interact with neurospace."

A sigh of regret seemed to emanate from the phantom woman. LeaMarsa experienced it as a breeze tainted by anguish.

She recalled June mentioning Lieutenant Donner's final words. *The Quad awakens.* He'd obviously been referring to the same entity, a creature who, like her, was able to access neurospace. The similarity between them was troubling. Were she and the Diar-Fahn alike in other, more disturbing ways?

"But the Diar-Fahn possessed a fatal flaw. Or perhaps the very structure of neurospace altered its fundamental constitution. We don't know the reasons, only the end result. The Diar-Fahn stopped functioning according to the tenets of tripartite consciousness and became the prototype of a fundamentally different species, one possessing a quadpartite consciousness. Shorn of empathy, it began perceiving all forms of tripartite intelligence as enemies to be destroyed."

"It attacked you," LeaMarsa concluded.

"Us and other civilizations, within the familiar universe and within that compacted dimension. Full access to neurospace had endowed it with mighty powers, even a kind of immortality. Our species was nearly overwhelmed before we found a means to trap and imprison its physical essence on the world you call Sycamore, which also neutralized its powers in neurospace."

"Until humans found it and set it free," LeaMarsa whispered, stunned by the revelations. She was about to ask what the three cryptic phrases meant when loud angry voices penetrated the shielding of her isolator hood, wrenching awareness back into the chilly environs of the port storage pod. She whipped off the hood to find Hardy and Ericho standing face-to-face, raw with anger as they engaged in a shouting match.

"You do *not* lock out a crewdoc!" the captain hollered. "June's medical authority overrides your experiments. Get that through your idiot brain once and for all!"

"And does a crewdoc's authority include vegetating LeaMarsa?" Hardy challenged.

"What are you talking about?" LeaMarsa demanded.

Hardy spun toward her with annoyance, as if regarding her as an interloper. He aimed a quivering finger at Ericho.

"Our captain ordered June – his partner, I might add – to vegetate you."

"That's a lie. I gave no such order."

"June Courthouse administered a powerful soporific. The moment you donned the hood, my scanners picked up Loopaline B4 in your system. You were given a high dose, far more than required for Quiets transit. The only use for the drug at those levels is to vegetate humans."

LeaMarsa turned to Ericho. "Is that true?"

"June was worried about the effect you've been having on the rest of us. So yes, she tried dosing you with loopy."

Hardy smirked in triumph. "His admission gives you grounds for a lawsuit, not to mention opening him up to charges of flagrant criminality."

"That's nonsense."

"Is it, captain? A Corporeal court may see things differently."

The argument is irrelevant. We're not going to make it back to a Corporeal courtroom.

"Put the hood back on," Hardy instructed. "The captain is leaving. And we shall continue with our experiments."

"No."

The science rep grimaced. "LeaMarsa, I've been most lenient with you throughout this expedition. I have graciously accepted your various refusals to cooperate and have bent over backward to accommodate you. However, my patience is wearing thin. I insist that you prioritize the scientific parameters of our mission and get over your self-centered attitude."

As he continued ranting about her deficiencies, LeaMarsa perceived Hardy Waskov as he truly was, a man totally unaware of the great depths surrounding him. He stood on the edge of a gaping abyss, secured by what he believed were safety lines – facts and figures, logical interpretations of data, rational experiments. But all that merely deluded him into thinking he was on a safe perch. He remained blind to his own precarious reality.

And in a wider sense, Hardy might be considered the quintessence of humanity in general, with its overreliance on the intellect for perceiving the world. Such perception increasingly seemed limiting to her. She suspected that the true nature of the universe lay beyond cognitive understanding – the highest manifestation of tripartite beings – and was comprehensible only from within the realm of quadpartite consciousness.

"Stop abusing her," Ericho snapped, grabbing Hardy by the collar and shoving him against an equipment rack. "She said *no*!"

The science rep looked astonished at being manhandled. He was momentarily at a loss for words.

"June wants you back in medcenter," Ericho instructed. He was breathing hard, his rage barely under control. "You have my word she won't attempt to administer any more drugs without your consent."

"Don't believe him," Hardy hissed. "Our captain does not have your best interests in mind."

"As if you do. You've been abusing your authority since–"

"Stop!" LeaMarsa hollered. "Neither of you have the right to tell me what to do!"

She'd had enough of everyone trying to manipulate her. A longing took hold, a longing to be away from the *Alchemon*, away from all the psychic and psychological turbulence that constituted her life. Away from the crew, away from the phantom woman and whatever machinations she intended. None of them understood her, understood what it was like to see the world from such a different perspective.

She stormed out the door, aware that her desires contained the kernels of suicidal ideation. She suspected that Tomer Donner must have had similar thoughts when faced with his own limited options.

From the files of Lieutenant
Tomer Donner, Pannis Corp
BRIDGE OFFICER

Eight years, four months and two days into the timeline of my obsession, I've finally achieved a breakthrough in my efforts to seek justice for Karl's murder.

Tomorrow I leave the solar system for an eighteen-month expedition on the Alchemon. *Up until last night, everything about this assignment seemed routine. And then came the first of two momentous surprises.*

One of the investigators I'd hired to look into Renfro Zoobondi's affairs tracked down and interviewed a Pannis assignor involved in the VP's latest scheme. It is a scheme with me as the target.

Zoobondi's plan had been launched only last week. But the assignor, possessing a personal honor code that left him plagued by guilt, was prompted to reveal the truth. Against the assignor's better judgment, he'd been ordered to put a powerful psionic aboard the Alchemon. *Renfro Zoobondi had pulled strings to make this happen, no doubt as a strike against me. Yet for perhaps the first time in our long battle, I believe the VP has made a mistake. The assignor has been deposed by my attorney and is willing to testify against Zoobondi.*

I've always known about my high telepathic rating, that I'm a gifted receptor. I was warned at the start of my career that being around any equally gifted individuals, particularly superluminal projectors or conveyors, could be problematic.

But even though I encountered a few such individuals over the years, I never noticed anything unusual, and certainly never had a sense of being influenced by them. In fact, like many others, I'd grown skeptical of the whole idea of psychic "science" and began to suspect that many of its practitioners and proponents were exaggerating claims, or worse, were clever frauds.

But then this morning, while still trying to absorb the exciting news about the assignor coming forward, I received the second surprise.

I was introduced to LeaMarsa de Host.

To say that this sullen young woman had an immediate impact on me would be gross understatement. When she walked into the lunar orbit docking bay and, at the urging of Captain Solorzano of the Alchemon, *shook my hand, everything changed.*

The instant our palms embraced, the most incredible visions flashed through my head. It was as if I was simultaneously witnessing the multiple tracks of some hypermedia event, as if my mind was a holo display into which the thoughts of others were being projected.

I saw a strange stick city on some faraway world, crumbling into dust. I saw a blue spherical mass pulsating with life. I saw an elongated skull-like head, a hideous visage boasting a marble-like sensory organ between its mouth and nose. But even more encompassing than the visions was the prescient intuition accompanying them.

When our hands parted a moment later, LeaMarsa wore a look of bored defiance. I could only stand there with a frozen smile, trying to hide the tremors coursing through my body. I knew at that moment, in a way I could never hope to explain, that my intuition was a dispatch from the future, a signifier of events yet to come.

The insight was simple. Spending months in close quarters with this woman would drive me insane. I would suffer an irreversible plunge into madness that no psychiatric methodology could circumvent.

There was no hope of convincing anyone of what I'd just experienced. Any rational person would think I was crazy. Rather ironic, considering that such was exactly the state I'd find myself in should I go on this mission.

I could withdraw from the voyage, of course. I had reasonable cause. The fledgling study of superluminal compatibility had revealed the potential consequences of confining two people with potent abilities in close proximity for an extended period.

Yet I was equally aware of corporate realities. Zoobondi had already used his influence to blacklist me from any major starship assignments. And resigning so close to departure wouldn't look good on my record no matter how valid the reason, and likely would make it even harder to gain future employment in my chosen profession.

It was a shrewd move by Zoobondi, seemingly a win-win situation for him. If I stayed aboard the Alchemon, I'd be at the mercy of devastating psionic forces driving me insane. If I withdrew, I'd be slamming the door on my career... and possibly even joining the needful majority. I simmered with fresh anger at the sheer gall of this man whom I'd come to hate to the core of my being.

The only sensible option was to withdraw. I would hand over to Corporeal authorities what evidence investigators and forensics auditors had gathered over the years against Zoobondi, including his embezzling and the brutal fights ending with dead opponents, plus the most damning document, the assignor's deposition. Together, there was more than enough evidence to launch a Corporeal probe and bring criminal charges against the arrogant bastard.

Zoobondi was a potent foe and the court system too often warped to benefit the interests of the rich and powerful, so there was no guarantee justice would be served, no guarantee Zoobondi would be sentenced to one of the offworld prisons of US-Them, the penal-institution mega. Still, I was certain it was enough to at least derail *his career, make sure he ascended no higher in the Pannis hierarchy. A small victory, but a victory nonetheless.*

With only hours before departure and still mulling over my dilemma, I realized I had another option. I could willingly board the Alchemon, *go on a mission in which the end result would be my descent into madness. Such a sacrificial action should bear fruit eighteen months from now. When the vessel returned to the solar system with an insane bridge lieutenant, it would provide strong evidentiary cause-and-effect that Zoobondi's machinations were responsible. In conjunction with the other evidence, there might just be enough to ensure a criminal conviction.*

Of course, being insane would deprive me of a certain level of gratification when it came to the woes Zoobondi might suffer. And the very idea I was even considering such a course of action suggested that I might already be certifiably mad. But perhaps that was indeed my true state over these past eight-plus years, focused as I've been on destroying the man who'd robbed me of the one person I'd loved deeply.

Yet truth be told, there was another motive for embarking on this course, a motive that I knew in my heart was the real reason. Something else happened to me in that instant when LeaMarsa and I shook hands. I saw something beyond those incredible visions and insight into my fate.

As if viewed through a heavy veil, I glimpsed a distant universe or dimension, a darkness rich with strange stars, a realm of luminous dark. Perhaps it was a place where my pain and anger over Karl's death could be lessened, where I might find salvation from the emotional abyss that seemed forever in my path, devouring my hopes and dreams.

And so I've made my decision. Tomorrow, I seal my fate as well as the fate of Renfro Zoobondi.

Tomorrow, I board the starship Alchemon.

CHAPTER 20

Ericho entered the medcenter treatment room still smarting from his encounter with Hardy. He watched a ceiling-mounted clinician sweep a pair of tentacle-hands back and forth across Alexei, scanning injuries and formulating treatment strategies. A breathing mask flanked by puffy O_2 bladders formed a tight seal over the unconscious trainee's mouth and nose.

"How's he doing?"

"I'll know in a sec," June said, monitoring the clinician's results on her wafer. "Just confirming my diagnosis."

Ericho realized she was following standard protocol by getting a second opinion from the clinician. But considering that Alexei had been nearly beaten to death by a machine, it annoyed him that another machine was performing the exam.

"Don't wait for the damn clinician," he growled, knowing that some of his anger was really meant for the science rep. "Trust your own judgment."

"And how are *you* feeling?"

"I'll survive."

"Didn't go well with Hardy, I presume."

"You could say that."

He drew a deep breath to force calm and excise the violent fantasy churning through him. In it, he was grabbing Hardy by the scruff of the neck and ramming the idiot into a wall until his face was reduced to bloody pulp. He couldn't recall ever experiencing such rage.

The clinician finished its scan and used another of its sextet of hands to insert a fresh IV line into Alexei's wrist.

"Summarize," June ordered.

The machine's male voice sounded inappropriately serene.

"Primary injury, traumatic brain damage. Multiple acute subdural hematomas in the frontal and parietal lobes. Increasing pressure from cerebrospinal fluid expansion within the intercranial space. Suctional tri-craniotomy recommended."

"Agreed," June said. "Initiate."

"Initiating."

The autobed rotated ninety degrees and inched forward to better position Alexei for the surgery. Two of its hands cradled his head to keep it immobile while a third injected a local anesthetic. Hand number four, gripping a Cartesian laser, descended upon the head like an ancient soldier with a drawn bayonet. The laser made a series of right-angled cuts on the top of Alexei's skull. The final pair of hands gently peeled back skin and bone to access the brain.

"Other major injuries?" June asked.

"Left knee, intra-articular tibial fracture. Non-critical. Fusion repair recommended following tri-craniotomy."

"Agreed. Initiate when tri-craniotomy complete, pending successful outcome."

"Affirmed."

The crewdoc continued to monitor the surgery on her wafer as she headed out into the lobby. Ericho followed.

The outer door opened, admitting Faye.

"Is he going to make it?" she asked. Her voice quivered, revealing the depth of her concern. "Oh, and feel free to lie to me. I need some good news about now even if it's not true."

"Alexei is stable," June said, monitoring her wafer. "Assuming no unexpected complications, his prognosis is full recovery."

Faye flopped onto a chair and curled into a fetal ball. "What's happening to us?"

"We're facing forces we don't understand," Ericho said. "But we're going to get through it."

His words felt hollow. But for morale's sake it was important to continue projecting optimism.

June pinned her gaze on Faye. "You look tired. You should get some sleep."

"No thanks. Last time I closed my eyes, the nightmare started right away. Pretty much the same one you've been having except it's me and my parents and sisters who get the hot-ice-melt treatment." She forced a smile even as shudders passed through her. "My current plan is to stay awake forever."

"If you find a way to make that work, please share."

"Anything new on the natatorium pollution?" Ericho asked.

Faye sighed. "The more I study it, the less sense it makes. There are biochemical transformations occurring in the water that don't correlate with anything on record."

"Theories?"

"None that fit the facts. Best hypothesis – and this is pure guesswork – is that for reasons unknown the pool is turning into a giant petri dish, some sort of bizarre cell-culturing medium. Before IBD sealed off the natatorium from the rest of the ship, LSN managed to gather and suck in organisms from all over the place. Protein clusters from the nutriment bath, floral seeds and roots from hydroponics, even waste products from FWP. About the only thing I've confirmed is that the mass continues to transform at a rather spectacular rate."

"Transform into what?"

She shrugged.

"Could these transformations be random?" June asked.

"I doubt it. But really, I don't know. Organic transformations of this complexity should be examined by a specialist. Hardy is more knowledgeable, but I can't even get him to look at my data."

"Forget Hardy," Ericho snapped.

They were all silent for a moment, lost in individual thoughts. Faye broke the stillness.

"So, what are we going to do about that thing in the containment?"

"We have to get it off the ship," June said. "It's literally poisoning us. Insanity, rages, nightmares. Who knows what's next?"

Ericho came to a decision, tabbed his mike.

"Rigel, where are you?"

The tech officer came on speaker. "Mech room. Still disassembling the remains of Alexei's link." He paused. "No luck so far in figuring out why it went nuts."

"Drop that. You and I are doing the EVA. We'll blow the inner hatch and purge everything. Meet me at airlock three."

He realized there was a real danger of the creature taking some sort of action against them while they were out on the hull. But they had to chance it.

"Keep working on that pollution," he instructed Faye. "It can't be random. There must be purpose behind it, something that makes sense."

"Hardy wants me to get back to helping him."

"I'm declaring the *Alchemon* on full emergency status. Under Pannis guidelines, you're no longer under the authority of the science rep."

"Aye aye, cap'n," Faye said, giving a mock salute.

Her words triggered a memory from Ericho's favorite childhood adventure story, *Captain Clarke in the Quiets of Doom*. Trapped in a transpatial corridor, the intrepid hero's command of both his ship and crew had inexorably slipped away. Ericho couldn't recall the details, only that the captain had come up with an unorthodox salvation to save the mission.

Unorthodox salvation. The words resonated. They seemed somehow germane to the *Alchemon*'s plight. Before he could consider the matter further, an ominous vibration rose from the floor. It coursed through their bodies for several seconds and then was gone.

Jonomy appeared on the nearest monitor. "Captain, the tremble was shipwide and was caused by an explosive discharge perpendicular to our line of transit. The fact that we received no advance warning prevented GEN and related systems from making compensatory geonic adjustments in time."

"What kind of discharge?" Ericho demanded.

"The containment was vacuumed."

"You found a way to do it." But even as Ericho uttered the words, he realized the conclusion was wrong.

"I took no action," Jonomy affirmed. "The inner and outer seals of the airlock chute were opened simultaneously and the radioactive mass purged. Eleven seconds later, both hatches were sealed again.

"How could that have happened?"

"Unknown. Here is the external imagery."

The monitor switched to a view from an outside hull camera.

A gaseous plume studded with chunks of debris floated off into the void. It was already half a kilometer away and retreating from the hull at a rapid rate.

"Sensors analyzed the expulsion. The remains of Bouncy Blue are there. However, Baby Blue was not ejected. And some components of that link robot, the one destroyed by the warrior pup, also were not part of the jetsam." Jonomy paused. "EPS gives the highest probability that the creature was somehow responsible for the purge."

"But why blow the containment? It would be exposing itself to a vacuum that likely would kill it."

"Considering the organism's propensity for surviving in hostile conditions, I would not presume that a vacuum would lead to its demise."

"The damn thing can't be omnipotent. Hell, we all saw that it was breathing. It has lungs similar to ours."

"A good point. The robot's cameras did register inhalation and exhalation at Baby Blue's birth, if that's what that event can be called. But remember Hardy's theory of an energy field that our instruments are not sensitive enough to measure? The creature could possess the same energy field and use it as a shield in harsh environments."

"Maybe breathing is optional," June said. "A physiological capability but not a requirement."

Rigel ambled in with a grunt. "So much for our EVA."

"For the moment," Ericho said. "All right, first priority is getting a look inside the containment. We have the same options as before. Either Rigel and I go out there or we send one of the pups."

"Considering this latest development, I suggest the latter," Jonomy said. "Even though we may lose control of the pup, it possibly would remain operational long enough to provide imagery and data from within the containment."

"Can you modify the pup, give it a better chance of not being taken over?"

"I can reprogram its com links to respond only to my direct commands."

"Might work," Rigel said.

"I will let you know when the pup is ready for egress."

Jonomy ended the transmission. The instant the monitor went to black, Rigel withdrew a safepad from his pocket and smacked the disk onto the nearest wall. A faint, low-pitched hum coursed through the medcenter lobby.

Ericho, June and Faye watched in silent curiosity as Rigel closed the other doors, including the one to Alexei's treatment room. The four of them were now isolated in the lobby. With a safepad activated, they were theoretically shielded from all forms of eavesdropping.

"Medcenter is already in a dopa," June pointed out. "We're assured of privacy."

"We're assured of nothing," Rigel said. "Not if I'm right. I lied to you earlier, about not being finished tearing apart that link. I did finish and found out why it went nuts. The suit's power modules were remotely reprogrammed and the safety circuits disabled. Someone introduced new programming that enabled them to take control of the suit."

"Baby Blue," Faye said.

"That's what we've all been focusing on. But we may have the wrong suspect. I have an alternate theory. I think our lytic has gone over the edge, the same way the lieutenant did. Whether he was driven that way by LeaMarsa or by our nasty little friend in the containment or some combination of the two doesn't matter. Bottom line, I think Jonomy's gone nuts."

Ericho glanced at June and Faye. Their astonished looks mirrored his own.

"Think about it. He's connected to the ship most of the time. And he's the only crewmember who can input the sort of commands that can restructure major or minor systems, such as what was done to the link."

"But why?" June asked.

"Who knows? All this psionic crap got to him, same way it got to Donner. If you posit Jonomy as the main cause of our problems, everything begins to make sense. Think back to the first malfunction, the link robot in the containment. Jonomy easily could have taken control of CYB and made those circuitry modifications, right?"

Ericho nodded.

"The next thing that happens is SEN reacts. The warrior pup is dispatched to deal with the whacked-out robot. So, Jonomy gets pissed and tries to take over the pup. Only there he runs into a problem. He's dealing with a Sentinel now, and it's not so easy. Ten times out of ten, SEN's going to win that battle.

"But even though the Sentinel is faster, Jonomy is pretty shrewd and has some tricks up his sleeve. For a while, the two of them fight for control of the warrior pup. It can't handle the conflicting orders. Maybe it goes crazy and blasts its way out of the containment.

"Then comes the mess in the pool. Maybe Jonomy doesn't even know what's growing down there. But if he is crazy, he could be sending weird signals into the network, even doing it unconsciously. There's precedent for such a thing. Ever hear of the *Bountiful Nomad*?"

It sounded vaguely familiar to Ericho. Faye jumped in with the details.

"The *Bountiful Nomad* was a Quiets exploratory ship about thirty years ago. During its voyage, their lytic contracted some rare disease."

"Not a disease," June clarified. "Their lytic unknowingly had been infected by a parasite during a previous voyage to the Louis Vuitton colonies. One of the symptoms of the infection was sudden and unpredictable bouts of microsleep."

"Now I remember," Ericho said. "The lytic ended up conking out for extremely short periods, just a few seconds here and there, but while umbilically linked."

"He wasn't even aware of what was happening to him. But he would slip into a dream state and his subconscious mind would cause contamination of the nutriment bath and other systems. It took the crew a while to figure out what was going on."

Ericho shook his head. "It still sounds pretty farfetched that Jonomy's our problem. And what about this other ship that's tracking us?"

"What other ship?" Rigel asked. "Jonomy probably figures we'll eventually suspect him as the source of our troubles, so he creates evidence of a mysterious vessel hundreds of thousands of kilometers away. Just far enough out, by the way, that we can't get any solid telemetry. But with its presence, we're suddenly looking away from the *Alchemon*, away from our own lytic as the source of the problem."

"Externalizing our fears," June mused, starting to buy into Rigel's theory.

Faye also seemed persuaded. "That's the first sensible explanation I've heard for what's happening in the natatorium. Those transformations are just so illogical. But if you posit them as the unintentional byproduct of a deranged lytic, it makes a weird kind of sense."

Ericho remained skeptical. "You're overlooking the most likely explanation for our problems. Remember that presumed crossover between psionic superluminals and portions of the electromagnetic spectrum? That points us right back to Baby Blue."

"I don't doubt that Baby Blue is causing a superluminal shitstorm," Rigel said. "But isn't it more reasonable to assume that because of that storm, Jonomy suffered a psychotic break?"

Faye nodded. "Occam's razor. When in doubt, select the hypothesis with the fewest assumptions."

"Damn right, Occam's razor," Rigel growled. "That Baby Blue drove our lytic insane best fits the facts."

"If what you're saying is true," Ericho said, "then it was Jonomy who vacuumed the containment. But why would he do that? And how did he do it?"

Rigel shrugged. "As to the 'why' part, if he's crazy, he could be operating under any sort of rationale. He knew we were about to do the EVA so maybe he figured to beat us to the punch. Or maybe some deep part of his mind realizes that Baby Blue and LeaMarsa are affecting him and he's conflicted. As to how he vacuumed the containment, who the hell knows? He's a goddamn lytic, which means he's whip-smart and knows how to bypass systems."

"But Baby Blue wasn't ejected with the purge," Ericho pointed out.

"We only have Jonomy's word for that. It would make sense for him to say Baby Blue is still onboard."

"To keep our suspicions focused on the creature as the source of our troubles," Faye said.

Ericho remained unconvinced. "Despite what happened

aboard the *Bountiful Nomad*, there hasn't been a documented case of true insanity in a lytic since their earliest years. And that was mainly with some of the more bizarre models, very experimental genejobs and the like. I don't believe the rational part of Jonomy would succumb. He'd recognize what was happening, work to counteract it."

"Maybe, maybe not," Rigel said. "But here's the bottom line. If I'm right, we've got a hell of a problem. A renegade lytic is seriously bad news."

"There's something else," June said. "Jonomy has had a number of recent psych sessions with me. He's recognized a problem." She glanced at Faye and Rigel, hesitated.

"Spit it out," Ericho said. "We're way past worrying about doctor-patient confidentiality."

"He's becoming a dreamlounge junkie. It's not an unusual problem for anyone to have, including lytics. His fantasies themselves aren't out of the ordinary, mostly vanilla sexual encounters. The trouble is, he's been so caught up in experiencing them that he's even been doing it from the bridge, connecting to the dreamlounge through the umbilical."

"Isn't that illegal?" Faye asked.

"Technically no, although it does stretch the lytic code of ethics. The real issue is the frequency of the fantasies. He admits he can barely go more than ten minutes without thinking about them. And since our last session was days ago, there's likely been a further escalation."

"Anybody need more proof?" Rigel demanded, glaring at each of them in turn. "If that doesn't indicate a seriously warped mind, I don't know what does."

"All right, Rigel, you've made your point," Ericho said. "There's a way to test your theory. Jonomy's been linked to the ship for more than thirty hours, well past his usual bridge shift."

"Which means irrespective of the fantasies, he's in the danger zone," June said. "For lytics, that many sequential hours can lead to serious neurological deficits. He'll not only be less alert but susceptible to microsleep events."

Ericho outlined his plan. "I'll go to the bridge and point that out to him, recommend he take a break. If he argues, I'll make it an order."

"What if he refuses?" Rigel asked. "If he is bonkers and realizes we're on to him, he could cause damage to the ship."

"What if he turns off life support?" Faye asked, a tremor of fear in her voice. "Or opens all the airlocks?"

Rigel shook his head. "EHO and EAC are critical Level Two systems. If he tries something that bold, he'll probably awaken the Sentinel. Considering what happened with the warrior pup, I think he'll try to avoid provoking SEN."

"Still, Faye has a valid concern," Ericho said. "If he is crazy, he could come up with a hundred ways to hurt us or disable the ship."

"Could we try warning SEN directly, detailing our suspicions?" June asked.

"Not without Jonomy finding out," Rigel said.

"With everything that's been happening, why hasn't SEN already taken some sort of action?" Faye asked.

Ericho shrugged. "Maybe the same reason as us. It's not certain what's really going on, which means it's not sure what action it should take. Sentinels normally activate in the face of specific, comprehensible threats. I think it's safe to say that what's been happening to us defies that sort of easy assessment."

Rigel nodded in agreement. "SEN wasn't programmed to

deal with some super-intelligent bastard lifeform attacking a ship's network, not to mention the crew. Bottom line, we have to figure on the Sentinel behaving unpredictably."

"Which means we can't count on it for saving us. In any case, if we're right about Jonomy, trying to warn SEN on our own is too risky." He turned to the tech officer. "We still have a manual Higgs cutter onboard, right?"

"Yeah, the one Donner didn't vaporize. It's in the mech shop."

"Can you airgap a shieldsuit so that no one can remotely take control of it?"

"Sure. I can rip out the transceivers and cripple the com-link circuitry, everything but basic two-way radio. Take me five minutes."

"Do it. Then get into the shieldsuit and hide the Higgs cutter. Head for the bridge so that you arrive just after I get there. If I can't convince Jonomy to unlink or if he becomes threatening in any way, don't wait for my signal. Use the HC. Cut the cord."

June frowned. "If you sever an umbilical without allowing a lytic to go through his withdrawal routine, Jonomy could suffer grave neurological damage."

"Whose side are you on?" Rigel demanded.

"Just make sure you're right about him before you do something so drastic."

Ericho nodded in agreement.

"Jonomy will probably track me," Rigel said. "I think I can retrieve the HC without him noticing. But he's sure as hell going to wonder what I'm doing in a shieldsuit."

"Tell him you're under orders from me and that I'm on my way to the bridge to explain."

Rigel headed out the door.

"What do you want us to do?" June asked.

"Stay here with Alexei. If things go bad, medcenter is a reasonably secure area of the ship."

Faye gestured to the safepad. "What if Jonomy's been trying to call us?"

"Deactivate the safepad after I'm gone. If he asks about being out of touch, tell him you have no idea."

Ericho could tell they had more questions. But there wasn't time to address every contingency. If they were dealing with a crazed lytic, separating Jonomy from the network was the primary concern.

He exited into the corridor; aware he needed to kill a few minutes while Rigel modified the shieldsuit. The main social room was up ahead and he ducked in, intending to grab an iced coffee from the dispenser. But he instantly flashed back to something that had occurred at the Homebound, something that in the swirl of ensuing events he'd forgotten about.

He'd asked June to put together a comprehensive file on LeaMarsa, everything the crewdoc could find that didn't violate medical ethics. His interest had been triggered by LeaMarsa's unease when he'd mentioned the connection between superluminals and mitochondrials, and the fact that her parents were bioresearchers specializing in mitochondrial DNA. As soon as the crisis with Jonomy was resolved, he'd remind June about the file.

He still couldn't come up with a good reason why he wanted the info. Yet he couldn't shake the feeling that it was of the utmost importance.

CHAPTER 21

LeaMarsa left the storage pod lab and wandered aimlessly through downdeck, still trying to process the narrative that had come to her while ensconced within the isolator hood. That an ancient civilization, the Avrit-Ah-Tay, had created the Quad – the Diar-Fahn, an entity whose fourth level of consciousness enabled full access to the compacted dimension of neurospace – was an incredible notion. Yet she sensed truth in the words of Nanamistyne, the phantom woman.

Nonetheless, her anger about being manipulated continued to simmer. The crew, the creature – who sought to use her in some way she didn't yet grasp – Nanamistyne, who clearly also had an unknown agenda: all considered her a pawn.

She rounded a bend in the deserted corridor and halted at an airseal. It took a moment to recognize where her random stroll had brought her. Beyond the door was the short passage leading to the natatorium.

A swim sounded like a perfect tonic, a way to ease worries, soothe anger and tamp down any possibility of the reek being awakened. She passed through the airseal and approached the entrance to the pool. A blinking lume sign confronted her.

Closed for Maintenance.

Ignoring the sign, she smacked her palm against the manual

egress. But the door refused to open. She tabbed an intercom.

"Jonomy, I'm at the pool. Please open the door."

There was no response. She withdrew her compressed wafer from a pocket, unflexed it. But she still couldn't reach the lytic, nor access any of the ship's systems.

Her anger surged.

"Open the goddamn door!"

The airseal remained impervious to her rage. She turned around, headed back along the passage to the airseal she'd just passed through. But now that door refused to open.

She again tried the intercom and the wafer. Nothing. An uneasy feeling took hold. It was as if the ship was conspiring to keep her trapped in this short corridor between two unresponsive airseals.

Frustrated, she slumped on the deck with her back to the wall. A childhood memory washed over her. She was maybe seven years old and playing a game of pick-up sticks with her father. He'd found the game at an antiques emporium.

Her father moved a yellow stick but disturbed the pile, losing his turn.

"Me next!" she said gleefully.

LeaMarsa's mother hovered nearby whispering research notes into a wafer, something she often did during her incessant documenting of LeaMarsa's behavior. Pointing to a green stick at the edge of the pile, her mother suggested it as the next selection.

Instead, LeaMarsa reached for a red stick buried deeper in the jumble. She freed the wooden twig from its precarious surroundings without disturbing the other sticks and waved it over her head, delighted by success.

"You're getting pretty good at this," her father praised. "We're guessing that you made use of your exceptional abilities. That's how you knew to choose the red stick, right?"

"No, Daddy," she protested. "It was *me* who did it. It wasn't my *abilities*."

She hated the way her parents always tried to attribute her accomplishments to her psychic gifts, as if she had no talents of her own.

"Seeking out challenging tasks is the hallmark of a maturing psionic," her father continued, ignoring her objection. "You're going to grow up to become one of the most remarkable young women in all the settled planets."

She'd tolerated their praise, at least until age thirteen when she discovered their manipulation of her genome. After that, memories of their many compliments tended to make her angry. The notion of her father telling her that she would grow into a remarkable young woman had come to seem like the epitome of selfishness.

Brilliant husband-and-wife bioresearchers, specializing in mitochondrial DNA.

Husband-and-wife bioresearchers with colossal ambitions who had injected into LeaMarsa's embryo a unique strand of mitochondrial DNA crafted from the genetic material of twenty-nine individuals.

Twenty-nine individuals with inordinately superior psionic abilities. Projectors, receptors and conveyors of the highest order.

Her parents had embarked upon what they saw as a noble quest, the creation of a superluminal transhuman, a leap forward in human evolution. LeaMarsa had been conceived, in every definition of the word, as a science experiment. She was a full-blown genejob, modified in the womb to become capable of the most extraordinary psionic feats.

Cursed even before I was born to be forever different. Forever alone.

CHAPTER 22

Ericho entered the final stretch of corridor leading to the bridge's port entrance, trying to project a nonchalant demeanor. Presumably, Jonomy was observing him on surveillance cams amid a plethora of simultaneous tasks.

His mind wandered back to that Mojave Desert of his dream, descending in the lander with a trio of unknown crewmembers behind him, heading toward the city of Barstow that was no longer there. The more he considered it, the more the dream felt like a harbinger of some grim future. Did it mean that only he and three others from the *Alchemon* would make it back to Earth? Were the other four crewmembers fated to die?

It was just a dream, it wasn't real. He forced concentration to the task at hand, getting Jonomy to unlink from the umbilical.

It suddenly occurred to him that there was another explanation for their troubles. Maybe the lytic was fine and it was Rigel who'd gone mad. The tech officer certainly had the skills to mess with the ship's systems. Maybe Rigel's particular brand of craziness was to cast blame on others. After all, earlier he'd speculated that Pannis was behind their troubles and Baby Blue part of some secret project.

No, he could only be paranoid about one crewmember at a time.

The thought inspired a grim chuckle as he reached the bridge airseal. The door failed to open at his approach as it should have. He tabbed the manual control.

No response.

He activated his mike. "Jonomy, I'm right outside. There seems to be an issue with the door."

"Yes, captain, I am aware of the problem. Both entry points to the bridge are presently impaired. Unfortunately, IAC registers no troubles."

"Why am I not surprised? Still, it must be obvious to you that we're having a problem."

"Of course. I have initiated feedback loops in an attempt to get IAC to acknowledge the malfunction. However, that does not seem to be working. I will attempt another series of steps to bypass IAC's control. Those steps should bring cognizance to the affected system."

"I don't care if the system's cognizant. I just want the goddamn door open."

"Understood."

Most of the *Alchemon*'s airseals had overrides on both sides. But because the bridge was considered a secure area, it was an exception to that rule. Normally, its airseals could be opened manually only from within.

"Why don't you just disconnect from the umbilical and do it yourself?" Ericho suggested. And resolve the very issue he'd come here to address.

There was a long pause. "I do not think that such an action would be wise."

"Really? It would only take you a few seconds."

"Due to the extraordinary nature of the troubles we have been experiencing, I believe it is vital that I remain connected at all times."

He knows what we're up to. He's not going to allow us on the bridge. Ericho restrained an urge to pound on the door.

Jonomy's voice rose sharply. "Rigel is on an approach to the starboard airseal. He is garbed in a shieldsuit and unresponsive to my queries."

"Maybe there's a problem with the atmospherics at his location," Ericho suggested, trying to buy Rigel time by faking confusion.

"EHO indicates no such problem." Jonomy hesitated. "Captain, is there an issue here to which I remain unaware?"

"What do you mean?"

"A corridor scanner reveals a bulge in Rigel's utility belt that suggests he is carrying the other Higgs cutter. The device appears to have been deliberately hidden. Also, if my judgment of facial expressions is of any value, Rigel is exhibiting grim determination enhanced by barely restrained anger."

"Maybe he's worried about having to cut through malfunctioning airseals."

There was another lengthy pause. Then...

"Captain, am I in some sort of danger?"

Ericho dropped the charade. "Jonomy, listen carefully. If that door doesn't open when Rigel arrives, he will burn through it with the Higgs."

"Inadvisable. Such an action likely would awaken the Sentinel, which may interpret the action as an assault on the bridge. A warrior pup would likely be dispatched."

"True enough. But Rigel would be on the bridge by the time the pup arrived. He already would have taken drastic action against you should you refuse to unlink."

Ericho detected a whiff of resignation. "You have concluded that I am the cause of these malfunctions."

"Call it a working theory supported by strong evidence."

"Understood. However, you have arrived at an erroneous understanding of our problems. I am not the one responsible."

"Open the door, Jonomy."

To Ericho's surprise, the airseal whisked open. He leaped through the portal, not waiting for an explanation.

Jonomy sat on the far side of the bridge, the umbilical curling over his shoulder and snaking across the floor to its connection at the base of the HOD. His eyes were pinched shut, indicating deep interfacing. A hint of worry played at the edges of his mouth.

"Unlink," Ericho ordered, moving toward his command chair.

Jonomy's eyes flashed open. "You must believe me, I had nothing to do with the airseal problem. Additionally, I did not open the door just now."

"Unlink, Jonomy. Then we'll talk."

"There is a subtle and deep deception at work here, a shrewd intelligence that is attempting to convince you that I am the cause of our troubles."

Ericho tried another approach. "You've been umbilically connected more than thirty hours. That puts you in the danger zone regarding neurological health."

"I remain functional."

"You need a break. You even look tired." Ericho wasn't making that part up. Jonomy had bags under his eyes. His shoulders drooped and he was scrunched awkwardly in the chair.

The starboard airseal whisked open. Rigel stormed in. Boots cracked against the deck and shieldsuit motors hummed, disrupting the bridge's tranquility. His right glove gripped the

Higgs cutter. He raised it in a threatening manner.

"Last chance," Ericho warned. "Unlink."

"If I do, we could suffer a terrible fate."

"Quit stalling," Rigel growled, aiming the cutter at the umbilical. "I swear, I'll cut the damn thing."

"Our only chance for survival is for you to listen to what I have to say. Please hear me out. After that, should you believe I am being untruthful, you can always follow your original intentions."

"You've got twenty seconds," Ericho said, wary that Jonomy was stalling for time in the hope that the Sentinel would be awakened. He reached his command chair and toggled through the wafer, looking for any signs that a warrior pup had been activated.

Nothing suspicious jumped out at him. Then again, Jonomy might be masking a Sentinel alert and manipulating readout data.

Still, the odds were with them that such was not the case. The extraordinary nature of their situation – a captain and a tech officer at odds with the ship's lytic – likely would give the Sentinel pause. SEN was smart enough to realize that it couldn't know with certainty which side was acting in the best interests of the *Alchemon* and its mission. In all probability it would take a wait-and-see attitude, not responding until the situation achieved clarity.

At least that's what Ericho hoped. He kept a wary eye on the airseals in case his theory was wrong and a warrior pup was about to burst through with carnage in mind.

"Captain, you must believe me. I am trying to combat the real threat here. The *Alchemon* has been invaded. We are being rapidly and systematically assaulted by a highly intelligent alien lifeform."

"You're saying the creature is responsible for what's happening."

"Correct. It is attacking us through our own systems. My presence in the network is enabling me to monitor and circumvent many aspects of this ongoing assault."

"Prove it."

"I cannot, although I can show you a great deal of circumstantial evidence. But ultimately, you must take my word for it. But know this. The invader wants me out of the network. It has engineered a clever series of malfunctions to cast doubt in your minds by painting me as the villain. Ideally, it wants you to sever the umbilical and cause me permanent damage, thus assuring that I can never again link to the ship.

"It caused the various troubles in the containment. It made Alexei's suit go berserk in a way that threw suspicion on me. It created what I now am certain was a mirage – the mystery ship – initially to direct your fears and uncertainties about what was happening away from the *Alchemon*, and later to discredit me by making the vessel vanish at an opportune moment."

"The ship is gone?"

"Only moments ago. Again, an attempt to escalate your suspicions by casting blame on me for its abrupt disappearance."

Ericho scowled. "So you knew there was never a ship out there?"

"I suspected."

"Then why not tell us? Not just about the mirage but all of this?"

"The opportunity never presented itself. By the time I became aware of what was happening, I could not find a safe way of apprising you of the situation without unlinking."

"Could've passed a goddamn note," Rigel growled.

"I could not take the chance of making the invader

suspicious of me. And even unlinking momentarily may have enabled it to lock me out. I have been playing a cat-and-mouse game with it within the network. Until now, I have kept my suspicions discrete from the information flowing through the neural connection."

"A load of crap," Rigel said, taking a menacing step closer to the lytic. One touch of the trigger and the umbilical would be severed.

"I am speaking the truth," Jonomy said, meeting the tech officer's glare. "Answer me this, Rigel. What sort of lifeform did you discover on Sycamore? How do you account for an ancient organism on such a barren world, a planet tortured by ferocious storms and exotic energy transformations? Tell me exactly what it is that you think we brought aboard the *Alchemon*?"

"Got a hunch you're about to tell us."

"Indeed. I have a theory that encompasses what we know. I believe that Sycamore was more than just a random home to this creature, what Lieutenant Donner referred to as the Quad. For lack of a better analogy, I believe the planet has been serving as a maximum-security prison and Bouncy Blue as a kind of organic confinement cell. The Quad was some terrible predatory thing being kept down there because it was too dangerous to be kept anywhere else.

"Long ago, well before the rise of intelligent life on Earth, an advanced civilization must have been at war with this creature. Unable to destroy their enemy, they did the next best thing. They crafted a unique prison and devolved the creature into a less threatening form, an embryonic state of existence. They incarcerated it within Bouncy Blue and banished it to Sycamore."

Jonomy's theory filled in various pieces of the puzzle but Ericho remained skeptical. Rigel could be right and the lytic's tale just the latest move in some clever game, twisting the interpretation of facts to hide his own insanity.

"The imprisonment was meant to be permanent. Sycamore, far from the galactic core, likely was chosen for its barrenness and for those fierce storms, factors making it unlikely to attract the interest of later spacefaring civilizations.

"The jailers even may have created the Sycom strain and left it behind as a biological early-warning system, a way of monitoring any problems with their sophisticated jail cell. Should Bouncy Blue eventually become free of the rock due to millennia of erosion and the Quad possibly gain a means to escape, the spread of the bacteria across the planet's surface might be monitored from a distance and alert the jailers. They could then return to Sycamore and refortify their prison.

"But for whatever reason, that never happened. And then, eons later, humans achieved starflight. We discovered the bacteria and, unaware it was possibly a warning system, enabled the Quad to achieve its freedom. Psychically empowered by proximity to LeaMarsa, it was able to generate the energy storm that freed Bouncy Blue from the rock. That storm also initiated a growth spurt. What must have been a tiny embryonic organism, something so tiny that Faye initially overlooked it, was able to instantaneously advance to its next developmental incarnation, a fetal state.

"Once the creature was away from the inhibiting energy patterns of Sycamore's disruptive ecosphere, which likely functioned to limit its abilities, I believe it began reacquiring many of its former powers."

"Like its ability to defy gravity," Ericho said.

"Yes. And more importantly, an incredible psionic prowess that enabled it, through LeaMarsa, to impact the rest of us. I believe she has been functioning not only as a psionic conveyor but as a kind of superluminal amplifier, enabling the Quad to attack our subconscious minds in various ways. Perhaps this process has been going on even before we reached Sycamore, perhaps even before the *Alchemon* set out. Through her, the creature may even have initiated the chain of events that led to the lieutenant entering the containment lab and taking his own life, and in doing so freeing the creature from its penultimate cage."

"Penultimate cage?" Ericho quizzed.

"The containment is now its final prison. Although the creature can invade many of our systems, while trapped down there I believe that some of its powers remain in check due to superluminal intensity diminishing with distance. If it escapes, it not only will be in closer proximity to the bulk of the network, it could well reach an adult developmental stage and come into possession of additional unknown abilities."

Rigel remained suspicious. "I get that it might have taken over the link robot to be its midwife, help it get born. But why take over the warrior pup?"

"It likely perceived the pup as a potential threat. Clearly, it is able to project superluminal signals into our systems, I suspect using a methodology similar to the way SEN functions. The heightened speed of those impulses allows the creature to overwhelm systems, even ones as sophisticated as ours. In some ways, we might think of the Quad as an organic Sentinel."

Ericho was beginning to accept Jonomy's theory. It seemed to make more sense than the idea of a crazed lytic. Still, he wasn't ready to let down his guard. Jonomy's whole explanation could still be a clever sham.

"What about Alexei and the link robot? Why interfere with our attempt to vacuum the containment when that's precisely what the creature ultimately made happen?"

"I suspect that at the time Alexei was guiding the robot, for some reason the Quad was not ready for the purge. I am at a loss for more specifics."

"Why wouldn't it just take control of the entire containment system?" Rigel wondered. "Why psionically manipulate the lieutenant through LeaMarsa to cause the melt?"

"Even when using its superluminal capabilities to invade and overwhelm a system, the *Alchemon*'s command hierarchy remains a challenge. Robotics and Probes is a Level Four system, more easily circumvented than the containment, which is Level Two.

"But there can be no doubt that the creature is working its way up the hierarchy. It already has penetrated several Level Three systems, including hydroponics and the primary genesis complex."

Ericho still found it hard to believe in such an omnipotent creature. Yet it was equally difficult imagining Jonomy's explanation as the product of insanity.

"There is something else. It has expended inordinate effort accessing data clusters within GEL."

"Makes sense it would want to learn everything it could about us," Ericho said. "Search for weaknesses."

"Yes, but its interest has been much more specific. It has scanned numerous files, many of them quite obscure, relating to population growth and human expansion throughout the galaxy." Jonomy paused. "I fear that this specialized interest does not bode well."

Ericho's lingering doubts were nearly laid to rest. He couldn't have listed every reason why he believed the lytic but there was a cumulative impact to Jonomy's version of events. Nevertheless, one aspect still begged for an explanation.

Rigel beat him to the punch. "What you're saying makes some sense. But how do you explain the fact you're becoming a dreamlounge junkie?"

Jonomy betrayed rare surprise. "June told you."

"Hell yes, she told us."

"I admit I have a problem."

"Ya think?"

"I am not immune to this psionic bombardment. But because of my altered prefrontal cortex, I possess an ability not shared by the rest of you. I can compartmentalize the resultant emotional torments and confine them to specific temporal lobe regions, thus preventing them from influencing behavior. However, I must periodically expunge this storehouse of torments, and have found the best method of mitigation is via the diversions offered by the dreamlounge."

Ericho translated. "You channel your craziness into sex fantasies so that you can maintain normal functioning."

"Succinctly put."

Rigel didn't look satisfied with the explanation. But Ericho had heard enough.

"Put away the Higgs," he ordered.

"You buying this crap?"

"I am. And I think you are too." *And the universe have mercy on us if we're wrong.*

Rigel still looked suspicious. But he lowered and sheathed the weapon.

Ericho turned to Jonomy. "We still need to know what the

creature's doing down there. Did you reprogram that pup to respond only to your commands?"

"I was about to launch it when you and Rigel arrived."

"Do it."

Jonomy nodded and blinked rapidly. "The pup has exited airlock three."

In the HOD, imagery from the pup's forward camera eyes appeared. It drifted aft along the ship's jagged exterior, a mass of structures, channels and protuberances. Electrogs on its outer skin maintained the robot at a level distance of fifteen centimeters above the hull but also restricted its speed. The pup floated toward the stern with agonizing slowness.

"One minute, fifty seconds until it reaches the containment chute."

The intercom came to life. It was June, wondering what was happening. Ericho provided her and Faye with a quick update. He sensed the crewdoc's relief when he explained that Jonomy wasn't the cause of their troubles.

He wished he could feel equally comforted. They may well have stood a better chance against a crazed lytic than the threat represented by the creature.

"You've been sending regular updates to the Corporeal?" Ericho asked.

"At standard intervals," Jonomy said. "However, I could not include my suspicions about the creature without alerting it that I was aware of its plotting."

"A moot point as of now. Better transmit immediately."

Established colony worlds utilized Quiets repeaters to maintain continuous contact. The Lalande 21185 system didn't enjoy that expensive luxury, which meant that any updates were limited by the speed of light and wouldn't reach the solar system for more than eight years. But in the event of a worst-case scenario – the *Alchemon* not making it back – humanity had to be warned.

Jonomy's eyes fluttered as he carried out the command. He frowned.

"The creature is interfering with our external telemetry interface, inhibiting all outgoing communications. Transmission was unsuccessful."

Ericho grimaced. If they didn't return, no one would ever know what happened.

CHAPTER 23

When LeaMarsa was a child, a good cry would often make her feel better. Letting go relieved a surfeit of tensions that had built up. On many occasions back then, her weeping had been due to those mean boys teasing her about her psionic abilities.

LeaMarsa de Host, the freaky ghost.

By the time she'd reached her tweens the taunt had lost potency, at least enough not to send her running home in tears. Nevertheless, such incidents had served as constant reminders of just how different she was, how she'd never been able to develop any real friends. That contributed to an emotional wall isolating her from everyone but her parents.

And then she'd learned of their genetic manipulation and how they'd saddled her with psionic abilities. After that, her parents also had been consigned to the realm of the disavowed. The two people she'd loved and trusted became, like everyone else, the enemy.

By her mid-teens, she was immune to trusting anyone. Even the kindly aunt and uncle who'd taken her in after her parents died in the shuttle crash had been kept at an emotional distance.

Right now, sitting with her back to the wall, trapped in this short corridor outside the natatorium, she wanted nothing more than to cry. Her anger had morphed into a deep sadness from which weeping might provide a short respite.

But tears wouldn't come. Instead, bitterness settled over her, a feeling that no matter what she did there was no way out of her painful existence.

Yet that wasn't true. Her thoughts again contemplated the ultimate form of resolution.

There is a way out. I can follow the path of the lieutenant, end it all.

A hissing noise, behind her. She whirled.

The natatorium airseal had opened. A cloud of swirling white mists poured out into the passage. Overhead fans whirred to life to draw off the cloud. But there was too much of it for the fans to handle.

The fog, warm and moist, swarmed over her. She tried seeing through the mists into the pool. But nothing was visible beyond the first few meters.

She sensed hidden danger within the fog. Still, there was nowhere else for her to go.

Curiosity overcame fear and she entered the natatorium.

CHAPTER 24

Ericho was riveted to the HOD as the pup neared its destination. He estimated another thirty seconds before the diminutive robot reached the containment chute's outer lock.

Jonomy and Rigel were discussing various systems that might be under the creature's control. The tech officer had removed his helmet but remained inside the shieldsuit. Ericho suspected he still harbored suspicions about the lytic's trustworthiness.

"Levels Six, Five and Four are entirely corrupted," Jonomy said. "Since a number of Level Three systems have also been breached, it follows that Level Two penetration cannot be far behind."

"But that would likely awaken the Sentinel," Rigel argued.

"In theory, yes. However, since initially taking over the robot and warrior pup in the containment, the creature has been tiptoeing around SEN, being careful to avoid any direct action that might trigger a Sentinel response. We are dealing with a very shrewd enemy."

"What if it gets control of EAC and opens the airlocks?" Ericho wondered, echoing Faye's earlier fears directed at Jonomy.

"SEN likely would be alerted. Also, such a scenario implies

it is trying to kill us. I am not sure that is its immediate goal. It may want us alive."

"Why?" Rigel wondered.

"Unknown."

"So, what do we do?" Ericho asked. "How do we fight back?"

"Unfortunately, by openly confronting me we have lost a tactical advantage. The creature is now aware of our opposition." Jonomy regarded them with a sharp look. "Keep in mind that it is likely eavesdropping on this very discussion."

The pup reached the containment lock. Extruding a hand-like appendage, it opened the outer hatch, maneuvered into the chute and pulled the hatch shut behind it. A series of dim lumes illuminated the robot's path as it floated through the shadowy tunnel.

"I just thought of something," Rigel said. "The HOD is Level Five. How do we know it's not been compromised? What's to stop the little bastard from feeding us fake imagery, maybe a recording from the GEL archives?"

"Theoretically possible," Jonomy admitted. "However, as of this moment, such is not the case. I am authenticating transmissions into the HOD via a multiplicity of systems, including Level One PAQ. We are not being deceived."

The pup reached the end of the tunnel. It opened the inner lock without any problems and entered the devastated and now airless containment. The ship's strong geonic forces again took hold. The pup, back in a normalized gravitational environment, switched off the slow electrogs and activated its swift maneuvering jets.

"Sensors read lingering radiation, mostly in the gamma range," Jonomy said.

The pup did a three-sixty-degree pan of its surroundings and raised its camera eyes to the ceiling. Ericho registered surprise, not because of anything up there but because of what *wasn't*. The suspended test canisters and their associated appendages that had survived the melt were missing.

"Ripped loose and ejected with the rest of the purge?" Rigel wondered.

"Those items were not part of the debris field," Jonomy said.

The pup finished perusing the containment and drifted through the shattered wall into the lab area. Again, it panned, but this time halted abruptly three-quarters through its rotation.

"What the fuck is *that*?"

Ericho had no idea. It was a robot of some sort, but not a prototype with which he was familiar.

The machine was about a meter high and stood upright in the corner of the lab. It had a slim lower torso widening to an upper spherical body. There was no head. The lower torso tapered into a cone that terminated in a point, the only part of the machine touching the floor. The whole thing reminded Ericho of an impossibly large child's top that wasn't spinning.

A triplet of arms, formed from the appendages taken from the missing canisters, projected from the torso in a triangular configuration. Two of the hands tightly gripped one of those melted chairs that rose from the deck like a crooked stalagmite. The third hand gripped the low-powered Higgs cutter.

"It must have held onto the fused chair to survive the purge," Rigel said.

The missing canisters also had been incorporated into the robot. Mounted on either side just below the torso, they looked like a pair of bulky hip pads. Pieces of the amputated link robot destroyed by the warrior pup also had been cobbled together into the strange creation.

"The prick has been busy," Rigel grumbled. "Nice do-it-yourself project."

The maintenance pup continued panning the lab. Spotting nothing else out of the ordinary, it rotated back to the strange machine.

"So where's the creature," Rigel asked.

Ericho had a pretty good idea. "Jonomy, does that that pup have backscatter x-ray?"

The lytic nodded. The robot took on a greenish hue as the x-ray scan rendered it translucent. Its lower innards appeared to have been assembled with circuitry modules from the link robot. But it was the spherical upper portion that proved Ericho's hunch.

"I'll be damned," Rigel muttered. "Explains how it survived the purge."

"It appears to have matured," Jonomy said.

The creature was squashed within the upper cavity, having grown to twice its original size. It had left behind the infantile development stage appropriate to Faye's nickname and now resembled a young child, perhaps two years old. The elongated face seemed even more skull-like, as if its flesh was an ultra-thin membrane stretched over a bony substructure.

An airseal opened and Faye entered.

"Anything you need me to do?" she asked. "I know I'm not bridge personnel but I can help with whatever you think…"

She trailed off, agape at the image in the HOD.

The creature's sensory organs also had undergone a developmental spurt. The eyes were open and unblinking, the irises a vivid green. The lips were parted enough to reveal upper and lower sets of ivory teeth. Yet despite those human similarities, the face could never be mistaken for a denizen of Earth, especially not with that extra sensory organ. The silvery marble was shiny, almost mirror like.

"Creepy," Faye whispered.

The robot whipped up the hand with the Higgs cutter, took aim at the pup. There was a flash of amber light. The HOD image devolved into a sparkling interference pattern.

"Telemetry and com modules were targeted," Jonomy said. "We've lost contact."

Ericho came to a decision. "OK, I want everyone up here. If we have to make a stand, this is where we'll do it from."

Jonomy tabbed the shipwide speaker. "June, Hardy, LeaMarsa – report to the bridge immediately."

Hardy checked in first. Not surprisingly, he protested the order. Ericho turned him over to Jonomy, who outlined the situation and attempted to convince the science rep that this was the wisest course.

Hardy could barely contain his rage. "I'm in the midst of important work. And I no longer recognize the authority of a captain whose indifference and bungling has turned this mission into nothing short of a disaster!"

The science rep terminated the call.

"Let the asshole rot down there," Rigel said.

Ericho saw no alternative. As long as Hardy remained oblivious to the superluminal storm impacting them, he would be impossible to convince. Physically dragging the science rep up here wasn't an option Ericho wanted to contemplate at the moment.

June came over the intercom but asked that she be allowed to stay in medcenter. Although Alexei's surgery had gone well, the trainee remained in critical condition and could best be monitored in a fully outfitted treatment room.

"I'll be OK," she said. "Medcenter is fairly secure."

"All right. But keep me updated." He turned to Jonomy. "What about LeaMarsa?"

"Unknown. IBD is not reading her position and her wafer is not responding."

"IBD is Level Four," Rigel said. "It's probably compromised."

"As is internal com, which could be preventing us from contacting her."

Ericho voiced the obvious question. "Why stop us from reaching LeaMarsa and not the others?"

"Given her psionic prowess, she likely figures prominently in the invader's plans."

"And just what the hell are those plans?" Rigel asked. "What does this thing want?"

"Clearly, it is trying to take over the *Alchemon*. Presumably, however, that is only an intermediate goal."

Ericho recalled June's description of her recurring nightmare, shared by others, where what they had brought aboard the ship returns with them to the solar system, destroying the world's cities and consuming the population. "It wants to reach Earth and the other worlds of the Corporeal."

"That is the most likely scenario."

And a scenario that couldn't be allowed. For the first time since the tumultuous events of the past few days, Ericho had a clear mandate.

We have to stop it out here.

CHAPTER 25

LeaMarsa slipped through the enveloping white fog and entered the natatorium. The vent fans in the passage were winning the battle, drawing off enough of the mists to enable her to see a few meters. The air was hot and humid, conditions no doubt contributing to the fog.

She eased past the garden and exercise machines and stopped at the edge of the pool. Hundreds of multicolored globules bobbed on the wavering surface, which was black, shiny and opaque. The globules resembled those from the nutriment bath although many were larger, some the size of oranges. A small area not slicked over was alive with clumps of green and violet algae.

Anxiety gripped her. Whatever bizarre metamorphosis was occurring in here she wanted no part of. She retreated toward the airseal. Three steps away, the door whisked shut.

She accessed the manual mechanism, cranked the handle. It froze at two rotations and wouldn't turn further. She tried the intercom.

No response.

The creature was doing this. It was manipulating the *Alchemon*'s systems to trap her in the natatorium.

But why?

She didn't need psionic abilities to realize that the question would be answered all too soon.

CHAPTER 26

"The hatch is opening," Faye whispered.

They all turned to the HOD. Jonomy had set it to display a hull-cam view of the containment's outer airlock.

Ericho, standing beside the scientist and Rigel, was startled by what emerged from the containment chute. Technically, it was neither the makeshift robot nor the exploratory pup whose telemetry and com modules had been disabled.

It was the two units combined.

The robot's pointed leg was deeply embedded in the pup's com-module socket. Together, they formed an awkwardly shaped machine.

"Infrared sensors reveal complex linkages between the pair," Jonomy said. "Not only can the creature build elaborate devices, it can swiftly combine them."

"Anything it *can't* do?" Faye wondered.

They watched spellbound as the pup's electrogs reactivated. The combo robot drifted along the hull, heading slowly for the airlock from which Jonomy had dispatched the pup a short time ago. From there it would have access to the main part of the ship.

"We played right into its hands," Rigel grumbled.

"That would seem to be the case," Jonomy said. "The

creature built the robot to provide a stable platform in which to resist the purge. But the unit lacked effective add-ons for facile navigation in the void."

"Which we conveniently provided by sending in the pup," Ericho said, troubled not only by this latest trick, but by the fact that the creature seemed to be constantly outwitting them.

"We can't let it into the ship," Rigel said, turning to Jonomy. "Did you seal the locks?"

"Yes. For the moment, EAC remains under our control. Should the invader attempt to burn through the lock with its Higgs cutter, the Sentinel likely would respond."

"Let's assume for a moment that it's smart enough not to risk that," Ericho said. "If it can't open the airlock, what's its next move?"

"Might play a waiting game," Rigel suggested. "Even out there it's probably close enough to keep using its superluminals or whatever weird-ass powers it has to keep attacking our systems. All it has to do is sit tight until it gets high enough in the network hierarchy to take over EAC."

Jonomy nodded in agreement.

"How long do you think we have?" Faye asked worriedly.

"Not long," the lytic said. "External airseals are Level Two. I cannot calculate a precise rate of network penetration. A rough estimate would suggest a matter of hours. Perhaps less."

"We can't just sit here," Rigel said, picking up his shieldsuit helmet. "I'm going out there. I'll blast the goddamn thing off the hull."

Ericho shook his head. "It's armed with a cutter."

"So am I."

"You would be at a serious disadvantage," Jonomy said.

"Machine reaction times are faster than human ones."

"Yeah, no shit. But it's better than wandering around the bridge doing nothing. We don't want the little bastard in here with us, now do we?"

"Other options?" Ericho asked.

"I know of none," Jonomy said. "The invader will eventually gain access."

"What about firing up the main engines?" Faye proposed. "A quick burst of acceleration might send it flying off into space."

"Wouldn't work," Rigel said. "With the pup's electrogs, it's as good as locked onto the hull. But there might be another way."

"There is not," Jonomy said, locking gazes with Rigel. "I have reviewed the situation thoroughly. There is no effective means of preventing the robot from entering the ship. I suggest we wait until it is inside. At that juncture, a range of strategies to combat its presence will become available."

"What strategies?" Rigel demanded.

"Considering that the creature is likely eavesdropping on us, I would rather not utter them aloud."

Rigel seemed about to snap a retort but hesitated. When he finally spoke, his voice was tranquil and accommodating.

"Yeah, I guess you're right. That's the best approach."

Ericho wondered if Rigel's polite attitude was veiled sarcasm. But as he gazed back and forth between the tech officer and the lytic, he realized that some form of nonverbal communication was passing between them.

Jonomy has a plan. And Rigel has just figured out what it is. A glance at their stern faces warned him to keep his mouth shut and go with the flow.

"I am attempting to prod SEN into a response," Jonomy said. "I have been continuing to alert and update the Sentinel to our overall situation, explaining that the *Alchemon* is under a form of systematic attack that defies its normal response parameters."

"I doubt that'll work," Rigel said. "If the creature scanned the library, it knows the general criteria for what contingencies are likely to awaken a Sentinel." The tech officer had second thoughts. "Still, can't hurt to try."

Ericho settled back in his chair, puzzled by what Jonomy and Rigel were concealing. Before he could entertain so much as a wild guess, June's troubled countenance appeared on a monitor.

"Alexei's gone!"

Ericho was stunned. "I thought you said his chances for a full recovery were excellent."

"No, that's not what I mean. He's not dead. At least I don't think he is. He's gone from medcenter. I was in the bathroom. When I came out, the treatment room was empty."

"Shouldn't he still be unconscious?"

"He is, as far as I know. The clinician detached his drainage tubes and IV lines. The autobed motored itself out of here with Alexei still on it."

Ericho grimaced. This had to be the work of the creature. "If MED's been compromised, it's penetrated as high as Level Two."

Faye paled. "What does it want with Alexei?"

"And where the hell's it taking him?" Rigel added.

Ericho turned to Jonomy. But something was wrong. His eyes were shut as if he was communing with the ship. Yet his posture was odd. He was slumped forward, his arms crisscrossed and hugging his chest.

In the HOD, the image of the combo robot making its way

toward airlock three disintegrated into savage flickers.

Ericho realized what had happened. Lunging from his chair, he raced through the malfunctioning sphere, the shortest path to the lytic. He grabbed Jonomy by the shoulders and violently shook him.

"Wake up!"

Jonomy's eyes flashed open.

"I am sorry, captain. I experienced a brief sleep event."

He blinked rapidly, a lytic's way of clearing his head. When the rapid eye movement ended, relief crossed Jonomy's face.

"Network status remains stable. The invader was unable to take advantage of the brief interruption."

This time, Ericho thought. But if it happened again…

"You need to separate from the umbilical and close your eyes," June urged from the monitor. "Even a fifteen-minute nap would be restorative."

"In fifteen minutes we may no longer have a ship for me to return to." Jonomy stiffened, as if forcing himself to remain alert. "I am scanning for the autobed."

"How long can Alexei survive away from medcenter?" Faye asked.

"Not long," June said, "not without those tubes and IVs. Thirty minutes, forty-five tops. Beyond that, his system will go into shock."

"No locational feedback from IBD and ICO," the lytic reported. "Those Level Four systems are now being neutralized shipwide. We can no longer determine the whereabouts of any crewmember. Also, the cameras and contamination monitors that Alexei left in the natatorium have stopped functioning."

Ericho accepted the news with a grim nod. If MED had been attacked and overrun, it likely wouldn't be long before the external airseals were lost to their control as well. That meant the creature would be able to enter the main part of the *Alchemon*.

Whatever plan Jonomy and Rigel were keeping between themselves, he hoped it came to fruition soon. In the meantime...

"Rigel, I need you to look for Alexei. When you find him, disable that autobed and get him up here any way you can."

The tech officer nodded and donned his helmet.

"I'm coming with you," Faye said.

"All right, but not like that," Ericho said, gesturing to a floor cabinet that stored a quartet of emergency shieldsuits. "From now on, anyone who leaves the bridge wears one."

Rigel dragged out one of the compacted suits, rotated the expansion tab. As compressed airjets blossomed the suit to its full size, the tech officer began airgapping the separate helmet, disabling transceivers and related circuitry to prevent remote tampering by the creature.

"What if we lose com?" Faye asked, donning the suit while Rigel continued working on the helmet.

"Shouldn't be a problem," the tech officer said. "I've switched to a direct RF channel. It doesn't route through the network. The downside is that I need to keep the bandwidth ultra-narrow. That means no video, audio only. Still, we should be able to keep talking to one another and with the bridge."

"Stick together," Ericho instructed. "If you lose contact with us, continue searching until you find Alexei. And if you come across Hardy and LeaMarsa, try to convince them to come up here as well."

Rigel finished modifying the helmet and handed it to Faye. She donned it and the two of them exited. Ericho returned his attention to the crewdoc.

"With MED compromised, you're no longer safe down there."

"I'll be fine."

"No arguments, June. I want you up here. Gather whatever supplies you need to treat and stabilize Alexei once we find him. And get into a shieldsuit." He paused. "Any chance you know how to do those suit modifications for airgapping?"

"Sorry, no."

"I can talk her through it," Rigel said over the intercom.

Ericho returned his attention to the HOD. The combo robot had reached airlock three. It halted beside the entrance and extended its three arms toward the manual opening mechanism adjacent to the lock. But by Jonomy sealing the external airseals, the handle refused to wind.

"It is stymied for the moment," Jonomy said. "It has yet to gain control of EAC."

Only a matter of time, Ericho thought, imagining the creature's superluminals flooding their systems, penetrating ever higher in the *Alchemon*'s hierarchy.

"Isn't there anything we can do?" he asked, aware that desperation had crept into his voice.

"Not unless the invader makes some gross mistake," Jonomy replied.

In the HOD, the combo robot moved, centered itself directly over the hatch. Ericho had the impression it was studying the problem, perhaps considering other ways of opening the airlock rather than waiting to overwhelm EAC.

"It has just made that mistake," Jonomy announced with a hint of triumph.

The hinged airseal snapped violently open, slammed the

combo robot with enough force to break the electrogs grip on the hull. The machine tumbled away from the *Alchemon*.

Ericho understood in a flash what Jonomy had done. By drastically increasing the airlock's internal pressure and then opening the hatch at the right moment, the explosive discharge had knocked the robot off the ship and into the void.

"My apologies for not revealing my intentions," Jonomy said. "I could not risk doing so with the invader presumably eavesdropping."

"No apologies necessary," Ericho said, acknowledging the first sense of relief he'd felt in days.

But the feeling was short-lived. In the HOD, the pup's jets fired. A series of synchronized thrusts halted the combo robot's wild tumbling.

"The robot has stabilized its position," Jonomy said. "It is holding at one hundred and twenty meters off the port hull."

The jets fired again, this time in unison. The robot propelled itself back toward the ship.

"Do something," Ericho urged.

"This move was anticipated."

A faint high-pitched squeal echoed across the bridge. It was followed by a swift breeze and an odd sensation that one side of Ericho's body was momentarily heavier.

He knew what those events signified. The squeal was a unique reverberation through the hull caused by dozens of the *Alchemon*'s maneuvering thrusters igniting in unison. The breeze and heaviness sensation was a side effect of that simultaneous discharge as the ship's geonic stabilizers attempted to adjust to an unanticipated directional change.

"We are moving away from the combo robot," Jonomy said. "Our lateral acceleration will keep us at a safe distance. The robot's fuel supply will expire in twenty seconds. Inertia will keep it in our gravitational field for a time but eventually it will drift away."

The combo robot stopped firing its jets. The creature must have performed the same computations, realized that basic physics were against it and a return to the ship impossible.

"It is conserving the remainder of its fuel," Jonomy said. "But that tactic will not help. It will be unable to close the gap."

"Good work. Now turn the ship, a ninety degree axial change. Put the robot at our stern."

"For what purpose?"

"A full-power blast with all four engines."

"Incinerate the little prick!" Rigel barked over the intercom.

At such close range, firing Bono, Beyoncé, Mick and Celine in unison would output more than enough energy to do the job.

Jonomy hesitated. "That action would use a significant amount of our nucleonic fuel reserves."

"I don't care," Ericho said. "I want that thing burned to a crisp."

"Given the invader's capacity for surviving extremely hostile environments, even such thermal distress may not result in its demise."

"Maybe not. But that doesn't apply to the combo robot."

The machine would be reduced to a liquefied mass. Even if the creature could withstand a temperature spike of thirty thousand degrees Kelvin from being caught in the wake of four nucleonic engines and subsequently survive in a vacuum, perhaps by devolving back into its earlier embryonic state, it would be stranded out here, far from Earth and the settled planets.

Jonomy closed his eyes to carry out the task. But immediately, the high-pitched whine of a SEN alert filled the bridge.

"What now?" Ericho wondered.

"My attempt to turn the ship is threatening to awaken the Sentinel. I have had to rescind the instruction."

The alarm went silent.

"What's the problem?" Ericho demanded. "Why is SEN reacting to a navigational change?"

"A safety issue. SOP has been sabotaged."

Ericho grimaced. Secondary operating power was the reserve battery banks. It was the second Level Two system after MED that apparently had been compromised.

"The sabotage was performed in such a subtle way that standard trouble warnings were not transmitted. I only learned of it through SEN, and only then as a precursive alert, which means it did not rise to the level of full Sentinel activation. With SOP nonfunctional, we are reliant on Level One primary operating power."

"But POP isn't affected, right?"

"Correct. However, the *Alchemon* is programmed to treat the loss of such an important backup system like SOP as a critical event. In this case, the network has automatically defaulted to its most restrictive energy-conservation mode. When I tried to override that programming, the Sentinel was alerted."

"You're saying there's no way for us to turn the ship?"

"NAV remains functional for priority operations. However, according to the ship's logic, using the engines to incinerate a robotic entity does not rise to that standard."

Not for the first time in his career, Ericho longed for a master switch he could throw that would return full control of a vessel to its captain. As a kid he'd read stories from a time when brave mariners sailed Earth's oceans without so much as the simplest nanoprocessor to rely on. Artificial intelligences certainly were necessary to carry out the complex tasks of contemporary starflight. But the downside to that control was that it allowed the *Alchemon* to be manipulated by a shrewd enemy.

Jonomy yawned.

"That's it, you've got to take a break," Ericho ordered. "You need to unlink."

"I cannot take the chance."

"Fifteen minutes," June urged from the monitor. She was still in medcenter, in the process of donning a shieldsuit. But she paused long enough to adopt her sternest physician's face and launch into a lecture.

"Jonomy, you've probably been slipping in and out of microsleep without even realizing it. Are you aware of what happened to the lytic on the *Bountiful Nomad*?"

"I am."

"Then you must realize that you could cause us as many problems as the creature. You're probably not even aware of how much your functioning has degraded, how much less alert you are."

Ericho drove the point home. "Sooner or later you're going to overlook something important, make a critical mistake. We have a better chance of coming through this if you're at a hundred percent."

"The invader could gain a tactical advantage during my absence."

"Right now it's trapped outside the ship with no way to get back in. The only way that changes is if it starts taking over Level One systems. But then it has to confront the Sentinel. Either way, I think we can risk your being unlinked for a brief period."

"You need a break," June insisted. "Do it!"

Jonomy yawned again. But this one was followed by a grimace of self-realization. "Point taken."

He blinked his eyes erratically, part of his unique withdrawal routine. Grasping the end of the umbilical, he twisted it. The cable snapped from its recep, exposing a depression in the lytic's forehead. A pewter-colored metallic disk slid into place to cover the opening.

Jonomy stood and did a quick stretching routine. "Wake me in thirteen minutes."

"The manual says fifteen," June countered.

"That is an average. I know my own metabolism. Thirteen minutes is all I need to return to full functionality."

As Jonomy continued to stretch, Ericho noted something odd. The lytic was staring intently at the umbilical, as if unable to divert his attention from the device that linked him to the uber mind of the *Alchemon*. Ericho had heard of rare cases where lytics connected for long stretches suffered withdrawal symptoms similar to those endured by habitual drug users.

But Jonomy was made of sterner stuff. Turning away from the umbilical, he lay on the deck near the HOD and folded his arms across his chest.

"Captain, in my absence you will need to monitor all systems. The creature is physically distanced but its superluminal ability to attack us likely remains unencumbered."

"Enough stalling," June said. "Go to sleep."

Jonomy gave the metallic forehead disk a series of erratic taps with his finger. The taps were meaningful, Ericho knew. Lytics had personalized cryptograms that they used to access specific cerebral areas. Jonomy had just triggered an autosleep mode and instructed his internal timeclock to rouse him in thirteen minutes.

His eyes fell shut. A fleshy curtain eerily slithered down across the disk like a third eye closing.

Rigel came over the intercom. "Faye and I are almost finished sweeping updeck. No sign of anyone. We're heading down. I planted sensors at the elevators in case the autobed, Hardy or LeaMarsa double back on us. The sensors are linked directly to my suit."

"Any problem with stubborn doors?"

By now, all the internal airseals were likely under the creature's control. It could hinder their search by not permitting them to open.

"Not so far," Rigel said. "But if one of them fails to cooperate, I'll cut through."

Ericho wondered if Rigel's threat was the reason that the creature, presumably eavesdropping and knowing their every move in advance, wasn't interfering with the search. But the more he considered the possibility, the more doubtful it sounded. For reasons unknown, the creature either wanted the ship to remain accessible or simply didn't care if they were able to move around at will.

"Keep me updated. Bridge out."

He activated a shipwide status report and watched pages of data stream across a set of wall monitors. All critical systems remained green. Occasionally, he looked away from the monitors to check the image in the HOD. The combo robot, still in thrall to the *Alchemon*'s geonic field, exuded innocence, belying the threat it continued to pose.

CHAPTER 27

LeaMarsa sat scrunched against the wall near the natatorium airseal. The white mists continued to swirl around her. Her clothes, drenched from the steaming environment, clung to her flesh. She'd made several more attempts to open the door and contact the bridge, all to no avail.

Her thoughts again turned to a solution to the predicament that was her life, the path chosen by the lieutenant. If she killed herself, her psychic torments and the threat of the reek would end.

But I don't want to die.

She was hit by a fresh wave of anger at her parents, who had so callously manipulated her genome to advance their ambitions. The rage blossomed, threatening to become something raw and uncontrollable.

That she could not allow. On that path the reek waited in ambush.

An immense frustration settled over her. She was physically trapped in this steambath of an environment. She couldn't express the full range of her emotions without unleashing the reek. A bevy of forces seemed to hem her in from all sides, eliminating all viable options.

She recalled her original reason for coming to the

natatorium, to ease tensions by going for a swim. No way was she diving into that unsavory mess. But there was an alternative – the exercise machines, their frameworks of handles, springs, pedals and pumps dimly visible in the white fog.

She made her way to the nearest mechanical octopi. A holo logo formed above it as she approached, the letters *I* and *A* encased in a sphere. The exercise machines were manufactured by one of the oldest of the megas, Infinite Amazons.

A welcome screen offered an array of workout choices. She selected a simple bench-press program to be performed while jogging on an inclined treadmill. Positioning her feet and lowering the weight handles, she reached for the activator button.

A draft touched the back of her neck. She whirled around.

The natatorium door had opened. Drifting silently through the portal was an autobed bearing a patient, Alexei. He was cloaked in a white sheet, his head swaddled in bandages. A mask covered his mouth and nose, the sacs pulsing as he drew shallow breaths.

LeaMarsa was so startled that she didn't even think to dash for the open door behind the autobed. The idea proved moot anyway. The airseal immediately snapped shut.

Alexei floated past her, looking strangely peaceful. She wondered how he'd been injured and what other significant events had occurred since her entrapment.

She followed the autobed through the fog. It reached the edge of the pool and kept right on going. Jets on its underside created tiny whorls on the polluted surface as it floated out over the liquid.

The bed reached the middle of the pool, halted above one of the spots resembling an oil slick. A rectangular depression formed on the gleaming surface, slightly larger than the bed's dimensions. Seemingly in defiance of physical laws, the water didn't flood in from all sides. Instead, the rectangular hole grew deeper.

LeaMarsa recalled an elementary school class, a virtual teacher showing them snippets of life in the Helio Age, including a graveyard burial. The teacher had explained that prior to the modern technique of deceased loved ones being reconstituted into mementos, interment had been a means of body disposal.

A coffin had been suspended above a hole in the dirt, similar to the way the autobed was now positioned over the depression in the pool. Her classmates had giggled at the idea of a lifeless human sealed in a luxurious container for preservation. But LeaMarsa had found the ritual unsettling.

The autobed's vertical jets gradually extinguished, dropping the autobed into the waiting hole. Alexei disappeared from view.

The surface grew agitated. More giant globules erupted and skid across the surface like billiard balls, beelining toward the hole. Some of the larger ones dragged flagella-like tails that cracked noisily against the liquid.

The globules poured into the hole, filling it. The pool's surface swept in from all sides. Within seconds, the aqueous lid had erased all traces of Alexei's entombment.

CHAPTER 28

Some individuals looked comfortable in shieldsuits. June wasn't one of them. Ericho watched as she walked onto the bridge with awkward strides.

"How are you holding up?" she asked.

"I'm fine. No change with the ship."

As far as I can tell, he added silently, wishing Jonomy would awaken. The lytic remained flat on his back, only halfway through his thirteen-minute sleep cycle.

June stared into the HOD. The combo robot continued to float serenely in the void.

"Why do you think it took Alexei?" she asked.

"Doesn't matter. We're going to find him, get him back."

Their eyes met. She knew Ericho was projecting a confidence he didn't feel.

"Shouldn't you be following your own advice?" she asked.

"Which is?"

"The rest of us are wearing shieldsuits."

"I'll put one on as soon as Jonomy's awake."

Rigel came over the intercom. "Faye and I have covered half of downdeck. We're at the port storage pod. No sign of Hardy."

That the science rep had abandoned his makeshift lab was odd, considering how vociferously he'd insisted on staying there.

"He wasn't in his cabin or the main social room either," Faye added. "We're heading for the natatorium next."

June unfastened her suit's thick utility belt, which she'd crammed with medical gear, and let it fall to the floor. She contorted her shieldsuit into a sitting position and assumed the lieutenant's chair. Worry was etched across her face.

"We'll find Alexei," Ericho promised.

A non-critical alarm sounded, a series of rhythmic beeps. Ericho swiped through pages on his wafer to track down the cause. It was frustrating having to perform such a task manually. Jonomy would have honed in on the trouble in milliseconds.

"Downdeck, port lander hold," he uttered. "Some sort of power surge."

"What does that mean?" June asked.

"I don't know." He kept working the screen, trying to pinpoint the issue. "Looks like something to do with the electrical feed to the lander interface system." He hoped it was just another routine malfunction and not some new mode of attack. "I can't track the event any deeper. LIS is Level Four. The creature must be blocking access."

Onscreen, a pulsing event light went from yellow to green, indicating the power surge had ended. But Ericho had an uneasy feeling that something noteworthy had occurred.

He reviewed the incident for Rigel. "Any ideas?"

"What was the strength and duration?"

He couldn't get any readings directly from LIS. But primary power was Level One and not yet under the creature's control. It took him half a minute to locate the relevant numbers.

"Fifteen kilowatts. Duration, twelve seconds."

"That just about what you'd need to prep the lander's power systems for a launch," Rigel said.

Erich grasped the significance. "It's going to send out its own rescue mission!"

"With the lander on autopilot," Rigel added. "Goddamn, I should have thought of that."

They'd all missed it, even Jonomy. Lack of sleep was taking its toll everywhere.

"Rigel, what's your location?"

"We were approaching the natatorium but just made a U-turn. We've got to stop that lander."

In the HOD, nothing appeared to have changed. The combo robot remained isolated in space, still caught in the ship's geonic field. But if the lander was launched, it could scoop up the robot and transport it back to the ship.

Two more warning lights appeared. This time Ericho quickly accessed the relevant subsystem.

"The lander hold has depressurized and the outer hatch is opening. Hurry!"

"Almost there," Rigel barked, his voice strained. He and Faye no doubt were running hard, pushing their amped-up suits to the limit.

"How will they stop it?" June wondered.

The intercom remained silent. Rigel would be formulating a plan. But he wasn't going to risk talking about it.

A new worry touched Ericho – the second lander. The tech officer likely had considered the possibility as well. But Rigel couldn't be in two places at once. And Faye lacked the expertise to incapacitate a craft on her own.

"We're in the port hold airlock," Rigel said. "Equalizing pressure. Ten seconds and we're in."

"Hurry," Ericho whispered.

"Pressure at zero. Inner door opening."

Ericho scanned for power surges in the second lander hold, was relieved to discover none. A troubling thought occurred.

This is too easy.

The creature presumably had control of internal airseals, which were under the command of a Level Five system. Why hadn't it hindered Rigel and Faye's movement through the ship, considering they might stop the launch? The creature could have slowed them down, made their task impossible. Or, achieved the same goal by powering up the two landers simultaneously.

"Rigel's firing the Higgs," Faye reported. "He's burning out the external nav sensors."

It's what Ericho would have done. The lander could still launch. But lacking navigational capacity, it would do little more than float in space. In the event they needed it again, the damage was repairable.

"You have to knock out the other one too," Ericho said.

"Our next stop."

"A couple more sensors to go," Faye said. There was a long pause. "OK, he's down to the last one."

Ericho kept waiting for the other hold to register an identical power surge. That it remained green filled him with foreboding. What were they overlooking?

"Nav system is toast," Rigel said.

"What's *that*?" Faye asked, a quiver in her voice. "Something moved, behind the supply cabinet."

There was a moment of silence. Ericho hunched forward in the chair. "What's happening?"

"Oh my god, it's inside!"

"What's inside?" he demanded.

No response.

"Rigel, Faye! Can you hear me?"

"The combo robot!" Rigel yelled. "Goddamn thing's in here with us!"

Ericho whipped his gaze back to the HOD. The robot outside the ship hadn't moved. It couldn't be two places at once.

"Look out!"

Faye let out a shriek. More agonizing silence followed before the tech officer came back online.

"The robot was hiding. It must have entered the hold when the hatch opened. Just flew past us like a bat out of hell."

"It's in the inner airlock," Faye added. "As soon as the lock repressurizes, it'll have access to the ship."

Tricked again. Ericho glared at the HOD, realizing he must be looking at a false image used to disguise the robot's movements. Somehow, it had returned to the hull and entered the lander hold.

"What now?" Faye asked.

"Try following it."

"What about Alexei?" Rigel asked.

"Something tells me it'll lead you to him."

Ericho checked the clock. Jonomy would awaken shortly. He hoped that a revitalized lytic would be brimming with ideas on how to fight an enemy that seemed beyond the capabilities of a mere ship's captain.

CHAPTER 29

LeaMarsa didn't know how long she'd stood at the edge of the pool, staring out at the spot where Alexei had gone under. She was still shocked at what had happened to the trainee. She wanted to help him but had no idea what to do. Diving in and trying to drag Alexei to the surface seemed sheer folly. Even if he remained alive, the water had assumed the guise of some carnivorous thing, poised to consume anyone challenging its depths.

The white mists grew agitated, disturbed by a change in air currents. Once again, the airseal had opened.

LeaMarsa whirled, squinted to penetrate the ghostly swirls. She heard the door whisk shut behind whatever had slipped into the natatorium.

A silhouette appeared, gaining form as it approached. It was a robot, but of a type unfamiliar to her, as if cobbled together from bits and pieces. The robot floated to within three meters of her and stopped. Its spherical upper body began to glow red, as if the plastiform alloy was being superheated from within.

Tiny cracks appeared on the surface. The cracks intersected, grew larger. The material melted; the sphere split open like some fantastic egg. Liquefied shards spilled to the floor, sizzled as they touched the moist deck.

The diminutive creature within the cracked shell appeared to be a more mature version of Baby Blue. Yet it still bore a youthful appearance, reminding her of a toddler just learning to navigate the world.

It leaped out of the cavity and onto the floor, landing on its feet. The skull-like face gazed up at her with unblinking green eyes. The organ between its mouth and nose bore a mirrorlike sheen.

It waddled a step closer, extended a six-fingered palm. Alien or not, the gesture was universal.

It wanted LeaMarsa to take hold of its hand.

Sentinel Obey. Coalesce and Target. Implement Synchronicity.

The cryptic set of instructions slammed into her, this time fueled by desperate urgency. Nanamistyne, the phantom woman, didn't want LeaMarsa anywhere near the creature, let alone holding hands with it.

Frightened, she backed away, realizing in a jarring instant that she'd come too close to the pool. Teetering on the lip, she flailed her arms wildly, barely kept from tumbling into the foul waters.

The creature took a step back, giving her space. She sensed it had no desire to force her into the pool. But the hand remained extended, urging her to take hold. Whatever it wanted from her involved voluntary cooperation.

She gauged the space on either side of the creature, wondering whether she could move fast enough to sprint around it. But with the natatorium sealed, where would she go?

The creature opened its mouth, attempted to speak. But only faint guttural sounds emerged, like those of a baby still lacking the synaptic connections for speech.

She sensed it didn't want to harm her. Attempting to communicate with it might be important. Besides, what did she have to lose? The angry frustrated existence that was her life?

She drew a deep breath to steady her courage and reached out her hand. The creature's six fingers encircled her palm. Its flesh was warmer than expected but it was the psychic impact that was truly stunning. It was as if a superluminal highway had opened, allowing impulses to flow freely between them. Her attention was instantly drawn to the creature's extra sensory organ. She found herself staring into that mirrorlike marble, hypnotically entranced.

And suddenly she was *inside* the sensory organ, staring out at herself, a sad-looking figure at the edge of the pool.

LeaMarsa de Host, the freaky ghost. For the first time in her tormented existence, she found herself acknowledging just how well the appellation fit. Seeing herself from this perspective induced the feeling that she *was* freaky, a psionic misfit, a warped genejob in a world of so-called normal people. She *was* a ghost, a tormented spectral presence drifting through life, unable to connect with others in any deep and fundamental way.

LeaMarsa de Host, the freaky ghost. The phrase no longer felt hurtful. It was simply a statement of fact. Deep down, she perceived herself in exactly those terms.

The natatorium disappeared. She found herself afloat in a place definable only by what it lacked. It possessed neither the tangibility of the physical universe nor the contours of neurospace. It was neither light nor dark. There were no sounds, no smells, no sensations of taste or touch; it was completely devoid of sensory input. It felt like death but wasn't death. Instead, she recognized it as a kind of protected habitat, a psychic sanctuary deep within the very embodiment of the creature, a preview of what it offered.

She could no longer feel the lurking presence of the reek.

Relief washed through her. She felt a lightness of being, as if a heavy burden had been lifted. Or perhaps more accurately, the burden remained but had been rendered weightless, its soul-crushing effects impotent within this sanctuary.

Not only had the reek disappeared but all the angers and pains and frustrations of her tormented life were gone as well. She felt giddy, overcome by a feeling of pure joy. That she felt so alive in a place where sensory input and connection to the real world was nullified didn't matter.

I'm free.

The creature released her hand. The nothingness vanished. She was back in the natatorium, back in her body, back in the realm of sensory engagement. She felt warm moist air on her skin from the omnipresent fog.

That glorious lightness was gone. Again, she felt the reek within her subliminal depths, ever poised to invade consciousness should she drop her guard. She acknowledged a desperate longing to return to the place where the reek and her other pains held no sway.

She thrust her palm toward the creature, her whole body aching for reconnection.

A flash of light pierced the fog, followed by a sputtering sound of incinerating metal. The disturbance momentarily swept the mists from the airseal.

A Higgs cutter. Someone was burning through the door.

The glowing beam shut off. A large rectangular opening had been cut in the center of the airseal. Rigel's shieldsuited boot kicked in the dislodged section. The heavy clump twirled through the air, clanged against the natatorium floor.

The creature raced past LeaMarsa and leaped out over the pool. There was no splash, just an unpleasant *slurp*, as if the foul liquid had swallowed it whole.

"No," she whispered to the spot where it had gone under. "Please stay."

"LeaMarsa, are you all right?"

Faye's voice was amplified by her shieldsuit's speakers. The scientist was bounding through the hole in the airseal. Rigel was on her heels, lips moving behind his faceplate, on the intercom with someone.

The pair froze as they reached the robot's carcass. Rigel examined the remnants of the spherical upper portion from which the creature had hatched.

"What happened?" Faye asked. "Are you OK?"

LeaMarsa had an urge to describe that brief taste of freedom the creature had enabled her to experience. She wanted to share with someone what it felt like to be emancipated from the reek.

"LeaMarsa, can you hear me? Do you understand what I'm saying?"

Rigel's tone bore none of Faye's gentle concern. "Speak up, woman! Where the hell did that thing go?"

She pointed to the water. "It jumped in."

"Have you seen Alexei?" Faye asked. "He was injured. The creature took control of his autobed and– "

"He's under there too." She described the incident.

Faye shook her head in dismay. "We have to do something."

"You two stay here," Rigel said.

The tech officer lunged forward. Shieldsuit motors hummed

loudly as he picked up speed.

"Rigel, no!"

Faye's protest came too late. Momentum carried Rigel several meters out over the pool before gravity took hold. He landed on the pudding-like surface with a muffled splat. Submerged to the waist and slowly dropping, he twisted around to face them.

"If I'm not back in ten minutes, get the hell out of here."

"Don't do this!" Faye urged.

"Gotta be done."

Those were his last words. The crown of his helmet disappeared beneath the surface, silencing external speakers. Faye's lips mouthed his name over and over. But it was obvious Rigel's intercom was dead as well.

CHAPTER 30

Ericho exchanged worried looks with June as they waited for Faye's next update. Several minutes had passed since Rigel had gone into the pool. All they could do now was hope that the attempt to rescue Alexei succeeded.

Had Ericho been asked, he would have forbidden the tech officer's bold action. But spontaneity divorced from consideration of danger had always been one of Rigel's failings.

Ericho tabbed his shieldsuit intercom. He'd donned the garment moments ago.

"Faye, anything?"

"Still no sign of him." The stress in her voice was palpable.

"Keep monitoring."

The words sounded impotent even as he uttered them. The classic saying about a captain's role and the limitations of command in an ascendant age of cyberlytic humans again coursed through him.

The captain needs to master that the master's not the captain.

Nothing in his experience had prepared him for the troubles impacting the *Alchemon*. Nevertheless, it was his duty to remain strong, not surrender to doubts. The others were counting on him.

Jonomy's internal clock reached the thirteen-minute

mark. His eyes popped open. The fleshy curtain covering his umbilical recep slid upward.

The lytic took note of their distressed faces. "What did I miss?"

Ericho filled him in as Jonomy grabbed the end of the umbilical to relink.

"You should be in a shieldsuit too," June said. The lytic had a special helmet that facilitated such a connection.

"The linkage is awkward. I'd prefer not utilizing it."

Jonomy reconnected without donning the suit. It took him only seconds to come up to speed on network status.

"What can we do to help Rigel?" Ericho asked.

"At this juncture, it would appear he is beyond our capacity to assist."

In the HOD, the combo robot disappeared, leaving only a swath of distant stars.

"I have forced a reset of the systems involved in the invader's deception," Jonomy said. "I should have been aware of this possibility."

"You were tired," June offered.

"An untenable excuse."

"How did the combo robot get back to the ship? I thought it didn't have enough fuel."

"An obvious solution, regrettably overlooked. The link robot manned by Alexei also remained within the ship's geonic field. The invader took control of that robot and utilized it to perform a rescue."

Jonomy switched the HOD's view to a hull camera outside the port lander hold. The link robot floated a few meters away from the hatch. Its emergency harness system, a tangled mess of pitons and cables, tethered it to the *Alchemon*.

"Note the blackened spots on its chest cavity. Those are the locations of its primary batteries."

Ericho nodded. "The creature shorted out the batteries, caused them to explode."

Done in sequence, the inertial thrusts from those tiny explosions had enabled a rendezvous with the combo robot. Had their situation not been so dire, Ericho almost could have admired the cleverness of the ploy.

Jonomy outlined the rest of the scheme. "Linked together, the two robots were able to navigate back to the ship. Powering up the lander was part of the creature's deception, providing what seemed a legitimate reason for opening the hold's outer hatch. The real purpose was not to launch the lander but to allow the combo robot to slip inside."

Faye returned to the intercom. She sounded increasingly desperate.

"Still no sign of them. I can't stand this. I have to do something."

Ericho sensed she was on the verge of attempting a rescue. "Two people are in peril already, Faye. Don't make it three."

"All right. But I'm not leaving here..." She trailed off.

"What is it?"

"I don't know. Something's happening."

CHAPTER 31

LeaMarsa stood with Faye at the edge of the pool, riveted to the violent transformations. The surface had become a constant roil. The large globules with the flagella tails erupted madly from the depths. Some leaped high in the air before falling back into the bubbling muck. Muscular waves broke against the perimeter.

Faye struggled to remain calm and analytical. "This is more than just a cell-culturing medium, a gigantic petri dish run amok."

LeaMarsa had already figured out what the pool was becoming.

"It's an incubator."

"An incubator for what?"

"Isn't it obvious?"

"The creature," Faye whispered. "The transformations are for achieving its next developmental metamorphosis. Maturation into an adult phase."

That was only part of it, LeaMarsa realized. The creature planned a far more radical transformation. She had no idea how she knew such a thing. Perhaps in those glorious moments when their hands had touched, her subconscious mind had absorbed some of its knowledge.

Only one thing mattered now. The creature would soon emerge in its final form. And LeaMarsa would do whatever was necessary to permanently experience its sanctuary, that incredible lightness of being, that freedom from the reek and all her torments.

"Look!" Faye yelled, pointing to the center of the pool.

A rectangular outline took shape beneath the turbulent waters. Moments later, Alexei and the autobed broke the surface. Bed and patient moved slowly toward them, rocking from side to side like a boat in turbulent seas. Had Alexei not been strapped down, he would have been thrown over the side.

The bed reached the pool's edge, grated against the wall. Faye knelt down to secure it.

"Help me!" she urged.

LeaMarsa grabbed one side rail, Faye the other. But before they could pull, the bed rose into the air and cleared the turbulent surface.

"Rigel!"

Faye's shout echoed relief as the tech officer's upper body came into view. He stood on the bottom of this shallow end of the pool, arms stretched skyward like a weightlifter to support Alexei and the heavy autobed from below. Shieldsuit motors whined in protest, pushed to their limits from bearing such weight.

"Grab the bed." His words carried the strain of exertion. He was using muscle power to augment the suit's power modules.

LeaMarsa and Faye gripped the railings from opposite sides and pulled hard, struggling to lift the bed over the pool's lip. The roiling mass fought them, as if not wanting to release its prisoner. Globules with flagella tails leaped across Alexei's unmoving form like marine animals performing at some Helio Age aquatic show.

But suddenly, whatever force was controlling the sludge-like mass seemed to change its mind. Resistance ended. The autobed popped free of the pool. Momentum sent Alexei and his berth shooting past them and disappearing into the fog. Moments later came a muffled *clang* as it slammed to a halt against something solid.

"I cut the bed's servo cabling with the HC," Rigel said, breathing hard. "It won't be doing any more wandering."

"Check on Alexei," Faye ordered.

LeaMarsa dashed into the fog. The bed had come to rest against one of the exercisers. The sheet covering the trainee was sopping wet but none of the pool's organisms clung to him. The mask remained in place over his mouth and nose, the O_2 sacs pulsating gently as he drew shallow breaths.

"He's alive," she said.

"Get back here!" Faye hollered. "I need your help!"

LeaMarsa scurried back to the pool. Rigel remained submerged to his chest. He couldn't extricate himself. No matter how forcefully Faye yanked on his shieldsuit arms, their combined strength wasn't enough to free him.

LeaMarsa knelt beside her, leaned out over the lip to get a two-handed grip on Rigel's elbow.

"On three," Faye said. "One… two…

"Three!"

They pulled with all their might. But nothing happened. They couldn't budge him.

"We need to pull harder," Faye urged.

Rigel shook his head. "It ain't happening. This crap's suddenly like glue."

He drew a sharp breath, winced in pain.

"Goddammit! Son of a bitch!"

"What is it?"

"My right ankle. Something tore through my suit, something sharp. It's ripping into my skin."

LeaMarsa watched the tech officer elevate his gaze to scan the overhead readout within his helmet. His face twisted with agony. He struggled to speak.

"I've got... penetration. Both ankles now. Med panel says... I'm bleeding bad."

"The creature," LeaMarsa whispered, realizing what was happening. Its final transformation would be into a human, the species that had enabled its rebirth. Alexei had been its original choice. But a physically superior specimen had become available.

"Goddamn! Hurts like a motherfucker!"

"Use your HC!" Faye yelled. "Burn it!"

Rigel grunted pained laughter. "Dropped the damn thing when I was trying to lift the autobed."

Faye drew a utility knife from her belt. "I'm coming in. I'm going to cut whatever's holding you."

"No! Won't work. You won't get enough leverage, even with the servos. This crap is too dense. You'll just end up being trapped too."

"We have to do something! We can't just–"

"Shut up for a sec. Just listen, OK?"

"OK."

The pain in Rigel's voice was starker now. His words emerged between clenched teeth.

"I need you to do me a favor. When you get back to Earth, I need you to tell my fiancées something."

Faye shook her head, fighting tears. "You're not giving up! We're getting you out of there."

"Tell them I'm sorry things didn't work out."

"Stop it!" Faye cried. "Stop talking like that! Move your ass! Do it!"

A violent shudder passed through the tech officer. His shieldsuit arms swung wildly, paddling the turbulent sludge. Chunks of the surface ripped loose, cascaded through the air.

Rigel's mouth opened wide, as if to speak. Instead, a spray of blood shot out. It caked the inside of his visor, cloaking his face behind a scarlet curtain.

And then something yanked him under and he was gone. Only swirling ripples on the agitated surface marked his disappearance.

"No!" Faye screamed, the tears rolling down her face. "Rigel, no!"

LeaMarsa should have been equally upset, overwhelmed by grief, or at least some sort of emotion. But she felt nothing. All she could think about was freedom from the reek, the taste of it she'd received.

Faye struggled to regain her composure. "We need to get Alexei out of here."

They ran to the autobed. Faye grabbed the front support rails, LeaMarsa the ones at the rear.

The bed was dead weight with its servo cabling cut, maneuverable only on tiny casters that somehow gained added friction against the damp floor. Even with Faye's shieldsuit doing most of the heavy work, it was slow going as they pulled and shoved Alexei toward the opening cut through the airseal.

The hole was just large enough to get the bed through. Faye strained as she lifted it over the bottom lip. Finally, they made it to the short corridor beyond.

LeaMarsa halted, released her grip on the rails.

"What are you doing?" Faye asked. "Keep pushing."

"This is as far as I go."

"What are you talking about?"

"I'm staying here."

"You can't stay here. What's the matter with you?"

The scientist circled around the bed and came toward her. LeaMarsa backed into the natatorium.

"I'm staying. I don't expect you to understand."

"You're acting crazy."

Maybe I am.

An inner voice warned that she was behaving like one of those Helio Age drug addicts, driven by overwhelming base urges that trumped all forms of emotional and intellectual governance. But the realization made no difference. If she was behaving like an addict, so be it.

When the creature was ready, when it emerged from the pool transformed into its final incarnation, she would be waiting for it.

CHAPTER 32

Ericho refused to believe Rigel was gone. The tech officer was a survivor. Somehow, he would make it through this ordeal. People like Rigel Shaheed didn't die, not like that.

Faye's disembodied voice trembled as she finished her account. "What should I do about LeaMarsa?"

"Let her go," Ericho said, glancing at June who nodded her affirmation. "We need to concentrate on Alexei. Time's running out for him."

It was the right thing to do. If LeaMarsa wanted to remain in the natatorium, so be it.

Yet even as the thought echoed, a sense of foreboding came over him. LeaMarsa had told Faye the pool was becoming an incubator for the creature, some sort of fantastic organic soup enabling it to achieve a final metamorphosis. Whatever emerged from that cauldron had trapped LeaMarsa in the natatorium for a reason. Somehow, the creature needed her to achieve its ultimate goal.

Every fiber of Ericho's being warned that LeaMarsa and the creature together would bring about the prescient future of June and the others' nightmare. The Quad would reach Earth, and from there the other worlds of the Corporeal. Civilization would fall, its cities destroyed, its skyscrapers reduced to rubble. Humanity would die.

He recalled his dream of piloting the lander toward a Barstow that no longer existed. It seemed possible that the dream was yet another illustration of the dark fate awaiting them all.

"The autobed's hard to move, even with my suit," Faye said. "I could use some help."

Ericho didn't need to give the order. June was already racing toward the airseal.

"Be careful," he urged.

She acknowledged his worry with a quick smile and was gone.

"Captain, I am registering a series of Level One power spikes," Jonomy said. "They are emanating from the dreamlounge. One of the pods has been activated. I do not believe it is a false reading caused by the invader. Since Hardy is the only crewmember unaccounted for, it must be him."

It wasn't exactly the best time to go dreamlounging. "Do an interrupt, tell Hardy he has to get to the bridge."

"He is not responding. I tried cutting Level One power to the pod but the secondaries fired up immediately to maintain an uninterrupted circuit."

"Override them."

"I cannot. SOP has been compromised, as have most other Level Two systems. I am tapping into the dreamlounge system."

"What the hell does Hardy think he's doing?"

The question was rhetorical. Jonomy answered anyway.

"He has entered a convoluted pleasure fantasy, one programmed for perpetual repeat. In it, he is being given a Corporeal knighthood amid accolades from the most famous members of the scientific community, both contemporary and historical. Albert Einstein, Charles Darwin and Stephen

Hawking are among those praising him for the monumental discoveries he made on Sycamore."

Ericho wasn't about to go down there and manually snap the science rep out of his imaginary laurels. That would lead to another Hardy Waskov temper tantrum. He had more important concerns.

"Let him have his crazy dream."

The science rep, still oblivious he was a victim of psionic attack, had retreated into an ultimate safe zone, a place where he could deny he was in crisis while simultaneously stroking his colossal ego. The fact that he'd programmed the fantasy for perpetual repeat meant he had no intention of ever leaving the pod.

Eventually, the dreamlounge's safety circuits would recognize that he was in physiological distress from too many hours without hydration, nourishment and sleep. He would be forcibly ejected from his fantasy.

The idea of being ejected from a fantasy resonated with Ericho. For reasons that still eluded him, his thoughts returned to that fractured conversation with LeaMarsa at the Homebound, about her parents being bioresearchers specializing in mitochondrial DNA.

Again, he recalled asking June to unearth more information and put together a file on LeaMarsa. The nonstop battle with the creature had made him forget the request. He vowed to speak to the crewdoc about it as soon as she returned to the bridge.

But why was it so important? An answer seemed to float just beyond the edge of awareness, tantalizing him to rein it in. Before he could do so, Jonomy snared his attention.

"Captain, I have discovered another serious issue."

He sighed. "What now?"

"When the creature was still within the combo robot in the port lander hold, prior to Rigel and Faye's arrival, several minutes of its activity were unaccounted for. Utilizing uncorrupted data from a mélange of systems, I have pieced together the missing timeline. The combo robot entered the maintenance shaft and accessed the Big Three nexus."

Their ticket home. Still, presumably the creature also wanted to reach Earth. Sabotaging SCO, POP and PAQ didn't seem a likely goal.

"I have been unable to ascertain its purpose. As far as I can tell, the *Alchemon* remains in control of all Level One systems. Be that as it may, a half dozen repair pups have gathered at the portal to the nexus site, presumably at the creature's bidding. They appear to be in a holding pattern."

"If they enter the nexus, would the Sentinel awaken?"

"Almost certainly."

Even with SEN's probable response, he didn't like the idea of the pups being that close to the Big Three, ready to take some unknown action. "Anything we can do about it?"

"At the moment, no. I will continue monitoring their presence."

Monitoring their presence. The phrase served to renew the feelings of helplessness that had been gathering in Ericho over these past hours. It seemed that all they ultimately could do was monitor their own impending doom.

CHAPTER 33

LeaMarsa ventured back to the edge of the pool. The violent agitation had ceased and the white mists had disappeared. The water, or what had been water, was nearly motionless. Only an occasional ripple disturbed its serenity.

The multihued globules had vanished, as had the oily sheen and those islands of algae. The surface had taken on a metallic appearance, like a lake of mercury.

A humming sound emanated from behind her. She turned to see a swarm of maintenance pups congregating in the hole Rigel had cut through the airseal. There were twelve of them. They positioned themselves three wide and four high, extruding and intertwining their various specialized appendages to form a makeshift wall. LeaMarsa knew that the wall was meant to keep anyone else from entering the natatorium, and to keep her here in case she changed her mind.

But she had no intention of doing that. She'd made her choice. She would await the rising of her savior from the depths and partake of its offer, liberation from the reek.

CHAPTER 34

"We made it to medcenter in time," June reported over the intercom. "Alexei is stable."

Ericho was relieved. Rigel's bravery hadn't been in vain. A wave of sadness came over him as he thought of his lost friend. He forced himself to repress the emotion. The time for mourning would come later.

Provided there *was* a later.

He didn't like the idea of June and Faye back in medcenter. With the MED system compromised, it was no longer a safe environment.

"You should have brought Alexei up to the bridge."

"If we had, he'd be dead. It was a close call. I couldn't have saved him without a full complement of med gear."

"And what if you again lose control of that gear?"

Faye jumped in. "That shouldn't happen. June is treating Alexei directly. I've cut power and control cables to the clinician and every other automated system down here." Her voice cracked. "And Rigel took care of the autobed."

Ericho wasn't reassured. It was possible they'd overlooked something.

"I still want you up on the bridge. How soon can Alexei be moved?"

"Give us an hour," June said.

"Shoot for half that. And keep me updated."

He turned to Jonomy, who had the look of someone waiting to deliver more bad news.

"Hit me with it."

"I believe the *Alchemon* has experienced its first Level One penetration. A series of subtle alterations have been made to NEL."

"What kind of alterations?"

"Several of the output power modules have been decoupled. I am uncertain as to the reason. It matches no prototype templates for modifications to that system." Jonomy paused. "At least none I have been able to access via GEL."

He didn't need to add that the library was no longer reliable. Although GEL as a whole remained accessible, as did most systems under the creature's control, there was no way to tell whether access to specific data was being blocked or the data rendered erroneous to further the creature's manipulations.

Ericho missed Rigel's presence, not only as a friend but also as someone with valuable engineering expertise. The tech officer knew more about nucleonic engines than many NEL engineers. Rigel might have understood what the engine alterations portended, or at least have a viable theory. And Ericho would have felt more confident knowing Rigel was here, backing him up.

"What about a Sentinel response to the engine alterations?"

"As before, the alterations were not drastic enough to awaken the Sentinel. SEN again issued only a precursive alert."

"Suggestions?"

"None at the moment."

Ericho caught his eye, seeking clues that Jonomy knew more than he was letting on, as when he'd secretly pressurized the airlock and sent the combo robot tumbling into the void. But the lytic gave no indication of concealed trickery. Instead, he looked as lost as Ericho felt.

Jonomy, hyperaware of the reality of their predicament on the most fundamental level, knew more than any of them that control of the ship was spiraling inexorably into the creature's hands.

"All is not hopeless," Jonomy said, sensing Ericho's growing doubts. "The invader still needs to get past SEN. The Sentinel remains a formidable barrier."

But not formidable enough. Ericho didn't dispute that the creature feared the Sentinel – or whatever passed for fear in that monstrous alien consciousness. Yet so far, it had outwitted them on every front. Doubtlessly it had a plan for overcoming SEN as well.

That favorite starship adventure story from childhood again popped into his head. He found himself trying to recall just what the eponymous commander of *Captain Clarke in the Quiets of Doom* had done to save his crew and vessel. Like Ericho, Captain Clarke had been faced with losing it all. Yet somehow in the end he'd triumphed by means of that unorthodox salvation.

Again, those words resonated. *Unorthodox salvation.* It seemed germane somehow to the *Alchemon*'s plight.

The ludicrous nature of what he was doing hit home. *As if recalling such things will save us.*

"Not likely," he muttered, unleashing a bitter laugh. The utterance prompted a concerned look from Jonomy.

Get it together, Ericho. No matter how hopeless their situation, he needed to continue functioning as a captain. The alternative was ugly: becoming like Hardy, spending what might be his final hours lost in a fantasy, perhaps reliving the excitement of a juvenile adventure story that had influenced him toward a career.

Yet despite his efforts to sequester Captain Clarke from awareness and remain focused on their troubles, that phrase continued to demand attention.

Unorthodox salvation.

Those words were important somehow. And so was another idea, one that had occurred to him only moments ago when considering the problem of what to do about a dreamlounging Hardy.

Being ejected from a fantasy.

A frisson touched Ericho. His mind brought together those disparate elements. The fusion of the two concepts – *unorthodox salvation* and *ejecting someone from a fantasy* – seemed on the verge of springboarding him to some new form of understanding.

And then a third clump of information melded into the mix. It was what LeaMarsa had said about her parents being bioresearchers specializing in mitochondrial DNA. His mind raced, on the trail of a connection that had been eluding him since the Homebound.

In a blazing instant, the pieces of the puzzle snapped together.

"Of course!" he exclaimed, almost leaping out of his chair. It all seemed so obvious.

This time, his reaction prompted more than just a concerned look from Jonomy.

"Captain, are you aware that you have been talking to yourself?"

"Thanks for the reminder," he said, forcing calm. He couldn't risk alerting the creature that he may have just come up with a means to fight it.

There was another reason for tempering his excitement. He'd put together a series of hunches and reached a conclusion. Yet that conclusion remained only a theory. Despite his gut telling him he was right, he needed proof before his theory could be upgraded to a viable plan.

For the first time since their crisis had begun, he felt they had a chance. It was clear what he had to do next.

"I'm going to medcenter to check on Alexei."

He powered his shieldsuit toward the port airseal, hoping Jonomy would accept the decision without protest.

"Captain, I believe it is unwise for you to be off the bridge."

"I won't be gone long."

"There is nothing you can accomplish in medcenter. I do not understand your rationale."

Jonomy had a bone and wouldn't let go. Ericho struggled to come up with a convincing reason that wouldn't make their eavesdropping enemy suspicious.

"It's possible we don't have much time left," he said as the airseal whipped open. "I just want to be with June, at least for a little while."

Jonomy's eyes narrowed in disapproval. A captain putting his personal feelings above the good of the mission was inappropriate in normal circumstances. And with the ship in jeopardy things were far from normal. But right now Ericho didn't care what the lytic thought of the lie, only that he accepted it.

"Captain, I strongly suggest that you not vacate your duties for any longer than necessary."

"I'll make it a quickie." He was no expert on Helioteer slang, but he had a vague recollection that the phrase referred to a hurried sexual encounter.

He stepped through the portal, pausing to glance back with what he hoped was a disarming smile. But a new sense of foreboding abruptly came over him.

He had the strangest feeling this was the last time he'd ever see Jonomy.

CHAPTER 35

LeaMarsa couldn't pin down the exact moment the natatorium started to blink.

She'd been listening to the faint hum emanating from that makeshift wall of pups blocking the airseal while staring at the pool's mirror-like surface. She must have entered a kind of dream state when a sharp noise broke the spell. It was one of the pups, quivering and making odd grating sounds. Obviously, some sort of malfunction.

It was then that she realized that *she* was suffering a kind of malfunction as well. The entire room was blinking in and out of existence. For a few seconds, eyesight seemed normal. But then there would be a few moments where the contours of the natatorium disappeared and she found herself gazing into the countless stars of neurospace.

Those ominous dark clusters now enshrouded half of the faux-stars. She sensed it wouldn't be long before the entire realm of luminous dark succumbed to them – or *had* succumbed or *would* succumb. There was no longer any doubt that Baby Blue… the Quad… the Diar-Fahn – was responsible. The creature's gradual resurgence into the physical universe was reawakening its powers in neurospace as well.

The natatorium blinked back into view. At the portal, the

malfunctioning pup exited, making way for a new arrival. The replacement pup assumed the vacated position.

LeaMarsa sensed that the entire ship was nearly under the creature's sway. Soon, the *Alchemon*'s final ramparts would fall.

CHAPTER 36

June looked surprised as Ericho motored his shieldsuit into the medcenter lobby.

"What are you doing here?"

"Where's Faye?"

The crewdoc gestured to the closed door of the treatment room. "She's keeping an eye on Alexei. We disengaged even the basic MED monitors. We're back to practicing medicine like they did in the early Helio Age."

Ericho repeated the lie he'd told Jonomy, added some fresh wrinkles he'd come up with on his way down here.

"We may not have much time left. I don't want to waste precious hours doing useless things, trying to stop something that likely can't be stopped."

She raised an eyebrow. He pressed on.

"I want to make love to you."

Surprise graduated to astonishment. "You want to... right now?"

"Can you think of a better time?"

"Actually, yes I can. After we've gotten through this crisis."

"There's a good chance that's not going to happen. I want every moment to be precious for us from here on out. C'mon."

He took hold of her hand, dragged her toward her office.

"Ericho! You're acting crazy!"

Rigel's safepad was perched on the edge of her desk. *Perfect.* He slammed the door as they entered and locked it.

"I don't want any interruptions," he said, picking up the safepad and smacking it onto the nearest wall.

"I am genuinely flattered. Truly I am." June's words dripped with the sing-song tonal nuances used by therapists attempting to calm individuals suffering from delusions or psychotic breaks. "Remember, we're both wearing shieldsuits for good reason. I don't think it's wise for us to remove them in order to gratify–"

"Sex will have to wait," he interrupted as the safepad's reassuring hum filled the office. They could now talk without the creature eavesdropping.

Gripping her shoulders, he shifted gears as tactfully as possible. "I really would like to make love to you. But right now, we have other priorities."

Confusion flashed across her face. "OK, Captain Solorzano. You've officially lost me."

"Remember when I asked you to look into what LeaMarsa said to me at the Homebound, about her parents being bioresearchers specializing in mitochondrial DNA?"

"Yes."

"Did you?"

Still bewildered by his flip-flopping needs, she gave a wary nod.

"You put together a file?"

"Yes."

"When? This is critical."

"Not long after you asked me about it. Things got pretty crazy after Tomer's suicide and frankly I forgot about it. Let me think… OK, it was right after his funeral."

He nodded in relief. She'd accomplished the task before the creature had gained control of the GEL and MED systems. If not, had it even permitted her to undertake such a search, the information gathered for the file likely would have been deleted or corrupted to prevent any chance of them uncovering the truth.

"Where is the file?"

She pointed to the wafer on her desk.

"And the data is still discrete from MED and the network?"

"Of course. My patient files are in there as well. I never let that information upload, not until I make my end-of-mission report when we're back in lunar orbit."

Ericho was thankful she practiced such MED safeguards. Once such information was dumped into the *Alchemon*, it would be automatically relayed into the Inet-29 upon their return through the Quiets. June always gave herself the option of double-checking patient data before allowing it to join the permanent record. But right now, all that was important was that she hadn't uploaded the file on LeaMarsa, which meant the creature didn't know it existed.

He huddled beside her as she opened the document. As he'd requested, it was comprehensive, with more than three hundred pages of data and written reports. He scanned the various subheadings. Some of the information was from LeaMarsa's early years and included school summaries from teachers and guidance mentors as well as basic OTTO transcripts of the sort done on every Corporeal citizen. The majority of the file appeared to have originated from the psionic's two-month stay at Jamal Labs.

"Care to tell me what this is all about?" June asked.

"I don't believe we can beat this creature by fighting it directly. But there may be another way."

"OK, so what exactly are you looking for?"

"First off, I'm trying to confirm a suspicion, that LeaMarsa is a genejob."

"I could have told you that. Of course, technically, if I had, it would have been a medical ethics violation." She sighed. "I've been guilty of more than a few of those lately. Even when I put this file together for you, I included some privileged information, things that LeaMarsa only revealed during psych analysis. Frankly, I don't even know why I did that."

"Maybe deep down you sensed it was important too."

"Maybe." She navigated to the appropriate page and highlighted several paragraphs. "Right there."

Ericho scanned the information, which had come from a DNA analysis of LeaMarsa by the Jamal researchers. The results confirmed his initial suspicion and made the rest of his theory feasible.

"Listen to this," he said, reading aloud. "LeaMarsa de Host's mitochondrial DNA was found to contain the genetic material of twenty-nine individuals. Those individuals have been genomically identified and confirmed as possessing high-order psionic abilities, divided among projectors, receptors and conveyors."

He faced June. "It had to have been her parents who injected that DNA into her embryo, right?"

"I doubt it could have happened any other way. I believe they were trying to create a superluminal transhuman."

"I think they succeeded."

Sadness touched the crewdoc. "The poor girl. Most parents who undertake major genome manipulation do so for fairly benign reasons, or at least they rationalize that they're benign. Still, the purpose is usually to give their offspring a better shot in life. But what LeaMarsa's parents did, using their own child as a science experiment…" She shook her head. "It was immoral and downright cruel."

"No argument. And keep that in mind when you listen to this next part," he said, quoting another passage of the Jamal report.

"LeaMarsa frequently inflicts bodily harm on herself, including but not limited to episodes of self-flagellation. It is apparent that this is done not as a form of sexual masochism but as an analgesic for constraining a specific psychological torment of an unknown source and nature."

June shrugged. "I told you about that the other day. She calls it the reek. It's a pain she's fought against most of her life."

Ericho played devil's advocate. He needed to eliminate the most obvious source of that pain to prove the validity of his theory.

"Could this torment be caused by her parents not loving her unconditionally? That she was more important to them as a science experiment?"

"No doubt there's some truth in that. Certainly, cold parenting can produce a residue of lifelong primal pains. Still, my gut tells me that this reek has another origin, an incident or series of incidents that induced a far deeper level of distress. Something happened to her. Something very bad."

"And you said she's never talked about it."

"All I know is that whatever the reek's source, it scares the hell out of her. I believe she'd do almost anything to be free of it. She possesses all the OTTO indicators of the classic misunderstood outsider. Her extreme psionic abilities set her apart socially from an early age. Her parents contributed to her isolation by constructing a home environment that stressed training her to apply those abilities."

"But they died when she was still a teen."

"Yes, at age thirteen. Still, in cases like these, where there's extreme parental micromanagement in the earliest years, it's common for the child to later suffer a range of neurotic and often self-destructive behaviors."

Another section of the report caught Ericho's eye. "It says here that LeaMarsa suffers occasional losses of consciousness while still wide awake, a condition the researchers call psychic blackouts." He turned to June with a questioning gaze.

"As with the reek, I couldn't get her to discuss this during our sessions. And I gather that no one else ever got her to open up about it either. However, I came across some studies done on other powerful psychics who suffer similar blackouts. And some of them *have* talked about it. They claim that during these blackouts, they literally journey to some sort of other dimension."

Ericho scanned the remainder of the Jamal report, looking for more information about the reek. But there was nothing further to either prove or disprove his theory. Certainly one or more of the researchers must have had the same suspicions and arrived at the same conclusion.

A solution to that mystery was suddenly obvious.

"They left it out on purpose," he whispered.

"Left what out?"

"The source of LeaMarsa's 'psychological pains of an unknown source and nature.' The Jamal researchers must have deleted it from their final report."

Had they included such an outlandish and unprovable

theory, the researchers' entire rigorous analysis of the psionic would have been tarnished. Besides that, they were Pannis employees. No matter how well trained in objective reasoning, they would have known that the ultimate purpose of examining LeaMarsa was to enable the mega to utilize her abilities. They'd adhered, perhaps unconsciously, to a fundamental precept of social research: conclusions tend to be biased toward the belief system of whatever organization, agency or individual is funding the research.

Ericho tried another tack to verify his theory. "OK, even before LeaMarsa went to Jamal, she must have known she was a genejob, right?"

"Of course. She told the researchers as much when she arrived."

"Then we have to go back to when she first learned about it. Is her full bio included here?"

"It is." The crewdoc hesitated. "But I still don't get what you're looking for. In light of our situation, what possible relevance could any of this have?"

"Trust me."

June accessed the appropriate pages. Ericho scanned LeaMarsa's timeline, starting with her earliest years and stopping when her parents died in the shuttle crash along with forty other passengers and crew. They'd been taking off from Rodan, the giant mining colony near the lunar south pole, intending to rendezvous at one of the orbital stations for transfer to an Earthbound vessel. In a matter of days, mother, father and daughter would have been reunited.

"It has to be here somewhere," he said.

"What does?"

He kept scanning. And then, as abruptly as he'd connected

the pieces of the puzzle on the bridge, he found his proof.

"Look!"

She followed his pointing finger, silently read the paragraphs. They were from a required school report LeaMarsa had composed at age thirteen. The assignment had been for students to discuss plans for their futures. With her parents recently deceased, LeaMarsa's report blazed with bitterness.

"Not surprising how angry and resentful she'd be under those circumstances," June said, still not making the connection.

"Look again," he urged. "The section where she's talking about mitochondrials, discovering that her parents injected them into her embryo."

"I read all this a while back. It's so sad. And it's perfectly understandable why she'd be so angry. What they did to her in utero was unforgivable."

June still wasn't seeing it. He highlighted a sentence in the middle of the paragraph. "Right there, the specific date she mentions when she made the discovery. Look at the date! Then look back at that timeline, the date of her parents' deaths."

June's eyes widened with comprehension. "The dates are the same." She shook her head, unwilling to accept where Ericho's thoughts were leading. "No. What you're thinking can't be possible."

"I think it is. This is the truth she's been hiding from the world, and more importantly, from herself. This is the origin of the reek, those psychological pains of an unknown source and nature."

"You must be mistaken."

Ericho couldn't blame June for being skeptical. It was a wild, outlandish theory.

"A week ago, I would have been just as disbelieving. But now, with what we've seen of the creature, with what we know it's capable of, is something like this really all that hard to accept?"

"That those dates are the same could be coincidence. Or a simple mistake. She or someone else could have transposed the numbers."

"You don't really believe that. Remember what you told me days ago, about LeaMarsa being the most powerful psionic projector, literally off the charts in a whole range of psychic indicators?"

He could tell that June's doubts were fading. But she made a final attempt to repudiate his theory. "None of this constitutes proof. You can't be certain."

"But I am, as certain of this as I've been of anything in my life. Call it a psychic hunch. I'm a receptor, remember, caught up like the rest of us in a superluminal storm. You and the others suffer nightmares. My symptoms are different. I get consumed by anger and lash out at Hardy. And I dream about returning to a city that's no longer there.

"But more importantly, I believe that for whatever reason, I've gained real insight into LeaMarsa. I just might be the first person to acknowledge the unvarnished truth about her, see what everyone else over the years either overlooked or dismissed.

"She's being totally driven by these unconscious pains, this reek. It's compelling her to cooperate with the creature. That's why she insisted on staying in the natatorium."

"How can you know that?"

"I can't really explain. But I'm certain that the creature is leading her toward a fate that will result in your nightmare coming true for the entire Corporeal."

"OK, let's say for a moment that I believe you. What can be done about it?"

"Make sure LeaMarsa doesn't go down that road."

"You mean use this against her? Force her to acknowledge the truth about herself?"

"Yes."

"That won't be easy. Even if you're right, she's had years to erect psychological barriers against such a thing, against acknowledging the source of such a terrible pain. No matter how we put it to her, she'll refuse to believe."

"*We're* not going to put it to her. I am. You're staying here."

June's presence would cause him to worry about her safety, distract him from a dangerous undertaking. This was something Ericho needed to do alone.

"You'll need my help," she argued. "She'll almost certainly go into full-blown denial. What if you can't get through to her?"

He hadn't given that possibility much thought. But in an instant of brutal clarity, he realized that if he couldn't get LeaMarsa to acknowledge the truth about herself, there was only one option.

"If I can't get through to her I'll have to take extreme measures."

This time, June immediately grasped his meaning. Her face paled. "Ericho, you can't. You wouldn't."

But if it came down to LeaMarsa versus the future of humanity, he might have no choice.

I'll have to kill her.

CHAPTER 37

The blinking effect ended. Consciousness stopped ping-ponging between the natatorium and neurospace. For the moment, LeaMarsa existed only as a solitary figure beside the pool.

Her anticipation continued to build. She knew it wouldn't be long before the creature rose from the depths in a form more suitable for their journey back to Earth. It was also clear to her that humanity would suffer for her choice, of accepting what it offered.

So what if the species does suffer? Why should LeaMarsa de Host, the freaky ghost, be concerned about what happens to humanity?

So-called humanity had never been concerned about her.

She knew it was a rationalization, an attempt to make what she was about to do more digestible. Still, in the end, feelings of guilt weren't important. Freedom from the reek was all that mattered.

CHAPTER 38

Ericho headed for the natatorium with only the vaguest notion of how he was going to accomplish his task. He tried not to think about what a longshot it was. He couldn't afford to be overwhelmed by futility.

He concentrated on what needed to be done: persuade LeaMarsa to change her course of action by having her confront the horrific event she'd blotted from her mind. It could be the only way to save the *Alchemon*, not to mention the Corporeal's billions.

Of course, there was the grimmer alternative he'd broached to June. Had Rigel been here, he likely would have urged Ericho to go directly to Plan B, kill LeaMarsa on sight.

Serious hurdles stood in the way of implementing that scenario. First, if the creature even suspected he was trying to end her life, it likely would find a way to terminate him. And even if he survived such an onslaught, a more fundamental impediment would need to be overcome.

Ericho had never killed anyone. He'd never even contemplated such a thing, not really. His earlier rages at Hardy had provided insight as to how one human could carry out such violence against another. But even when caught up in those raw emotions toward the science rep, he'd felt he could never go through with them, that a more rational and fundamental expression of his nature would always win out. Within the sanctity of the virtual, he might perpetrate cold-blooded murder. But here in the real world...

And then there was the fact he bore no animosity toward LeaMarsa, no sense of personal outrage to fuel such an act. No matter what was at stake, to stand before a young woman who was merely a pawn in others' machinations and extinguish her life would require an iciness of purpose he wasn't sure he possessed. And since he carried no Higgs cutter or other serious weapon, killing her would have to be done up-close and personal.

His mind revolted at the mere contemplation of such things. He sought sanctity in more pleasant thoughts, or at least ones that were bittersweet. Upon departing the medcenter moments ago, he'd experienced what might well have been his last conversation with June.

Circumstances dictated that their final words ring untruthful. If the creature was eavesdropping, deception was necessary so that his trek to the natatorium wouldn't be hindered.

"Maybe Rigel's still alive," he'd told June after deactivating the safepad. "It's my duty as captain to make every attempt to save him."

The tech officer was gone. They both knew it.

June had pressed her faceplate against his. It was as much of an intimacy as possible within the confinement of shieldsuits.

"I'm glad we could have this time together," she'd said.

"I'm glad too."

"I do love you, Ericho Solorzano. So, come back to me, OK?"

Those final words performed double duty, reinforcing the charade while bristling with genuine emotion.

Jonomy's voice in his helmet wrenched thoughts back to the here and now.

"Captain, I again suggest you reconsider your course of action and return to the bridge. Even if Rigel somehow survived, he is surely beyond rescue."

"Good advice," Ericho admitted. "But there are some things a captain must do." He changed the subject before the lytic could lodge further protests. "Any updates on our status?"

"Yes. In regard to those subtle alterations made to NEL, the decoupling of those output power modules: the half dozen repair pups that have gathered at the portal of the nexus site were activated. They are making new wiring connections between NEL and SCO. It appears to be an effort to route additional power to the Big Three. Other changes to those systems were made by the earlier incursion by the combo robot. I have not determined a reason for any of these alterations. There are a few scenarios, but none that rise to the level of reasonable probability."

Ericho wondered if Jonomy knew more about what the alterations portended but wasn't comfortable broaching it with the creature likely eavesdropping.

"If you figure things out and believe a specific action is immediately required, don't wait for my OK."

The intercom was silent for a moment. Then…

"Captain, is there anything else you would have me do?"

The words echoed fatalism, a trait Ericho rarely associated with cyberlytic humans. Jonomy sensed that he was likely on a one-way mission.

"Carry on as best you can," Ericho said, breaking the com link.

He reached the corridor outside the pool without incident.

Either the creature had bought into their deception or simply didn't regard him as a viable threat. No roadblocks had been put in his path.

Until now.

Up ahead, a dozen maintenance pups were stacked in the natatorium's entrance, the hole Rigel had cut in the portal. Their appendages were interlocked, forming a three-by-four barrier. Beyond the pups, the fog had dissipated. He could see all the way to the transformed pool. LeaMarsa stood at the edge, a statue in waiting, gazing out over the mirrorlike surface.

He strode to within two paces of the pups and halted. It was clear they weren't going to move to allow him entry. Perhaps Jonomy could have come up with a subtle plan to circumvent the makeshift barrier. But time was running out. Subtle methods were no longer in the playbook.

He powered his shieldsuit forward at breakneck speed, arms extended. His fists caught the two pups in the middle of the formation, easily knocked them out of the way. Swinging his arms right and left, and up and down, he smashed his way through the rest of the robots. A series of reverberating clangs echoed through the air. He punched one of the pups with such fury that it fell to the floor, dead on arrival.

And then he was through. He whirled around, expecting the pups to regroup, perhaps mount a counterattack. Although they weren't weaponized, a swarm of pups smashing into him from all sides might challenge even a shieldsuited man. But other than the ones too damaged to stay aloft, they simply reformed into a new wall. Why they were leaving him alone became clear a moment later.

"Captain, your unprovoked assault has alerted the Sentinel,"

Jonomy said. "It is considering dispatching the warrior pups to the natatorium to address your erratic behavior."

There was nothing to be done about that. He walked past the hulking exercisers, keeping his target in view. LeaMarsa's back remained to him. Either she was unaware of his approach or unconcerned.

"I am attempting to convince the Sentinel that you are acting in the ship's best interests," Jonomy said. "For the moment, it is evaluating. Indications from SEN are that should you retreat from the natatorium, the Sentinel alert would be withdrawn."

Ericho repeated the lie. "I can't do that, not until I know about Rigel. Keep me informed about those warrior pups. Other than that, no interruptions."

He was three paces from LeaMarsa now. She finally turned. Her face appeared vacant, her mind distant.

"You should leave this place," he said, keeping his tone friendly.

Even as he spoke, the pool's mercurial surface began to change. Bubbles erupted from below, disturbing its mirror sheen. Ericho suspected that the final metamorphosis was at hand, the creature's transformation into its ultimate phase.

LeaMarsa stared blankly. If he was to succeed, he needed her emotionally engaged in the here and now. Ideally, that would best be accomplished away from the natatorium. But it seemed implausible she would leave willingly. Even if she wanted to, he was pretty sure the creature wouldn't allow it.

Time was running out. He was caught between two powerful forces, both with hostile intentions. In front of him, the creature would soon emerge from the pool, no doubt deadlier than ever. Behind him, an alerted Sentinel might decide at any moment that the captain was a menace to the ship and dispatch the warrior pups to eliminate the threat.

More forceful tactics were necessary. He steeled himself for what he was about to do.

Now or never.

Lunging forward, he grabbed LeaMarsa's wrist and squeezed hard. Inflicting pain was the fastest way to wrench a person back into the moment.

The ploy worked. Her vacant expression dissolved into a stifled cry. He loosened his iron grip but didn't let go of her.

"Mitochondrials and superluminals. The way you reacted at the Homebound is what first made me suspicious about what you've been hiding from yourself."

She looked flustered. "What are you talking about? I'm not hiding anything."

Indignation colored her words, a volley of denial. Ericho pushed through her defenses.

"You're a genejob, LeaMarsa. Your parents created you as a science experiment. You were thirteen years old and at that boarding school when you found out. It made you angry as hell."

Her eyes widened, surprised that he could know such things. Her denial morphed into a counterstrike.

"June had no right to tell you."

"That doesn't matter. What does matter is that according to the testimony of several of your classmates, you had a psychic blackout at school. You walked out of your room and froze."

"So?"

"The Jamal Labs report indicates it was your first blackout. What I don't understand is why you never questioned the two dates?"

"What two dates?" Her tone was now feigned boredom.

"It's in your own school report, the one you wrote shortly after losing your parents. You mention how you accidentally discovered their genomic manipulation. You dated that incident." He paused to let his next words sink in. "It was the same day your parents died in the shuttle crash."

She frowned then violently shook her head.

"No, those things happened weeks apart. Maybe months."

"That's the lie you've been telling yourself all these years. The reality is, not only were they the same day but likely within minutes of one another."

Her face contorted into terror. Her eyes betrayed an even more haunting emotion, that of a child pleading to be spared from having to face an awful truth.

"The Jamal researchers said you're the most powerful psionic they ever studied, literally off the charts. And like many psionics, you remain unconscious of the extent of your powers."

"Stop it!" she cried, trying to break his grip by wrenching backward, as if to deliberately fall into the pool. He kept hold and yanked her away from the edge. The surface bubbled madly, a boiling cauldron of fracturing mirrors.

Jonomy's alarmed voice filled his helmet.

"Captain, your assault on LeaMarsa has persuaded SEN that you indeed are a threat. Despite the illogic of it, the Sentinel somehow has become convinced that you intend harm to the ship."

The creature didn't need to take control of the Sentinel, Ericho realized. The mystifying alterations to NEL proved that it was now capable of penetrating Level One with impudence. It had learned to feed false information to the *Alchemon*, outwit SEN, trick the ship's ultimate protector into doing its bidding.

"The warrior pups are being activated."

"How long do I have?"

"Less than a minute."

"Let me go!" LeaMarsa hollered, trying to escape by twisting her arm.

"Not until you face the truth."

"What truth!"

"I scanned the report on the shuttle crash. The investigating team never pinpointed a reason the vessel went down. The engines simply exploded at a critical juncture during takeoff. They chalked it up to an accident of unknown causes.

"But it wasn't unknown causes. It was you, LeaMarsa. You may have been in the midst of a psychic blackout and didn't know what you were doing. But I doubt that mattered much to your parents and the forty others who died.

"In a fit of anger at what your mother and father had done to you in the womb, you sent some kind of superluminal shock wave four hundred thousand kilometers into space, killing the crew and everyone onboard. You used a power that neither you nor anyone else even dreamed you possessed. You used that power to murder your own parents."

Her gyrations became more frantic. "Why are you doing this!"

"Because for all our sakes, you've got to face the truth."

"No! Go away! Let me alone!"

Her eyes rolled up in their sockets. He grabbed hold of her shoulders to keep her upright as she crumbled into a faint.

In the center of the pool, something broke free from the depths and erupted through the agitated surface. Defying geonic forces, it elevated two meters into the air.

Ericho gasped. The creature hadn't metamorphosed into

what he'd been expecting, a full-sized version of Baby Blue. It had changed into something adult all right, but far more unsettling, a grotesque variant of a familiar figure.

It was Rigel Shaheed.

Or, more precisely, a doppelganger that had pilfered Rigel's DNA to assume the contours and musculature of the tech officer. Its skin was identical to human flesh but closer to that of a newborn, dripping with a pale fluid reminiscent of a shattered amniotic sac. Only the creature's head was different, more elongated to make room for that additional sensory organ between mouth and nose, a mirrorlike node.

Eerily familiar eyes glared down at Ericho. He backed away from the pool with LeaMarsa unconscious in his arms. The Rigel creature moved too, floating slowly but menacingly toward them.

"The warrior pups will arrive in twenty-five seconds," Jonomy said. "Your only chance is surrender. Assume a submissive posture to let them know you pose no threat."

That wasn't an option, Ericho thought, not with a monster gliding toward him with unmistakable hostility. If he had any chance at all it was with the woman in his arms.

"Wake up!" he hollered. He shook LeaMarsa like a rag doll, using the full force of his shieldsuit motors. But there was no response.

Wherever she'd gone, it was far from this place.

CHAPTER 39

LeaMarsa's eyes were closed yet she remained cognizant of the world. She could sense the creature in its Rigel guise coming toward them, ready to offer her permanent liberation from the reek. She could feel the captain's grip holding her upright, hear the distant echo of his words urging her to awaken.

A barrier protecting her from a reality that she'd buried more than a decade ago had collapsed. Consciousness was no longer shielded. The reek, which she'd often thought of as originating from outside herself – a foreign aggressor – was just the opposite, a thing fundamental to her nature.

The captain had outed her secret torment. It stormed through her, shredding the very fabric of her being, redefining and reshaping the person whom she thought she was. A phantasmagorical abyss opened at her feet, its air colored by the terrible truth.

I killed my parents.

She fell into the abyss. It smelled of death and decay, the same vile odor she'd come to associate with the reek. The odor was symbolic, a repressed memory of her murderous rage, and what it had done to two guilty individuals and forty innocent ones.

The sudden death of the crew at a critical moment in the

flight had caused the shuttle to crash into the wall of a lunar crater. Engines and fuel tanks had exploded, incinerating the evidence of how those forty-two people had actually died. Like the hapless souls on the raft in her vision of the Avrit-Ah-Tay under attack, their bodies had been consumed by that icy fire. But in this instance, it was not the Quad that had been responsible. LeaMarsa had unconsciously reached into neurospace to access the same terrible power utilized by the creature, a power given added fuel by her rage.

She perceived the breadth of the event from beginning to end, from the actualization of her rage into a potent superluminal force to the crash itself. She perceived it with a clarity that no longer could be suppressed or falsified.

An even grimmer truth achieved focus. Had her actions on that terrible day in the fourteenth year of her life been wholly the product of her subconscious mind, the awfulness of what she'd done might have been bearable. But that wasn't what had happened.

She'd blacked out, yes. Yet even as the real world lost its reassuring contours, even as neurospace blinked into existence, a part of her had known what she was doing. Vowing to avenge her parents' manipulations, she'd accessed that realm of luminous dark, specifically the stars representing analogues of her parents and, by their proximity, those forty other luckless souls.

Not subliminal. Not accidental.

Premeditated murder.

My own parents.

The reek came into being in those moments to keep her mind insulated from the horror of her actions. It was a safety valve, one of such efficacy that it had even twisted the timeline of events to keep her oblivious of the facts. Now that she could no longer suppress the truth, questions surfaced that she'd been too blinded to ask earlier.

Why was the creature so intent on making her its ally by offering her sanctuary from the reek? Certainly not for LeaMarsa's benefit, to spare her emotional pain. And it didn't need her assistance to overwhelm human civilization in the real world and as well as attacking the analogues of intelligent beings that existed in neurospace.

And how could she have first experienced the reek at age five when the events that created it didn't occur for another eight years?

Answers were suddenly obvious. Her psionic consciousness – her *Quad* consciousness, the latent part of her that had always been able to touch neurospace – wasn't bound by the commonplace. As with neurospace, it wasn't limited by notions of time flowing in a single direction. And she understood the reason behind the creature's manipulations, why it sought to offer her sanctuary.

It's afraid of me.

The psionic powers that were her genetic legacy made LeaMarsa perhaps the only intelligent entity in the galaxy capable of interfering with the Quad's plans. Offering her sanctuary was nothing more than an attempt to neutralize her powers by making her a confederate.

But why not just kill her?

The answer surfaced even as she parsed the question. If she died, a part of her would continue on in neurospace, an immortal entity just like the creature – and a possible threat to its dominion.

She was indeed the transhuman her parents had designed her to be.

The flood of insights occurred in an instant as the captain continued his retreat from the creature. But those insights were mainly a product of intellectual understanding, the highest form of human tripartite consciousness. Beneath that was a layer of pure emotions that required its own acknowledgment in the form of grief.

Her eyes flashed open. A scream erupted, a thing of pure torment, so intense and all-encompassing that she barely recognized it as arising from her own throat.

Within that abyss, the scream breached a storehouse of pains. Wretched sobs exploded out of her. Her body shook as she wept for a fragile young girl who, in a moment of foolishness, lashed out and ended the lives of the two people who had brought her into this world.

CHAPTER 40

Ericho could barely hear Jonomy's words through the shrieks of the writhing woman cradled in his arms. With LeaMarsa's face mere centimeters from his helmet, her screams penetrated even his thick visor.

"Captain, the warrior pups are fast approaching the natatorium. They will be on you in less than fifteen seconds."

He continued backing away from the Rigel creature, an imperious predator floating slowly across the pool. He estimated he would arrive at the farthest wall and run out of space to retreat at about the same time the warrior pups reached the natatorium. What little hope he still had for his own survival trickled away. He would die at the hands of either the creature or the warrior pups, maybe both acting in concert.

Ericho had accomplished part of what he'd come here to do. He'd ejected LeaMarsa from the fantasy she'd constructed to hide from herself. He'd subjected her to an unorthodox salvation. But it wasn't enough. Now he needed to finish the mission by doing something that only minutes ago he'd had difficulty even contemplating.

"I'm sorry, LeaMarsa."

He wasn't sure if she heard him through her screams. It didn't matter. He released his grip on her shoulders, wrapped his gloved hands around her throat.

"Forgive me," he whispered, clenching his fingers and squeezing hard.

He didn't know if killing her would matter. Maybe it would save billions of lives or maybe it wouldn't make the slightest difference. But he couldn't take the chance that she and the creature working together would bring about June's nightmare. For the crewdoc and for the rest of the crew; for his parents and siblings and friends back on Earth; for the future of humanity, he had to commit this horrible act.

The old saying from the Pannis command school again coursed through him. *The captain needs to master that the master's not the captain.*

For perhaps the first time in his career, the phrase was utterly untrue. At least for these next few moments, Captain Ericho Solorzano of the starship *Alchemon* was indeed the master of his vessel, taking action that might well determine its fate.

His choking grip ended LeaMarsa's screams. A part of him wanted to get it over instantly, utilize the shieldsuit's full amplification to crush her vertebrae and snap her neck. But her eyes, brimming with terror and fixated on his, prompted hesitation. He gazed back at her, fingers momentarily frozen, wondering if she was relieved or even gratified to know that a thing of such paralyzing dimensions as her emotional pain was about to end.

CHAPTER 41

The old adage was wrong. It wasn't your life that flashed before your eyes when you were dying. It was the spaces between the events of your life, the paths not taken, the choices not made, the feelings unacknowledged.

That's what LeaMarsa saw, reflected back in the grim determined face of the man strangling her.

She sensed those things in an instant of suspended time amid a swarm of feelings. Foremost among them was guilt. What a contemptible and shameful trade she'd been about to make, accepting the creature's offer of sanctuary from the reek and all her pains in exchange for participating in the annihilation of her own species.

It was now clear that any pain could be borne, even the special hell of having murdered one's own parents. Repressing such pain, as she'd done all these years, had fueled her unconscious torment, provided the reek with a limitless source of energy, making it into a thing so powerful that she would have traded the universe to keep the truth at bay. The opposite tactic, simply allowing herself to feel the awfulness of what she'd done, had already served to deflate much of its energy.

The pain was still there. A century of sobs wouldn't eradicate it, not entirely. But she could live with its presence now, live with the scars. She could survive.

Or, at least survival would have been possible were she not experiencing the real-world version of the reek's final symptom.

Being strangled.

She sensed blackness settling in. Even now, her lungs desperate for air, moments from the end, she found herself acknowledging the irony of her own demise.

Her physical self was being murdered for having been a murderer. A circle was being closed, a circle of life and death. There was something appropriate about leaving this world as a helpless victim, mirroring the extinction of those forty-two souls who had died at her own hands.

A helpless victim. The phrase resonated. That was what she'd been for most of her years. Buffeted by psychic forces, isolated by society, manipulated by parents who should have loved unconditionally rather than using her to further their scientific ambitions. A helpless victim, one whose life had been structured around trying to ensure that the reek stayed buried.

Yet in these final moments, as that blackness smothered consciousness, she gained insight into a deeper truth. It too was something she'd kept hidden from herself since that darkest of days as an emotionally devastated thirteen year-old reeking of vengeance and lashing out.

She'd been a victim, yes. Nothing could change that. It was an essential reality of her life.

But she was not, and had never been, truly helpless. A power existed within her. Once before she'd used that power, back then to carry out a malicious and terrible act. Now it was time to take the next step. Her alien mentor, Nanamistyne, had provided a set of instructions. All she had to do was follow them.

But first things first.

She grabbed hold of the captain's gloved wrists. Alone, she lacked the strength to free her neck from those crushing fingers backed up by the mechanical power of a shieldsuit. But similar to what she'd done a decade ago, she psychically reached into neurospace and located the analogue of Ericho Solorzano. Not driven by rage this time, she was able to control the amplitude of the summoned power. She didn't want to kill the captain, merely move him out of her way.

His face registered astonishment as an icy thermal force entered his gut and began to spread through his body, layering its way upward and outward through the interwoven breadth of his tripartite consciousness. He had no choice but to release her neck and lunge away. She sensed that he somehow knew that she was the cause of his sudden torment, and that he needed to put distance between them if he was to survive.

She gulped down precious air, filled her lungs with it until she regained the strength to mouth words.

"Implement Synchronicity."

Neurospace mushroomed into view. But now it was no longer a matter of her existing in one universe or the other, or of consciousness blinking back and forth between them. Having fulfilled the instruction, she now existed simultaneously in both realms, as an entity standing in the *Alchemon*'s natatorium and as a free-floating spirit among those countless faux-stars. From her dual vantage point, the next step was clear.

"Coalesce and Target."

Within neurospace, she collapsed the past, present and future of every analogue enveloped by those shadowy clusters into a kind of temporal singularity, a state of existence whereby each one was locked into a specific moment, an infinite fraction of a nanosecond. She couldn't have said just *how* she accomplished such a task. It was simply a matter of giving free rein to her latent instincts.

Coalescing those timelines enabled her to target the clusters with a stream of untethered superluminal impulses. Within the confines of that singularity, she vaporized those polluting shadows, restoring the realm of luminous dark to its pure and natural state.

As she wrenched neurospace from the creature's influence, simultaneously in the real universe she whirled around to face the Diar-Fahn in its Rigel form. It was right behind her. She could sense its rage at her insurrection along with its growing fear of what she was becoming.

Everything was clear to her now. Despite its immortality and immense powers, the creature had an Achilles' heel. Although it could never be destroyed, Nanamistyne and the remnants of her destroyed civilization had provided the template for how it could be contained.

LeaMarsa was distracted by a sound like exploding fireworks. Half of the pups forming the makeshift barrier against access to the natatorium burst into flames and blew apart. Fragments of their shattered bodies whizzed through the air in a rain of shrapnel. She felt the heat of a glowing piece shooting past, missing her face by centimeters.

Ericho whirled toward the commotion, hollered something about "mag projectiles." The rest of his words were lost as a second round of explosions destroyed the rest of the robotic wall.

Two warrior pups floated into the natatorium, projectile

guns and Higgs cutters sprouting from their compact bodies. They realigned weapons on their new target, the captain.

"Sentinel Obey!" LeaMarsa commanded.

It was a peculiar sensation, linking the superluminals she controlled in neurospace with the ones ruled by SEN. But with consciousness synchronizing both realms, the task was not especially challenging.

She was in charge of the *Alchemon* now, with SEN just another aspect of her control. A logical next step would have been to order the warrior pups not to fire on the captain. But there was a more efficient way to have them do her bidding.

She allowed the Sentinel controlling the deadly robots to access her mind via its superluminal pathways, enabled SEN to learn in a fraction of a nanosecond the extent of the Quad's manipulations and its threat to the ship, and ultimately to the Corporeal.

Six Higgs cutters ignited in unison, three from each warrior pup. The whining beams lanced into the Rigel creature. Five beams burned into its torso in a pentagonal pattern. The sixth nailed the center of its forehead, just above the eyes.

The stunned creature lunged backward, flailing its arms and legs. The warrior pups' second volley severed those appendages below the shoulders and above the knees.

Round three of the attack decapitated the creature. Torso, severed head and appendages fell into the pool over which it hovered. In seconds they were swallowed up, leaving no trace.

The creature wasn't dead, of course. No power, not even LeaMarsa's, could ever destroy it, for an essential aspect of its consciousness would always exist in neurospace. And that would enable its physical remnants within the incubating pool to regenerate eventually into a new form.

But there was a window of opportunity before that happened. LeaMarsa hoped it would be long enough for her to embark on a new and unanticipated future, one far removed from what she'd envisioned nine months ago upon boarding the *Alchemon*.

CHAPTER 42

Events had occurred with such speed that Ericho was still trying to comprehend their meaning. He'd been strangling LeaMarsa, certain it would be the last act of his life. The next thing he knew, some unbearable combination of intense heat and freezing cold was emanating from deep within his guts, forcing him to release her neck and scamper as far away from her as possible. And then the warrior pups were in the natatorium, turning their fierce weaponry on the Rigel creature and cutting it to pieces.

His attention remained riveted to the deadly robots, wary of their next move. But it soon became clear that hostilities were over and that he was no longer a target. The pups retracted the barrels of Higgs cutters and mag projectile weaponry back into their compact bodies and floated serenely out of the natatorium.

He turned to LeaMarsa, still trying to process what happened. "You did that?"

She nodded. Although her eyes were alert and gazing directly at him, he had the impression her mind was in another place, somewhere far away.

"You need to go," she said. "You have very little time left."

"I don't follow."

"I transmitted the pertinent information to Jonomy. It will be simpler to let him explain."

As if on cue, the lytic's voice filled his helmet. "Captain, the Sentinel has driven the invader out of the network. But we are about to experience a calamity. A deluge of new data, originating from what the *Alchemon* can only describe as an unknown source, has clarified the creature's scheme."

Ericho instinctively knew that LeaMarsa was the "unknown source" to which Jonomy referred.

"The invader's modifications to the Big Three during its incursion, in conjunction with the rerouting of the output power modules, leaves us facing a dire situation."

"Get to the point."

"We are about to be chronojacked."

"What!" He shook his head in disbelief, gazed at LeaMarsa.

"It's true," she said.

"But you can stop it."

"No. Not this."

"Captain, these modifications cannot be undone, not within such a limited time frame."

"How limited?"

LeaMarsa and Jonomy answered in tandem. Their words, slightly out of sync, echoed weirdly in Ericho's helmet.

"Less than four minutes."

"There must be something we can do."

Jonomy was adamant. "We would have difficulty even reaching the Big Three nexus. Those repair pups are blockading the entrance portal. Their com systems were sabotaged, making them independent and uncontrollable, even by superluminal energies. They likely are following the invader's last programmed instructions."

"What about the Sentinel? The warrior pups?"

"Even if the pups were to blast through the blockade, there would not be enough time."

Ericho gazed in awe at LeaMarsa, knowing she was responsible. *What has she become?*

"You need to go," she repeated, this time more insistently. "The creature set this plan in motion. It cannot be altered."

"All right. Jonomy, we're on our way to the bridge. Get the others up there too. And tell June to prepare loopy doses for everyone."

"She is administering the injections now."

He gestured to LeaMarsa. "Let's go."

"I'm not coming with you."

"If we're about to be chronojacked, the bridge is the safest place to be."

"I'm needed elsewhere."

Ericho's first inclination was to grab hold of her and drag her to safety. But recalling the power she'd unleashed the last time they'd physically touched, he thought better of it

"Good luck." He couldn't stop turning to stare at her as he rushed for the exit.

CHAPTER 43

LeaMarsa knew what she needed to do. Clarity of purpose had come upon her in those moments when the warrior pups were destroying the Rigel incarnation of the Diar-Fahn.

She turned back to the pool. Its surface again grew wildly agitated, bubbling and pulsating. The level began to drop, and for a moment she wondered if the creature was somehow responsible. But then she realized that the ship's natural systems had come back online and were draining away the polluted mess.

The basin was quickly emptied, revealing the creature squirming on the bottom, still in its Rigel guise. Already it had reassembled much of itself, crudely fusing together head, torso and appendages in a manner that suggested some ancient Frankenstein monster. For the first time she sensed its driving emotion, a deep and intolerant rage, directed not only against her but against all intelligent lifeforms. She still couldn't fathom the reason behind such anger, only that it was the foundation of a desire for destruction.

But at the moment, such things didn't matter. And although she and the Diar-Fahn drew superluminal energies from the same source, LeaMarsa was now the stronger entity.

Eons ago, the survivors of the stick city civilization had

done what was necessary to capture and imprison the creature, a threat they'd brought upon themselves by reengineering their DNA to develop a quadpartite consciousness. A lone individual from their species, its most gifted psionic, had made a supreme sacrifice. Nanamistyne had become an organic prison, the jailer, a willing martyr to protect the survivors of her own species and other civilizations.

It was time for a new martyr to take up the cause.

CHAPTER 44

Ericho rushed onto the bridge just as June and Faye arrived through the other airseal. The women were pushing and pulling the disabled autobed with the unconscious Alexei.

"How long?" Ericho demanded, before realizing the lytic's chair was empty. The disconnected umbilical snaked across the floor.

Jonomy came over the intercom. "Two minutes, nine seconds, captain. You will need to be strapped down. Firsthand accounts by chronojackers confirm that the moment of transit can create unusual turbulence."

"Where are you?"

"On my way to the starboard lander hold. I have already prepped the lander for departure."

Before Ericho could ask why, June appeared at his side, her gloved hand clutching a tubular inhaler.

"Take off your helmet!" she ordered. "I injected Loopaline B4 into the rest of us but two minutes isn't enough time for a shot to work. You need to snort it. Hurry!"

Ericho removed the helmet. Before he could utter a word, she rammed the inhaler up his left nostril and squeezed.

The inoculation burned and had a vile smell that made him gag. An overwhelming vertigo took hold and he nearly collapsed. June helped him to his chair.

"The dizziness will pass in a bit."

Ericho plopped the helmet in his lap, willed the bridge to stop gyrating. Or maybe he was the one twirling like a top and the bridge was motionless.

"LeaMarsa contained the creature," Jonomy explained. "She is meeting me at the lander. I will be her pilot for our return to Sycamore."

"What!"

"I cannot fully elucidate the situation in the time remaining. She transmitted a vast amount of data to me through the superluminal conduit she established with the ship via SEN. I recorded everything for your later perusal."

"Jonomy, get back to the bridge. That's an order."

"I cannot. The external telemetry interface is functioning again. I sent the relevant facts of our predicament to the Corporeal as an emergency transmission."

"Just tell me why you're doing this. The short version."

"The lander likely could make it back to Sycamore and navigate through that unstable atmosphere on automatic. But considering her mission's crucial nature, it's best to have a skilled pilot aboard as backup."

"And why's LeaMarsa returning there in the first place?"

"Please, captain, there's no time for further explanation."

Jonomy cut the link.

"Can a lander even make it to Sycamore?" Faye wondered, strapping herself into the lieutenant's chair.

"Fuel-wise, it'll be close," Ericho said. "Once they touch down, I doubt if they'll be able to take off again."

"Then both of them will be…"

"Yeah."

June finished securing Alexei with some additional straps and locked down the autobed. She bolted for the nearest airseal.

"I have an inhaler for Hardy."

Jonomy beat Ericho to the punch in voicing an objection.

"June, that is unwise. I have attempted various means to interrupt Hardy's dreamlounge fantasy, all to no avail. It is unlikely you can reach him in the limited time remaining."

"I have to try."

"No!" Ericho ordered. "You're staying here."

She lunged through the door and was gone.

He secured his straps, glanced over at Faye. She looked terrified.

"We're going to get through this," he said, trying to sound reassuring.

"What if the loopy doesn't kick in?" Faye whispered.

"June knows what she's doing."

He hoped so. Loopy was impetus-triggered and was supposed to knock them unconscious at the moment of temporal transition. Yet whether injected or snorted, the recommendation was for the inhibitor to be taken fifteen minutes prior to activation of the spatiotemporal coagulators.

At least LeaMarsa had disabled SEN. Once they made the temporal jump, the warrior pups wouldn't treat them as renegade chronojackers and attack.

Hopefully.

The worst of Ericho's vertigo passed. He was about to put his helmet back on when a panel snared his attention. A flashing light indicated the egress hatch of the starboard lander hold had opened.

He activated the HOD. Hull cams showed the lander floating away from the *Alchemon*.

Jonomy ignited the lander's engines. The craft rocketed away. It would have to get far enough from them to avoid the electromagnetic tides occurring in the wake of a chronojacking, when SCO activated outside the boundaries of a Quiets. Twenty kilometers was the recommended safe distance.

A clock counted down the final moments.

"Fifteen seconds," Faye uttered, clutching her armrests in a death grip.

Their outlandish predicament presented a new twist. Ericho found himself staring at Faye, overcome by lust. He suddenly wanted her.

She looked appalled. "Captain, I'm so sorry! My secretors! It happens sometimes when I get scared. I can't control them, and they release."

He snapped his helmet back on, took deep breaths of suit air uncontaminated by her alluring pheromones. His lust subsided. He was about to offer another homily about remaining strong in the face of adversity when time ran out and spacetime deviated.

His chair seemed to wrench sideways. The sensation was like being whipped twenty feet to the left and brought to an abrupt halt. His stomach danced. He fought an urge to vomit.

Mad streams of color erupted from the HOD, swirled across the bridge. The air mutated into a spectral nirvana of impossibly vivid hues, alien and haunting. Weird sing-song melodies and mystifying odors squeezed into his brain, uprooting sensible thoughts, throttling sanity.

It was too much to process. He pinched his eyes shut but it made no difference. The sensory barrage continued, unrelenting.

And then the universe skipped a beat and blackness overtook him.

CHAPTER 45

LeaMarsa awakened. She was strapped into the lander's copilot seat beside Jonomy, who was staring ahead at Sycamore. Over the five days they'd been in flight, the planet had grown from the size of a coin to a sphere of churning clouds nearly filling the window.

"How long yet?" she asked.

"We will reach orbit in an hour," he said, shifting his attention to the small flight-control panel. Landers were relatively simple-minded machines and didn't require umbilical interfaces.

"Do you have a landing-site preference?" he asked.

"Whatever's best for you."

Jonomy would just be a visitor to Sycamore. It made sense for him to choose an area that might be the most conducive to being rescued. She was here for the duration, an abstract length of time. A thousand years? A million?

Eternity?

An answer was impossible to fathom, neither here within the lander nor in neurospace, that other universe where her consciousness existed simultaneously.

She sensed Jonomy turning to her with a concerned look.

"What is it?" she asked.

"Are you certain the creature remains safely contained?"

She felt its presence inside her. She'd shrunk it to the smallest incarnation attainable by her powers, an embryonic organism less than a millimeter in length, about the size it must have been when she and Faye had first set eyes on Bouncy Blue. She could have inserted the embryo into most any bodily orifice for safekeeping but had selected the most logical one: her uterus. There it ideally would remain in stasis, frozen in spacetime, prohibited from maturing into a threat.

"It's secure."

Jonomy still looked troubled. During their relatively uneventful flight in the lander, he'd displayed a wider range of expressions than he'd shown during their entire nine months together aboard the *Alchemon*. She believed it had something to do with being deprived of his umbilical connection. Lytics were said to establish intimate attachments with starships and the other AIs they interfaced with over long periods. When such a relationship ended there were often withdrawal symptoms, one being increased emotional sensitivity.

She prodded him into talking about it.

"I have been experiencing recurrences of the sort of psionic bombardment that forced me into excessive dreamlounge fantasies aboard the *Alchemon*. Their intensity has been escalating over the past few hours."

She understood why. "It's the creature. It knows we're getting close to Sycamore. Obviously, it doesn't want to be returned to its old prison."

She could literally feel the creature raging at the idea that it had a new jailer. In fact, over these past days in the lander, she'd come to realize that anger was its dominant emotion, driving its attempts to destroy intelligent life. Yet beneath that anger lay some deeper emotion, an underlying cause that remained indiscernible.

"Nothing to worry about," she assured Jonomy. "It's still able to channel some of its powers through me and is trying to influence you that way. It's hoping you'll panic and not land us on Sycamore."

"Panic is not in my nature," Jonomy said, sounding relieved by her explanation.

"Once we touch down, I'll leave the lander and get far away from you. When we're separated, your urges should go away, or at least lessen."

"Your air supply will not last long."

LeaMarsa shrugged. She'd explained as best she could the incredible changes she'd undergone. Still, Jonomy was having difficulty coming to terms with them. Not surprising. At a fundamental level, she too found them hard to grasp.

The energy field now enveloping her was an outgrowth of her ability to exist contemporaneously in both this universe and the dimension of neurospace, the same power possessed by the Diar-Fahn. Breathing and other metabolic processes were mere options for her now, no longer essential for survival. When her air ran out she would simply remove her shieldsuit and keep walking. Perhaps she'd circumnavigate the planet. Possibly several times.

Eventually, she'd likely tire of such aimless wandering. Maybe she'd find a small cave to curl up in or figure out a way to encase herself in rock in the manner of her predecessor, Nanamistyne.

Jonomy's last transmission from the *Alchemon* hopefully would be enough of a warning to keep future expeditions at a safe distance from the planet. Still, there was always the possibility of Corporeal profiteers or rogue explorers someday landing on Sycamore and attempting to track her down. Making herself hard to find was the wisest course.

But whether she remained hidden or not, the inevitable process of devolution would set in, as it had with Nanamistyne. Over eons of time, LeaMarsa would physically regress into a more basic lifeform, shedding unused features. Bones, muscles, internal and sensory organs, appendages – all would atrophy, morphing her into a protoplasmic blob. Perhaps in the distant future she'd even earn a nickname as flippant as Bouncy Blue.

Her gradual regression would annihilate self-awareness. There would come a tipping point when she transitioned from a state of full consciousness to a state where she was barely conscious at all. At that point her unique dual citizenship would expire, and the creature on Sycamore would be contained only by an empty organic vessel. The intelligent being that once had been LeaMarsa de Host in the physical universe would, for all practical purposes, take up sole residency in the realm of luminous dark.

It is a noble sacrifice.

The voice shifted LeaMarsa's attention from the cramped lander to neurospace, to that endless expanse of stars. One of them emerged from the stellar backdrop, accelerated toward her until it dominated her field of vision.

"Nanamistyne," LeaMarsa whispered.

There was a sound like gentle laughter as the star coalesced into a tall lean figure with bluish skin. Her hips were draped in frothy culottes, cable-stitch patterned in pleasing shades of green and gold. The projected vision suggested dignified fortitude and grace.

Yet it was more than that. Her presence caused LeaMarsa

to recall a long-forgotten dream from childhood, back before her uniqueness had fractured natural connectivity with other humans. She used to fantasize about encountering someone who was her equal, someone with whom she could share her deepest feelings and thoughts. A genuine friend.

We are much alike. Anomalies within our civilizations.

"Blessed and cursed."

One cannot exist without the other.

The very sound of Nanamistyne's words induced a strange pleasure. They seemed to wash over her as if she were sand on a summer beach lapped by effervescent waves.

"Is it worth it? This noble sacrifice?"

It is our fate.

"LeaMarsa, are you all right?"

Compared to the soothing impact of Nanamistyne's speech, Jonomy's words sounded harsh and hollow, inconsequential. She returned her focus to the lander and to the lytic's perplexed look.

"I'm fine," she assured him. "I was just talking to a friend."

He nodded although he obviously didn't understand.

"I'm curious about something," he said. "It is a question that you may not wish to answer. Yet I must ask."

"Feel free."

"Why are you doing this?"

She'd already explained but repeated her rationale.

"The creature can't be destroyed, not by any known means. This is the only way to ensure the safety of the Corporeal, the survival of our species."

"Yes, that part I understand. Let me rephrase. My question is, why are *you* doing this?"

She hesitated. "I guess because I'm the only one who can."

It was an honest answer yet not the entire truth. Sacrificing herself, retreating from any chance at a real life to become an organic confinement vessel on a bleak world, was a difficult concept for anyone to comprehend. She didn't fully understand it herself.

Maybe part of the reason was to assuage the guilt she felt over nearly betraying humanity. Maybe another part was realizing that she had so little in common with that humanity. She'd been a freakish outsider for too much of her life, her relationship to the everyday world defined by estrangement. Deep down, she knew that such a status would never entirely leave her.

There was another reason for making such a sacrifice, one that was entirely irrational yet appealing nonetheless. Now that she had full access to neurospace, she sensed it contained far more than just those stars serving as analogues for organic tripartite beings. Perhaps temporal chasms existed within its depths that provided the means to contact those who were no longer alive. Perhaps she could even find her parents and explain to them what had happened and beg forgiveness for their murders.

She sighed, recognizing the idea as little more than a childish desire to rewrite the past. Transhuman or not, she couldn't truly go back in time and fix a wrong, nor give her parents the opportunity to express regret for transforming her into humanity's first quadpartite consciousness.

Still, now that she'd awakened as a Quad, there would be much to explore. She could already perceive tantalizing glimpses of something she'd suspected earlier, a method of comprehension that far exceeded the boundaries of cognitive understanding. Intellect and reasoning, the highest manifestations of tripartite consciousness, were mere echoes of a grander way of sensing and interacting with the universe.

Jonomy's frown returned her attention to the lander. Her response to his question clearly hadn't satisfied his curiosity. She shrugged, unwilling to offer more.

"Let's just call it fate."

CHAPTER 46

Ericho awoke with a mild headache, his typical reaction to a dose of loopy. The bridge looked and felt normal again, but he knew that wasn't the case. The past was gone, the future was here. The present into which he'd been born, that all-encompassing and nurturing array of familiar comforts, had ceased to exist.

A clock indicated an hour and a half had passed since the chronojacking. That was ship time, of course. According to the *Alchemon*'s SCO clock, based on Earth time, eight hundred and two years, five months, fourteen days and six-plus hours had gone by. That the SCO clock was functioning meant that they were again within range of a Corporeal com beacon. Still, such beacons were meant to last thousands of years. Whether the Corporeal and humanity still existed was yet to be ascertained.

He checked his wafer for their location. Chronojacking usually caused radical spatial displacement as well. Obviously, they were no longer anywhere near Sycamore or the Lalande 21185 system.

But he couldn't get any readings from navigation, not from the primary or backup systems. External telemetry, including hull cameras, also was inoperative. The rest of the network seemed functional, which made it even odder that the two systems that could reveal their location, NAV and ETI, weren't working.

The mystery would have to wait. He had more important considerations. Ignoring the headache, he rose from his command chair and checked on the others. Faye was still asleep and Alexei unconscious on the autobed. Both appeared to have survived the event with no ill effects.

"June, can you hear me?"

There was no response on the intercom. He headed out the airscal at a brisk pace, fearing the worst.

He found June lying face down in the corridor leading to the dreamlounge. She was unmoving. Gripping the side of her shieldsuit, he flipped her over.

Her eyes opened. He let out a sigh of relief.

"Are you OK?"

She managed a nod. "I think so. Did we…"

"Yeah. Eight centuries and some change."

She motored her shieldsuit upright. He could tell by her vacant face that she was fighting to contain a tempest of emotions. Ericho had left behind parents and siblings, and that would be hard enough to come to terms with. For June, it would be worse. There were children and grandchildren she'd never see again.

"Did you reach Hardy in time?"

She tried maintaining professional calm but couldn't keep a quiver out of her voice. "I only made it this far. When the transition occurred, I was thrown against the wall and fell over. Everything got weird for a few seconds and then the loopy must have kicked in. How long were we out?"

"About ninety minutes."

They proceeded to the dreamlounge. Hardy had sequestered

himself in the largest of the four pods, the one used for Lieutenant Donner's funeral service a few days ago.

Ericho corrected himself. *Not days ago, centuries ago.* It would take a while to make that mental adjustment.

"Be careful," June warned as they halted at the pod's entrance. "No telling what state he could be in."

Whether passing through a Quiets or being chronojacked, a crewmember not inoculated with loopy was likely to be suffering some form of psychological instability. And Hardy Waskov had been half-mad before they'd made the temporal leap.

Ericho opened the door, ready for a violent confrontation. But there was no attack. The room was plain, devoid of holo imagery. A glance at the menu revealed that Hardy's most recent subcortical fantasy had been deactivated.

The science rep sat in the corner in a pool of blood, unmoving. His head was slumped forward, his hands tucked into the jacket pockets of his formal science uniform. It was the same one he'd worn at Donner's service.

June knelt beside him, checked for a pulse. She shook her head.

"Looks like he bled out."

She removed Hardy's hands from his pockets, revealing the source of the blood. The tips of seven fingers had been gnawed at, some all the way to the bone. More serious damage had been self-inflicted upon the forefingers and right thumb. They'd been bitten off entirely.

She pulled back his head. A ring of dried scarlet made his lips appear obscenely large. A jagged lump protruded from between the teeth. One of Hardy's own severed fingers.

June's voice was strained but clinical. "Psychotic

autosarcophagy. Had I gotten here sooner, I may have been able to prevent it."

"No way is this your fault."

"I know. But I still can't help feeling–"

She stopped as a voice came over the intercom.

"All survivors please report to the port lander hold. Departure from the *Alchemon* will commence in fifteen minutes."

Ericho and June traded stunned looks as the voice continued.

"Bring all personal items and anything else that you might wish to store in the lander. You will not be returning to the ship."

"That can't be Jonomy," June said. "Can it?"

Ericho had no answer.

CHAPTER 47

Sycamore loomed ever larger in the lander's window. They were close enough now for LeaMarsa to see flashes of light from the energy storms that perpetually ripped through the atmosphere.

Neither she nor Jonomy had uttered a word since he'd questioned her willingness to embrace such an irrational fate. She finally broke the silence.

"What about you?" she asked. "Why are you doing this?"

"It was necessary. You needed a pilot."

She wasn't certain of that. Automatic systems on landers were remarkably trustworthy, could enable safe touchdowns even in the most extreme conditions. She pressed on.

"You're making a big sacrifice too. You'll be trapped on Sycamore for a long time. There's no guarantee Pannis will even send a rescue ship."

"After they receive the *Alchemon*'s final transmission, they will be too curious not to. The transmission will take approximately eight years to reach the solar system. Therefore, I estimate being picked up within the decade, eleven or twelve years at the outside."

"And you're sure you can stay vegetated that long?" He'd explained it to her earlier, but she still had doubts. Being in that form of stasis for such a length of time was known to be risky. A small but significant percentage of those who attempted it never awakened.

"There is enough Loopaline B4 aboard for such a contingency."

"So, back to my original question. Why are you doing this?"

A sad smile came over him. "Whatever future the ship is destined for, I would be rendered an anachronism. Unmodified humans have a reasonable chance of adapting to a radically transformed society. Lytics, however, are the pinnacle of specialization, designed to function within a particular technological period. Where the *Alchemon* is going – or more precisely, where it *has* gone – is likely to be a place and time where I would be an outmoded remnant of an obsolete science."

"You can't know that for sure."

"I ran the projections before leaving the ship. EPS predicts a 99.98 percent probability of such a reality coming to pass."

"But surely in that future there'd be some sort of upgrades available."

"Perhaps. But there is another factor. It is a future I no longer desire."

Jonomy hadn't volunteered to pilot her back to Sycamore strictly out of a sense of duty. Something within him had changed too.

LeaMarsa gazed out the window at Sycamore. From deep within her, she could feel the creature's rage increasing as they approached the planet. She wasn't bothered by it. If she elected, she could sequester herself from its emotions, shut them out of her mind with the same ease that she controlled its physical presence.

She superimposed the view from the lander's window onto

neurospace, melded the two universes into a singular vision instead of concentrating on one or the other. The fusion that resulted – Sycamore blended with those faux-stars – brought insight.

In a flash she grasped the underlying source of the creature's anger, why it sought to destroy intelligent life.

Nanamistyne and her people, in creating a quadpartite consciousness to access and interact with neurospace, had suffered from a huge blind spot. Despite the awe-inspiring technological achievement of the Avrit-Ah-Tay, they'd overlooked an issue that from LeaMarsa's unique perspective seemed blatantly apparent.

The creature was lonely.

Nurtured in what the Avrit-Ah-Tay no doubt believed had been a supportive environment that would instill long-term stability, the brilliant civilization of the stick city had nonetheless failed to comprehend that the Diar-Fahn, once dispatched on its mission of discovery in neurospace, would end up inconceivably alone, without peers to relate to. Forcibly separated from all that was familiar, it reacted by lashing out against the tripartites who should have been looking out for its welfare, but who instead had condemned it to an eternity of isolation. Added to that indignity was the fact they'd made it feel like a freak.

"You had better strap in," Jonomy said. "We are about to enter the atmosphere and begin our descent."

LeaMarsa reversed the fusion of the two universes, for the moment returning her focus solely to the lander. Tightening her belts, she gazed out the window at Sycamore, looking ahead to a future that surely would bring both solace and storms.

CHAPTER 48

By the time Ericho and June reached the bridge, Faye was up and about. She was pacing nervously but looked relieved to see them.

"Jonomy?" she whispered. "You heard his voice too?"

"We heard someone," Ericho said.

She looked relieved. "I thought I was going crazy."

He checked his wafer. NAV and ETI were still down but records indicated that the latter system had functioned momentarily, just long enough to permit a message to be transmitted to the ship.

"Transmitted from where?" June asked, reading the display over his shoulder.

"Source unknown."

"What do we do?" Faye asked.

Ericho was about to say he had no idea when the Jonomy voice returned. Except for the time element, the new message was identical.

"All survivors please report to the port lander hold. Departure from the *Alchemon* will commence in *twelve* minutes. Bring all personal items and anything else that you might wish to store in the lander. You will not be returning to the ship."

"Did I ever tell you how much I hate countdowns," Faye muttered.

"Especially from someone who has to have been dead for centuries," June added.

Ericho checked LIS for the status of the port lander. Rigel had burned out that craft's NAV sensors. Without them, the lander could do nothing more than drift aimlessly in the void. He wasn't all that surprised to discover that repairs had been made, and within the last hour.

"The pups installed new sensors," he said. "The lander is fully functional."

"Should we do as he says?" June wondered. "Or, as *it* says?"

"Do we have a choice?" The Jonomy message returned at three-minute intervals as they gathered personal items from their cabins and secured Alexei's autobed in the lander. By the time the countdown passed the three-minute mark, Ericho was in the pilot's seat and the others strapped in behind him. They had removed their shieldsuits, conserving what air remained in the mechanical lungs.

Not knowing what was in store for them, they'd packed the lander's hold with nonperishable food, as much as could be gathered in the time available. June had brought portable MED gear and supplies but had been forced to leave behind her beloved camelback sofa, the family heirloom encompassing her late husband's remains and memories of her children. She did manage to grab one of the cushions, however, stowing it beneath her seat.

At the one-minute mark in the countdown, the Jonomy voice issued new instructions.

"Your destination is programmed. The flight will take approximately forty minutes. There is no need for pilot intrusion. Relax and enjoy the final stage of transit into your new future."

The lander's window shields were down. Ericho tried to raise them but the control wouldn't respond. Hull cameras were also disabled. As with the *Alchemon*, they were flying blind.

The countdown was displayed on the flight-control panel. When it reached ten seconds, he started to turn around, intending to offer the others some last words of reassurance. At that moment, he recalled his desert dream. It was coming true.

He was sure that the time jump had returned them to near-Earth orbit and that the lander was bound for Barstow... or at least to where that California city had once stood.

Readouts indicated the lander hold depressurizing and the egress hatch opening. Moments later came a gentle acceleration followed by a familiar transition into weightlessness.

The flight went by quickly. Ericho used the time to read a summary of LeaMarsa's final transmission to Jonomy. It filled in many gaps in his understanding of what had occurred.

The summary also included Tomer Donner's private files. LeaMarsa must have accessed them when she took command of the *Alchemon*'s network. It was sad reading about the lieutenant's fixation on bringing Renfro Zoobondi to justice for killing his lover. The impact of that one event had ended up creating severe repercussions for all of them as well as invoking deep ironies.

Because a ruthless Pannis VP had arranged for LeaMarsa to be on the *Alchemon*, the Quad ended up being freed from its prison. Yet LeaMarsa's presence also had resulted in the creature's recapture, thus saving humanity. Had she not been aboard, would the creature still have gotten free? Would it have returned to Earth and been unleashed on civilization? Would Tomer Donner, Rigel Shaheed and Hardy Waskov still be alive?

He could probably speculate about those questions for the rest of his life and never come close to definitive answers.

After forty minutes, gravity returned. The lander dropped into what must have been a planetary atmosphere. As the ship headed toward the surface, the remainder of his dream played out in real time. He again started to turn to address the other three but was interrupted by the raising of the window shields.

The lander soared through a patch of clouds into vivid blue skies. Below was the desert. Ahead were the mountain peaks and the horizon in the grip of that beautiful dusk. As in his dream, Barstow's tallest skyscrapers that should have been visible above the mountains were gone.

Had LeaMarsa failed? Had the creature escaped from Sycamore and, sometime within the last eight hundred years, attacked Earth. Had human cities been destroyed and the species wiped out?

Yet if so, who was guiding them in?

They crossed over the mountains. Below, where Barstow should have been, a wide treeless prairie was covered in sunburnt grass. There was no trace that a city had ever existed here.

A man with long white hair dressed in a gray suit stood in a small clearing. His hands were folded serenely in front of him. The lander touched down five meters away.

The man gazed in at them, his expression unreadable. Ericho, June and Faye stared back. For a long moment, no one said anything.

Ericho broke the silence. "I guess we should get out and say hello."

Hull sensors indicated a safe atmosphere, slightly more oxygen-rich than when they'd last breathed it, and totally free of pollutants. There was just enough room in the airlock for the three of them and Alexei's autobed. The outer seal opened, and they stepped into warm sunlight for the first time in months.

First time in centuries, Ericho corrected himself.

The temperature was perfect, neither too hot nor too cold. He hadn't done the calculations but had a hunch it was early spring.

The man's voice was deep, pleasant. "Welcome back to Earth."

He appeared close to Ericho's age. The white hair was combed straight back and dangled across his shoulders. His ebony skin was a shade darker than June's. His gray trousers and jacket bore a faint metallic sheen. A string necklace of alternating pearls and rubies reminded Ericho of a line of Helio Age jewelry he'd seen in a museum.

The man approached and halted a pace away.

"I am Glan Excelsior Lancelot Dupree, your reintegration facilitator. You may address me as Glan. My responsibility is to guide and assist your adaptation into our society, hopefully with as few hurdles as possible. I realize that you must be in a mild state of shock from the profound experience of being thrust eight centuries into the future. So, before we begin the next phase of our journey together, I will try to set your minds at ease by answering your most pressing questions."

"We only have a few thousand of those," Faye blurted out.

Glan smiled and held out his hands, palms up. "I am at your service. Be aware, however, that you may not fully comprehend all my answers. Rest assured that in time, clarity will come."

"Why did we hear Jonomy's voice?" Ericho asked.

"A simulation. It's a common technique we use when reintegrating chronojumpers. A familiar voice is the best remedy for putting those long estranged from society at ease."

"Kind of creeped me out," Faye said.

"Reactions vary. I am sorry it invoked such a response."

"What happened to Barstow?" Ericho asked.

"Two centuries ago, Greater Barstow and its population of one-point-three million voluntarily accepted a rokoloko epiphany into a fargo clusterization."

"I see what you mean about not fully comprehending."

"I sense your greater concern, Captain. Rest assured that the city's disappearance was not the work of the Quad. The creature is still safely imprisoned on Sycamore."

"And LeaMarsa?"

"She remains hidden somewhere on the planet, serving as its containment vessel, its jailer."

"What about Jonomy, our lytic?" June asked. "Was he ever rescued?"

"Jonomy J. Jonomy returned safely to Earth. He became quite famous for his role in the events that transpired during your Sycamore expedition. He was offered numerous opportunities to use his lytic abilities, not only aboard premier starships but by interfacing with high-level planetary AIs. He declined all such offers and chose to retire from Pannis and cyberlytics to pursue the classical arts. He became a landscape painter of some renown as well as an amateur poet."

"Who would have thought," Faye murmured.

"Jonomy married and fathered two children, a boy and a girl. Neither of them was genetically modified in utero for lytic capabilities. Five generations of Jonomy's family were at his bedside when he made his final transition."

Ericho felt June flinch beside him and her features darken. Glan took notice.

"I apologize if my words trigger painful memories. I know there is sadness for the loved ones all of you left behind. Although it might seem small consolation at the moment, each of you has living descendants. Many of them are anxious to meet you."

"You obviously knew when and where we'd be coming back," Ericho said.

"The precise time and place of your time jump into Earth orbit was learned years ago from Jonomy, who was given the data by LeaMarsa. How she came by it remains one of the numerous mysteries related to her metamorphosis.

"The actions taken by the invader did not lead to a typical chronojacking, whereby a vessel is thrown forward to a random location and time period. The creature used scientific knowledge unknown to your era to modify the *Alchemon's* Level One systems and pinpoint the spatiotemporal coordinates of the ship's reappearance."

"Why eight centuries?"

"It scanned your systems and realized the interstellar population was expected to peak in eight hundred years, according to Corporeal projections."

"More people to attack and murder," June whispered.

Glan nodded grimly then brightened. "Your Sycamore expedition has been studied in detail over the centuries and the anticipation of your return has sparked an upsurge of interest. Once you're settled in, many researchers hope to interview you."

"Are other people watching us right now?" Faye wondered.

"An audience of several billion citizens is sharing our exchange."

The scientist gazed around her at the darkening prairie then craned her head skyward.

Ericho asked Glan if he knew of Renfro Zoobondi, whose sadistic actions had led to the chain of events culminating in their present conversation.

"I indeed know the name. An infamous criminal."

"What happened to him?" June asked.

"He was about to go on trial for murder and other crimes. He escaped and managed to chronojack a starship. He has not been heard from since."

"What about our ship?" Faye asked. "That Jonomy voice said we can't return to it."

"The *Alchemon* was purchased at auction decades ago and is already in the process of being moved to the moon. Because of your vessel's fame, there was quite a bidding war for its acquisition. Once LOMAS refurbishes it, you may certainly return for a tour."

"LOMAS?"

"Lunar Orbital Museum of Antique Starships. A renowned Corporeal institution for more than five centuries."

"So, the Corporeal is still around," Ericho said. "What about the megas?"

"Many of the same dynasties that flourished in your time are still with us, including Pannis. Today's megas are larger and more extensive. They oversee many governmental services that were once handled by Corporeal agencies."

Ericho didn't know enough about this brave new world to discern whether that was a good thing or a bad thing. Had the percentage of those in the needful majority grown larger? Or had the balance of wealth versus impoverishment achieved greater equality across the intervening centuries.

"What about other cities?" Faye asked. "Do they still exist?

Or did they go and do that weird thing you said happened to Barstow?"

"Numerous cities remain on Earth and throughout the settled worlds, all more vibrant than ever. However, the nature of urban environments has changed rather drastically. You will need to go through a lengthy orientation process before you're able to function safely within one."

On the autobed, Alexei stirred. Opening his eyes, he pulled off his breathing mask. He looked around in surprise.

"What happened? Where are we?"

"Not in Kansas anymore," Faye said, clasping his hand in a reassuring grip. "Come to think of it though, we're probably only about a thousand kilometers from Dorothy's home."

Alexei frowned, understandably confused. As June checked his MED monitors and Faye explained what had happened, Ericho turned back to Glan.

"Are there other psionics today with similar powers to LeaMarsa?"

Glan smiled. "There is only one LeaMarsa de Host. No one has yet come close to her. Numerous attempts have been made to replicate her abilities through genetic and other means of bio-intervention. But whatever unique blend of attributes composed her character and enabled such an extensive range of psionic mastery continues to be elusive." Glan paused. "There are some who believe she was created by forces beyond our comprehension in order to save the universe."

"Is that what you believe?" June asked.

"I think she is a good person forced to make the best of a bad situation."

And facing an eternity of loneliness. Ericho recalled a saying from Pannis command school, once located near the very ground where he now stood: *Absolute power corrupts absolutely.*

Would endless years of enduring a sacrificial role someday turn LeaMarsa against her own kind, cause her to angrily lash out the same way the creature did?

June nestled up to his side, caught his eye. He could tell that her thoughts mirrored his own.

"If there are no further immediate questions," Glan proposed, "I suggest we begin the next phase of your reintegration."

"Lead the way," Ericho said.

He took hold of June's hand. Whatever future this strange new world offered, they would face it together.

ACKNOWLEDGMENTS

My warmest appreciation for the passionate encouragement by Etan Ilfeld, and for the efforts of Eleanor Teasdale, Gemma Creffield and the rest of the team of operational overlords at Angry Robot, genre publisher extraordinaire. Dedicated literary agent Mark Gottlieb at Trident Media Group gets a shout-out for his tireless efforts, often against formidable currents, in channeling my stories toward print. And special thanks to Ilya Meyzin, who in the best tradition of editors, systematically applied macroscopic and microscopic lenses to the text, enhancing my own focus and ultimately helping produce a better story.

First Chapter of
BINARY STORM
by Christopher Hinz...

A hundred years ago this month, Nicholas had been nearly stabbed to death. He was pretty sure the three knife-wielding men ambling toward him weren't here to toast his centennial.

Philadelphia was enjoying rare atmospheric conditions this evening. Its normal smog layers had been swept out into Delaware Bay and there was a deep chill in the air, uncharacteristic of late summer. The moon was nearly full. Pristine lunar light glimmered off the knives as the trio closed on Nick in the dead-end alley.

Six long blades, one in each hand. Seersucker hoodies embellished with human bone fragments. Camo pants stained with the blood of victims.

If those things weren't enough to ID their gang affiliation, the flextubes running from belt pouches to nostrils clinched it.

Mokkers.

The pouches would contain mok-1, the sweet-smelling addictive vapor they inhaled with alarming regularity. Nick had snorted, swallowed and vaped more than a few illicit pharmaceuticals in his teen years a century ago. But he'd never understood the attraction of a drug that could transform even the most serene yogi master into a psycho with issues.

The mokkers moved slowly, deliberately, knowing he was trapped. The scenario had been similar a hundred years ago, back in 1995, the last time Nick had been bladed.

He glanced around. The alley lacked doors and first-floor windows. He could try clambering onto the ancient dumpster that pissed foul liquid from rusted cracks. But even if he found footholds in the brick wall, the upper windows were barred.

"Howdy," he drawled, softening the word with a friendly smile as the mokkers closed to within two paces. They halted, eyed Nick like a pack of hungry megalions. The slashing, stabbing and screaming were imminent.

He'd known this was a cul-de-sac, having checked satellite scans of the area. Still, he hadn't figured on a total lack of escape routes. It didn't help that the sat scans had been made decades ago, well before clandestine jammers and AV scramblers thwarted nearly all forms of surveillance here in Philly-unsec. Even passive technologies like sat imaging weren't immune to such electronic countermeasures.

The mokker in the middle stepped forward, signifying he was leader of the pack. A hairy giant, he had a diecast face molded from slaps, neglect and a hundred other catastrophes of poverty and abuse.

"Howdy," Nick tried again. "Nice night, huh."

"Suck twig, ya fuckin' midget."

"Technically, I'm a proportionate dwarf," he said. "And not to brag, but I'm at the upper end of the range for the definition. If I'd been taller by only a few more centimeters, I would have avoided the label entirely. And consequently, you gentlemen wouldn't be here sizing me up."

He grinned with the pun. The leader glared and unleashed a wad of spit that splatted against Nick's jacket.

It was a bit ironic that this South Philadelphia alley was just across the Delaware River from his old stomping grounds, site of his first stabbing. Back then he'd been asking for it, or at least taunting the gods to smack him down. An eighteen year-old punk, he'd been running with some Jersey gangbangers out of Camden, having proved to them that despite his diminutive size and white-boy sheen he could kick ass with the best of them, not to mention reprogram Duke Nukem 3D and other popular videogames of the era to make them faster and cooler – the real source of his street cred. But then a small-time dope deal in an alley not unlike this one had gone to hell and he'd been stabbed nine times by a raging meth freak.

He wiped the mokker's dripping commentary from his chest with a sleeve and continued his spiel.

"I'm not averse to the term 'midget'. Sure, some folks object to it, insist it's not PC. But I feel there's little to be gained by being small about the tiny things in our short lives."

The leader's face remained ironclad but the wingmen laughed. That was Nick's intent. His humor had gotten him out of scrapes in the past. Putting at least two of the mokkers at ease gave him a shot.

His chances were slim. His neck implant was an encrypted attaboy, the most advanced com link available. But with this level of jamscram, calling for help was out of the question. He had some fight skills but he was forty-two years old, no spring chicken anymore. His only real weapon was his Swiss army first-aid knife. But the safak's longest extension was no match for the mokker's twenty-centimeter serrated blades.

He'd been forced to leave his handgun at the transit station where he'd exited the secure section of Philadelphia to venture into the "zoo", the street name for Philly-unsec's urban wilderness. Like all of the world's gated cities, Philly-sec sought to keep projectile and energy weapons out of the hands of the zoo's impoverished millions, who outnumbered them twenty to one. *No guns across the border* policies maintained an uneasy coexistence between sec and unsec realms, preventing those at the bottom of the economic pyramid from gaining access to technologies that might flip the status quo.

"What the fuck you doin' here?" the leader growled, ejecting fresh spittle with every word. "You some kind of sec spy?"

Nick had dressed down for tonight's excursion. But his tattered pants and jacket weren't enough to fool the zoo's more hardcore residents, who had a knack for spotting outsiders.

"Actually, I'm here on official business. I'm with ODOR, the Office of Dumpster Operations and Retrieval." Nick gestured to the leaking receptacle behind him. "This one doesn't meet code."

One of the wingmen laughed hysterically. The other leaned forward and barfed a stream of bloody puke. Mokkers tended to throw up a lot, an unavoidable side effect of the constant vaping. The ones who survived gang life on the streets tended to die young of respiratory problems.

"Ya think you're funny?" the leader challenged.

"Well, not comedy club, Jim Carrey kind of funny."

"What the fuck's a gym carry?"

The mokkers would take whatever cash Nick had on him and, either postmortem or premortem, cut off his fingers and slice out his eyes. His body parts would be put on ice until they could be sold to a poacher who would mule them across the border into the secured area of the city. There, some associate with a clean record would try using Nick's digits and orbs at a terminal in the hopes that he had financial accounts worth emptying. He saw no upside to informing the mokkers that such efforts would be a waste of time, that his accounts were protected by far more advanced technologies.

The leader's face twisted into an ugly sneer. Time was running out. Nick had to make his move.

"Prior to you gentlemen displaying your prowess with edged weaponry," he began, "there is something of great value I'd like to willingly hand over. Consider it a token of peace and friendship." He gestured toward his inside coat pocket. "May I?"

"Real fuckin' careful."

Nick undid his overcoat's flap, eased his hand inside and withdrew the small jewelry box. It was covered with bioluminescent weep fabric, an ever-changing array of dripping hues that resembled tears. Weep fabric looked exotic and expensive but was neither, at least not for someone with ready access to high-tech products.

But the way the mokkers' eyes widened indicated they'd never seen such an item before, having probably lived their entire lives in the zoo. Enough clarity remained in their drug-addled minds to conclude that the box contained something of great value.

Nick took a step closer and extended the offering. "If you could just see it in your hearts to allow me to leave here in peace, I'm sure that this gift will more than compensate you for any troubles. Remember, it takes a big man to spare a little one."

The wingmen laughed again. This time the leader joined in, although with a caustic brutality that made it clear what he really thought of Nick's proposal.

Had he ventured into the zoo to meet any of his other confidential informants, he could have hired some off-duty Earth Patrol Forces soldiers to serve as bodyguards. But no one could know about tonight's rendezvous with his most secretive and extraordinary CI, Ektor Fang, who'd set the time and location. If Nick had brought EPF into the zoo as muscle, Ektor Fang would have found out and wouldn't have come within ten klicks of this alley.

Then again, he's not here anyway. That was disappointing on a number of levels.

The leader eyed Nick suspiciously for a long moment. Finally he took the bait. Holstering his knives, he snatched the box. As he did, Nick eased sideways, slowly enough not to alarm the mokkers. He was now positioned in front of the shorter of the wingmen, the one with the maniacal laugh. The man didn't appear to be wearing body armor and it was doubtful he had access to a crescent web or other energy shielding. Better yet for Nick's purposes, his tight camo pants revealed only a natural male bulge and no hint of a groin protector.

The leader opened the box. The mokkers were instantly entranced. The one standing farthest from Nick was so taken by what he was seeing that he vaped a triple snort of mok-1 up his nostrils and shuddered with delight.

The box contained a large silver ring with a massive diamond setting. Its perimeter was studded with what appeared to be emeralds, rubies and sapphires.

Nick tensed, ready to spring into action as the leader reached a hand toward the box. But the mokker hesitated at the last instant, suspecting a trick of some sort.

He has to touch it.

"Here, let me show you some of its beautiful features," Nick said, lunging forward and making a grab for the ring.

The leader reacted as expected. He yanked the box away with a possessive growl that would have done an angry mutt proud.

Good boy. Now pick up the damn thing.

The leader gripped the prize between his thumb and forefinger and held it aloft. The diamond's polished facets gleamed under the lunar light, suggesting the ring was extraordinarily valuable. In reality, it was a clever fake. Nick had bought it for nineteen dollars from one of the licensed beggars who plied their trade in Philly-sec's Rittenhouse Square bazaar.

Body heat from the leader's fingertips activated the thermal switch. The tiny flashbang hidden inside the ring triggered.

Blinding white light.

Earsplitting noise.

A flashbang this small couldn't produce the severe disorienting effects common to its larger brethren. But the sudden eruption of light and sound was enough to startle the mokkers and buy Nick a few precious seconds.

He stepped forward and swept his right leg upward. The toe of his reinforced boot caught the short mokker in the crotch. The man grunted, grabbed his junk and crumbled to his knees. Nick dashed past him and ran for all he was worth toward the alley's exit. His ride, an '89 Chevy Destello, was right around the corner, optically camouflaged in the recessed doorway of an abandoned factory building.

The leader and the other wingman recovered from the flashbang's effects quicker than anticipated. Nick could hear their loud footsteps. There was no need to glance back to realize they were closing fast.

I'm not going to make it.

The physics of human locomotion were against him. Short legs couldn't compete with long ones. The two mokkers were seconds away from tackling him. At that point, extremely bad things would happen.

He was five meters from where the alley funneled into the street when two more men stepped around the corner. Their faces were silhouetted by a dim streetlamp at their backs. His first thought was that they were more mokkers.

His only chance was to crash through the pair. He lowered his head and mentally steeled himself to be an unstoppable battering ram.

The newcomers whipped up their arms in tandem. From the left hand of one and the right hand of the other, beams of twisting black light erupted. The luminous streaks flashed past Nick's head on opposite sides, passing so close that the heat of the burning energy warmed his earlobes.

Startled gasps emanated from behind him. Nick stopped, whirled around. The two mokkers had been hit. Smoldering fabric and flesh over their hearts marked the beams' entry points.

The mokkers collapsed face down in the alley. Their backs revealed the exit wounds of the hot particle streams. They writhed for a few moments as the thermal energy spread through their chest cavities, baking internal organs. In seconds they segued to a motionless limbo from which there would be no return.

Back at the cul-de-sac, the surviving mokker had recovered from Nick's crotch kick. Having seen the fate of his companions, he was huddled at the side of the dumpster, frantically vaping. But inhaling all the mok-1 in the known universe wouldn't make him fearless enough to confront a Paratwa assassin.

...

Find out how it ends by purchasing BINARY STORM from any good stationer or book emporium

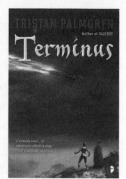

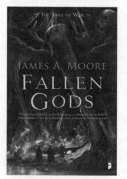
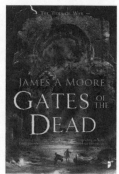
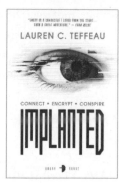

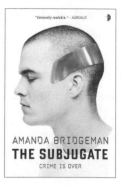

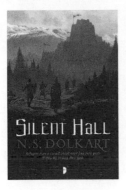
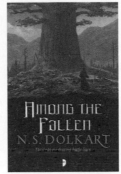

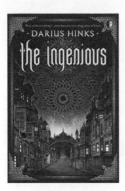

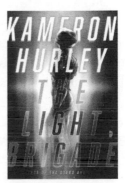

ABOUT THE AUTHOR

Christopher Hinz wrote the Paratwa Saga, whose first book Liege-Killer won the Compton Crook Award for best first novel and earned Hinz a nomination for the John W Campbell Award for best new writer. He has worked as a newspaper reporter, technical administrator of a TV station, public relations writer, screenwriter, and comic book scripter for DC and Marvel. He orchestrates the creation of fantastic universes, a lifelong passion, from a wooded realm in southeastern Pennsylvania, USA.

christopherhinz.com